SCRUBBED MIND

A ZORDI WORLD NOVEL

SECRETS
TRILOGY
—3—

SCRUBBED MIND

MELISSA LAM

12Bunnies
Publishing

Developmental editing by: R. D. Langr
Editing, cover design, and proofreading by: Enchanted Ink Publishing
Author photo by: AB-Photography.us
Logo art by: A. Krause Studio

www.authormelissalam.com

For my Rooly.
I love you, but please don't read any of Mama's books. Ever.

CONTENTS

Playlist xi
Content Warning xiii

Chapter 1   1
Chapter 2   14
Chapter 3   22
Chapter 4   33
Chapter 5   40
Chapter 6   49
Chapter 7   52
Chapter 8   57
Chapter 9   67
Chapter 10   79
Chapter 11   84
Chapter 12   88
Chapter 13   97
Chapter 14   104
Chapter 15   115
Chapter 16   120
Chapter 17   127
Chapter 18   136
Chapter 19   144
Chapter 20   155
Chapter 21   161
Chapter 22   171
Chapter 23   181
Chapter 24   190
Chapter 25   196
Chapter 26   204
Chapter 27   210
Chapter 28   214
Chapter 29   225
Chapter 30   230

Chapter 31   236
Chapter 32   243
Chapter 33   252
Chapter 34   264
Chapter 35   279
Chapter 36   290
Chapter 37   300
Chapter 38   303
Chapter 39   316
Chapter 40   329
Chapter 41   344
Chapter 42   349

Acknowledgments   359
About the Author   361
Support Indie Authors   363

PLAYLIST

Chapter 8: "Train Wreck" JAMES ARTHUR
Chapter 10: "Incomplete" BACKSTREET BOYS
Chapter 13: "What It's Like To Be Lonely" TYLER WARD
Chapter 14: "No More Sad" NIGHTBREAKERS
Chapter 15: "Leave a Light On (Acoustic)" TOM WALKER
Chapter 16: "Save My Soul" JoJo
Chapter 16: "My Love Won't Let You Down" LITTLE MIX
Chapter 18: "Back To" NIGHTBREAKERS
Chapter 19: "Bruises" LEWIS CAPALDI
Chapter 21: "A Year Ago" JAMES ARTHUR
Chapter 23: "Tattoo" LOREEN
Chapter 25: "Quarter to Midnight" NIGHTBREAKERS
Chapter 26: "Treat You Better" SHAWN MENDES
Chapter 33: "Come Back Home" CALUM SCOTT
Chapter 33: "Love Is Gone (feat. PVLN)" VERMILION
Chapter 34: "Take Your Sweet Time" JESSE MCCARTNEY
Chapter 35: "Fake Smile" NIGHTBREAKERS
Chapter 35: "This Love (Taylor's Version)" TAYLOR SWIFT
Chapter 41: "All That Really Matters" ILLENIUM & TEDDY SWIMS
Chapter 42: "Emily" JAMES ARTHUR

CONTENT WARNING

Packing List for This Emotional Journey:

- **Earplugs**—these naughty words are loud enough to wake up your neighbors.
- **Tissues and ice cream**—for those tearful moments crying over pregnancy loss.
- **A sober friend**—someone's gotta balance out all the drug and alcohol abuse.
- **Therapist on speed dial**—just in case the brief suicidal thoughts hit a little too close to home.
- **A fan**—things are about to get hot and steamy from these spicy scenes.

1

TREY

I BANG A FIST AGAINST THE WOOD TABLE. "WHERE IS SHE?"

The Keeper sitting across from me sighs. With the long sleeve of his navy-blue uniform, he rubs the fingerprints off the golden nameplate pinned to his upper chest. It reads ORTIZ. "Mr. Grant, if you don't want to cooperate with me, I'm happy to ask the Enforcers to put you back behind bars until you do. Now answer my question."

I burst out of my metal chair. It falls behind me with a *clank!* against the hard floor of this stuffy interrogation room. This bullshit little space is barely bigger than a bathroom stall. Plus, it's musty, it's windowless, and, most of all, it's Arella-less.

"I've been cooperating with you for the last three days!" I shout at the useless example of a Superior in front of me. "Now I'm done cooperating, because every time I ask you where she is, you refuse to answer. If you don't tell me now, I'll tear this whole place apart until I find her!" *And that's a fucking promise.*

Ortiz leans back in his chair and chuckles. "This prison is packed with Enforcers whose powers aren't subdued by perrizo—while yours are. How do you plan to tear this place apart without your gifts?"

Each injection of perrizophine forced onto every inmate is supposed to last twelve hours. To ensure there's never a chance an inmate's perrizo has worn off before their next injection, doses are handed out like candy every eight hours.

I never realized how much I relied on my Empath power until now. I have to pay attention to people's facial expressions and body language to guess how they're feeling. Even then, it's just a guess. When I get outta here, I'm never talking shit about my mind power ever again. And I say *when* because it's a matter of when, not if.

Three days ago, I woke up in a large holding cell, surrounded by the remaining **ZIRDA** (Zordinary Innovations Research and Development Agency) agents and double that number of Royals, the chaotic assholes who think all Zordis are better than Ordinaries, just because we were born with powers—something outside of our control. The Enforcers stated that if we could prove we hadn't broken any laws, they'd let us go.

One by one, they took us into an interrogation room. Depending on our answers to their questions, a Detector on the other side of the wall either confirmed that our words are true or that we've lied.

On day one, every Royal was taken out of the holding cell, interrogated, then relocated to separate cells to await their trials that will determine how long they'll be incarcerated for. Depending on the severity of their crimes, they could be trapped in prison for the rest of their lives. I hope that's the case for all of them.

As for the **ZIRDA** agents, they were also interrogated on day one, then released within twenty minutes of their interrogations starting. I'm not that great at math, but I'm good enough to know that three days is a hell of a lot longer than twenty minutes.

The first **ZIRDA** agent to be freed was Ruby. She was also the only person left I knew by name. Everyone else I knew by name had been killed: Dash the Speeder, who helped me get Arella out of Shadow Ridge by making sure the hidden tunnel was safe. Carlos the security guard, who helped fend off the Royals while I got Arella to safety. Pixie the Ear Blower, who was barely twenty years old and one of the bravest people I've ever known.

The youngest to die was Katie. She's the one I owe the most. She preloaded some perrizo guns for me, which was crucial in our escape. Katie is also the one who pushed Arella out of the way when a Royal tried to stab her with a knife. Sadly, Katie ended up on the other end of that knife.

I barely had time to process Katie's death before Aunt Jodi, in Victor's body, stabbed me in the side. Then Victor, in Jodi's body, tackled her to the ground. They tried to kill each other until the Enforcers showed up seconds later, but it was too late. Victor—who I thought for all my life was my uncle but was really my dad—had already stopped breathing.

Jodi had suffered some injuries too—a few blows to the head and a dagger to the chest. She didn't make it long enough to see the prison's Healer. I did, though, and now I don't even have a scar to memorialize that battle.

I'd like to say I've had a moment to mourn the loss of my dad, but I've been too busy trying to figure out what the zovernment has done with my girl and wondering why they're still keeping me here when they've already deemed me innocent.

They're not holding me for being a Royal, nor are they holding me for committing crimes as a ZIRDA agent. Surprisingly, they aren't holding me for exposure to an Ordinary either. After their many questions, all of which I answered with the truth, they determined that since I used my powers to protect Arella and only did it *after* she'd already found out about the existence of Zordinaries, they're dropping the charges.

So if I'm not being convicted for anything, why am I still

here? More importantly, why am I talking to a Keeper? Keepers are high-level zovernment officials who make the laws. Enforcers are the ones who enforce those laws. The people who were arrested with me were all interrogated by Enforcers, which makes sense because this is mid-level Enforcer work. So why is there a *Keeper* sitting in front of me?

Ortiz points at my knocked-over chair. "Pick that up, sit your ass down, and answer my question."

Glaring at the man, I scoop up my chair and set it upright with a *clank!* Then I plant myself back onto the metal and cross my arms with a huff.

"What else do you know about her immunity?" Ortiz asks for the third time. Since he's so insistent about getting my answer to this question, I'm gonna assume *this* is why they're still keeping me around. Arella must be an anomaly to the zovernment too.

"I've already told you everything I know."

Like it did the last two times I said that, a device on the wall glows red with the word LIE. Whoever that Detector is who keeps pressing that LIE button on the other side of that wall needs to stop.

This Keeper already knows I was sent on a mission to find out the source of Arella's immunity. He also knows I never found it. I told him that she was able to project her immunity onto me multiple times. I even told him the way she did it was by imagining waves of water drenching me. I've told him everything I know—except one thing.

What I haven't told him is that I was able to break through Arella's immunity walls by making her orgasm. I don't want the zovernment knowing that, for two reasons: First, I don't want them to take advantage of that knowledge and scrub her memories. Second, they've already let me off the hook for fake-dating an Ordinary. I doubt they'll be as relenting if they find out I had sex with her too.

Sadly, getting locked up for that is the least of my worries.

My biggest concern is that they'll find out Arella and I were able to conceive, even though it's biologically impossible for us to do so. I still have no idea how that happened, and it doesn't matter. What matters now is that the Keepers don't find out about it. Who knows what they'll do with that information. If it's anything close to dissecting Arella to study her reproductive organs, fuck that. This is why I need to know where she is, because if they've already locked her up for research, then I need to bust her out.

"You can't tell lies in here." Ortiz folds his hands together over the table. "So how about you stop wasting—"

Knock-knock.

The door unlocks, then opens to reveal a slender Asian woman in a fancy-ass burgundy suit. Her heels clack against the floor as she lets herself into the room. "Thank you for your time, Mr. Ortiz. You may dismiss yourself."

Ortiz lets out a scoff and wrinkles his face together. "Excuse me? I'm in the middle of an interrogation. Who are you?"

In a sweet tone, the twenty-something woman says, "I'm Mia Wang, Executive Keeper."

"Executive Keeper?" Ortiz chuckles under his breath. "Yeah, right. Those people never come out from behind their desks."

"I assure you, Mr. Ortiz, when needed, we do *come out from behind our desks.* I am here to speak to Mr. Grant. Therefore, you are no longer needed." Mia gestures a shooing hand out the door again.

Ortiz remains in his seat. "You can't be serious. Where is your badge?"

Without hesitation, Mia pulls back the left collar of her silky shirt and suit jacket. Right over her heart is the *official crest of the Keepers* branded into her skin. It's something I've only ever seen in books. Only the highest level Executive Keepers get that symbol branded onto their skin. They're the

Executive Keepers who are allowed more information than the other executives and the lower level Keepers—like this toe-jam sniffer who's just dropped his jaw.

It doesn't take more than a second for Ortiz to hop onto his feet and scurry out the door. With an apologetic smile, he closes and locks my precious exit behind him.

Mia makes her way to Ortiz's newly vacated chair and sits. With a smile, she says, "How are you today, Mr. Grant?"

I'm not fooled by her gentle voice or the way she just asked that question like she actually cares about my answer. "Been better."

"I hear you've been pretty concerned about the Ordinary the Enforcers found you with."

Concerned is not the right word for it. Obsessively tormented over her well-being is more accurate. "Where is she?"

Like Ortiz, Mia doesn't answer me. "I only have one question, Mr. Grant. Once you answer it, you'll be free to go."

My heart thrashes like it's trying to escape from my chest. Whatever this lady wants to ask me can't be good. "What do you mean by *free to go?*"

"As in, you're welcome to leave." She says that too casually. Like, *waaay* too casually.

"After I proved my innocence, you Supes have kept me drugged up here for three days while interrogating me for hours on end. All of a sudden, an Executive Keeper with the official crest shows up and tells me I just have to answer one question, then I'll be *free to go?*"

"Yes, sir."

I can't think of what information this woman wants from me that would grant me my freedom. "What's your question?"

"My question is: When Miss Rance was kidnapped, did you feel the glimmer?"

My eyes go wide because that is the farthest thing from what I expected her to ask me.

Since falling in love with Arella, I've felt the glimmer three times. The first time was when she was attacked by spiders. The second time was when she was in a bad car accident. The third time was after she realized she was kidnapped. Each time, nausea took over my body, my limbs went numb, and my chest felt tight like someone had a vise grip on it.

"Your honesty is important, Mr. Grant." Mia stares me down with an impassive look.

Without my Empath power, I can't even begin to figure out what this woman is up to. A Zordi can only feel the glimmer when their *soul mate* is in danger. We're taught in Zordi school that our kind is meant to be with *only* our kind. So why did this Keeper even think to ask if I felt the glimmer with an *Ordinary*?

Does the zovernment already know it's possible for us to be soul mates with Ordinaries? Does that mean they also know it's possible for our kinds to reproduce together? Based on what this Keeper is asking me, yes.

Why does it not surprise me to find out that the zovernment spreads false information? I guess after finding out that Aunt Jodi stole Victor's body for over twenty years and that my uncle is actually my biological father, nothing can shock me now.

I must be taking too long to answer, because Mia says, "I'm just looking for a simple yes or no, Mr. Grant. Did you feel the glimmer when Miss Rance was kidnapped?"

Should I lie? If I do, that stupid device on the wall will glow red again. Why does knowing if Arella is my soul mate or not matter anyway? And why is it so important that they had to send an Executive Keeper to ask me about it? In America, the Executive Keepers are based in New York City. Did this lady come to California all the way from New York just to ask me *one* question?

I repeat her words in my head. *When Miss Rance was*

kidnapped, did you feel the glimmer? Suddenly, it hits me: The keyword here is *when.*

"No," I say, because technically, I didn't. Arella was sedated in her sleep before she was taken, so she didn't know she was in danger until *after* she woke up. The glimmer doesn't activate if the person in danger doesn't know they're in danger.

Mia glances at the wall, where a light glows green with the word TRUTH. She narrows her eyes at me as she thinks for a moment. She's smarter than I thought, because within a few heartbeats, she clears her throat and asks, "Did you ever feel the glimmer *after* she was kidnapped? Maybe once she woke up from the sedatives the Royals injected her with?"

I go silent again. How do they know Arella was drugged? Did they interrogate her too?

My hesitation makes Mia stare at me. "Again, Mr. Grant, your honesty is important."

I lean back into my chair and side-eye her. "Important for what?"

"That's classified information."

"Classified?" I scoff. "Like how you Keepers are keeping millions of Zordis away from their possible Ordi soul mates?"

A slight smile turns up the corners of Mia's lips. "So you admit you felt the glimmer?"

I lean over the table and lower my voice. "How can you live with yourself? We have the right to be with our soul mates, even if they're Ordis."

Mia leans toward me as she, too, lowers her voice. "That's a small price to pay to keep our kind safe, don't you think? Can you imagine what would happen if we openly told the general public that it's possible for Ordinaries to be our soul mates? Our kind would expose themselves left and right in retaliation. Then once the Ordinaries find out about us, they'll want to get rid of us again.

"Our kind cannot survive another mass genocide. Plus, it'll

be harder for our Scrubbers to do another worldwide scrub. People have more technology now than they did back then. The Ordinaries will come after us with more than just poison. Knowing where Miss Rance is will be the least of your worries."

I hate to admit it, but this Keeper is right. Ordinaries are not ready to know about the Zordi world again. They're too fearful of anything they don't understand. There would be more than just murders and genocides. The world would erupt into chaos.

Mia presses her back against her chair. "Final question, Mr. Grant, then I will see you out the door."

"You said I only had to answer one question, then I was free to go. I've answered it. Now let me go."

She ignores me. "Did you know she was pregnant with your child?"

I try to keep my face impassive because I don't want to give her an answer. Unfortunately, my silence and lack of shock are all the answer she needs.

Mia's chair squeals as she pushes it back and stands up. "Thank you for your time today, Mr. Grant. I'll walk you outside."

I stay where I am. "That's it?"

"Yes, sir. That's it." Her heels *clack-clack-clack* as she heads toward the door.

What is going on? This Keeper just found out that I broke the second most enforced Zordi law—to never engage in sexual activities with an Ordinary—and now she's just gonna let me go? Wait . . . why the hell am I questioning this? If she's freeing me, why am I still sitting here?

Fifteen minutes later, I'm out of my z-prison jumpsuit and wearing the clothes I was arrested in: some light-wash jeans and a gray polo with a slit in the side from where Aunt Jodi stabbed me. All the bloodstains have been washed out, which I'm not mad about. Some of that blood was Katie's, and I don't need to walk around with a display of sacrifice all over me.

When I step out of the bathroom in my laundered outfit, Mia says, "Follow me."

At the prison's main entrance, a gray-haired man in a light-blue Enforcer uniform waits for us with my leather jacket neatly folded in his palms. On top of my jacket is my wallet.

"Thank you," I say as I shove my wallet into my back pocket, then slip into my jacket. With it on, I feel closer to normal, although I won't feel completely normal until I'm holding Arella again. That's why the moment the Enforcer disappears behind a door marked MAIN OFFICE, I turn to Mia.

"Where is she?"

As if she can't hear me, Mia opens one of the double doors, then holds it wide for me. Sunlight shines onto my shoes, the first glimpse of the outside I've had since being arrested. I'm about to take a step out when I stop. What if this is a trick? Having sex with an Ordinary is a huge offense. To the zovernment, *for a ZIRDA mission* is not a valid excuse for breaking the law. Why are they just letting me go?

"Are you hesitating because you'd rather stay behind bars?" Mia asks.

Fuck that. I step out into the bright September sun and squint. It only takes a second for my Zordi eyes to adjust, then I can see clearly. I'm no expert, but based on where the sun is, I'd say it's three o'clockish.

Mia joins me outside, then clicks the door shut behind her. "What time was your last dose of perrizophine?"

"Around ten this morning."

"Great. That dose should wear off around ten tonight. When it does, drink lots of Healing Water. It'll help counteract some of the side effects from coming off a long period of being under perrizo. Since your time here was short, I expect your side effects to be minor compared to the people who leave z-prison after decades of being locked up. If the side effects become unbearable, try eating some bananas. For some reason, they help."

Healing Water. Bananas. Got it. Now back to the important stuff. Since the way I asked my question before didn't yield results, I reword it. "Do you know where Arella is?"

Mia ignores my question again. "Do you know where *you* are?"

"The z-prison in Corcoran."

"Correct. On the outside of these brick walls is a van waiting to take you home. We don't normally give inmates rides. Given your situation, I pulled some strings to arrange it for you."

My situation? What does that mean? Is she talking about how I didn't know I was going to be released today, or that I don't have any family to come pick me up? Either way, I appreciate the ride.

Mia continues, "The driver has specific instructions to take you home and nowhere else, so don't even try."

"In other words, don't ask him to take me to wherever you're keeping Arella?"

Mia lets out a big sigh. "Mr. Grant, we aren't keeping Miss Rance anywhere. She's safe at home, where she has been since this morning."

Since this morning? That means they've kept her for the last three days too. Is that why they're finally letting me go? They finished their studies on her, and now they don't need to keep me locked up anymore? That's some bullshit.

I try not to sound angry. "Why did you guys keep her for that long?"

Mia blinks up at me with an expression I can't read. For a second, I think she's about to answer my question, until she turns back toward the doors and opens one. "If you know what's good for you, Mr. Grant, you'll stay away from her."

My anger comes out this time. "Why did you guys keep her for that long?"

"Don't forget about the bananas, okay? They really do help." Without another word, she disappears behind the door, and it clicks shut.

I think about rushing back in and demanding that she tell me what they did with Arella for three whole days, but I doubt that will help anything. Plus, now that I know where my girl is, I feel a pull to head straight there.

Three and a half torturous hours later, the van driver drops me off outside my home. No matter what I said to him, he refused to take me to Arella's apartment.

I race to open my garage. The loud door lifts to reveal only my car. *Shit.* I'd forgotten I ditched my motorcycle on the side of a road after I got Arella out of Shadow Ridge. My bike would have been faster, but my car will do.

Since running inside to find my keys will waste precious time, I plant myself behind the steering wheel and wave a hand at the ignition. Nothing happens, so I do it again. Then I facepalm myself. *I'm such an idiot.* If my empathy power isn't working, then my telekinesis isn't either.

I sprint through my house to find my keys. Once I do, I'm back in my car with the engine started.

THE OUTSIDE OF ARELLA'S APARTMENT LOOKS THE SAME AS IT always does. The car I bought for her is parked in her usual spot. I pull my Lexus right up next to it, then half run, half stumble toward her door.

Knock-knock-knock.

My hands shake against my leg as I wait for the door to open. I'm itching to hold her. I need my world to feel right again.

When the barrier keeping her from me finally opens, my heart fills with relief. There she is, and she looks unharmed. Her long chestnut hair cascades down her shoulders in soft waves. The hem of her white sundress falls just above her knees. Her eyes are warm and gentle—the way they always are. She looks like an angel. Partly because she's so beautiful, partly because I can't believe she's finally standing in front of me.

"Arella." Her name comes out breathily as I scoop her into my arms and crush her against my chest. "I've been so worried about you. Are you okay? Please tell me you're okay."

She doesn't return my hug or melt into my body the way she normally does. Instead, she goes stiff. Then she pushes herself out of my grasp and takes a step back. "Um, yeah? I'm okay."

I keep examining her arms and legs, looking for any signs of cuts or bruises. "Did they hurt you?"

She cocks her head to the side and creases her eyebrows together. "Um, no?"

I slap a palm over my heart. "Oh, thank fuck. I'm so glad you're—"

A movement on Arella's couch catches my attention. Someone I've never seen before stands up and stares at me with narrowed eyes and a crumpled forehead. White male in his early twenties, light brown hair, looks like he keeps up with his workouts, and he's got a french fry sticking out of his mouth. Two fast food bags sit on Arella's coffee table along with two fountain drinks.

I hook my thumb toward the guy. "Who the fuck is he?"

Arella blinks at me. "Better question: Who are *you*?"

2

ARI

I wake up from the anesthesia surrounded by a handful of nurses and doctors.

"The procedure went perfectly," one of them says from behind a light-blue medical face mask. "I'm gonna help you get off this bed and into this wheelchair. Then I'll bring you right back to your boyfriend."

Things are still fuzzy as I'm wheeled back to the same pre-op room I was in earlier. There, the nurse helps me back into the bed.

"How did it go?" Caleb asks the nurse. He's stationed on a chair in the corner when he stands to come hold my hand. I offer him a warm smile as our fingers intertwine.

We didn't plan to get pregnant, but when I told him the news, he was thrilled. We were in the midst of talking through possible names when we got the terrible news that we'd lost our baby.

Since I was already over nine weeks along and the baby wasn't coming out naturally, I opted for a D and C. Caleb has been supportive and loving throughout this entire experience. He promised he'd treat me to some burgers for dinner since I've had a huge craving for fries lately.

"Everything went splendidly," the nurse says with a bright smile. "Zero issues."

Caleb gives my hand a light squeeze. "That's awesome. Thank you so much for taking good care of her."

The nurse turns back to me. "Remember, you'll be sore and have some light bleeding down there for about two weeks. After that, your body will return to normal. Do you have any questions before we start the process of discharging you?"

"Nope," I say as the fuzziness begins to leave my head.

"Great. You rest up then. I'll come back in a bit when the anesthesia has fully worn off. After that, we'll get you up and walking, then you'll be ready to head home."

The nurse is right, I am a little sore down there.

I feel slightly more at ease by the time Caleb and I are back home. Together, we sit on the couch to enjoy our dinner. Typically, we eat at the kitchen table, but I want to sit somewhere more comfy while I devour my fries.

"It's been a while since we've had In-N-Out," Caleb says as he unwraps his burger.

"The last time was back when we first met." I shove some fries into my mouth, then let out a satisfied *mmm*. "We had In-N-Out on our third date."

He counts on his fingers. "That was only three months ago. I suppose that's not *that* long ago, but it sure feels like it."

I feel the same about my relationship with this beautiful man. We haven't been together for that long, but it sure feels that way. In only three short months, Caleb and I have gone from being strangers on the side of a highway, to going on a few dates after he helped me fix my flat tire, to falling madly in love, to finding out we were going to be parents, to losing our baby. I can't imagine going through all of that with anyone else.

Knock-knock-knock.

Caleb eyes me with his mouth full. "Are we expecting anyone?"

"It's probably Javina," I say as I wipe my fingers off on some napkins. "She texted me before my surgery, saying she'd stop by after she gets off work."

When I open the door, it's not Javina. Instead, a man with dark chocolate hair and a stubbly beard stares back at me. He lets out a tiny breath of relief as our eyes lock. Relief from what? I don't know. I'm about to tell him that we aren't interested in whatever he's selling when he says my name.

"Arella." It comes out breathless. In a flash, he wraps his arms around me and clutches me against his firm chest.

I freeze. How does this man know my name? And it's my full name too. Everyone calls me Ari. Barely anyone even knows that Arella is my full name.

"I've been so worried about you." The snug way he wraps his muscular arms around me sends a warmth down my spine. His hold feels desperate, possessive, and protective—three things I don't expect to feel when being hugged by a man I've never seen before. "Are you okay? Please tell me you're okay."

It takes me a second to regain myself. When I do, I push the man away and step back. "Um, yeah? I'm okay."

His gaze skims my body up and down. "Did they hurt you?"

Did *who* hurt me? The doctors who performed my surgery? How does this man know that I just had surgery? "Um, no?"

He slaps a hand over his chest and lets out a breath. "Oh, thank fuck. I'm so glad you're—"

Behind me, Caleb must move, because the man's eyes dart away from me. Then his entire face crinkles together. With a thumb pointed at Caleb, he says, "Who the fuck is he?"

This guy sure has a potty mouth. "Better question: Who are *you?*"

The strange man drops his jaw. It takes him a second to say, "W-w-what?"

I don't think I stuttered, but I repeat myself anyway. "I said, who are you?"

His eyebrows press together so hard, it makes his forehead wrinkle. "What do you mean?"

I feel like *who are you?* is a pretty straightforward question. What does he mean by what do I mean?

"Arella, it's me, Trey."

"I'm sorry. You must have the wrong apartment." Even as I say that, I know it's not true. This guy is staring at me like he can't comprehend why I would ask who he is, and he just held me like he's been desperate to for days. Plus, he knows my full name. This man is exactly where he thinks he should be.

Caleb steps up behind me and places an arm around my shoulders, protectively pulling me back. "Who are you?"

He has barely gotten the words out when this Trey guy leaps into our apartment and shoves Caleb away so hard, he's launched backward several steps. Even more protectively than Caleb just did, Trey pulls me behind him and stands in front of me like a shield.

"Don't you dare touch her."

Caleb throws his arms up in surrender. "Hey, now. No need to get violent, okay? We'll give you whatever you want. Just don't hurt my girlfriend."

"Your *girlfriend?*"

I step away from the crazy man. "Who are you?"

The man whips his attention back to me. "Baby, it's me, Trey. Trey Grant." He points at his chest. "*I'm* your boyfriend, not him."

I keep my voice calm so I don't aggravate this man any further. "I'm sorry, but I've never seen you before in my life."

"What?" At first, he stares at me with his mouth slack. Then I see it in his eyes the moment something clicks for him. He gasps with his entire body jerking backward. "You've been scrubbed."

Scrubbed? Am I supposed to know what that means? I flick

my eyes up to Caleb. The look on his face tells me he doesn't know what *scrubbed* means either.

Trey closes the distance between us in two large steps. With rough hands, he grabs my face. "Baby, look at me. We can beat this, okay? Whatever they did to you, you can fight it. Look into my eyes. Try to remember me."

My body stills. I don't want to move, because I'm afraid of what's going to happen if I do. I don't know what this man's intentions are, nor do I know what he's capable of. He's built like he could fight off truckloads of soldiers. "Um, could you, please, take your hands off me? You're scaring me."

Trey gazes into my eyes as if he's trying to figure out if I'm serious. When he realizes I am, his shoulders droop and his arms fall to his sides. "Arella, please. Try to remember me. If there's anyone who can do it, it's you."

Caleb still has his hands up in surrender. "Look, buddy. I think you should leave."

Trey ignores Caleb and keeps his attention trained on me with a desperate look on his face. "Arella, come on. You can fight this. We met on the side of a highway, remember? You had a flat tire, and I helped you put a new one on."

How does this guy know how Caleb and I met? And why is he claiming that's how I met *him*? Now he's *really* scaring me.

He keeps talking. "We started dating after that and—"

Caleb cuts him off by rushing to my side and pulling me behind him. "Ari, go call the cops. This guy is a psycho."

"I'm not a psycho!" Trey shouts. "I'm telling the truth!"

Caleb scoffs. "You're the literal definition of a psycho. Unstable and aggressive."

What is Caleb doing? When someone is being crazy, the last thing you should do is call them crazy. It only makes them more crazy.

"Arella, will you just look at me? You know me. Deep in there somewhere, you know me."

I eye the man up and down, trying to entertain the idea

that I *might* know him. Tall, light skin, dark hair, broad shoulders, a leather jacket. The more I stare at him, the more I'm certain I've never seen him before. He's got a gorgeous face that was carved by gods. I'd remember a face like that.

"I'm sorry," I say. "I don't know who you are."

"WHAT HAPPENED AFTER THAT?" JAVINA ASKS. SHE SHOWED UP barely ten minutes after that Trey guy left. We're sitting in the living room with Caleb as I finish telling her the whole story.

"Caleb told him to leave before we called the cops," I say. "Without another word, the guy got right back into his car and left."

Javina shakes her head, huffing. "Why do the weirdest and worst things always happen to you, Ari? As if your abusive ex isn't enough, last month, you got into a bad car accident. Then this week, you lost your baby. Did you piss off the karma gods or something?"

After my car accident, I was sent to the hospital by ambulance. I came out with some whiplash, stitches, and bruises. My parents were killed in a car accident. I'd pick wearing a neck brace for two weeks over death any day.

While I was away from work, Caleb took good care of me. He brought me food, cleaned for me, and treated me like a queen. I don't know how I could have gotten through it without him.

"That man was a psycho," Caleb says from the floor. Javina and I are taking up my small couch, so there's no room for him up here. He always says he prefers to sit on the floor, but I know he's just being gracious. He never sits on the floor when it's just us. "He kept grabbing you. I was afraid he was going to hurt you."

I wasn't. Trey's tight grasp on me felt too protective for me to think he had intentions to hurt me. Yes, the man scared me, but mostly because he claimed to have met me the same way I had met Caleb.

"What did you say his name was?" Javina asks.

"Trey Grant," Caleb says.

Javina thinks, then gasps. "Oh my god! I know him!"

I blanch. "You do?"

"Yes! I mean, not personally, but I know *of* him." From the coffee table, Javina grabs her phone. A few seconds later, she shows me a Google image page. "Is this him?"

The blue-gray eyes that stared at me earlier look back at me from Javina's screen. "That's him."

Caleb pushes off the floor and leans closer to Javina. "Lemme see."

Javina shows him her screen.

Caleb points a finger at her phone. "Yeah, that's the guy. Who is he?"

"He's a musician," Javina says. "He's in a band called Flames in the Night. They play at a bar in downtown LA every weekend. Rachel and I were there a few months ago for the first time. I've been watching all their music videos on YouTube ever since."

"Okay . . ." Caleb pretzels his legs back together. "That doesn't explain why he showed up here, claiming that *my* girlfriend is *his* girlfriend."

"Yeah, that's weird." Javina shrugs. "At least now you know who he is."

Later that night, after Javina heads home, Caleb leaves for his night shift as a security guard at the Los Angeles County Museum of Art. The alone time gives me freedom to do my own Googling.

Trey Grant's Wikipedia page is the first link that pops up when I type his name in. I read the entire thing word for word. What I gather from the limited information is that Trey seems to be a normal guy who loves music. He's been with his band for four years, and they released a few cover albums together before releasing an original album. They're known for being a diverse group of talented individuals who went viral on YouTube with their music. He even has a foundation that supports children with deceased parents, in honor of his parents passing away when he was young. There's nothing on his Wiki page that suggests he's an escapee from a mental hospital.

Naturally, my research gravitates toward the next best thing: social media. Because of my ex, I deleted all my social media accounts when we broke up, so I have to create new ones to be able to continue my research. Once I do, under a made-up name, I scroll through Trey Grant's platforms.

At first glance, it doesn't look like he manages his own accounts. He must pay someone to run his pages for him, because the content is full of candid pictures of him playing guitar, sitting behind a piano, or singing to a large crowd. As for his other band members, their content is a little more personal, with pictures of the things they're eating and videos of them doing silly dances.

I head to YouTube next. It only takes me one video to become captivated by Trey's sultry singing voice. It sounds familiar, but at the same time, so new. Still, I don't find anything that suggests he's a weirdo.

Judging from the video comments, Trey's fans think he and the half-Hispanic woman in his band are dating—or, at the very least, friends with benefits. It also sounds like he has a reputation for being a bit of a bad boy.

That triggers me to take my research back to Google, where I type, *Trey Grant criminal record.*

My heart thumps wildly as I pull up his past charges: two counts of disorderly conduct and one charge for fleeing the police. Obviously, this man has a history of being violent and doing things he shouldn't. Knowing that, I'm surprised he left as willingly as he did. However, that probably means he's bound to reappear soon.

3

TREY

"She's been scrubbed!" I meant for that to come out a little less panicky.

"What?" Liz stands on the other side of her open front door, giving me a furrowed look. "Who's been scrubbed?"

"Arella. They took her, then they interrogated me in z-prison for three days before finally letting me go. I just went to her apartment, looked straight into her eyes, and she didn't recognize me. They fucking scrubbed her!"

Liz puts her gloved hands up, palms forward. "Wait, wait. Let's start from the beginning. Who's Arella?"

I gasp. "No! Not you too!"

Liz side-eyes me like she's trying to figure out if I need to get checked into an asylum. It's the same look Arella gave me earlier. "Why don't you come in and sit down, T?"

I get only two steps into Liz's house before my legs buckle and I fall to my knees. *This can't be happening.* I can't breathe. My throat feels like I'm swallowing sand. *Is everybody scrubbed?*

Liz grips my arm and helps me to my feet. "Come on, T. Let's get you on the couch, then I'll get you some water. Once you're calm, you can tell me everything."

It takes me a while to become calm enough to speak again.

I start off by telling Liz about my **ZIRDA** mission and how, over time, I fell deeply in love with Arella. Then I tell her about the baby, Arella's kidnapping, and how I found out that the person I thought was my uncle was actually my biological father, who was actually Aunt Jodi the whole time.

Liz ogles me like I'm telling her a horror story. "Oh my god. That's a lot to process."

"Oh, I'm not even done yet."

"There's more?"

"Yep. I found out today that the zovernment already knows that our soul mates can be Ordinaries. They also know that we *can* reproduce together. They only tell us we can't so our worlds don't mix again. They don't want to have to deal with another mass genocide, so basically, they've conditioned us to think Ordinaries aren't an option."

"Wait." Liz shakes her head like she can't believe what I just said. I don't blame her. A part of me is still trying to believe it too. "Does that mean there are a bunch of half-Ordi, half-Zordi people walking around?"

"Um, that, I don't know. I didn't even think to ask because I was so fixated on getting to Arella. Oh, by the way, when I got there, she was with some dude who claimed to be her boyfriend."

"Damn." Liz blows out a long breath. "In my memory, you called me up and said you needed a break from band stuff. You told me you were going to hop onto your bike and travel around for a week or two. Then you asked if I could tell Monique so you didn't have to hear her yell at you about it."

At least when the Scrubbers altered Liz's memory, they gave her a fake one that's reasonably believable. If that had actually happened, my band manager definitely would have yelled at me for taking two weeks off without notice.

I clear my throat as I prepare to say something stupid. "I have to go back."

"Back where?"

"To the prison."

"What?"

I knew it was stupid. "I don't mean behind bars. I mean that I need to go back so I can beg them to unscrub her."

"Is that even possible?"

"Fuck if I know, but I'm gonna find out."

———

THE SKY IS DISMALLY DARK BY THE TIME I PULL MY VEHICLE UP to the z-prison's guard booth. The barrier arms are down, blocking my car from going any farther.

I told Liz not to come with me, but she insisted. She gawks out the window at the empty road stretching ahead of us, then at the gigantic building at the end of it. "I've never seen a z-prison before. It looks kinda eerie."

I roll my window down at the same time an Enforcer in his light blues peeks his head out the booth window.

"Sorry," he says from under a gray mustache. "Visiting hours are over."

The zense in my chest tingles from his nearness. "I'm not here to see an inmate. I'm here to see Mia Wang." *That is, if she's still here.* She could be back in New York by now.

"I dunno who that is, but either way, y'all can't be here right now."

"She's an Executive Keeper. I was just here earlier today and spoke with her. I need to talk to her again."

"This is a z-prison, sir, not a zovernment office. If you're trying to talk to a Keeper, go bother them instead."

"Find me someone who can get me in contact with Mia." *Oops.* I didn't mean for my words to come out so demandingly. I'm just still on edge from hearing Arella ask me, *Who are you?*

"Excuse me?" The Enforcer screws his face together as a tiny wave of anger floats into my head. The perrizo is slowly wearing off, but it's not fully out of my system yet. If it was,

I'm sure I'd be sensing heavier emotions from this man. "You have no right to be making demands around here. If you're trying to see a Keeper, an Executive Keeper at that, you've come to the wrong pl—"

Ring. Ring.

The Enforcer slides his window shut, then picks up the booth phone and holds it to his ear. There's a long pause as he listens to whatever is being said on the other line. He nods a few times, says words I can't make out, nods again, then hangs up the phone.

The window slides back open. "Miss Wang will meet you out here in ten minutes. Stay in your vehicle until she arrives."

"Thank you." I roll my window up, then turn to Liz. "She must have known I was coming. This oughta be good."

The ten minutes I'm forced to wait feels like ten hours. Eventually, a black Cadillac Escalade with blinding headlights rolls down the road and stops on the other side of the barrier arms. The front passenger door pops open, then Mia Wang slides out. She's still wearing her burgundy suit and matching high heels. Whoever is driving the vehicle remains in the car with the engine running.

Mia approaches my window as I roll it down. She bends at the hip to meet my eyes. I'm about to ask her how she knew I was coming when she says, "I'm a Seer. Besides, even if I wasn't, I had a feeling you'd be back."

"Is that why you're still here?"

"You were my main reason for coming to California, but I had other things to take care of here. Things I'm not doing right now because I'm standing outside, talking to you. You've got some nerve, Mr. Grant. We've had to make quite a few exceptions for you. Dropping charges for exposure to an Ordinary. Dropping charges for having sexual relations with an Ordinary. Getting you that ride home. And now this. Do you realize you can't just show up to a z-prison and demand to speak to a Keeper? Given your situation, I'm allowing you one free pass, so make it count."

I step out of my car and shut the door behind me. I expect Mia to be a little intimidated because I'm a full head taller than her, but the woman doesn't look fazed at all. I guess she didn't get that official crest branded onto her chest for nothing.

I cross my arms. "What did you do to her?"

Mia sighs as she tucks some of her long black hair behind an ear. "Didn't I tell you to stay away from her?"

"Did you really think I was gonna listen?"

Mia sighs again, heavier this time. "How about we go for a walk?"

I bend to peek my head into the car. "You cool to stay here for a bit?"

Liz nods. "I'll be fine."

Mia gestures down the road leading away from the prison. She doesn't say anything as we fall into steady steps side by side. Maybe she's waiting for me to speak first, so I ask my question again.

"What did you do to her?"

"You already know what happens to Ordinaries who get exposed to our world. Why are you surprised the same thing happened to her?"

Because I didn't think it was possible to scrub her. Erasing and altering memories is a mind power that would affect Arella internally. She's immune to that. "How did you do it?"

"With a Scrubber, of course."

"Yes, but how?"

Mia chuckles under her breath. "Mr. Grant, if you know how to pleasure a woman right, then you should already know that it's possible to bypass her immunity walls." She throws up a hand, palm forward. "Before you get too worked up about that, no, we did not sexually violate her."

I let out a breath because that's exactly what I was about

to accuse the zovernment of doing. "What did you do instead?"

Mia's heels clack against the road as she pulls all her long hair to one shoulder. "Do you know what happens to the human brain during climax?"

"I dunno. Dopamine, I'm guessing."

"Correct. That, along with a bunch of other hormones, are released. Most importantly, the brain shuts down the control center that has to do with fear. Getting a person to orgasm is not the *only* way to shut down that control center. As you've already figured out, when those fear controls are put into overdrive, she gains the ability to control and project her immunity. So it's simple: Shut down the fear and her invisible shield comes down."

That makes a ton of sense now that I think about it, except . . . "How did you shut down her fear?"

"Our zoctors did it with the right mix of drugs and hormone injections." Mia puts another hand up. "Don't worry. She was under anesthesia, and she doesn't remember a thing."

Since the zovernment knows so much about how to scrub an Immune, I'm going to assume Arella wasn't their first. I wouldn't be surprised if the zovernment was or is hosting research sessions on Immunes in a secret facility somewhere.

"What about when Arella woke up?" I ask. "Wouldn't she have questioned why she was put to sleep by a bunch of people she didn't know?"

"The Ordinary had a Zordi fetus inside her that stopped developing. She would have had to undergo a surgery for the removal anyway, so we took the liberty of doing both procedures at the same time."

I swallow hard as I'm flashed back to the short moment when I thought I was going to be a dad. I hadn't felt that kind of happiness in . . . well, ever. I've always wanted a family, and the idea of having my own had brought me more joy than I realized it would. Then Arella told me our baby was gone.

I'll never forgive Jodi for all the things she's taken from me. First, my parents, even though she claims she didn't cause the explosion. Then she kidnapped Arella, killed my unborn child, and murdered my dad in front of me. Selfishly, I wish Jodi hadn't died. She's now free of the demons that turned her into the monster she was, instead of suffering with them like I am.

I keep my feet moving as I ask, "Am I right to assume that this isn't the first time an Ordinary has gotten pregnant with our kind?"

Without hesitation, Mia nods. "Yes. While it *can* happen, it doesn't happen very often, and very rarely does the baby grow to term. Even when Ordinaries reproduce with other Ordinaries, one in every four pregnancies ends in a loss. When it comes to Ordis reproducing with Zordis, losses happen ninety-nine percent of the time."

"So what you're saying is that the chances were pretty high that we would have lost our baby anyway?"

Another nod. "Most likely."

I'm not sure if that information is comforting or depressing. If the zovernment knows that only one in every hundred pregnancies between our kinds grows to term, that means it has happened enough times for them to have gathered that statistic, which means Mia probably knows the answer to my next question. "When those babies are born, are they half Zordi?"

Mia side-eyes me with a slight smile creeping onto her lips. "Are you asking because you're wondering if Miss Rance is part Zordi?"

"The idea has crossed my mind."

"Like I said, it's rare for a Zordi and Ordi baby to grow to term, but when they do, they're born as one or the other—never both. Miss Rance is full Ordinary, which means it is in your best interest to stay away from her."

I open my mouth, about to ask the question that's burning in my mind, when Mia throws her hand up, palm forward. "No, Mr. Grant, we cannot unscrub her." The way this woman knows what I'm about to ask before I ask it is a little unsettling. "Do you realize that your situation was one of the biggest scrub jobs the zovernment has had to do in decades? This wasn't like erasing the memories of all the people at an Ordinary school when a Zordi child got too emotional and lost control of their powers. This wasn't a situation where someone simply used their powers in public, thinking no one was around. Your situation was much more than that.

"Your face was plastered all over the news as a kidnapper. Even people who lived out in the middle-of-nowhere Montana heard about the man who disappeared and took his ex-girlfriend with him. People were looking into your criminal history and your past, and your fans went wild on social media. If we didn't erase all evidence of this incident from the Internet and alter everyone's memories, you would have come home to news reporters on your front lawn, waiting to get a statement. The FBI would have gotten involved, which comes with the risk of exposure, so we did what we had to do.

"Most importantly, we did this big scrub to protect the Immune. We couldn't allow her face to remain plastered all over the news. If there's attention on her, it's only a matter of time before the Royals discover her again and try to use her for her immunity."

I guess that's a positive. If the world doesn't remember Arella, that means the Royals don't either. That means she's safe.

"Do you know what makes her immune?" I ask as I turn around to head back toward my car.

Mia follows me. "I don't."

I give her a narrowed look.

"You don't have to believe me. That doesn't change the

fact that the zovernment doesn't have an explanation for her immunity."

From the tiny waves of calmness I'm sensing from Mia, I think she's telling the truth. Now it's time to ask the other question that's been burning on my mind. "Why didn't I get scrubbed?"

"Because if you forget everything that happened, how will you ever learn to never make those mistakes again? Need I remind you, Mr. Grant, you had an illegal relationship that resulted in high-level exposure and nationally televised news."

I throw my arms up, letting them flop to my sides. "So what am I supposed to do now? Just move on with my life as if I never met her?"

"That would be the wisest decision, yes."

"But she's my soul mate," I say as if it'll change anything.

"That's a small price to pay to avoid all the chaos that comes with worldwide exposure. Think of this sacrifice as your duty to our people."

That's some bullshit. I feel no sense of duty to the Zordinary community. The only thing I feel is a need to be with Arella, but she's with that other guy, which reminds me . . . "Who's that guy who claims to be her boyfriend?"

Mia sighs heavily. "For the record, I was against replacing you in her memories with another man, but the Scrubber insisted it was necessary. Apparently, the memories you created with her became such deep core memories that they were quite hard to fully erase. Therefore, the Scrubber altered them to reflect someone else."

A light flickers on in my chest. If Arella's memories run that deep, maybe there's a chance I can get her to remember me.

"May I ask you a question now?" Mia asks.

"Sure," I say through a sigh.

"Did Miss Rance ever feel the glimmer?"

"Is it possible for her to?" I thought the glimmer was something that's unique to only Zordi bodies.

"It is possible. Despite what you're taught, a soul-mate connection is not something that's limited to only Zordis. Ordinaries with Ordinary soul mates *can* sense when their partners are in danger. Their symptoms just aren't as severe, and they usually ignore them. However, if an Ordinary makes a soul-mate connection with a Zordi, they will experience the glimmer like any other Zordi does. And before you ask, no, we have no idea why that is. We can only assume that because one of the soul mates on that connection is a Zordi, the glimmer affects the Ordinary the same."

"So what you're saying is that the glimmer exists between both our kinds, but we Zordis just have a stronger connection to it?"

"Yes," Mia says with a firm nod. "Actually, that's a great way to put it. I'm going to use that at my next meeting with the other execs."

"To answer your original question, no, I don't know if she ever felt glimmer-like symptoms. If she did, she never mentioned it."

The glimmer exists to warn us that our soul mates are in danger when we're not around them. It's not as strong when we are already with our soul mate when something bad happens since we already have that knowledge. Whenever something bad happened to me, I was already with Arella, so if she did feel anything, she was too busy fighting off ice balls to pay attention to it.

"You realize that this is cruel, right?" My words come out partly angry and partly choked. "You're aware that Arella is my soul mate, yet you guys scrubbed her, and now you're telling me to just forget about her."

"What's done is done, Mr. Grant."

Well, fuck me then.

When I return to my car, Liz perks up, ready to hear everything. "So? How'd it go?"

I put my car into reverse and back away from the guard booth. The whole time, Mia watches me from outside the Escalade, as if making sure I'm actually leaving.

It's not until I'm at least a mile away from the prison that I say, "Basically, the Keeper said I'm shit out of luck and that I need to move on as if none of it ever happened."

"What? But Arella is your soul mate."

"That doesn't matter to them. They only care about keeping Ordinaries from knowing about our world."

While I drive us back to LA, I go into some details about my conversation with Mia. The whole time, Liz is quiet while she takes it all in.

Once I'm done, she says, "I think we both know you're not gonna stay away from her."

I chuckle humorlessly. "You know me too well."

"So what are you *actually* gonna do?"

My answer comes easily. "I'm gonna get her to remember me."

4

TREY

DESPITE HOW MUCH I WANT TO SHOW BACK UP AT ARELLA'S apartment, Liz convinces me to sleep on it.

Around noon, I wake up on Liz's couch, feeling like shit. My mind is hazy, and my body aches from head to toe.

I stumble into the bathroom like I'm hungover, even though I haven't been drinking. After a quick piss, I stare at myself in the mirror. The skin around my eyes is dark purple. I look like I either lost a bar fight or have some weird skin condition.

Liz's footsteps thump down her stairs as I make my way back to her uncomfortable couch. I didn't want to sleep here last night, but I also didn't trust myself to stay away from Arella.

"Holy balls!" Liz clasps an ungloved hand against her chest. "What happened to your face?"

"I think it's a side effect from coming off perrizophine."

"You look like the Joker."

"Thanks, Liz." I huff. "You're just the person everyone needs when they're going through one of the worst times of their lives."

"Sorry, T. I'll, um, be right back." Her footsteps thump

back up the stairs. A minute later, she's returned to the living room with her makeup bag in hand. "I did a quick search on the z-net. It sounds like Healing Water and bananas can help."

So I've heard. "You got any?"

"Yep." Liz disappears into her kitchen, then comes back with a cold bottle of Healing Water and two bananas. "Sorry, they're a little overripe."

"I'm not picky." I take the bananas and peel one open. Then I inhale half of it in one bite and wash it down with some Healing Water. "I'm gonna try to talk to her today—without that other guy there."

Liz unrolls her makeup bag over the coffee table. "Does he live with her?"

"Fuck if I know." I swallow down the rest of the banana, then peel open the second one.

"Whatever you do, T, just don't scare her again. Try to see it from her point of view. To her, you're just a crazy guy who showed up on her doorstep yesterday, claiming to be her boyfriend."

I slump my shoulders, feeling the weight of the world on them. "But to me, she's my everything."

"Yes," Liz says tenderly, "but she doesn't know that. How would you react if some chick you've never seen before showed up on your doorstep, claiming to be your girlfriend?"

I take a small bite of my second banana and actually chew it this time. "I'd probably think she's some deranged fan with an unhinged obsession."

"Exactly."

I didn't mean to freak out Arella. How was I supposed to know her memory had been wiped? If I had known, I might have handled things a little differently. "Okay, I'll try to be calm."

When my car pulls up to Arella's apartment complex, I'm not calm. I'm not even close to it. My hands are jittery, my throat is scratchy, and, worst of all, the skin around my eyes is still purple. No matter how much makeup Liz put on me, the purple was still visible. I ended up just washing off the makeup.

Thanks to the Healing Water and bananas, the body aches and that hazy feeling in my head have diminished. Before coming here, I stopped at home for a quick shower and a change of clothes. I hoped the purpleness would disappear during that time. It didn't, and I still look like shit, but I don't care because I need to see my girl.

Based on the way hundreds of emotions are shooting at me all at once, I'm gonna say my powers are back to normal. I draw in my range to a five-foot circle around me, turning the intense emotions screaming in the back of my mind into a low hum. Then I aim my gift at Arella's apartment.

No emotions come to me. That could mean one of two things: either she's not home or she is home and that other guy isn't. Only one way to find out.

Knock-knock.

A shuffle of feet comes toward the door, then stops. The barrier never opens. She must have seen me through the peephole and is now pretending she's not home. I didn't prepare for this. All I planned out was what I was gonna say once she opened the door. The thought never crossed my mind that she'd be too scared of me to open the door at all.

I knock again. In the gentle tone I would use if I was speaking to a wounded puppy, I say, "Arella, I'm not gonna hurt you. I just want to explain."

A short pause sits between us, then her firm voice comes from the other side. "If you don't leave, I'm calling the cops."

I suck in a deep breath as I try to calm my shaky hands. "Can I just talk to you? I promise I won't touch you."

There's another pause—longer this time. Then the bolt

lock clicks. The door opens, but it doesn't open all the way. A chain lock stops it, giving me only a three-inch view of the woman who completes me.

I crumple my eyebrows at the metal line blocking me from her. "Since when have you had a chain lock?"

"Since last night when my boyfriend installed one to keep crazy men from barging in again."

Hearing her call someone else her boyfriend hurts more than hearing her call me crazy. "I'm sorry about that. I didn't mean to scare you."

"Say what you came to say, then leave."

It stings that she's trying to get rid of me so quickly. I'm beginning to think getting her to remember me is gonna be harder than I thought. If she's not willing to listen to me, how can I explain anything? "Arella, I—"

"My name is Ari."

Ouch. I've always called her Arella, and she's always loved it. "Yes, that's what other people call you, but I don't."

"Why?"

"Because Arella is a unique name that suits you better than Ari."

She shoots me a dirty look. "Are you sure it's not just because you saw that it's my legal name and you didn't know I went by anything else while you were stalking me?"

"Is that what you think I've been doing?"

"How else would you have known how I met Caleb?"

"Who's Caleb?"

"My boyfriend."

Could you please *stop calling him that?* "I don't know how you met Caleb."

"Yesterday, you claimed that you and I met on the side of a highway. That's how I met Caleb."

"What? No, no, no." That must have been one of her core memories the Scrubber inserted Caleb into. What other core moments were altered? "Look, Arella, I—"

"It's Ari."

I refuse to call her that. *Ari* is not who she is to me. "Look, I know this is gonna sound insane, but you've had your memories erased. You know me. You just don't remember it. I met you on the side of a highway, then we fell deeply in love. I'm confident we had the kind of love that can't be erased."

"How can someone get their memories erased?"

When I ran through this conversation in my head, I knew she'd ask me that, so I prepared an answer. "You were in a bad car accident. You hit your head and got amnesia. Now you've forgotten me and you think that other guy is your boyfriend, but he's not."

"If that's the case, then why weren't you at the hospital after my car accident?"

I didn't prepare for her to ask me that. "Um, I couldn't be there."

"Why not?"

"Well, um, because I was in prison." That's probably not the best answer, but it's partly true, and I've got nothing else.

"Prison? For what? Stalking women?" Her words drive an invisible dagger straight into my chest.

"Of course not."

"Then what were you arrested for?"

"Um . . ." I think hard, trying to come up with a version of the truth. "I was doing things I shouldn't have done in public."

"Why isn't that on your criminal record?"

"Because they dropped the char—Wait, you looked up my record?"

She lets out a little *pfft*. "A strange man shows up at my door claiming to know me. Of course I'm going to look him up."

"I *do* know you, and I can prove it. Ask me anything."

"I'm not going to play this game." She's about to shut the door on me when I stop it with my foot.

"Arella, please, just hear me out."

"It's Ari," she says sternly. "And that's the last time I'm going to remind you."

Fuck. I need to stop calling her Arella. It's not benefiting me. I throw my hands up, palms forward. "Just ask me anything about you. I'll know the answer."

"The only thing that's going to prove is how good of a stalker you are."

"Then ask me questions even a stalker wouldn't know. I'll get them right."

Her shoulders rise and fall as she sucks in a breath and thinks. After a moment, she says, "What's the only food I'm allergic to?"

"Huh?"

"I said, what is the only food I'm allergic to?"

Well, fuck. I'm only one question in, and I'm already failing. "Ar—I mean . . . I'm sorry. I—I don't know the answer to that."

"I thought you said you *know* me?"

"I do. I just . . ." I shove a hand through my hair. "Of all the meals we've had together, you've never mentioned being allergic to anything. I guess I just assumed you didn't have any allergies."

"Okay, answer this one then: Where's my birthmark?"

"Your birthmark?"

"Yeah, you know, a mark on someone's skin they've had since birth. If you know me so well, where's mine?"

I rake my fingers through my hair again as I think back to all the times I had the privilege of seeing Arella naked. I can't recall seeing any marks on her skin. "I—I didn't realize you had one."

"I thought you said we were in *love.* If we were, you must have seen me naked and saw my birthmark. It's in a pretty obvious place."

This is not going the way I hoped it would. "It's probably

not *that* obvious, because I've kissed every single inch of your body, and I swear to you, I've never seen a birthmark."

That quiets her. I wish I knew what she was thinking. The blank look on her face tells me nothing. "One more chance. If you get this wrong, then you either leave or I'm calling the cops."

"Deal."

"What was the name of my childhood dog?"

Dog? She's never mentioned having a dog. I've never seen a picture of her with a dog either. I slump my shoulders. "I . . . I don't know. With how often you moved, I didn't even realize you had a dog."

She blinks up at me from behind her long black lashes. The look in her eyes kills me. There's no recognition in there anywhere. "We had a deal, sir. You leave or I'm calling the cops. Maybe your old prison cell is still vacant and they'll give it back to you."

With that, she slams the door in my face.

5

———

ARI

I'M IN THE MIDDLE OF TELLING JAVINA ABOUT MY INTERACTION with Trey earlier today. Caleb is at the museum, so it's just me and her, hanging out in my kitchen.

"Where was Caleb when Trey showed up?" Javina asks as she cracks open a can of root beer and takes a sip.

"At the gym."

"I see. So what questions did you ask Mr. Obsessed-with-you?"

I lean back against the counter and fold my arms together. "I asked him what food I'm allergic to, where my birthmark is, and what the name of my childhood dog was."

"Childhood dog? I didn't know you had a dog."

"I never did. I don't have a birthmark either, and I'm not allergic to any foods."

"Ahh . . ." Javina says when it clicks. "Trick questions on the spot. I like it. What were Trey's answers?"

"He got them all right. He said of all the meals we've had together, I never mentioned being allergic to anything. He said he's kissed every inch of my body and he's never seen a birthmark. Then he said with how often I moved, he didn't realize I ever had a dog."

40

"So he *does* know you."

Pfft. "Lucky guesses."

Javina shakes her head, then takes another sip of her soda. "I dunno 'bout that, babes. If someone were to ask me those questions, I woulda taken shot-in-the-dark guesses. Your allergies? Peanuts. It's the number-one food allergy people have. Your birthmark? It's on your back. It's a big area, and tons of people have birthmarks there. Your childhood dog's name? Bub. No matter what people name their dog, everyone calls their dog Bub."

Knock-knock.

Javina and I freeze.

"Who's here?" I ask, even though I've got a good feeling who it is.

"Stay here." Javina sets her root beer onto the counter, then heads to the door. She steals a peek through the peephole, then whispers, "It's him."

I stay where I am and whisper back, "Don't open it."

My best friend sucks at listening. "Don't worry. I've got this." With the chain lock in place, Javina slides the door open until it clicks against the metal.

"Javina," Trey says. I can't see him, but I recognize his voice. Hearing it just kicked my heart rate up.

Javina tilts her head to the side. "You know who I am?"

"Yeah, you're Arella's best friend. Your favorite color is pink. You enjoy spa days, massages, and you like to call me *pretty boy.*"

Javina glances back at me with a *what the hell?* look. I flash her the same look back. How does this guy know what Javina's favorite color is or that she enjoys spa days? She hasn't had one in almost a year. Is that how long he's been stalking me?

Javina turns back to the man outside my door. "What else do you know about me, pretty boy?"

"Uh, you're dating Rachel. You drive that red Toyota Corolla parked right there. Um . . . ." He pauses to think. "I know that Arella keeps root beer in her fridge just for you, even though she hates root beer."

Javina glances back at me again with her eyes bulging out of their sockets. Without making a sound, she mouths, *What the fuck?*

"Look, I know this must be weird for you since you don't remember me. I'm sure Arella has told you all about me by now. I know you're protective of her, but I promise, I'm not here to hurt her. I just want to show her something."

"Show her what?"

"It's a picture of her and I. It's proof."

Javina holds her palm out. "Hand it over, pretty boy."

"Could you ask her to come to the door?"

Javina flashes me a silent *what do you think?* look. My head tells me I should call the cops, but my heart tells me I'm not in danger around this man. If he wanted to hurt me, he would have already.

Trey's breath hitches as Javina steps aside and I step into his view. Earlier, he looked like he was recovering from two black eyes. Now the purple is gone. His skin looks perfect. Not a single out-of-place wrinkle or any signs that he's ever had a blemish.

His eyes are an ocean blue of somberness and fear. Why is *he* the one who's scared? He's the stranger who keeps showing up at *my* door, knowing things he shouldn't, and spewing out made-up stories of me losing my memory.

"Here." Trey hands me a wallet-size photo of him and I staring lovingly into each other's eyes. In the photo, I'm wearing a dress that's currently hanging in my closet. Around my neck is a necklace I've never seen before. It's a pair of golden angel wings around a huge sparkly heart-shaped diamond. "Four days ago, you were wearing the angel-wings necklace in this picture. It's a necklace I bought for you, and it's got an engraving on the back with my initials on it. Besides this photo, it's the only other thing that exists that's proof I'm telling the truth. Please tell me you have the necklace somewhere."

"I don't," I say as I hand the photo back to him. He doesn't take it. "Great job with the photoshop, though. That woman looks just like me."

"Because it *is* you. You just don't remember taking the picture."

"Right, because I lost my memory after a *bad car accident.* If that was true, how do you explain that Javina doesn't remember you either?"

His arm muscles flex as he scratches the back of his head. I try my best not to stare.

"Okay," he says, "I might have lied about the car accident thing. That's not actually how you lost your memories."

"Then how did it happen?"

"Um, I can't say. But if you could *try* to remember me, maybe you'll remember how that happened too."

I throw the photo at him. It falls flimsily to his feet. "Take your photoshopped picture and leave."

I'm about to shut the door on him when he shouts, "Wait! I can prove this wasn't photoshopped. You wrote a note on the back." He picks up the picture and hands it to me again.

Out of curiosity, I accept it. My lungs constrict as I read the note written in pen:

I love you, Trey. You are right.
We do belong together.
—Arella

It's in my loopy handwriting with my signature.

I was freaked out before. Now I'm terrified. How does he know what my handwriting looks like? How many times did he practice writing in my handwriting before he perfected it on the back of this photo?

Over my shoulder, Javina stares at the note. "I dunno, babes, that looks pretty legit to me. It's either real or a hella-good forgery."

"It's not a forgery," Trey says. "I swear."

"You've already admitted to lying about the car accident," I say. "How can I trust that you aren't lying about this too?"

"I only lied about the car accident because I can't tell you the truth about how you lost your memories. If I do, they'll put me back behind bars."

"Who's *they*?"

"The, uh, the government."

I press my eyebrows together. "What?"

"Yeah, I know it sounds weird, but again, if you can try to remember me, maybe—"

He gasps as I rip his photoshopped picture in half, then half again.

I toss the pieces at him. "Go away, and stop coming back. The next time you do, I won't hesitate to call the cops. This is your last warning."

"Nooo!" He falls to his knees, grasping at the photo pieces on the ground. "No. No. No." His breaths become shaky as he gapes up at me with the ripped-up picture in his palms. Disbelief mixes with the tears glistening over the surface of his eyes. "Why did you do that? This is the only thing I have of us."

"There is no *us*! I don't know who you are! Now leave!" I slam the door shut and twist the bolt lock.

My silent apartment feels too silent. I thought telling him off would feel good, but it doesn't. Instead, I feel . . . I'm not sure what the right word for it is. It's like I'm a sailor not at sea who knows I'm supposed to be in the water, but I don't know why. Meanwhile, something keeps pulling me back to shore.

Javina beams at me. "Damn, girl. That was spunky."

After letting out a long breath, I sneak a glance through the peephole. Trey is exactly where I left him: on his knees, with the photo pieces in his palms. Except now, he's got tears rolling down his cheeks. He looks like he's barely breathing as he stares at the ripped photo.

My heart breaks for him. I must have really hurt him. Then again, he's a stalker. A lunatic. A deranged man. Whatever I want to call him, they all point to the same thing: This guy is off his rocker.

"Is he still there?" Javina whispers.

"Yeah," I whisper back.

"What's he doing?"

"I don't know. He's just . . . staring at the ripped picture." I feel the need to apologize, but for what? I don't owe him anything.

Eventually, Trey stands and wipes his damp face off on his shirt. Then he stares at the ground with a desolate look in his eyes. His chest rises and falls with each breath he struggles to suck in. I've never seen someone so sad. He's either a really good actor or he actually believes the crazy story he's been feeding me and is truly hurt by what I just did.

With a blank look in his eyes, he turns on his heel and walks away.

At the living room window, I pull the blinds back a tiny bit to see him slowly dragging his feet toward his car like they're weighed down by a ball and chain. He's still got that bleak expression on his face as he opens the driver's door and sits behind the wheel.

Then he just sits.

And sits.

And sits.

The whole time, he stares at his steering wheel and barely blinks. He's in his car for so long that Javina gets tired of peeking out the window with me and heads to the couch with her root beer in hand. As for me, I'm not planning to leave this window until he's gone.

"Seeing a man that pretty look so sad hurts me," Javina

says. "I'm about to go out there and offer him a blow job just to wipe that godforsaken frown off his face."

I'm still holding the blinds open just enough for my right eyeball to see outside. "He could just be putting on a show."

"A show for who?"

"For me—to make me feel bad for him so I'll believe his crazy story."

Javina sucks in a breath through her teeth, shaking her head. "I dunno, babes. Your handwriting on the back of that picture looked hella real to me."

"But how? I don't recall writing a note on the back of a picture I never took."

Javina gasps so loudly, I drop the blinds. "Oh my god. What if he's from an alternate universe?"

"A what?"

"You know, a world like ours, but not. Maybe whatever he was imprisoned for was so bad that his universe banished him to our universe. And in his world, you were his girlfriend, but he doesn't realize he's been banished, so he thinks you're his girlfriend, when really, his real girlfriend is back in his universe."

"Javie . . ." I say with a *come on* face, "that sounds even crazier than the lies he's trying to feed me."

"Hey, if it's possible for D. B. Cooper to jump out of a flying plane with a bag full of cash and never be seen again, then alternate universes are possible too." She gasps again. "What if that's why no one ever found D. B. Cooper or his parachute? What if he parachuted through a portal into another universe?"

I roll my eyes at her. "Maybe it's time we lay off the true crime shows for a while."

In the parking lot, an engine starts. I peek through the blinds again and catch a glimpse of Trey driving away. "He finally left."

Javina finishes the rest of her root beer, then stares at the empty can in her hands. "Don't you find it a little odd that he knows you don't like root beer and that you keep it in your fridge just for me?"

I join her on the couch. "That's what stalkers do; they watch you until they know every little detail about you."

"Yeah, but that's a pretty *specific* thing to know, and something you can't find out just by sitting outside someone's house. Also, I'm not gonna lie; calling him *pretty boy* feels right."

"What are you trying to say?"

She shrugs a shoulder. "I dunno. I'm just thinking out loud. Anyway, I should dip out. Will you be cool on your own?"

"Yeah, I've got a chain lock now."

Javina disappears into my kitchen to toss her can into the recycling, then heads to the front door to slip her shoes on. "Call me if pretty boy comes back, 'kay?"

"Okay." Now that I'm hearing her call him that again, I suppose it does sound right.

Javina opens my apartment door, then gasps.

I shoot up from the couch. "What?"

"He left the pieces of the photo on the ground." Javina picks them up and holds them out to me. "Here. Put these under a microscope."

"Why?" I open my palm for her to drop the pieces into.

"To look for alternate universe dust, duh. If this picture came from his world, there's probably evidence of it on there somewhere."

I roll my eyes as I chuckle softly. "Okay. I'll get right on that."

Once Javina is gone, I return to the couch to examine the photo. I don't have a microscope, but I do have packaging tape. On the coffee table, I arrange the photo pieces to reflect their original form. Then I stick a large piece of transparent tape over the picture. After cutting off the excess tape, I sit back to investigate the mended photo.

Javina is right, the handwriting does look legit. The photo looks real too. I stare closer at the necklace I'm wearing in the picture. I don't recognize it. Trey claims I was wearing this necklace four days ago. If that's true, where is it now?

6

ARI

I haven't seen Trey in over three weeks. At least not in real life. In my dreams, he's the star of the show.

It's been happening a few times a week. One of my dreams was of us at a restaurant together. Trey and I had just finished our pastas when he asked me to dance with him. After I refused, he frolicked around the dance area by himself with an invisible woman in his arms. The whole time, I laughed until my belly hurt.

Another one of the dreams I had was of us baking snickerdoodle cookies together. Trey and I were in a kitchen I didn't recognize, when suddenly, we were throwing flour at each other. It ended with us making out until I was breathless.

My dream last night was a terrifying one. I was getting dressed in my bedroom when I saw a spider. Usually, one spider doesn't freak me out; I'll simply grab a shoe and stomp on it. But this spider was huge—so big, I could see the little hairs on its legs.

Suddenly, it wasn't just one spider anymore. There were tons of them. Hundreds, maybe thousands, came crawling out from every crevice of my bedroom. I screamed and jumped onto the bed, but they followed me there. Then they were crawling on me like they were trying to eat me alive. I kept wailing and screaming until I was lifted off my feet and rushed out of my apartment. The person who saved me was Trey.

Why am I suddenly having dreams about this man? And why so frequently? I haven't told anyone about my dreams. Not Caleb, and especially not Javina. I already know what my best friend will say. It'll be something along the lines of Trey being from an alternate universe and how his presence here is causing my dreams to be snapshots of things that happened in his universe.

Javina hasn't given up on the alternate-universe theory. She even came up with a name for the alternate version of me: Alterella. "You know," she said, "because he calls you Arella. Maybe in his universe, you go by your full name."

Javina's theory could be right. It would explain why Alterella signed her name as Arella instead of Ari.

I'm storing Trey's taped-up picture in a book that Caleb would never open. He doesn't know I have this photo, and I don't want him to know. He might trash it. I don't know why I'm so keen on keeping it or why I think to look at it as often as I do, but I can't bring myself to get rid of it.

Keys jingle outside my apartment door. I peek my head out from the kitchen just as Caleb steps inside and kicks his shoes off.

"Hey, muffin," he says as he shuts the door and secures the chain lock. I had left it off knowing he'd be home soon. He still has beads of sweat running down his forehead from his workout at the gym.

"Lunch will be ready in ten," I say.

"Sounds awesome. I'm going to take a quick shower, then I'll be right out."

After his shower, Caleb emerges from our bedroom wearing a pastel pink button-up. It's one of my favorite shirts on him because he always looks so happy in it.

"Smells good," he says. "What did you make?"

I set two bowls across from each other on our cozy kitchen table. "Quinoa salad."

Caleb plants himself into his chair, practically drooling. "Thanks. This looks awesome."

"How was your workout?" I ask as I sit and take my first forkful.

"Good. Rakesh and I worked on our upper body today. He's a beast. I could barely keep up with him."

Caleb has been best friends with Rakesh since they roomed together in college. They go to the gym together almost every day, even on Saturdays, like today. When they're not at the gym, they love to explore bookstores and go hiking together. If Caleb is not with me or at work, there's a pretty good chance he's with Rakesh.

"Did Rakesh ever hear back about that personal trainer position?" I ask.

"Yeah. He didn't get the job, but he applied at a different gym, and he already got an interview."

"Wonderful. I hope he—" My entire body locks up as my eyes land on a spider on the wall. It's big, it's black, and it's got hairy legs.

Suddenly, I feel it again, all those spiders crawling up my body. I feel their legs on my skin. They're attacking me! They're trying to eat me! They're . . .

The room tilts as I fall off my chair. When my body hits the floor, the room goes black.

7

———

TREY

THE SECOND THE NAUSEA HITS ME, I'M ON MY NEW motorcycle in a flash. As I race toward Arella's apartment, I pray to the glimmer gods that this one isn't life-threatening. I can't lose her this way, not when she doesn't know who I am.

Cars honk at me from all directions as I weave between them on my bike. This one revs up to speed faster than my old one, and I'm living for it.

My arms feel numb as Arella's apartment complex comes into view. Her car is sitting in the lot. *Thank fuck.* I had no idea where she was, and this was my best guess. If she wasn't here, I would have torn this city apart looking for her.

When I park, I yank my helmet off and chuck it in the grass. Then I shake my numb arms out as I sprint to her apartment door.

I pound on it. "Arella?"

"Just put the knife down," a man says calmly.

Arella shouts from the inside. "Get away from me, or I'll stab you!"

I pound on the door again. "Arella?" I'm about to wave a hand at the lock to open it when the door bursts open.

Arella stands on the other side with a kitchen knife in

52

hand. The moment she locks her eyes with mine, I see it—recognition. "Trey!"

My name. *She just said my name.* I didn't realize how much I was yearning to hear it come from her lips.

The knife falls from her hand, then she throws herself at me. She wraps her arms around my torso as she buries her face into my chest. Instinctively, one of my arms latches around her back as my other hand fists her soft hair.

Tears pool in the corners of my eyes. For the last three weeks, I've spiraled down hours of dark thoughts, wondering if I'd ever get my girl back. Now she's back. I don't know how, but she's back, and I'm never letting her go.

"Oh, Trey," she says into my shirt. "Thank God you're here."

My blackened world fades back to color. That constant knot in my chest loosens. My lungs feel less constricted. I'm sucking in air, and it no longer feels like a battle.

"Arella," I say into the top of her hair. "What happened, baby?"

She leans back and points at a wide-eyed Caleb standing in her living room. "I don't know. I woke up in my bed, then all of a sudden, this strange man walked into my room. He keeps saying I'm his girlfriend."

I glance at Caleb as if he knows what the fuck is going on. The look on his face confirms he's just as confused as I am. With one hand firmly around Arella's waist, I use my other hand to grab her face and force her attention back to me.

She looks straight into my eyes, and I see it again—recognition. It makes me so happy, a tear actually rolls down my cheek.

"Tell me, baby. What's the last thing you remember?"

"Like, before I woke up?"

I nod.

"Um, I—I don't know."

"Think, babe. Think real hard for me. Do you remember being at the Ridge?"

She doesn't hesitate. "Yeah."

"Do you remember us getting arrested?"

A nod.

"Do you remember when a bunch of Royals popped out of the woods and attacked us?"

"Yes. Then you got stabbed, and I was putting pressure on your wound when, all of a sudden, everything froze."

That was the last time I saw her before I was knocked out and woke up in z-prison. "Do you remember anything after that?"

She thinks for a moment. "Not really. The next thing I remember is waking up and this guy walking into my room."

I hold her tight against me. "It's all right, baby. I'm here now."

I get to hold her for all of two seconds before Caleb shouts, "What the fuck is going on?"

I wish I had an answer for him, because I want to know too. How did Arella suddenly get all her memories back? Well, *most* of them. She doesn't have any recollection of what happened after the Enforcers showed up.

"Ari, why are you letting this man touch you? He's a psycho."

Arella leans back and furrows her brow. "Who are you?"

"I told you already. I'm your boyfriend."

"No, you're not. *He* is." She gestures toward me, making my heart leap out of my chest. I didn't realize how satisfying it would be to hear Arella tell someone that *I'm* her boyfriend and not him. That title doesn't even fully encapsulate all the deep feelings I have for her, but I'll take it over being called her stalker.

"Wow." Caleb chuckles humorlessly. "You must have hit your head really hard."

I've been staring at Arella this whole time, but that

statement makes me flick my eyes up to Caleb. "She hit her head?"

"Yes. We were just sitting down for lunch when she saw a spider on the wall. Then she fell off her chair and hit her head on the floor. I picked her up, laid her in bed, and was just getting her a glass of water when she woke up and screamed at me to get out of our apartment."

"*My* apartment," Arella says with a scowl.

"*Our* apartment," Caleb says.

"What is happening right now?" Arella gapes up at me as if I've got the answer. "Who is this guy and why is he——" She lets out a painful scream. It retightens that knot in my chest. Her entire face crumples as she clasps her palms against her temples. She screams again, then her knees buckle.

I catch her as she slumps to the ground. "What's wrong?"

"My head. It hurts."

"Where?"

"All over. Something is pinching my brain and my temples."

In one swift motion, I scoop her into my arms and cradle her against me as I march toward her bedroom. Confused energy seeps into my mind from behind me. Caleb follows me and watches my every move as I lay Arella on her bed and cover her with blankets.

I have no idea why her head hurts. I'm going to assume it has something to do with how she suddenly remembers me, but how do I stop the pain?

"Ah!" She clasps her hands to her temples again. "Oh, God. My head."

I turn to Caleb. "Tylenol. Ibuprofen. Do you have either of those?"

With a nod, the dude disappears, then he returns with two pills in his palm.

I accept the white tablets from him and offer them to Arella. "Here, babe. Take these."

There's a glass of water on her nightstand that I hand to her as well. She takes the pills with a large gulp of liquid, then sets the glass back onto her nightstand.

"Maybe I should sleep it off," she says.

"Sure. Maybe that'll help."

She lays her head onto her pillow, then places a gentle hand over my forearm. "Will you cuddle me?"

I never enjoyed cuddling until I met Arella. Once I cuddled with her, it was practically all we ever did together. Hearing her ask me to cuddle her is like hearing a perfect chord on the grandest piano of all grand pianos.

Without hesitation, I kick my shoes off, then shrug off my jacket and let it drop to the carpet. Then I climb onto her mattress and slip under the covers with her. Arella scoots closer to me, then lays her head over my shoulder and rests a hand over my abs. I squeeze my arms around her as happy tears fall from my eyes.

I ignore Caleb's glare as I pull the blanket over Arella some more and tuck it under her back. Then I breathe in her intoxicating scent of lavender and springtime, allowing it to relax me. I haven't felt this at ease since . . . I can't remember. Since before Arella was kidnapped, that's for damn sure.

My girl tilts her head back to look at me. "Trey?"

I'll never get sick of hearing her say my name. "Yes, baby?"

"Don't leave me, okay? Stay here until I wake up."

It would take an act of God to make me leave her.

8

———

TREY

There's evidence of *him* everywhere. He's got clothes in the closet. Jackets hanging up behind the door. Colognes on the nightstand. A pair of his worn socks lying on the floor. I haven't gotten a closer look at the rest of Arella's apartment yet, but I can only imagine there's more of him around.

The Keepers sure went through a lot of effort to plant Caleb into Arella's life: altering her memories, moving him in, giving them a shitload of fake memories together. It was a good effort, but in the end, I was right. I had known my girl could fight it. I had known she could overcome the scrub. Her immunity probably played a huge part in that, but I'm going to give most of the credit to her inner strength—one of the first things about her I fell in love with.

Now that she's come back to me, I'm gonna make sure she stays. Fuck the Keepers, and fuck their stupid laws. If this isn't proof that they can't keep my soul mate away from me, I dunno what is.

Whenever Arella wakes up, we'll figure out a plan together. We'll run away to somewhere the zovernment can't find us. We'll start a family, and we'll grow old together.

Whatever Arella wants, she'll get. All I want, all I need, is to be with her. As long as I've got that, I'll—

"She knows you," Caleb says, cutting into my thoughts. He's stationed on a chair in the corner, where he has been since Arella fell asleep. Like a fucking creep, he's been watching me hold her for the last twenty minutes. No matter what I said, he refused to leave. "How does she know you?"

"Could you speak quieter?" I say in a low whisper. "I don't want you to wake her."

The pastel-shirt-wearing motherfucker has the nerve to cross his arms over his chest and shoot daggers at me with his eyes. "Answer my question, asshole. How does she know you?"

"Speak quieter, asshole, or I'll throat-punch you so hard, you'll never be able to speak again."

In a lower tone this time, he says slowly, "How . . . does . . . she . . . know you?"

"We met on the side of a highway."

"That's how she and I met." The dude narrows his gaze at me. "How is it possible that we both met her the same unique way?"

Maybe because you only met her after the goddamn Keepers placed you here. I don't bother coming up with an answer for him because I don't care enough. The only thing I care about is the woman in my arms.

After a long silence, Caleb speaks again. "The only reason I haven't torn you away from my girl is because she specifically asked you to stay. If she hadn't, I would have called the cops by now."

"Call her *your girl* again and I'll set you on fire." The guy probably thinks that's an empty threat, but my palms are already sparking up.

He scoffs. "You're kinda possessive of her for a man she didn't remember an hour ago."

"She remembers me now, so you can go fuck off." *Preferably over a cliff.* The tallest damn cliff he can find.

"How did she forget you?"

I let out a frustrated sigh. "Don't you have something better to do? Like, I dunno, fall into a pool of sharks?"

"Actually, sharks aren't as violent as people think. More people are killed by cows every year than sharks."

"That's great. Since you're such a know-it-all, why don't you go on *Jeopardy!?* I'm sure they'd love to feature you and your pastel-as-fuck pink shirt."

He shrugs with a grin I want to slap off his ugly face. "I'm just sayin', dude. If you're going to wish death upon me, you should wish for cows over sharks."

"Seriously, could you just fuck off?" *And take all your shit in Arella's apartment with you.*

It takes him a moment to finally stand. "Fine. I'm going to go finish the lunch that my *girlfriend* cooked for me, but the second she wakes up, I'm comin' right back."

As he exits the room, I imagine chucking a big-ass fireball at the back of his head. If I wouldn't get imprisoned for exposure, I probably would.

Finally, for the first time since we were in my parents' safe house, I'm holding my girl—alone. I relish how the sounds of her steady breaths calm me and the way she looks so innocently beautiful when she's asleep. She's an angel who was made specially for me, and she fits in my arms like we're two perfect pieces of a puzzle. Little does Caleb know, our puzzle doesn't have room for a third piece.

Barely five minutes pass before Arella stirs. I remain still in case she's just fidgeting a little, but she moves some more, then her eyes flutter open. When she tilts her head back to look at me, my heart sinks to my stomach.

The recognition is gone.

A high-pitched scream fills the room as Arella launches herself off the bed. "Get away from me!"

My world stops turning.

Caleb dashes through the open door, then my gut wrenches as my girl dives straight into his arms.

She points a shaky finger at me. "Caleb! He—the crazy guy—he's in our bed."

Our bed. That one little word jabs me in the gut. My breath hitches as Caleb protectively snakes his arm around my entire reason for existing.

"Calm down, muffin. Everything's okay."

Muffin? What the fuck?

"It's not okay!" Arella shouts. "The crazy guy is *in our bed*!"

I'd be fine going the rest of my life without ever hearing her say "our bed" in reference to Caleb ever again. Slowly, I slide off the mattress with my hands up in surrender. My movements only make Arella curl into this other guy more.

All the color that lit up my world a minute ago quickly fades. That pitch-black fog of depressive darkness floats back into me, clouding my vision.

Caleb cups her face the way I did earlier, forcing her attention to him. "What's the last thing you remember?"

"We were having lunch," Arella says. "Then I saw a big spider."

"What else?"

Her eyes cast down as she thinks. "Um, I think I passed out."

"You did, but you're okay now." Caleb pulls her closer to him. My body stiffens as she softens into his chest. "I've got you, muffin."

Seeing her in his arms like that is like watching a horror movie: It's terrifying, but I can't look away.

Caleb shoots me a glare. "Get out." He keeps his arms wrapped tightly around my girl as she turns her head to look at me. Still no recognition.

Swallowing hard, I keep my hands up in surrender as my eyes lock with hers. In the calmest voice I can manage, I say, "You just remembered me."

Her eyebrows dip. "What?"

"Just now, before you fell asleep, you remembered me."

"What are you talking about?"

I flick my gaze up to Caleb. "Tell her."

The dude blinks at me in silence, and it's all I need to know he's not gonna back me up. Why would he? To him, I'm the guy who's trying to steal his girl.

"Come on, man," I plead, "tell her the truth."

"Get out," he says.

He's a lost cause, but Arella isn't. That recognition earlier is proof that every moment we've ever shared together is still inside her somewhere. Maybe those memories are buried deep—way, way deep—but she can access them. There's hope. I can get through to her. I just have to figure out how.

"Arella, twenty minutes ago, you—"

"My name is Ari!" she shouts so loudly, I drop my hands and jerk back a step. I trip over my shoes and catch myself on her nightstand. "If you ever call me Arella again, I'm going to file a restraining order against you. Actually, I'm going to do that regardless. I told you to stop stalking me."

"I'm not stalking you. I'm telling the truth. Just now, you remem—"

"No! I don't want to hear you feed me a bunch of lies. Just leave, and stay away from me!"

My breaths come out shallow as all the hope I just had fades away. The disgusted look she's giving me is confirmation that no matter what I say, no matter what I do, she's not coming back to me.

She doesn't remember me.

End of story.

She doesn't remember the nights we spent cuddled in my bed, talking about her dream bakery until two in the morning. She doesn't remember taking me to her *thinking spot* under that giant oak tree—the place where we made love for the first time. She doesn't remember the battles we fought together to stay alive. She doesn't remember any of it.

Without her memories, this woman standing in front of me isn't Arella. Suddenly, it hits me that she's been right this whole time: Her name *is* Ari, because Arella is gone. Arella died the moment that Scrubber altered her memories to remove me. Unless she can remember us falling in love and all the hell we went through together, this woman in front of me is just a woman who *looks* like the woman I love.

The realization hits me like a baseball bat to the face. First my parents, then my Deaf mentee kid Elliott, my unborn baby, my dad, and now her. This is my fate, to lose anyone who has ever meant anything to me. What did I do to deserve this curse? I would never wish this torture upon anyone. Not even Aunt Jodi, who I hate with every piece of my broken soul. Who's next? Liz? The rest of my bandmates? My dog? I don't even have a dog, but if I did, I'm sure it wouldn't be safe either.

Tears collect on the surface of my eyes. I need to get outta here before they drip down.

I stare blankly at my shoes as I shove my feet into them. My breaths come out sharp as I pluck my leather jacket off the floor and slip my arms through it. I feel Ari's and Caleb's gazes on me as I force my feet to shuffle around the bed.

As I pass them, I keep my eyes glued to the carpet. I can't look at them. I shouldn't, anyway. I don't know them, and they don't know me. To them, I'm just a stranger in their home. I don't belong here.

I slam their apartment door shut behind me as I drag my feet outside. I'm about to reach my bike when I realize my helmet is missing. I twist on my heel and find it in the grass, exactly where I chucked it. My vision blurs with wetness as I bend to pick it up.

As soon as I pull the helmet over my head and my face is covered, I burst into a silent sob. It's the kind that consumes my entire body and shakes my shoulders. Tears roll down my cheeks in steady streams as I spend all my energy forcing my feet toward my bike. It's hard to move when the air feels like black sludge entering my lungs.

A door opens behind me. "Trey!"

Fuck. It's her voice. For a second, I think about turning around and scooping her up. I'd rip my helmet off and kiss her until she's breathless. She'd say my name again and look up at me with that precious recognition in her eyes.

But it's not her. It wasn't her when I showed up here after leaving z-prison, and it wasn't her I gave my photo to either. My Arella is gone, and no matter how much this woman sounds, looks, or even acts like Arella, she *isn't* my Arella.

That's why when she calls my name again, I don't stop. Actually, my slouchy walk toward my motorcycle turns into a dead run. I have no desire to talk to a woman who reminds me of someone I lost. Someone I have zero chances of ever getting back.

"Trey," she calls again as I straddle my bike.

The key is still in the ignition. I turn it, and the engine awakens with a soft rumble. I'm about to back out of my parking spot when she runs up next to me and places a hand over my forearm.

"Trey, wait!" Her touch doesn't feel like Arella's. It feels more like pain and heartache. "Can I talk to you for a second?"

I can't answer her with words, because if I do, they'll come out through a choked sob. Silent tears are still rolling down my cheeks, wetting the inside of my helmet. I'd wipe them away, but that would require removing my helmet. I can't let this woman see me cry. She wouldn't understand, and from what I know about her, she doesn't care to, so I simply pluck her hand off my forearm, give it back to her, then roll my motorcycle back.

Like Arella, this woman is difficult as fuck. She runs

behind my bike and throws her hands up. "Trey, please! Wait!"

With a sigh, I twist the key. The engine dies like the way I am on the inside with each passing moment I'm in this woman's presence.

She returns to my side. "I just want to talk to you."

I circle my hand in the air as if to say, *So talk then.*

"Can you take off your helmet?"

Holding back my sobs, I shake my head.

"Please? It feels weird to talk to someone when I can't see their face."

If this woman is anything like Arella, she won't give up until she gets what she wants. The faster I do what she asks, the faster I can get outta here.

Looking anywhere but at her, I reluctantly drag my helmet off and set it on my lap. A light breeze blows against my damp skin as I stare at the bike key I want to twist so badly.

Ari lets out a little gasp. "Oh, Trey . . ."

I bet she didn't expect to see me like this. I probably have red cheeks and even redder eyes. I drag the bottom of my shirt up to wipe off my wet face.

In the corner of my eye, I see her attention drop to my bare stomach. She stares at my abs while I dry my cheeks. Her fingers used to trail little figure eights over my abs whenever she rode on the back of my bike. She doesn't remember that, but I do. I'll remember it for the rest of my miserable existence.

"Oh, Trey . . ." she says again. I wish she'd stop saying my name. It's in Arella's voice, and I used to love hearing her say my name. Hearing it was like hearing my favorite song pop on the radio. Hearing it now is like hearing skips on a record player. It's still Arella's voice, but something is off about it. "I didn't mean to hurt you."

I bet if I could sense her emotions, they'd be somewhere between shock and pity. I don't want her pity. The only thing I ever wanted from her was for her to hear me out. For her to *try* to remember me. But she didn't want to hear me out. She didn't even want to try.

Arella never pitied me. Even when I told her about witnessing my parents' murder, the only way Arella ever looked at me was with understanding. I don't think I'll ever find that again.

Since this woman isn't getting to the point, I muster up the courage to force out some words. They come out more broken than I intend them to. "Just, uh, s-say what you came out to say so I can l-leave."

"Um . . ." In the corner of my eye, I see her rub the ends of her long hair between her fingers. Arella would do that whenever she was anxious. I'll miss seeing that. "Caleb confirmed that what you said is true. He said that I remembered you."

I'm surprised Caleb told her the truth. I didn't think he would.

"How did that happen?" she asks.

I keep my eyes glued to anything but her. "Don't you think that if I knew, I'd do anything and everything in my power to make it happen again?" *Permanently this time.*

She goes silent as my question sinks in. "Um, Caleb also mentioned that I said something about you getting stabbed. He said I remembered putting pressure on your wound. Is that true?"

Slowly, I nod, unsure where she's going with this.

"Where did you get stabbed?"

"In my side."

"Can I see it?"

Ah. That's where she's going with this. She wants physical proof that I was stabbed because simply hearing it from her stupid boyfriend isn't enough. Suddenly, I wish I hadn't been fixed up by the z-prison Healer, because then I'd have something to show her. Unfortunately, if I wasn't healed, I probably wouldn't be here.

Either way, having proof changes nothing. I know that now. Even if she saw the remnants of a stab wound, she still wouldn't remember me. She would still have another man waiting for her in their apartment. She would still have no recollection of us falling in love. Therefore, this conversation is pointless.

"I don't have a scar from it." I tap my fingers against my helmet, itching to put it back on.

She cocks her head at me. "How is that possible?"

"The same way it's possible for you to not remember a single thing about me."

"So, like, magic?"

It's offensive as fuck to call anything from the Zordinary world *magic*. Our gifts are passed down through genetics. There's nothing magical about that.

"Is there anything else you wanted to talk to me about?" I ask, a little clipped. I know I shouldn't be mad at her. It's not her fault I've been erased from her head, but all my energy is being used to keep my shoulders from shuddering. I only have so much energy left to say things nicely.

"I guess not."

"So can I go now?"

Her face drops, and I'm not sure why. What did she expect from this exchange? For me to have all the answers? I don't, and I'm more upset about it than she is.

She swallows thickly. "Yeah, you can go."

I waste no time dragging my helmet back over my head, then turning my bike key. The engine rumbles again. Ari steps back, giving me enough space to back out. Once I do, I ride away from her, leaving behind my entire heart in her hands.

It may not belong to her, but it belongs to her soul. Arella is still in there somewhere, and I want what belongs to her to stay with her.

9

ARI

"So?" Caleb says when I shut the door behind me. "Did you see a scar?"

I'm speechless. I'm not sure what I wanted from that encounter with Trey, but I didn't expect to come out of it feeling so confused and empty. I suppose I wanted answers, but all I've got is more questions.

I slump into my chair at the kitchen table. My quinoa is still waiting for me to eat it. I don't feel like eating though. "No, I didn't see a scar."

"So he was lying then."

The evidence—or lack thereof—sure points that way. However, I'm not convinced that's the whole story.

"Hopefully, that's the last we'll ever see of him," Caleb says. "I'll help you file that restraining order on Monday."

"Okay," I say impassively. I can't think straight. My mind is reeling.

Caleb told me that after I woke up from fainting, I freaked out and didn't know who he was. Apparently, I kept yelling at him to get out of our apartment. When he refused, apparently, I ran into the kitchen and threatened him with a

67

knife. Why would I do that? More importantly, why don't I *remember* doing that?

According to Caleb, Trey showed up shortly after, pounding on our door, and when I heard Trey's voice, I ran straight to him.

"You remembered him," Caleb told me. "You said something about how he got stabbed and you were putting pressure on his wound. Then you got these painful pinches in your head. He brought you to our bed, then you asked him to cuddle with you. I'm not gonna lie, babe. It was pretty fucking strange to see you talk to that man like you knew him."

Why don't I remember *any* of that? The last thing I remember is seeing that spider; then I woke up in my bed with Trey in it.

I stand with my bowl in hand. From a lower cabinet, I pick out a Tupperware container and spoon my lunch into it.

"You didn't eat much," Caleb says.

"I'll try eating more later." I snap the lid onto the container, then place it into the fridge, knowing I probably won't eat it later. As I close the door, the room spins around me and a wave of nausea hits me in the gut. A pair of strong arms catches me as I stumble backward.

"Muffin?"

"I'm okay," I lie. "Just got dizzy all of a sudden."

"You want to sit down?"

"Sure." The nausea whips around my stomach as Caleb leads me to the couch. We're only halfway into the living room when I feel like— "I'm gonna throw up."

In a flash, Caleb lets go of me and rushes into the kitchen. A trash bin appears in front of me just as I start hurling. My chest heaves as I cough up the little that's in my stomach.

Caleb holds back my long hair as I puke some more. Once the vomit has subsided, he helps me over to the couch. "Do you feel any better?" he asks.

"No," I say as I lay my head back. "My arms feel numb, and I feel like I might throw up again."

"That's it. I'm taking you to the ER."

THE NAUSEA HAS SIMMERED DOWN A BIT NOW THAT WE'RE AT the ER. The numbness in my arms is lighter too. The twisting knot in my chest hasn't disappeared though.

A small medical bed sits in the middle of my sterile room. A white paper sheet is draped over the top of the bed, and the air smells of lemony disinfectant.

"Take a seat, Miss Rance," says the nurse, who points two fingers toward the bed.

I do as I'm told while Javina plops into a chair. Since there's only one chair, Caleb leans his back against the wall, crossing his arms over his chest.

On our way to the hospital, I called Javina to ask if she could meet us here. Depending on how long this takes, Caleb will have to leave for work, and he didn't want me at the ER alone.

The nurse checks my temperature, then takes my blood pressure. After he tells me that everything looks normal, he says, "We only have one doctor in tonight. She's currently with another patient but should be around to speak with you shortly."

"No worries," I say. "I can wait."

"Thanks. I'm gonna go check in the next patient. Just holler at any of the nurses out here if you need anything."

The second the nurse slides the glass door shut behind him, Javina perks up. "Okay, tell me what happened!"

Together, Caleb and I tell her a shortened version of what happened with Trey. Caleb even tells her about all the stuff that happened while I was under some kind of memory spell.

"The way he stared at her while she slept creeped me the fuck out."

"I have a theory," Javina says. "I think Trey was banished here from an alternate universe and doesn't know it. With his presence in our world, I think Ari's memories are merging with the memories of the Ari from *his* universe. Maybe that's how she suddenly remembered him but she actually doesn't, because technically, those things didn't happen to her; they happened to Alterella."

Caleb arches his brow. "Alterella?"

"I know, I know. I'm a clever woman," Javina says with a flip of her black curls. "Anyway, what if traveling through alternate universe portals heals all wounds? Maybe that's how he doesn't have a scar from being stabbed."

The room goes silent as Caleb glances between me and Javina a few times. Then he hooks a thumb her way. "Is it just me, or is Javina making some sense?"

"What?" I blanch. "She's making no sense at all. There's no such thing as alternate universes."

Caleb shrugs a shoulder. "I didn't think so either—until you screamed at me to get out of our apartment, then laid in our bed with another man who you claimed was your boyfriend."

I can't believe Caleb is actually considering Javina's theory. Usually, he's so pragmatic.

"Shit, Trey can be *my* boyfriend if he wants," Javina says, fanning herself with a hand. "I'd willingly throw myself into a volcano if it means that hunk of delicious meat would belong to me."

I roll my eyes at her.

"I'll do some research on alternate universes tonight while I've got downtime on my shift," Caleb says. "Which reminds me, I've gotta get going. I still have to run home and get my uniform on before I head to work. Will you be okay with Javina?"

"Of course, love." We give each other a quick kiss.

Barely a minute after Caleb leaves, an Asian woman in scrubs strolls into my room with a friendly smile. "Hello, I'm Doctor Park. Could you confirm your full name and birthdate for me?" After I do, she washes her hands at the sink, then turns to me. "All right. Tell me why you're in today."

"I'm not really sure what's wrong with me. One second, I was putting food away. The next, I got really dizzy and—"

"Doctor Park!" a guy shouts from outside my room. "Emergency! Ambulance patient! Arriving now!"

"Please excuse me." The doctor rushes out of my room. She doesn't even bother sliding the door shut behind her.

Javina, as curious as ever, pops out of her chair and shuffles toward the sliding glass.

"Status?" the doctor says from a distance.

"Twenty-something white male," a man says. "Motorcycle accident. Witnesses say he rode straight into an oncoming truck at full speed. Thankfully, he was wearing a helmet. Broken arm. Unstable vitals. He's breathing, but he's coming in and out of consciousness."

"Which room do we have open for him?"

Their voices trail off as they head down the hall.

Javina slides the door shut, then heads back to her chair. "Sounds like a doozy. I hope the poor guy is okay."

Twenty-something white male on a motorcycle? It can't be. It'd be too much of a coincidence. Then again, it wouldn't be the hardest thing for me to believe lately.

"You okay, babes? You're lookin' kinda pale."

My lungs feel tight as I force myself to breathe. "Javie . . . um, Trey is a twenty-something white male who left my apartment earlier on a motorcycle."

She gasps. "You don't think . . . I mean, there's tons of people in this city. He can't be the *only* guy who fits that description, right?"

The air goes still around us. We must come to the same

conclusion at the same time, because just as I'm about to hop down from my bed, Javina jolts off her chair. Without a word, she goes to do the exact thing I was about to do: slide the glass door back open.

"Out of the way!" a woman shouts from down the hall.

Chaos erupts outside my room. Javina and I peek our heads out the door as a bunch of EMTs rush into the hospital with a man on a stretcher. They wheel him down the hall so fast, I don't catch a glimpse of him. I know it's Trey though. My gut is telling me so.

For the next hour, Javina talks my ear off about alternate universes. She even scours the Internet for articles about how other universes could work, and she reads them to me. The more she tells me about the possible trillions of galaxies and beings out there, the more I believe her.

"He could be from the future," Javina says. "Maybe in the future, they have things that can wipe memories and that's what his government did with you as his punishment for breaking the future's laws about falling in love with people from the past."

"I think I prefer your alternate-universe theory," I say. "It's a little more believable."

Eventually, Doctor Park returns, slightly out of breath. "I apologize for the wait. Whenever we get someone in by ambulance, those patients always come first."

"What's the guy's name?" Javina asks, because she has no boundaries.

"I'm sorry," the doctor says, "I can't share that. Patient privacy."

"Is he going to be okay?" I ask, because, like Javina, I'm too curious for my own good.

"I'm sorry, I can't tell you that either. Let's talk about you instead. Tell me why you're in today."

Since my weird symptoms from earlier are no longer

present and all my vitals are normal, the doctor determines that I simply need some water and rest.

"If the dizziness comes back, please don't hesitate to return," she tells me.

"Thank you," I say as I hop off the bed.

"You're good to go." The doctor sucks in a long breath through her teeth. "Now I'm off to see my next patient. I hope they're as nice as you two were about the wait."

Javina and I must be on the same page again, because we wait for the doctor to leave before we glance at each other in silent agreement of what we're about to do. She takes my hand as we exit the room, then she practically drags me down the hall—the same hall the man on the stretcher was wheeled down earlier.

"I'm so curious to know if it's him," she says.

"Me too." Even though I already know it's him, but I can't tell her that. I'll sound crazy if I tell her that my heart feels a strange pull to head this way.

We casually pass each room, where either the curtains are drawn shut or the people inside are not Trey. At the end of the long hallway, two people step out of a room. One is my nurse from earlier. The other is a woman I recognize as Liz Hart, Trey's best friend. His bandmate that all his fans say he dates on and off. She looks as beautiful as she does in their YouTube videos, maybe even more.

Javina stops dragging me down the hall and stops mid-step to turn to me. In a whisper, she says, "That's Liz Hart. She's in his band."

I haven't told Javina about all the research I've done on Trey, so I act like this is new information. "Should we ask her if he's okay?" I say instead.

Javina gives me an *I dunno* look.

"He's going to get admitted soon," the nurse says in a low voice as he slides Trey's room door shut. "He'll have to stay for at least a night. Depending on how he is tomorrow, he could be discharged, but that will be at his doctor's discretion."

"Am I able to stay the night with him?" Liz asks.

"Of course. Is there anything I can get for you in the meantime?"

"I'm good. Thank you."

The nurse heads toward Javina and me as Liz turns back toward Trey's room. She's just sliding the door open when I blurt out, "Liz?"

Her head whips up, and we lock eyes. For a split second, I regret what I just did, but it's already done, so, with Javina in hand, I head down the hall. This time, it's me who's dragging her.

"Hi?" Liz says warily as she slides the door closed.

"Um, hi," I say as we reach her. "I'm sorry to bother you. I just recognized you from down the hall."

"Oh, you're a fan. Um, now isn't really the best time."

"Actually, I'm not a fan."

That makes her tilt her head to the side and narrow her eyes at me. I suppose it sounds weird to say that I recognized her, yet I'm not a fan of her band.

Thank God for Javina. "She's not, but I am. I went to one of your shows a few months ago, and I've been watching all your music videos ever since. My favorite? The video for 'Fired Up!' The flames in it looked so real!"

Liz relaxes a bit. "That's because they *were* real."

Javina's mouth dramatically pops open. "Shut up. That wasn't just special effects?"

"Nope. One-hundred-percent real flames. Trey built that set all by himself, then set it on fire, just for our video shoot."

"That's so cool! Anyway, I'm Javina." My friend throws her hand out for a shake.

Liz accepts it with her satin-gloved hand. She wears cute gloves in all of her band's music videos. I didn't realize it was something she did in real life too. "Nice to meet you."

I offer her my hand. "Ari."

At first, she takes my hand and shakes it. Then she freezes. "Wait. Did you just say Ari?"

"Yeah."

She narrows her gaze on me again. "Is that short for anything?"

"Arella."

Her eyes go wide; then she blinks at me. Trey must have told her about me. I wonder what he said.

Finally, Liz and I let go, and I take a step back. An awkward silence fills the air as neither of us knows what to say next.

Again, thank God for Javina. "Is Trey okay? We saw him getting rushed in."

Liz sighs deeply. "Yeah, he's okay. He wasn't when I got the call from the hospital. They weren't sure if he was going to make it, but he's stable now."

"What happened?" I ask, desperate to know.

"They said Trey was on his bike when he crashed into a truck. Both parties were going over the speed limit. No one died, but Trey got banged up pretty bad. Actually, he's the only one who got hurt. What I don't know is how he lost control of his bike. I mean, to go straight into oncoming traffic?"

Judging from the timing, Trey's accident happened shortly after he left my apartment. At the time, he was upset, crying, and barely breathing right. Is that why he lost control of his motorcycle? Did he almost die because of me? Because I said things that hurt him?

I swallow thickly. "Is it all right if I see him?"

"He's asleep right now. He's under sedation."

"I don't need to talk to him. I just want to see that he's okay." *That he's alive.*

Liz thinks, then says, "Um, yeah, sure."

Javina takes a step back. "I don't need to see the man. You go, Ari. I'll be in the waiting room."

Liz reopens the glass door, then gestures for me to step inside. Trey's room is bigger than mine was, and filled with more machines. That same lemony disinfectant smell lingers in the air. Some cords dangle from Trey's upper body, and there's an IV sticking out of his arm—the arm that's not in a cast.

I don't know what comes over me. All of a sudden, I'm tearing up and my chest feels numb. It doesn't feel like the numbness that dominated my arms earlier. This numbness feels more emotional than physical. It doesn't make any sense though. I'm not emotionally attached to this man. Why does seeing him hurt and helpless affect me this much?

Liz gestures toward a chair. "You wanna sit?"

I don't take my eyes off Trey. "No, thanks. I won't be staying long." I feel the urge to apologize to him. Earlier, I yelled at this man to get out of my apartment. I even threatened him with a restraining order. Now he's all drugged up in an emergency room, with a broken arm, and I feel responsible.

"Sooo . . ." Liz says as she settles into the chair she just offered me. "You don't have to answer this if you don't want to, but, um, why are you at the ER?"

"I got really nauseous earlier and threw up. I wasn't sure what was wrong, so my boyfriend brought me here to get checked out."

"Nauseous?" Liz repeats with a lift of her brows. "And you threw up?"

"Yeah."

"Did it happen all of a sudden?"

"Yeah."

"Did your body go numb? Like, your arms especially?"

My body freezes. "Yeah . . . ? How did you know that?"

She blinks at me, then flicks her attention to Trey, then back up to me. "Lucky guess."

I want to ask her to clarify how she came to that highly accurate lucky guess, but I'm not sure how to word that question without sounding accusatory.

"Could I ask you something, Ari?"

I nod. "Sure."

"Do you believe in soul mates?"

What an odd question to ask someone you just met. I take a moment to think about it. *Soul mates.* What is the definition of a soul mate? Someone you're meant to be with? "I suppose I haven't put much thought into the concept."

Liz uses her gloved fingers to drag her reddish-brown curls behind an ear. "Well, I believe in soul mates. I believe that there's someone for each person in this world. Someone who sets our soul on fire when we're together and makes us feel like we're empty when we're apart.

"While I hope that everyone in this world is blessed enough to find their soul mate, I also believe that some may never find theirs at all. In addition, I believe that sometimes, even after we find ours, things can happen that tear us apart."

I crinkle my eyebrows together. "Why are you telling me this?"

She shrugs like there's no hidden meaning to what she's saying. "I was just wondering if you believe that even when soul mates are torn apart, somehow, in some way, they're still connected to each other, whether that's mentally, emotionally, or even *physically*."

Is Liz trying to tell me that Trey is my soul mate? I stare at the sleeping man. The man who has been the star of my dreams for the past three weeks. The man who's got me tearing up at the sight of him in a cast, even though I don't know him. The man who got into a motorcycle accident today after leaving my apartment, and around the same time, I suddenly got dizzy. Are our minds and bodies connected to each other's in some way? Some alternate-universe or futuristic way?

I shrug nonchalantly, ignoring the chill running down my spine. "Like I said, I haven't put much thought into the soul mate thing."

A soft knock sounds on the door, then the glass slides to the side.

The nurse flashes Liz a warm smile. "We're ready to take him upstairs."

Liz stands from her chair. "It was great to meet you, Ari. You really are gorgeous."

Why is she saying that as if Trey has talked her ear off about how *gorgeous* he thinks I am? My heart warms with the idea that he spoke about me to Liz in that way.

I steal one last look at him. He looks peaceful, even with all the cords and medical stuff surrounding him.

With a heavy heart, I force my feet out the door. The second I leave his side, my body yearns to go back.

10

TREY

My eyes flutter open. An IV is taped to my arm. It's hooked up to a bag of fluids hanging above me. I glance around and conclude that I'm in a hospital room. It sure smells like it.

My mind feels groggy. My body feels like I fell off a building. Maybe I did, because my right arm is in a cast. I want to sit up, but when I try to lift my head, it feels weighed down by sand.

Liz is sitting in a chair by the window, reading a book while munching on some pretzels.

"How long have I been here?" I ask.

My question makes Liz set her book and pretzels onto a rollable table, then pop out of her chair. Her shoes click against the floor as she drags her chair closer to my bed.

Once she's settled back down, she offers me a warm smile. "Hey, T-Bear. You've only been here for a night."

"Did I get a zoctor?"

"A doctor, but your hospitalization wasn't Zordi-related, so anyone could have treated you. After they discharge you, we can take a trip to Chinatown so you can see a Healer."

"That sounds good." With a few bottles of Healing Water, my arm will be fixed within days. With a Healer, it'll take five minutes, tops.

"How ya feelin'?"

Physically or emotionally? My answer is the same either way, so I say, "Shitty."

"As expected. You were hit by a truck, after all."

"A truck?"

"You don't remember that?"

The last thing I remember is the woman who looks like Arella rushing out to me from her apartment. She asked me about my missing stab wound. The next things I remember are bright lights and people shouting. That's about it.

"Liz." My voice comes out scratchy. "She remembered me."

"Huh?"

"It was only for a few minutes, but she remembered me." I go into the whole story. The entire time, Liz listens without a single interruption. Once I finish, I say, "I wish I knew what caused her mind to flip to remembering me, then back to forgetting me."

"Do you think that happens with everyone who gets scrubbed, or just her because she's immune?"

"If I had to guess, I'ma say it's just her."

A heavy cloud of anxiety floats toward me from Liz. She chews on her bottom lip as she picks at her fingernails.

I eye her, wishing I was a Mind Reader instead of an Empath. "What?"

"Oh, nothing." She waves a nonchalant ungloved hand through the air. "We can talk later. For now, let's just focus on getting you to full health."

"No. I want to talk now."

She hesitates. "Are you sure you're ready to have a serious conversation?"

"Yes," I lie.

With a long sigh, she leans in closer to me. "T, you've barely been eating, and you're always staring off into the distance with this blank look in your eyes. Getting you to come to band rehearsal is a battle, and whenever you perform, it's so robotic. At least you show up willingly to our writing sessions, but everything you write is so dark and depressing."

That's a very long-winded way of saying, *T, you've been miserable.* "How 'bout you stop sugarcoating what you're trying to say and just give it to me straight?"

"Okay, fine. When I got the call about you being at the ER and they told me what happened, I couldn't help thinking maybe . . . I dunno. Look, I don't want to accuse you of anything, but I don't want to assume either. Because you've been feeling so wrecked, I wasn't sure if—" She sucks in a deep breath and blows it out. I'd make this easier for her, but I'm not sure what she's trying to get at. "T, they told me you rode your bike straight into oncoming traffic."

Ah, I see now. "You want to know if I did that on purpose?"

"Yes. That's exactly what I want to know."

"I didn't," I say without hesitation.

Liz clasps a hand over her heart. "Oh, good. I was so worried that was the case. What made you lose control of your bike, then?"

My answer comes easily. Saying it out loud is harder. "I—" I clear my throat. "I, um, was having a panic attack."

"What?"

"You know, they're these moments when my heart races and I feel like I can't breathe, or move, or think, or anything. And whenever it gets really bad, my powers go haywire."

"I know what panic attacks are. I just didn't realize you got them, but I guess that makes sense. You've been through a lot of trauma."

With the arm that isn't in a cast, I drag the blanket draped over me a little higher up my chest. "I used to get them a lot when I was a kid. I thought I grew out of it, but I guess not."

"Did something happen to trigger this one?"

I swallow like there's something stuck in my throat. Knowing what triggered the panic attack is one thing; admitting it to someone is another.

Liz waits patiently while I gather my words.

"After she reverted to forgetting me, I came to the conclusion that my Arella is gone. Without her memories of me, that woman is nothing more than a woman who looks like her. Coming to that realization hit me hard."

I choke up, holding back a wave of tears. "Even now, there's still a part of me that wants to pursue my original plan of getting her to remember me. Obviously, she's still in there somewhere, but I don't know how to draw her out. I'm not even sure if it's possible to do so permanently, and everything I'm doing is only scaring away the woman who goes by Ari."

Liz goes quiet as she takes that all in. After what feels like a long time, she says, "So if you're not going to pursue her anymore, what are you going to do instead?"

A thunderstorm of pain crashes through me like it probably did when I ran into that truck. The only difference is that I'll remember this agony. I lose my voice as I whisper, "I have to let her go."

Liz offers me a sympathetic smile. "I'm glad you came to that decision without me having to tell you."

I eye her through slits. "How long have you known that was my only option?"

"I figured it out while I was sitting in your car outside the z-prison, waiting for you to be done talking to that Keeper."

"Why didn't you tell me sooner?"

"Because you suck at listening to me. You would have fought me on it, and you would have done what you did anyway."

She's right—as always.

"I dunno how I'm gonna do it, Liz. I've spent the last three weeks trying to stay away from her while I figure out a new plan to get her back. The entire time, I've been dying inside. She's all I think about. She's all I care about. She's all I want. How am I supposed to go on like this?"

11

TREY

I raise my fist to knock on Ari's door. I'm about to make contact when I stop, and my hand drops to my side. I shouldn't be here. I don't even know why I'm here. What am I trying to get out of bothering her again?

It's been two weeks since I got out of the hospital. It took me that long to realize that staying in LA wasn't right for me. Mostly, it's not right for Arella. The only thing I'm doing by being here is causing her pain and distress, and I don't want that. I want what's best for her. I want her to be safe and happy. Since she *is*—just not with me—I decided it's best to leave.

I made this decision yesterday. Since this would affect my bandmates the most, I told them first. They took it hard. Liz took it the hardest. She cried for over an hour, and I felt like an asshole for being the cause of her tears, but I have to do this. Liz was understanding about that, which only made me feel like more of an asshole.

Now I've got a brand-new not-totaled motorcycle sitting in the parking lot of Arella's apartment complex—*Ari's* apartment complex. Next to my bike is a backpack full of clothes and toiletries.

I have a few stops to make on my way off to wherever the fuck I'm going. I didn't plan for one of those stops to be here though. Somehow, on my way out of California, I ended up here. Now I'm standing outside her door like a fucking weirdo, refusing to knock while also refusing to leave.

I should just get this over with. Maybe she's not home. I glance back at the parking lot, where her car is sitting. That doesn't mean anything though. She could be somewhere with Javina or her—uh, boyfriend. I don't sense any emotions coming from her apartment, but that doesn't mean anything either.

I raise my fist to her door again, then stop. What if she yells at me? I'm not sure if I can take another bad interaction with her. Nor can I take hearing her call me *the crazy guy* in Arella's voice.

Again, why am I here? This woman has nothing to offer me that could make things better. To her, I'm a stranger, and it'd do me some good to remember that.

Still, a big part of me just wants to see her one last time. She still *looks* like Arella, even if she isn't. Seeing her again could be worth the heartache I'll feel from hearing her tell me to get lost.

I lift my fist back up to her door, then stop again. Once she opens this—*if* she opens this—what will I say? More importantly, what will she say back? Will she look at me like I'm a lunatic, the way she has been? Arella never looked at me like that. She always looked at me like she felt safe with me. This woman doesn't feel safe with me. Not one bit. I don't blame her either. When I see things from her point of view, I know her actions are justified. So are the actions of her—uh, boyfriend.

Still, if I leave LA without seeing her one last time, I'll obsess over it. I'll regret not knocking. I'll regret not trying to leave things with her on a good note. I'll be tormented over what could have happened if I had knocked. *If I had been brave . . .*

I bring my fist back up to her door, then pause. What if she calls the cops on me? She's threatened to enough. After waking up in her bed with me in it, I don't doubt she would hesitate to make that call this time. Do I really want to deal with the aftermath of that? What's worse—living with regret or living behind bars?

I drop my hand back to my side. I shouldn't be here. If she's in there and saw me pulling up on my bike, she's probably already called the cops. They could be here any minute. I should go before they arrive.

With a heavy heart, I stare at the door I used to shove her back up against. I used to pin her arms above her head and kiss her until our lips felt raw. I wish I would have appreciated those moments more while they were happening. Since my photograph of us is gone, those memories are all I have left. A part of me wishes I had never shown Ari that picture. Maybe then I'd still have it.

I'm not sure why the Keepers allowed me to keep that photo. It was in my wallet when I got arrested, and it was still in there when I got out of z-prison. They went through my entire house to get rid of anything that belonged to her, so I'm sure they went through my wallet too. Why would they let me keep a photo? To torture me? To rub it in? To make sure I'd always remember my greatest loss?

Last night, I spoke to Liz about the possibility of finding a black market Scrubber. It's illegal for them to scrub people outside the zovernment's permission, but I'm sure I could find one I could talk into erasing my memories. Everyone's got a price, and I'm willing to pay it. It'd make things easier. I could move on without this pain.

When I shared this idea with Liz, her response was "If neither of you remember the love you created together, then it'll be like it never happened. Is that what you want? Is that what Arella would want?"

I already knew I could never go through with getting scrubbed, for that exact reason. If everything Arella and I went through together only exists in my mind and I get rid of it, then it'll be like none of it ever mattered. I don't want that. I just needed Liz to validate that living with this physically debilitating hole in my chest is better than forgetting about the happiest moments of my life.

I place a palm against Arella's door and whisper to it as if she can hear me from the deep depths of where she's being suppressed. "I'm sorry, angel. This isn't me giving up on you, but I have to let you go. I know I promised to always fight for you, but I don't have any fight left in me. I think I'm doing the right thing. I just hope you see it that way too."

With that, I turn on my heel and force my feet to walk away.

12

ARI

THE SOUND OF A MOTORCYCLE PULLING UP OUTSIDE MAKES ME
race from my kitchen to the living room window. The engine
stops as I peel the blinds back to find Trey Grant yanking his
helmet off. He hangs it on a handlebar by its strap, then rests
his backpack on the ground against his bike.

His bleak expression matches the gray clouds as he
dismounts his motorcycle and makes his way to my door. His
arm is out of the cast, and I can't figure out why. It's only been
two weeks since he was in the hospital. There's no way his
broken arm healed that fast. An injury like that takes a month
to heal at best.

I tiptoe to the door and ready myself to open it. If Caleb
was here, he'd already be calling the cops. I probably should,
but I don't want to. Maybe it's naive of me, but I don't get the
feeling that Trey is here to hurt me.

I glance through my peephole to find him raising his fist to
the door. Then he stops. He's got that desolate look in his eyes
again. I have an overwhelming urge to do something to get rid
of it. His arm drops back to his side as he chews on his
bottom lip.

Why isn't he knocking? Why is he just standing there, staring at the ground?

A few moments pass before he raises his hand to the door again. After he knocks, I'll wait a few seconds before opening the door so it doesn't seem like I was standing on the other side, watching him.

But the knock doesn't come. His hand drops back down again.

He's thinking heavily about something. I wish I knew what. Judging from the pained look in his eyes, it's nothing good. Whatever he's thinking about, he keeps thinking for several heartbeats before lifting his fist again. It looks like he's about to knock, but he doesn't.

Instead, he chews on his bottom lip some more while he contemplates whatever he's contemplating. Maybe he's trying to figure out how he's going to say whatever he wants to say. He must figure it out, because for the third time, he lifts his fist to the door. And for the third time, he drops it back down.

Why is he hesitating so much? I've wanted to talk to him since I saw him in that arm cast. About what? I don't know. I just have this yearning inside me to hear his voice. I've been hearing it in my dreams. Last week, I dreamt of hearing him sing in the shower. In my dream, I didn't hesitate to strip naked. As I entered the shower, his breath hitched and his eyes glazed over. The next thing I knew, he crashed his lips against mine and pounded into me against the tile wall while I moaned his name and begged for more.

That's not the only sexy dream I've had about him. Last night, I dreamt that we were at my thinking spot and he was giving me a guitar lesson—at least, he was *trying* to give me a guitar lesson. It's nice to know that even in my dreams, I still suck at playing an instrument. Eventually, the guitar got thrown into the grass and he pinned me to the ground. We panted with desire as we tore each other's clothes off. Soon, that desire turned into a need. When he slipped his thick erection inside me, I gasped from his size. He filled and stretched me so much, it was painful at first. Once the pain went away, I couldn't get enough of him.

I woke up with that vivid dream so fresh in my mind that I slipped my hand under my panties and rubbed myself until I came. I didn't even feel guilty about the orgasm coming from the thought of another man doing me, because I hadn't had an orgasm like that in months.

I still haven't told anyone about my Trey dreams. They continue to play out in my head a few times a week, giving me snapshots of a life I never had. What if my mind is merging with the mind of Alterella's and I'm seeing moments she and Trey shared together? I cringe at myself for even considering that as a possibility, because it would mean accepting that my best friend's outlandish theory has any merit.

For the fourth time, Trey's fist rises to my door, but he pauses again. I almost open the door to put us both out of this misery. He came all the way here to see me at the risk of going back behind bars. Obviously, whatever he's got to say is worth the risk, so why is he hesitating? Maybe he doesn't want me to actually file that restraining order I've been putting off.

Once again, Trey lifts his hand to the door, except this time, it's not a fist. It's his palm. He keeps it there as he whispers something to himself. I can't hear what, but he looks tearful as he says it. Whatever he says, it's brief; then he turns and walks away.

I don't know what comes over me as I undo the chain lock and whip the door open.

"Trey?"

He's three steps away when he twists back around with his arms up in surrender. "I was just leaving. No need to call the cops."

"I wasn't going to."

"Oh." He drops his arms. "Thanks for not doing so

already. I'm sorry. I didn't mean to bother you." With a hard swallow, he heads back toward his motorcycle.

I can't let him go like this. I want to know what he came for. Without thinking, I blurt out, "I heard you're moving."

He turns on his heel with his brows knitted together. "How'd you hear that?"

"Javina told me. She read about it on your band's social media page this morning."

With a deep sigh, he shakes his head. "I specifically told my manager not to post anything for at least a month. I knew she wasn't gonna listen."

"Are you going to fire her?"

"I can't. She's too good at what she does, and there's no one else in this world who would ever put up with my shit."

That makes me chuckle. "Are you a hard man to handle?"

"According to Monique, I'm the worst. Now that I'm moving—and I only told her yesterday—I think she's gonna let me keep that well-deserved title."

The screenshot of the social media post Javina sent me didn't specify how long Trey will be moving away for. It also didn't say if he'd be working on new music with his band while he's gone. All it stated was that Trey would be moving for an undetermined amount of time and everyone will continue on without him until further notice.

I echo the most asked question from his fans in the comments section. "Are you quitting the band?"

"No," he says somberly. "Just taking a long break."

"Where are you moving to?"

A shrug. "I dunno."

"When are you moving?"

"Right now." He gestures toward his bike and backpack.

"That's all you're bringing?"

Another shrug. "I don't need much."

"So let me get this straight: You're moving *right now*, but you don't know where you're going?"

"Yep."

"It doesn't sound like you've thought this through."

"Welcome to every big decision I've ever made." He shoves his hands into his jeans pockets. "Anyway, this moving-without-a-plan thing isn't new to me. When I got kicked out at eighteen, I packed up what I had, bought a car, and went wherever life took me. The only difference now is that I've got a bike instead of a car."

I wonder who he lived with after his parents died and why that person would kick him out. I think about asking, but that seems like too personal of a question when we barely know each other. At least, *I* barely know *him*.

Instead, I ask, "Why are you moving?"

He stares at his shoes, then out at the parking lot, then up at the gloomy sky, then back at his shoes. "I just need a change of scenery, I guess."

I hold back the question I'm dying to ask: *Are you moving because of me?* I'd feel bad if the answer is *yes*. Los Angeles is big enough for the both of us. He doesn't have to leave.

Trey continues, "When I got kicked out, I was told to go 'find my place in the world.' I guess I'm still looking for it."

I draw up the courage to ask the question I want the answer to most. "Why did you come here?"

He looks anywhere but at me. "I'm not sure, but like I said, I'm sorry for bothering you."

"You didn't. *I* was the one who opened the door, remember?"

He offers me a tiny forced smile. It doesn't light up his face the way his smiles do in my dreams. It doesn't crinkle the corners of his eyes either. I wish I could see those smiles from my dreams in real life. I'd prefer it over this dark and wretched version of him.

Since I'm not ready for him to leave yet, I say, "Your arm sure healed fast."

Finally, he looks at me. "How did you know I broke my arm?"

"I was at the ER when you were brought in. I overheard the nurse telling the doctor about it."

His entire face drops. "Why were you at the ER?"

"I got sick, so Caleb brought me in to get checked."

"You got sick?" The pure concern lacing his voice makes my insides flutter. "With what?"

"I don't know. It came all of a sudden. I got dizzy and I threw up, but I'm fine now. It went away by the end of the night."

I can practically see the gears turning in his head as he blinks at me. "Around what time did that happen?"

The answer he's looking for isn't a time on a clock. He's wondering if I got sick around the exact moment he got hit by a truck. It's something that's been weighing on my mind over the past two weeks. I try not to think about it too much, because whenever I do, I get chills. How did my body know Trey was hurt, and why did it react in that way?

"It happened around the same time you got into your motorcycle accident." I give him a moment to see if he'll react. He doesn't. He just keeps gaping at me. To try to elicit a reaction, I add, "My arms went numb too."

He gasps, then quickly hides it behind clearing his throat. That confirms he and Liz know something I don't. I think about asking, but I don't even know what I'd be asking about.

Trey licks his lips, then drags a hand through his dark hair. Three nights ago, I dreamt that I ran my hands through his hair as he laid his head in my lap. I can't remember what we were talking about, but it made him laugh a lot. I'd like to hear that laugh in real life.

"I'm glad you're feeling better," he says.

"I'm glad you are too. You looked pretty rough that night —with your arm in a cast." I added in that last part as a subtle attempt to get him to explain his magical fast-healing arm.

He doesn't. Instead, he crinkles his eyebrows together. "You got to visit me?"

"Yeah. I recognized Liz out in the hall and asked if I could. She didn't tell you?"

He huffs out a breath. "Nope."

"She asked me a weird question that night." I'm getting tired of standing with the door open, allowing all my precious air conditioning to escape, so I step out and shut the door behind me. Then I lean my back against the door and stick my hands into my dress pockets. "She asked me if I believe in soul mates."

"What did you tell her?"

"That I haven't put much thought into the concept."

He shifts his attention to the ground. "I see."

"What about you? Do *you* believe in soul mates?"

"I didn't used to."

I arch my eyebrows. "But you do now?"

A nod.

"What changed your mind?"

He stares deep into my eyes, almost like he's trying to stare into my soul. "I met someone who didn't just change my mind —she changed everything for me. Before her, I didn't think I was capable of falling in love. Even more, I didn't think anyone could ever fall in love with me. She proved I was wrong, and being with her made me believe in soul mates."

"Liz told me she believes soul mates are connected to each other emotionally and physically. Do you believe that too?"

"Yes," he says without any hesitation.

"Do you also believe that not all soul mates end up together?"

He chuckles humorlessly under his breath. "I think you might have had the same conversation with Liz that she had with me last night. She told me that being someone's soul mate means your souls are perfectly matched for each other but it doesn't necessarily mean you'll end up together.

"She said that sometimes, soul mates are only together for a brief moment, like it's the right person but the wrong time or situation. She said that many things can tear soul mates apart, like geographical location, certain laws, death, and even unforeseen circumstances."

Do the unforeseen circumstances he's talking about have anything to do with falling through a portal into an alternate universe, tearing him away from Alterella?

I pull my long braid to one shoulder. "What do you think happens to those people who lose their soul mates? Are they just doomed to be alone forever?"

"That's the same question I asked Liz last night. She said most people never find their soul mates. Instead, they find a compatible partner, someone who makes them happy but they aren't a perfect match."

"So is that what you're going out in the world to find? A compatible partner?"

He sighs and runs a hand through his hair again. "No, I want to find my place in the world."

"What if your place in the world is the one you're about to leave?"

"If that was the case, then why do I feel like I don't belong?"

I imagine Trey as a lost soul, floating around the earth as a little orb, looking for a place to land. What if his soul never finds the place where he belongs? Will he just float around for all eternity? Finally, I say, "Well, Trey, I hope you find what you're looking for out there."

Somberly, he says, "Me too."

"Will you send me a postcard from wherever you end up?"

He gives me a slow nod. "Sure."

"Do you need me to write down my address for you?"

"Nah. I can figure it out."

"Okay." I place a hand on my doorknob but make no effort to turn it. A part of me doesn't want this to end;

however, Caleb will be getting home from the gym soon, and I don't want to find out what happens if he sees Trey here. He might actually push that restraining-order thing through. I don't know why, but I just don't feel like it's necessary. It especially isn't now that Trey is moving. "I suppose this is goodbye then."

Trey's entire face falls, and the dim light in his eyes turns dimmer. His shoulders go taut, then suddenly, he doesn't look like he's breathing anymore.

What did I say wrong? "Trey?"

He doesn't answer. I'm not even sure if he heard me.

I say his name again, a little louder. "Trey?"

His gaze flicks up to me, and my breath hitches. He's looking at me, but I'm unsure if he's actually *seeing* me. There's a hollowness in his eyes that wasn't there before. I feel a need to go to him, to cup his face in my hands and tell him that everything will be okay.

I resist the urge. "Don't forget about the postcard, okay?"

He blinks slowly, as if he's trying to process my words. Once he does, he swallows, then nods. "I won't."

"I'll look forward to getting it."

A long silence sits between us. I can't bring myself to go back inside. I know I should though. On the other hand, I want to soak up every second with this man. I want to understand him and know what happened to bring him into my life. Why do I feel this strong connection to him?

Trey clears his throat. "I can't leave. Not while you're still standing out here."

"Do you need me to go inside?"

He gives me a slight nod with that hollow look still in his eyes.

"Okay." I turn the doorknob my hand has been holding for a while. "Goodbye, Trey."

He doesn't say goodbye back. All he does is stare at me longingly as I step back into my apartment and shut the door.

13

TREY

It feels weird to leave a black bag full of cash on a stranger's doorstep. It took me a while to even find the right house. It looks different in the daylight.

I put a written note inside:

To the owner of the Nissan Altima I stole, I'm sorry for stealing your car and for any trouble that caused. I really needed it at the time, and I promised the person I was with that I would return someday to pay you back. This money should cover the cost of the vehicle, plus more.

My next stop is Chinatown in Las Vegas. I arrive at the traditional Chinese medicine shop about five minutes before closing time.

When I step through the front door, the scent of dried earth and spices fills my nostrils. The store no longer looks like a tornado ran through it. Now it features tidy shelves with containers perfectly facing forward, red paper lanterns hanging from the ceiling, and visible wood floors. Near the register sits a golden toy cat. It waves at me with one arm.

In the back of the store is an Asian man with graying black hair, stocking some shelves. "Can I hep you find someting?"

Tao doesn't recognize me, and I didn't expect him to. When I met him, Arella was with me. Anyone who interacted with Arella and me no longer has those memories.

I didn't plan out what I wanted to say, so I stutter out, "Um, is Li here?"

Tao heads down a hall, then shouts down the staircase. "Li! Another customer here to talk with you."

"Who?" a woman yells back.

"Aiyah. Just come up." Tao sighs as he reappears from the hall. "Our customers always prefer to talk to her, not me. Every time, she always ask who, like I know everybody's name."

A pair of footsteps marches down the hall, then Li steps into the light. She looks the same as last time: long black hair that falls past her shoulders, a gentle smile, and kind eyes.

Like she did before, she gasps with a hand to her chest. As she approaches me with slow steps, she keeps staring at me. I already know the words she's about to say.

"Are you Trey Grant?"

"Yep, that's me."

"Oh my god. You are so big, and tall, and very handsome. And you have strong arms." Also like before, she gives my bicep a squeeze. "Wow! I can't believe it's really you."

It's nice to know that some things don't change. Maybe if I had re-met Arella like a normal person, things might have turned out differently. Would she have fallen in love with me again? Would I have the same conversations with her that we already had before? Would I feel the déjà vu I feel now? Would she be standing here with me as I right my wrongs?

Then again, with that other guy in her life, she wouldn't

need me the way she did before. Back then, she needed me to show her that a man can love her with all his heart and treat her like she's gold. I hope Caleb is treating her right. Arella deserves to be loved, even if it's not me doing it.

I hold out a black bag to Li. "This is for you."

She accepts the bag and unzips it. "Oh no! We cannot take this."

"You can, and you will. This is money I owe you for helping me out six weeks ago."

As expected, she crumples her eyebrows together. Tao does the same.

With a sigh, I ask, "Do you guys have a few minutes for me to tell you a story?"

"Of course," Li says. "Tao, you close the store. I'll take Trey downstairs."

On my way to Vegas, I considered not telling them anything at all and just leaving the money at their door. By the time I arrived, I had come to the conclusion that they deserve to know why "Victor" stopped talking to them all those years ago. Also, I have to clear my dad's name. I can't let his best friends live out the rest of their lives thinking he was cruel enough to cut things off with my mother out of the blue, then cut them off too. My dad would have wanted me to do this for him.

It takes me a while to get through the whole story because Li and Tao ask for a lot of details. When I finally finish, Tao says, "Victor was always a good man."

"You know he loved you very much, right?" Li says. "He always looked at you like you were his entire world."

"I know that now." I wish I could say that the thought of my real dad loving me outweighs the bitterness I feel toward Jodi, but it doesn't. Because of her, I was robbed of the relationship I could have had with my father.

I leave Li and Tao with a promise to visit again in the future.

Back on my bike, I head northeast.

The next morning, I arrive in Colorado. At my secluded cabin in the woods, I have full intentions of getting sleep, but no matter how many times I toss and turn, I can't manage to shut my eyes long enough. Being alone with my emotions and having nothing to do is only making me feel more lonely.

Usually, I enjoy having a break from people's emotions rushing through me all the time. But without other people's feelings distracting me, this heartache is only getting worse. Being here isn't clearing my head like it did when I lost Elliott. Instead, it's making me imagine jumping off one of the nearby cliffs. But before I can talk myself into actually doing that, I pack up and leave. I still have unfinished business, so I can't rid the world of me just yet.

The next afternoon, I arrive in a chilly Bloomington, Minnesota. It wasn't hard for me to find out where Katie's family buried her. Not at all to my surprise, Katie was a well-loved person and her funeral was a heavily attended event. Her friends and family posted about it all over social media.

At the cemetery, I dismount my bike. Then I walk around with flowers in my hand for almost forty-five minutes before I finally find her name on a gravestone.

Katie Williams
April 4, 1995–September 19, 2014

A lump forms in my throat as I bend to lay my bouquet of flowers near her name. "Everything you did for us was so brave, Katie. Thank you for saving her life."

For the next few hours, I sit with Katie and reminisce over how she helped me plan Arella's escape in a supply closet, then later jumped in front of a knife to save a woman she barely knew. Arella won't remember the courage Katie showed, but I will. If Katie was here, I'd bet anything she'd have some words of wisdom for me. I could really use some right now.

Once my ass is unbearably numb, I stand up, shake out my legs, then hop back onto my bike.

The next early evening, I make it to New York City, where Pixie's family buried her. It takes me even longer to find her gravestone because the cemetery is ginormous compared to the one in Minnesota.

Anna Jung
Daughter, sister, aunt, friend.
September 6, 1994–September 19, 2014

Both Katie and Pixie died way too young.

I give Pixie some flowers. Then I sit with her for a while, remembering how she tortured my ears, then ended up sacrificing herself so Arella and I could run away.

The sky is dim when I finally gather enough willpower to stand up. Paying my respects to Pixie was the last thing on my to-do list. Now what?

My stomach growls and claws at me to fix the emptiness. I haven't eaten much since I left LA. Not that I ate much while I was *in* LA. I guess I could get something to eat while I figure out where to go next.

Later that night, I'm slouched in a booth at a burger joint with a basket of food getting cold in front of me. I've had a couple of fries, but they can't seem to go down right. They keep sticking in my throat.

"You 'ight, sweetie pie?" asks my plump Black waitress. A wave of concern rushes through me from where she's standing.

"I'm fine," I say without looking up at her.

"You sure? You been sittin' here for almost two hours, and there ain't a single bite outta yo burger yet." She stares at me as her mood drops. "Oh, baby. I know that look. Either someone died or you just got yo heart broken. Which is it?"

This woman is perceptive as fuck. "Both."

"I'm sorry, sweetheart. Is there anything I can do for ya?"

Can you turn back time? Bring back my dad? Get me my girl back? "No, but thank you."

"Why don't you try to eat a li'l bit, baby boy? It might make ya feel better."

"I'll try."

An hour later, I've gotten all of one bite out of my burger. The other patrons have left, and the staff is mopping the floors.

My waitress stops by my table again. "You need anything else, hon?"

"Just the check."

"No way. You ain't even eat nothin'. I ain't chargin' you for that. Why don't you just go on home? Maybe tomorrow will be a better day."

I would do that . . . if I had a home to go to. Nowhere feels like home when *she's* not there.

I leave a few hundreds on my table, then grab my backpack and head out into the darkness.

The street is busy with moving cars, couples strolling side by side, some guys on bikes, and a group of teenagers taking a selfie together. An old dude stands next to a parking meter, smoking a cigarette. The cool early November air blows his cigarette smoke into my face as I drag my feet past him.

I've never been much of a smoker. My substances of choice were always alcohol, pills, and injections. I wouldn't mind some of those right now.

As I make my way down the sidewalk toward where I parked my bike, I pass stores that are closed for the evening, and restaurant owners turning their glowing OPEN signs off.

Eventually, I reach a crosswalk, but I don't bother waiting

for the light to tell me when it's safe to go. If another truck hits me, maybe it'll actually take me out this time.

Liz would backhand my chest for thinking that. She would backhand me for thinking most of the self-harming thoughts I've had lately. She would also hit me for strolling straight past my motorcycle and into a bar.

An all-female band plays a sultry ballad from the stage as I hang my backpack on the back of a barstool and sit. The place is packed with men and women who are dancing, laughing, talking, whatever.

"Hey, handsome." Excitement spikes inside the pale-skinned bartender as she sets a coaster down in front of me. "What can I get you?"

"How 'bout a shot of whatever you feel like pouring?"

"Comin' right up." A few seconds later, she sets a shot glass with amber liquid in it onto my coaster. "This is—"

I don't let her finish telling me what's in my glass before I seize it. When I thunk it back onto the counter, it's empty. "Another, please."

"Sure." Without hesitation, she grabs a bottle and pours more liquid into my glass. When I thunk it back onto the counter again, she doesn't wait for me to ask; she just pours. I down my third shot, then gesture for her to give me some more.

She does, then asks in a cutesy little voice, "So where ya from?"

I drop the glass back down and wipe off my wet lips with the back of my hand. "California."

"Ooh." She leans against the counter, pressing her perky tits together. Her brunette hair falls off her shoulders to cover her cleavage. The woman is quick to grab all her locks and move them to her back. "Where in California?"

I'm not in the mood for small talk or her titties, so I point at my empty shot glass. "Another."

14

TREY

"Housekeeping," someone says from outside my hotel door.

I pry my eyes open to glance at the digital clock on the nightstand. The little red lines say it's just past noon, which means it's well past checkout time.

The ceiling looks like it's spinning. The back of my head throbs like I've been bashed with a sock full of coins. My bladder is about to burst, so I tear the blankets off me and stumble toward the bathroom.

My hotel door opens. An older woman strolls in, then gasps and covers her eyes. "Sorry! I'll come back later."

I glance at my morning wood swinging around. *Oops.*

After I'm done using the bathroom, I return to the bed, and my eyes go wide. A woman is lying on the side of the mattress I didn't wake up on. Her long brunette hair is sprawled out all over the pillow.

Fuck. What trouble did I get into last night?

I pluck my boxers off the floor and shove my legs into them. Then I find my jeans and shirt and put those on too. I make sure to be extra loud as an attempt to wake up the woman, but she doesn't even stir.

Begrudgingly, I kneel at her bedside and shake her shoulder. "Hey."

She doesn't move.

I shake her again—harder. "Hey."

Slowly, her eyes open. I think she's the bartender from last night, but I don't know for sure. I don't remember much beyond stopping at a liquor store before stumbling into the first hotel in sight. Did I ask this woman to come with me, or did she invite herself?

"Morning, handsome."

I don't bother with the pleasantries. "Did we fuck last night?" *Please say no. Please say no.*

Topless, she sits up and rubs her eyes. "We tried."

We tried? I push off my knees and onto my feet as I scan the floor for her clothes. "What does that mean? And please, explain in detail."

With a sigh, she catches the bra I toss at her. "It means you brought me here with the intention to fuck but you couldn't get it up."

What? That's never happened to me before.

"Don't worry," she says as she slips her arms through her bra straps. "I understand. You were really fucking drunk. You guzzled two liters of Karkov like you'd been trapped in the Sahara for days. And that was *after* all the shots you already had at the bar. I'm surprised you're not dead."

If only I could be so lucky. "I have a high tolerance." I pluck her shorts and panties off the floor, then toss them to her.

"You're a good kisser. If you weren't so wasted, I'm sure you would have fucked just as good."

I'm so disappointed in myself for making out with another woman barely three days after leaving LA. This isn't why I left. Thank fuck I can't remember it. The only kissing-related memories I want are the ones I have of kissing Arella. Drunk me probably thought getting laid would be a good way to get over her. Hungover me knows it wouldn't have worked. Nothing will.

"Do you need money for a taxi?" I ask as a hint that she should leave. I don't even know her name, and I don't care to.

"I'll be fine. I don't live too far from here. I work at that bar because I can walk there from my apartment. I would have walked home last night, but by the time you passed out, I was also too drunk to function."

I don't think I ever told Arella that I love how she doesn't drink. While we were together, her soberness kept me sober.

"Who's Arella?"

My attention flicks to the woman who's getting dressed like she's in a contest to see who can put panties on the slowest. "What?"

"You kept talking about her last night, saying things like 'You're not Arella' and 'You don't taste like Arella.' Is she an ex-girlfriend?"

I suck in a deep breath while also sucking in as much patience as possible. I can't be a dick to this woman. She did nothing wrong, except try to sleep with a guy who belongs to someone else.

The person I was many months ago would have definitely given her the night of her life last night. I'd probably be doing it again right now since she seems so willing, but I'm not that person anymore. I don't know who I am, but I'm not him.

I muster up the nicest tone I can. "Look, I don't wanna be an asshole, but last night shouldn't have happened. Also, it's past checkout time. I think you should go."

"Ahh." She nods in understanding. "She's your wife. Please tell me you're at least separated?"

If I was married to Arella, I wouldn't be here. I'd be at home with my wife, making sure she's happy, fed, and living any type of life she wants. I'd be asking her to make babies with me and thanking every star in the sky for each precious moment I had with her.

The bartender sighs. "Of course you're not separated. Why is it always *me* who finds the married ones?" She shakes her head at herself as she zips up her shorts. "Just my fucking luck."

I don't think I ever told Arella this either, but I like that she doesn't swear. I mean, she has, and she will occasionally, but it's not a habit of hers. I didn't appreciate that about her enough.

Finally, the woman grabs her small purse off the table by the TV, then slips into her shoes and leaves without another word.

———

AFTER ANOTHER WEEK IN NEW YORK, I CONCLUDE THAT THE booze isn't doing enough. Arella has never even been to New York, yet I feel her everywhere I go. The restaurants I force myself to eat at have food she would have loved to try. The stores I walk past feature flowy little dresses on the mannequins that she would've looked beautiful in. The bars I hop between play songs over the speakers that remind me of her.

I thought I could do this. I thought I could be a better man than I was, but it turns out, I can't. It's not like she remembers the man I was anyway. A man who stayed away from drugs. A man who could deal with his inner demons. Why bother trying to be him when she's not around to see it?

It's surprisingly easy to find z-drugs. All I had to do was download an app. Within two hours, I had jaderro in my hands, and the needles to inject it with.

As the liquid races up my veins, I lay my head back on a hotel pillow and wait for it to kick in. I went straight for the good stuff this time because if I remember correctly, jaderro is the shit that will knock me out for a couple of days. I've already booked this room for the next week and asked for no housekeeping. Hopefully, I can spend the next forty-eightish hours not thinking about her. And when I wake up, I'll do it again.

Usually, jaderro takes about two minutes for the effects to appear. It's only been thirty seconds, and my vision is already blurry, and my body's getting warm and tingly. My nose itches, but when I move my arm to scratch it, my arm feels heavy like my bones have pebbles in them.

The slight nausea will come next, but at least it'll be accompanied by the calm high. I wait for what feels like forever for that high to arrive. When it finally does, I'm euphoric, relaxed, and sleepy. My chest doesn't feel achy anymore, and my mind feels numb. *I could get used to this.*

<hr>

TWO WEEKS LATER, I STARE AT THE EMPTINESS OF MY NEW penthouse in Manhattan, wishing it was my house in LA with Arella in it. The only reason I signed the lease for a penthouse this morning is because it was the first available place I could find to rent in this goddamn city.

I tried nine different apartment buildings before I found this one. Every other place was either not move-in ready, the person in charge wasn't around, or they were already full with a wait list that's months long. I don't have months because Liz is coming to visit me tomorrow for Thanksgiving.

This isn't a surprise. She told me she'd be coming to visit over the holidays before I even left LA. I procrastinated on finding a place to live until the last possible day because, well . . . I'm an idiot.

Liz thinks I found this place two weeks ago and that I chose this city for the vibrant nightlife. In reality, I chose New York City because I happened to be here after I finished doing all the things I wanted to do. I guess one perk is that the many emotions rushing through my head drown out some of the achy ones in my chest. This is better than being at my lonely cabin, that's for damn sure.

Liz thinks I've been enjoying things like exploring Times Square and seeing Broadway shows. In reality, I've been hotel-hopping and getting wasted at the nearest bars. Any time a bartender cuts me off, I stumble into the next closest bar until those people cut me off too.

The thing about getting an Ordinary bartender is that they think ten shots is enough for me. I need the whole damn bottle to feel buzzed, another to feel drunk, and a third to feel nothing. Feeling nothing is my goal.

My other goal is to wake up alone. So far, I haven't found any more brunette surprises in my bed. All I ever find are empty bottles and a used needle.

Unfortunately, I can't do any of that shit tonight because Liz's flight arrives in the early morning. I need to be sober so I don't look like a wreck when she gets here. Plus, I have to make this place look like I've been living here for more than twenty-four hours.

So I head to the store.

The next day, Liz's face drops the second she enters my apartment. "What the hell is this?"

"It's called a penthouse," I say like a smartass, because that's not what she's talking about.

She drops her carry-on suitcase onto the floor, then backhands my arm. "Why is there nothing in here?"

"What are you talkin' about?" I rush to open my kitchen cabinets and gesture at all the dishes I bought yesterday. "See? I have stuff."

"T, you have zero furniture. My voice is echoing against your walls."

"I have furniture." I lead her to the bedroom, where a blow-up mattress is lying on the floor. "See?"

She flashes me an *are you serious?* look. "Haven't you been living here for, like, two weeks now?"

I'm about to spew out some bullshit excuses when she throws a gloved hand up. "Don't even start with me. Where do you expect me to sleep for the next four nights?"

I point at the air mattress. "We can't just share that?"

She rolls her eyes at me, then grabs my hand. "Come on. We're going shopping."

I don't move. "Liz, it's Thanksgiving day. Nothing's open."

"Haven't you ever heard of Black Friday sales? I'll bet tons of places are open today."

THE NEXT WEEK, I WOBBLE INTO MY NEWLY FURNISHED penthouse like I'm on a swaying ship. One hand clutches a paper bag, concealing the bottle I'm guzzling. My other hand steadies me against the wall as I kick off my shoes. I wave a hand at the door, and it slams shut behind me.

I take another swig as I half run, half fall into my bedroom. From under the bed, I drag out the cardboard box my silverware set came in. From it, I pull out my syringe and a little jar.

Usually, one dose will put me out for two days. Two days hasn't been long enough. Every time I wake up, I still wish I hadn't. *Let's see what a dose and a half can do.*

A minute after the liquid enters my bloodstream, my vision blurs and my body goes tingly again. I shove all my supplies back into the silverware box and re-hide it under the bed. Then I climb onto the mattress and lie back to wait for that euphoric feeling to take over.

Once my body finally relaxes and my mind numbs, I close my eyes and bask in the feeling of floating on a cloud.

What's she doing right now? Does she ever think of me? Probably not as much as I think of her. Probably not as fondly either. If she thinks of me, she probably thinks about how scared she was when she woke up and found me in her bed. If

I could, I'd turn back time to the moment I saw that recognition in her eyes. I'd figure out how it happened and make sure it stayed that way.

Fuck, I'm thirsty. I should get some water.

I pry my eyes open, then slap my palm over my face. It's so bright in here. Blindingly bright. Where did all this light come from? Did I somehow get transported next to the sun?

My skin tingles, but instead of tingling inside my body, it's tingling *outside* my body. I remove my hand from my face to find an army of little cockroaches no bigger than a thumbtack crawling up my shoulder and over my chest. I swat at them, but they don't go away. It's as if my hand goes straight through them. The little bugs continue crawling over me in a single-file line as if marching to the beat of a drum. Once they reach my other shoulder, they crawl over the bed, then over someone's hand.

I sit up with a jolt. A gorgeous woman has appeared on my sheets. "Arella?"

She's lying on the pillow next to mine, smiling up at me the sweet way she used to.

I gape at her. "What are you doing here?"

She doesn't answer me. Instead, she continues to lie there as the tiny cockroaches crawl over her the way they just did on me. In a single line, they start at one of her shoulders, then march across her chest until they reach the other.

I try to swat the bugs off her, but all my hand catches is air. Why isn't she reacting to them? If she's afraid of spiders, I'd assume she's afraid of tiny roaches too. Also, why did my hand go straight through her body?

"You're not really here, are you?"

Without a word, Arella pats the empty space next to her and gestures for me to lie back down. I do, never taking my eyes off her.

In silence, she caresses the side of my head, around my ear, then down my neck. I close my eyes and melt into the feel of her touch. Even if it's not real, it *feels* real, and that's all that matters.

I wake with a jolt. I'm nauseous as I trudge into the bathroom. When I come back out, my phone tells me three days have passed. Three whole days of feeling nothing. What a treat! And that was after I got to see my girl again. Now *that* was a treat.

I remember most of it. The whole time, she just caressed me. She never said anything. She never left me either. She just lay there, drawing figure eights over my abs. I haven't been that happy since . . . I can't remember. *Wait, actually, I do remember.* It was when she looked up at me like she knew me.

I can't wait to see her again. But first, I need to get something to eat, then I have an errand to run. After all that, I plan to come right back here so I can see my girl.

Since I've got a case of the munchies, it doesn't take me long to inhale the sandwich and bag of chips I get from a little restaurant down the street.

Once my stomach is no longer growling, I head into a souvenir shop to look for a postcard. Hallucinating Arella made me realize I never did the last thing she asked of me.

"Will you send me a postcard from wherever you end up?"

I guess since I have a place in New York now, this qualifies as the place I ended up.

I must stare at the spinning rack of postcards for too long, because a young male clerk comes up behind me and asks, "You need help pickin' one out?"

My problem is when she sees this in her mailbox, I want her to think, *The man who sent me this postcard is the man I'm supposed to be with, instead of the fuckwad I'm currently with.* Sadly, none of these generic pictures of the New York City skyline or the Statue of Liberty say that.

"Sir?"

I snap out of my thoughts. "Um, I can't decide. Could I just get one of each?"

"Sure." With a smile, the clerk plucks one of each postcard off the rack.

Back in my quiet apartment, I sit at my kitchen counter with my stack of postcards and a souvenir pen. I flip through the postcards for almost twenty minutes before deciding on the one that reads, *Greetings from New York City*. It features some artwork of the city's skyline and the iconic statue. No, it doesn't say, *Please come back to me*, but it's colorful and bright, and Arella likes that shit.

I stare at the back of the card for almost an hour before I write.

> ARELLA,
> I ENDED UP IN NEW YORK CITY. IT'S BUSY HERE, AND I THINK YOU'D LIKE THE BEAUTIFUL VIEW FROM MY APARTMENT. ITS BEAUTY REMINDS ME OF YOU. HOPE YOU'RE DOING WELL.
> —TREY

I lean back in my barstool to read it. On my third pass, I shout the F-word to my bare walls. I wrote her name as Arella without even thinking about it. She's going to get this in the mail and toss it straight into the trash.

I draw a big X through my note, then grab another postcard.

> ARI,
> I ENDED UP IN NEW YORK CITY. IT'S BUSY HERE, AND I THINK YOU'D LIKE THE BEAUTIFUL VIEW FROM MY APARTMENT. ITS BEAUTY REMINDS ME OF YOU. HOPE YOU'RE DOING WELL.
> —TREY

I sit back to read it over, then draw a big X through my words again. I can't tell her that the beautiful view reminds me of her. That sounds too forward. She'll think I'm still obsessed with her. I mean, I am, but I don't want *her* to know that.

With a long sigh and another postcard, I try again.

> ARI,
> I ENDED UP IN NEW YORK CITY. IT'S BUSY HERE.
> HOPE YOU'RE DOING WELL.
> —TREY

No, no, no. I can't sign my name! What was I thinking? What if her boyfr—no. What if Caleb sees this before she does and trashes it once he knows it's from me? I've gotta keep my name off it. She'll know who it's from.

> ARI,
> I ENDED UP IN NEW YORK CITY. HOPE YOU'RE DOING WELL.

There. That's good, right?

I read it again, then scowl at the postcard. It's so lame. Nothing about this screams, *I love you*. Most of all, it doesn't scream, *I miss you so much, it hurts*.

15

TREY

I'VE FIGURED OUT THE PERFECT CONCOCTION TO MANIFEST MY hallucinations of her and still remember them. I need exactly two bottles of vodka and a dose and a half of jaderro. Anything less than that and she doesn't appear. Anything more and I pass out before I can see her at all.

Whenever I do see her, she never says anything. She just lies there, caressing my face. Sometimes I talk to her. I tell her about the moments we've shared that live in my mind rent free. I tell her how much I miss cooking dinner with her in my kitchen. I tell her how much I used to love seeing her in my shirt that covered everything from her collarbone to her upper thighs. She never responds with anything but a sweet smile. Whenever I'm not talking to her, I just lie back and admire her beauty.

After I wake up from the high, I usually go get a sandwich. Then I write notes on a bunch of postcards I'll never send and fall into another high where I'm happy and get to talk to the only person who's ever truly healed me.

These postcards have turned into a therapeutic exercise. I write things on them I wish I could say to her. Then I shove them into my bedroom drawer and never look at them again.

I've just shoved my most recently written card into that drawer when I drop to my knees to dig under my bed for my supplies. This will be my last high for the week because Liz is coming to visit me for my birthday. Whenever I wake up from this one, I'll have to get my place cleaned up for her and pretend like everything is fine.

THREE DAYS LATER, LIZ STROLLS INTO MY PLACE WITH A SMILE. "Happy twenty-seventh birth—" She gasps. "Oh my god."

I'm in my messy kitchen, getting myself a glass of water, when I stop. "What?"

She drops her suitcase onto the floor, then stares at me with her anxiety nipping at my head.

I wait for her to explain why she's looking at me like that. When she still doesn't say anything, I urge her to. "Liz?"

"Oh, T. You're using again." She says it like a statement, not a question.

How the fuck does she know? I feign innocence. "Huh?"

"Don't play dumb with me. Did you forget that you were an addict when we first met? I know what you look like right after a high."

Well, shit. I only woke up a few hours ago. My eyes are probably still sunken, and my skin is probably a little gray.

Liz heads straight to my couch, then pats the space next to her. It's not a suggestion. It's a request. Reluctantly, I join her with my glass of water, feeling like a student in trouble with the principal.

"I'm not mad at you," she says, making it worse. "I just want to know what's going on. How long have you been using?"

I hang my head low as I place my water glass on the coffee table. "Not long."

"How long, T?" Of course, she's not gonna let me off the hook that easily.

I sigh heavily. Lying never works with Liz, so I go with the truth. "I started the week after I came to New York."

Her face screws together. "That was back in November. It's March."

"Yep."

Her jaw drops. "Were you using when I came for Thanksgiving?"

Yes. "Probably."

"Then you were using when I came for Christmas?"

Yes. "Most likely."

"T, why didn't you tell me?"

"Because I knew you'd make me stop. Why do you think I worked so hard to hide this from you?" *Obviously not hard enough.*

"Of course I'm gonna make you stop."

I shake my head. "I don't wanna stop."

"You have to."

"Why?" I say like a whiny child.

"Because it's not good for you."

A scoff. "I don't care what's good for me."

Liz rolls her eyes like that's the dumbest thing she's ever heard. Little does she know, I mean that statement with everything that's left in this dark and lonely hole in my chest.

"Which z-drug is it?"

"Jaderro." There's no use lying now. She already knows. I hate my body for giving her the clues so easily. I was able to hide it during her last two visits. Why couldn't I this time? Is it because I've been using it longer? Is it because I didn't wake up sooner? Is it because my apartment looks like a trash dump?

A sharp gasp leaves Liz's mouth. "Jaderro? T, that shit is the worst of the worst. If you inject even the tiniest bit too much, it can kill you."

I fucking hope so. Although, it hasn't killed me yet, so maybe I'm immune.

Liz scolds me. "Don't do that."

"Do what?"

"Look happy about the thought of dying."

It's not the dying part that would make me happy. It's the part where I could stop living this worthless thing I call my life. The air between us goes stale as my unspoken words stay behind my lips.

"Where is it?" she asks.

"Where's what?"

"Your supply."

I scoff-laugh. "Like I'm gonna tell you."

Before I can stop her, Liz hops onto her feet and storms into my bedroom. I catch her by her waist just as she tears the top drawer of my nightstand open—the drawer where I keep all those handwritten postcards. She doesn't know about those, and I don't want her reading them.

"Put me down!" she shouts as I throw her over my shoulder.

I march out of my bedroom, then wave a hand at the door. The wood slams behind me as I return Liz to the living room.

She smacks my back so hard, it stings. "Put me down, or I'll drench you with a waterball."

This time, I listen. I set her feet onto the carpet, then stand in front of her with my arms crossed. "I'm not letting you in there."

"You can't keep doing this, T."

"I can, and I will. It makes me happy, Liz. Don't you want me to be happy?"

"Of course, but this isn't the way." She doesn't get it. She's never done drugs, so she doesn't know what it's like. She doesn't know how good it feels.

"This *is* the way. It's the *only* way. When I'm high, I'm

almost as happy as I was when I was with her." Actually, it's not even close, but it's *something*. And something is better than nothing.

"But this isn't healthy for you. You need to find happiness another way."

I cross my arms over my chest like a challenge. "Fine. How?"

"Come back to LA."

"I can't." *But I want to so fucking bad.*

"Yes, you can." Liz softens her stance. "I miss you, T. The whole band and crew misses you too. It's not the same without you. Our band needs all five of us to function properly. It's not good for you to be alone out here. You need something to do and to surround yourself with people who care about you."

I miss my friends too, but not enough to make me move back. "Nope. Sorry. Can't."

"Like ever?"

"Maybe if she moved out of the state."

"What if she never moves?"

"Then I guess I'm never going back." If I do, it'll be too easy for me to end up sitting in my car outside her apartment, waiting for her to come out, just so I can catch a glimpse of her. Then I'll truly become the stalker she thinks I am.

Liz pouts a little. "When you told us you were leaving, you said it was only for a while. Not forever."

"But here in New York, whenever I get the urge to see her, I'll have a whole plane ride to realize it's a bad idea. Here, I can see her when I'm high and she never looks at me like she doesn't know who I am."

"Wait. You see her? As in, you hallucinate her?"

"Yes, and it feels so real! When she touches me, it's like she's really there. I'm happy again, Liz." I put my hands together like I'm praying. "Please don't take that away from me."

16

TREY

Two months later

"Happy birthday, angel. You're even more beautiful at twenty-three."

Arella responds the way she normally does: with a soft smile and her eyes glued to mine. Her long chestnut hair drapes over her shoulders in loose waves I want to claw my hands into and pull on until she's close enough for me to feel her warm breath on my lips.

I want to touch her, but whenever I do, my hand just falls to the mattress. That's why I usually stick to only looking at and talking to her.

"Sorry I haven't seen you in a while. Liz came to visit last week, and she thinks I quit jaderro last month. Thank fuck she's not a Detector. I probably shouldn't have lied, but she wouldn't get off my back about it. Deep down, I think she knows I haven't quit. How can I, when this is the only way I can see you?"

Arella's hand slides up my chest, leaving behind a trail of

tingles. Then she cups my face. I close my eyes and lean into her touch, indulging in how soothing it feels.

"This is all I need to be happy, baby. Just you and me here, where nothing else matters and no one's trying to hurt you or take you away from me."

Her hand stops caressing my face. I open my eyes, and she's gone. *Not again.*

I roll onto my side and throw my feet over the bed. Then I dig out the silverware box and ready my arm for another dose. My little glass jar is almost empty. It's got about a dose left. *Might as well finish it out.* Lately, the jaderro has been wearing off too fast, so I've had to shoot up in the middle of my hallucinations. It's annoying, but you gotta do what you gotta do.

The hallucination returns the same as it always does. First the bright light, then the cockroaches, then she shows up. This time, she stays a little longer than usual. I try to talk to her, but suddenly, the nausea overwhelms me. I lean over the side of my bed just as the vomit rises up my throat. It splatters over my carpet with bright stars and rainbow colors.

I wipe my mouth off with my hand, then turn back around to stare at my girl. Suddenly, she's not the only person I'm seeing anymore. Two people in suits have appeared in my bedroom. One is a woman whose blonde hair has a strip of purple in the front. The other is a man with a goatee. Behind them are more bright lights and neon colors.

"I told you he's getting bad," the woman says. "I really think it's time to intervene."

"But our job is to keep out as much as possible," the man says.

I cock my head at them. "Are you guys real?"

The woman continues like she didn't hear me. "If he proceeds like this, he's going to kill himself. What's more valuable? Keeping out or this?"

The man thinks, then sighs. "You're right. Let's do something."

Usually, Arella can hear me, but she never talks. These people are talking, but they can't hear me. *Strange.* That extra dose is really fucking me up. First the puke, and now two people in suits?

I blink a few times as if it'll reset my vision. Suddenly, a loud *pop!* sound cracks through the air, then the woman disappears. I blink a few more times, and after another loud *pop!*, the man is gone too.

I wake to the sound of something beeping. It's coming from outside my bedroom. *What the hell could be beeping?*

"Could you go check on the patient in six twelve?" a woman asks as the beeping stops. "She pressed her call light again."

Getting my eyes to open feels like trying to pry apart a stubborn mussel shell. Once I succeed, a blurry image of a dim hospital room appears. Cords are attached to my arm.

"Hey, T," someone softly says from my left.

I slowly turn my head to find Liz sitting on a chair at my bedside, with a closed book in her lap. "Where am I?"

"A hospital," Liz says nonchalantly.

"H-how did I get here?"

"Ambulance."

I squint at her. "Did I get into another accident?" I can't see why. I haven't ridden my bike in months. Anywhere I go, I walk. That is, if I go anywhere at all. Lately, I've been getting food delivered because the thought of having to put pants on is daunting. My trash is overflowing with takeout containers and pizza boxes.

Liz chokes up as she says, "T, you almost died."

"What happened?"

"I called you multiple times for two days straight, and when I didn't get a response, I booked the first flight out to New York. I broke my way into your penthouse, which wasn't hard, by the way. You left the front door unlocked. I found you lying on the floor next to a puddle of vomit."

That's odd. I'm usually pretty good about locking my door.

Liz continues, "At first, I tried to shake you awake, but you didn't respond. I exploded into tears, thinking I'd lost you. I hated myself for waiting as long as I did to fly over. When I realized you were still breathing, I called for an ambulance. You've been here for two days while your zoctor has pumped you full of medications I can't even pronounce."

I reach out and gesture for her to give me her hand. She takes her gloves off first, then places one palm into mine. "I'm sorry, Liz. I didn't mean to put you through that."

She falls into a quiet sob, making me feel like the shittiest friend ever. I can't imagine what that was like for her. To rush into my bedroom and find me unmoving on the floor? If it had been me with her, I would have lost my fucking mind.

"I'm so sorry, Liz," I say as if my apology can erase the panic she must have felt.

"T, please be honest with me. Did you overdose with the intent to . . ." She hiccups a tearful breath. "God, I can't even say it."

"I know what you're trying to ask. It's the same thing you wanted to know the last time I was in a hospital, right?"

She nods, wiping her tears off with a few fingers.

I debate lying to save her from the pain, but she can always see through my lies. "Liz, you and her are the only beneficiaries of my will. Everything I have would have been split between you two. That's millions for each of—"

"No! I don't want millions of dollars. I want you!"

I scoot over to one side of the medical bed, then tap the empty space next to me. Without hesitation, Liz climbs up and digs her face into my chest. As I circle my arms around her and pull her close, she cries even harder.

Usually, I'd offer to kick the ass of the person who made

her cry. This time, it's me, and I don't know how to handle that. Instead, I give her a soft kiss on her forehead.

"I'm sorry, Liz." I choke up as I kiss her forehead again and silently beg for her to stop crying. "I'm so sorry."

I don't think my apologies are doing anything. Her body is still shaking.

I end up turning two nurses away before her tears finally subside and I can breathe again.

"I can't lose you, Trey."

Wow. She hasn't called me *Trey* in a long-ass time. She only does it when she's being super serious.

"I don't have a family, T. You're all I've got. If I lose you, I won't have anyone."

"You could find a new best friend."

"Not one I can hold hands with. Not one I can have sleepovers with, where they'll hold me all night to keep the nightmares away."

Zordis can't dream, but Liz does. *Sort of.* Technically, they're the horrifying memories she's caught over the years, replaying in her head. It happens whenever she sleeps, and it wakes her up after only two or three hours of rest. Because she never gets enough sleep, she has to sleep every night like an Ordinary.

Back when Liz stayed over for Thanksgiving, we shared my bed. To help her fall asleep, we put on a movie. Normally, we cuddle during movies, so it didn't feel weird to cuddle in my bed while she fell asleep, and when she woke up in the morning, I was still holding her because I didn't want my movement to wake her. She slept through the night—a full seven hours—and she didn't have a single night terror.

The next night, we tried it again. I held her while she slept, and she got another full night of rest without a single replay of anyone's trauma.

When she stayed over for Christmas, we found out that if I left her while she was sleeping, the nightmares crept into her head within a few minutes of my disappearance. But one hundred percent of the time, if I stayed in bed and held her, the nightmares stayed away.

Like how Liz doesn't question how she can touch my hands without seeing my parents get blown up anymore, she doesn't question how this is possible either. There is still so much that Zordis don't understand about our powers.

I'm the only person Liz can touch hands with without seeing their traumatic past. I'm the only person who can keep her nightmares away too. Everything we have has happened over many, many years, and it all happened organically. Now that I think about it, I realize it'd be hard for her to rebuild our friendship with someone else and I'm angry with myself for almost taking that away from her.

Liz tilts her head back to look at me. She's not crying anymore, just hiccupping from the previous cries. "You've always said you'd do anything for me, right?"

I nod, knowing exactly where she's going with this. She's gonna try to convince me to go sober again.

"Remember when we first met and how I encouraged you to be sober?"

"Yep. You said there's a better version of me who exists under the drug habits and fistfights."

"Um, sure. That's not how I remember it, but if that's what you heard that got you to clean up, then sure. Either way, the point is that you quit the drugs cold turkey. If you did it once, you can do it again. The thing is that I can't just encourage you to quit. You have to *want* to quit. The only thing I can do is say things to help you want it."

"Lemme guess." I lean back a little to see more of her. "You're gonna say I need to quit so I can be here to help you keep the nightmares away?"

"Nope. Guess again."

Outside my hospital room, that beeping sound chimes

again. I ignore the commotion. "You're gonna tell me there's still that better version of me beneath the drugs?"

"Closer."

I think hard. "You're gonna say this isn't the man I want to be?"

Liz smiles up at me. "Even closer."

"I'm done guessing. Just tell me."

"I was gonna say this isn't the man *she* would want you to be."

That slams me right in the gut. I wasn't expecting Liz to say that, because she normally avoids bringing Arella up. Liz doesn't mind when *I* bring her up, because that means I'm choosing to talk about her. But Liz avoids mentioning her so I don't get that "sad and depressing look in my eyes."

I swallow hard. "She doesn't know me well enough to have an opinion on who she wants me to be."

"No, T. I'm not talking about Ari. I'm talking about Arella. Ari doesn't know you, but Arella does. You've said it yourself: Your girl is still in there somewhere. If she saw you now, what would she think?"

If Arella saw the terrible things I've done in the last six months, she'd be so disappointed in me. Getting wasted in bars until they kick me out, shooting poison up my arm, barely eating or doing basic things like drinking water or combing my hair. I've lost so much weight, my cheeks are sinking in. The thing is, though, Arella's not around to see me, which is why I don't care what type of man I am.

Liz continues in her same gentle tone, "If she suddenly reverted back to remembering you and came looking for you, how would it make her feel to find you like this? Is this the man you want her running back to?"

"But she's *not* running back to me, Liz. She's not even *walking* to me."

"But what if she was?"

17

———

ARI

ONE YEAR LATER

"WHERE ARE WE GOING?" I ASK FROM THE PASSENGER SEAT OF Javina's car. The air conditioning is on high to combat the intense heat from the early afternoon sun. I turn the vents to face me.

"I told you already," Javina says as she makes a left turn. "We're going to a softball game."

"Really?" When she said that earlier, I thought she was joking. Javina does that sometimes. She likes to answer questions with the wrong answer. Like yesterday, when I asked her what book she's currently reading, she said, "It's called *101 Ways to Kill Your Best Friend and Get Away with It.*" I just rolled my eyes and moved on. "Why are we going to a softball game?"

"I was gonna surprise you, but I'll just tell you. I entered a contest where if I won, me and a plus-one got to be extras in a music video. And guess what? I won!"

"No way!" Now I see why she told me to dress nicely. "What exactly does being an extra mean?"

"Don't worry, babes. There's not a lot of acting involved. Our only job is to sit on the bleachers and cheer."

A while later, Javina pulls into the parking lot of a softball field. The scorching June sun beats down on my skin as I exit her red Corolla. A pair of giggly young women in skimpy skirts strolls past us toward a table featuring a sign that reads, EXTRAS. CHECK IN HERE.

"Did the email say if we'd have a chance to meet the band?" the woman with pink hair asks.

"Nope," her friend says. "But I don't care. I'm not leaving here without a picture with Trey Grant."

I whip my attention to Javina. "Excuse me?"

She grits her teeth together with a guilty smile. "Oh, um, did I forget to mention that this video shoot is for a band called Flames in the Night?"

I meet her at the trunk of her car and slap her shoulder. "No, you didn't mention that, because that's something a *good* friend would have done. Why didn't you tell me that important piece of information?"

"Because then you wouldn't have come. Duh."

Actually, I would have. I've been suppressing this deep urge inside me to see Trey again for the past year and seven months. *Not that I've been counting . . .*

I still see him a few times a week in my dreams. Some dreams have repeated so often, I've memorized them. Like the dream where Trey is lying on the floor of a gas station office with a gash in his thigh so deep, I can see the inside of his leg.

Every time I have that dream, it happens the same: Trey always says, "I'll only slow you down. I'll probably bleed out anyway. Just forget about me and get outta here." I always fight with him until he allows me to bandage his wound, and then I help him stand and we drive away from the gas station in someone else's car.

In my free time, I've been doing research on dreams and what they could mean. The best explanation I could find to explain Trey almost dying in my dreams is that I'm afraid of losing him. But how can I be afraid of losing someone I don't have?

Javina takes my hand and leans into me with a low voice. "Look, Ari, you can be mad at me all you want, but I've been in love with this band for years. You know that Rachel and I were going to their shows almost once a month until they went on tour. Now they're back, and they're filming videos again.

"They don't ask for extras often. The two times they did in the past, I didn't win an invitation. Now I finally did! I know this must be weird for you, given the whole thing where he came from an alternate universe and thought you were his girlfriend, but could you please pretend like that didn't happen for a day and just enjoy this with me?"

"I'm not mad at you, Javie."

She leans back with her brows knitted together. "You're not?"

"No. I just would have appreciated a heads-up."

"Oh. In that case . . ." She flashes me a cheesy smile. "Hey, babes. Just so you know, we're gonna go be extras in a music video that Trey Grant's band is filming."

I roll my eyes. "Gee, thanks. I'm so glad you told me that *ahead of time* so I could mentally prepare to see the man who's been starring in my dreams for a year and a half."

"You're *still* having dreams about him?"

"They haven't stopped."

I finally told Javina about my dreams a few months ago because I wanted to get her opinion on them. Her crazy theory is that my dreams aren't dreams. She thinks they're Alterella's memories. Somehow, I knew she was going to say that.

Caleb still doesn't know about my dreams, and I don't plan to tell him. I don't want him reading into them as something with a deeper meaning. Despite what Javina says, I still think they're just dreams. At least, that's what I'm telling myself.

After we get checked in, we're ushered toward a set of bleachers facing a small diamond field. Javina and I have two seats smack-dab in the middle of the stands. Within ten minutes, the bleachers are full of other extras. The crew gave us blue pom-poms to wave. The bleachers on the other side of the field are full too, except the extras there have red pom-poms.

The Black woman who checked us in earlier stands in front of our bleachers with a microphone. "Hello, everyone! I'm Monique, the band's manager. Thank you for coming."

The crowd cheers with hoots and hollers.

"I love the enthusiasm! Two things before we get started: First, there is to be no video recording or pictures taken during the filming of this video. If any of the crew catches you with your phone out, you'll be asked to leave. No exceptions.

"Second, many of you have already asked me if there will be a photo opportunity with the band. The answer is yes. After we film all the scenes we need, anyone who wants to get a photo can line up on the other side of this dugout." Monique gestures toward the red team's dugout. A bunch of people wearing red jerseys are sitting in it. None of them are Trey. "Any questions?"

When no one raises their hand, Monique says, "Great. Now I'd like you to meet Mateo, the video director." She gestures toward the short Hispanic guy leaning against the fence. A Giants baseball cap covers his curly brown hair.

Mateo steps forward and takes the microphone from Monique. "Hey, hey! I'm excited to be here, and I need you to be excited too. Your only job today is to give us high energy. The band will be acting out a few rehearsed scenes on the field with some hired actors. I need you to act like you're at a real softball game. When someone on the blue team makes it on base, you cheer! When someone on the blue team scores a run, you scream! When anyone on the red team does that, you boo 'em. Got it?"

The people on my bleachers let out a high-pitched *whoo!* in unison. Javina is one of them. I shout out a loud *yes!*

"Awesome!" Mateo says. "The last scene we're filming today is of Trey scoring the winning home run. His job today is to actually hit a ball that far. Since that could take a few tries, we'll need you to be on your toes for that. The second he hits the ball out of the park, we need you on your feet, going wild. Can ya do that?"

The extras scream out again. Javina and I join them with cheers and claps.

"That's the energy I want!" Mateo says. "We'll begin this shoot in ten minutes."

With a wave goodbye, Mateo and Monique head toward the away team's bleachers. Once there, they give the away team a similar speech. Eventually, Monique heads back toward the parking lot while Mateo steps up to home plate.

A rumble of chatter comes from the home team's dugout. Unfortunately, I can't see any of the players from where I'm at. I'm anxious to see what Trey looks like now. Does he look the same? Different? Older? I've kept away from cyberstalking him, even though I want to often. I don't because I don't feel like I have any business doing that. But now that I'm here, my curiosity is flying through the roof.

The chatter in the dugout fades as a bunch of people wearing blue jerseys runs out onto the field. The fans on both bleachers cheer for them. The players I recognize are the ones in Trey's band. The drummer and bass guitarist head toward the outfield as the band's pianist trots toward first base. Then there's Liz. She heads to home plate, wearing catcher's gear. Still no Trey though. A guy from the red team carrying a baseball bat over his shoulder joins Liz at home plate, completing the scene to look like a real softball game.

Mateo glances around, then gestures toward the empty pitcher's mound. "Where the hell is pretty boy?"

Liz says something to the director, but it's not loud enough for me to catch it.

Javina leans over to me and whispers, "Apparently, I'm not the only person who calls him *pretty boy*."

"I'm right here," a deep sultry voice says, making my heart spark with heat.

Trey steps out of the closed-off concession stand wearing a blue jersey, dark jeans, and a baseball cap. My breath gets caught in my throat, and my hands are suddenly sweaty. I didn't expect my body to react like this at the mere sight of him.

The two giggly women at the front of the bleachers cheer for Trey as he jogs to meet with the video director at home plate.

Mateo says stuff I can't hear as he gestures toward the field. In unison, Trey, Liz, and the batter nod their understanding.

Since Trey's facing away from me, I can't get a good look at his face, but I can get a good look at his back, and it's not a sight to complain about. His body fills out his jersey in all the right places. GRANT is printed in big block letters over his thick shoulders. *Has he always been that muscular?*

"Pretty boy looks like he's been goin' to the gym," Javina says with a waggle of her eyebrows.

"Okay, people!" Mateo says into the mic as Liz kneels behind home plate and Trey jogs over to the pitcher's mound. "Let's do this! Cameras ready?"

The three guys with heavy cameras on their shoulders nod.

"Action!"

Once the batter is in position, Trey underhand throws the ball to him. The batter swings and misses. They do a few takes of this until the batter finally makes contact with the ball. It barrels toward left field as the people on the away team's bleachers make some noise.

The band's drummer races toward the ball and catches it in his glove with ease. The people in my bleachers pop up to cheer. I join them, waving my pom-poms in the air.

The next batter is a woman with her long blonde hair in a ponytail sticking out of her helmet. Trey pitches her the ball. She hits it, drops her bat, then runs until she makes it to second base. The red team cheers from the dugout as the fans on their bleachers do the same. Everyone on my side shouts out some boos.

An hour later, my throat is sore. I've never seen the filming of a music video before, so I didn't realize how much work goes into these things. They have to film things over and over again until they get the right shot.

During the scene where Liz has to slide home, they make her do it fifteen times before the director is satisfied with how the dirt looks as it kicks up behind her. I never would have thought little things like that mattered so much.

This whole time, Trey hasn't looked my way once. I don't think he knows I'm here. Javina mentioned that all the coordination to be here came from the band's manager. I doubt anyone from the actual band is part of that process.

I keep obsessing over what's going to happen when Trey does see me. Is he going to want to talk to me? If so, what will he say? What will *I* say? I'm not sure if I even want to talk to him. I mean, I do, but I don't. What if it's awkward? What if it ends badly? Or worse, what if he pretends like we don't know each other and just ignores me the whole time? I think that will hurt the most, even though it shouldn't. I shouldn't *want* to talk to him as much as I do, but I do. I shouldn't think about him as much as I do either, but I do.

"Last scene!" Mateo's voice booms over the speakers a while later. "Six-pack, you know what you gotta do?"

Trey nods from his position at home plate as he practices

swinging his bat. "Hit a homer, run around the bases, get water dumped over my head."

"Exactly. Easy peasy, lemon squeezy. We'll all be home in no time."

Trey chuckles from deep in his belly. It's a laugh I've heard in my dreams but never in real life. Hearing it makes my insides flutter. "You've got more faith in me than I do, Mateo. You saw how I did during rehearsal yesterday. I couldn't hit a home run to save my life."

"Yeah, but now you've got loads of people watching. I'm hoping the pressure will whip you into shape. Aaand action!"

A guy wearing red on the pitcher's mound readies himself, then tosses the ball toward home plate. Trey swings and misses, then shakes his head at himself.

"You've got this, Willie Mays!" Mateo shouts with his hands cupped around his mouth. "Let's try that again."

A woman on the side of the field throws the pitcher a new ball. He catches it in his glove, then readies himself again as Trey raises his bat into the air. When the pitcher releases the ball, Trey swings, and it's another strike.

"Try again," Mateo says.

Trey strikes out with the next ball.

And the next.

And the next.

"Come on, Pete Rose!" Mateo says. "You can do this!"

Trey chuckles beautifully. "I'm telling ya, man, I think my bat is broken."

Mateo puts the microphone up to his lips. "Let's pump him up, guys! Trey! Trey! Trey!"

Everyone in the bleachers, even the red side, joins in on Mateo's chant.

Javina throws her fist into the air each time she shouts his name. I cup my palms around my mouth and chant too.

Trey shakes his head at the crowd as he gestures for everyone to calm down. "Thanks, but I think this might be faster if someone else hits a home run and we just edit the person to look like me in post."

"No can do, buddy-boy," Mateo says. "We need this shot to look as authentic as possible. Now channel your inner Babe Ruth and knock this shit outta the park."

The giggly woman with the pink hair cups her mouth. "If you hit this next one, my friend will let you take her out on a date."

The friend playfully slaps the woman with pink hair on her shoulder. "Caitlyn!"

Trey turns to offer the ladies a warm smile. "Thanks for the encouragement, but I—"

His eyes lock with mine, then his smile drops. The world stills as he stares at me, mouth partly open. His intense gaze from those blue-grays steals my breath away. He's blinking at me like he's not sure if I'm real.

In the corner of my eye, I see the giggly women turn around to find out what he's gaping at. A few others whip their heads around too. Then suddenly, everyone's staring at me, making me want to curl into a turtle shell.

Trey rubs his eyes with his fingers, then glances back at me. We lock gazes again, and I almost wave at him as a peace offering. Before I get the chance to, he tears his attention off me.

With a shaky voice, he calls out, "Liz?"

She runs to him from the dugout. "What's wrong, T?"

He grips her forearm and says something to her I can't make out. Whatever he says, it makes her turn to look at the bleachers. When she catches sight of me, her eyes go wide, then she turns back to Trey. She says something in a low voice. He responds by sucking in a deep breath and nodding back.

Javina nudges my arm with her elbow. "I think they're talking about you."

I'm speechless. *I think so too.*

18

———

TREY

LIKE THE BESTEST FRIEND A MAN CAN HAVE, LIZ RUSHES TO ME as soon as I call out for her. "What's wrong, T?" she asks.

I grip her arm to steady myself as I lean toward her ear. "I swear to you, I haven't done drugs for over a year, but I think I'm hallucinating right now."

"What?"

My lungs feel full of shrapnel as I prepare to hear her tell me I'm losing it. "I see *her*. In the bleachers."

Liz turns to glance behind me, then her eyes go wide and she lowers her voice. "You're not hallucinating. I see her too. Are you okay?"

I draw in a deep breath of relief and nod. It's good to know I'm not hallucinating. "Did you know she was gonna be here?"

"Nope. Do you want me to get Monique to ask her to leave?"

"No." *Absolutely not.* I don't know why she's here, but I've been dying to see her. Whatever force of nature brought her here today, I'm grateful for it.

"Then do you think you can hit us a home run so we can all go home sometime, oh, I dunno . . . today?"

"Yeah, I'll try to pull myself together."

"I believe in you, T." With that, Liz returns to the dugout.

I resist the urge to glance back at the bleachers—at *her*. Instead, I suck in a long breath and slowly let it out.

I do it again.

Then again.

My zerapist told me that deep breathing can be helpful when I feel like I can't control my emotions. I need it to work right now. Otherwise, Liz is right and we'll be here all day.

If I had known Arella was in the stands this whole time, I would have tried harder to hit this homer. Now I'm determined to nail the next one.

"You good?" Mateo asks.

"Yep," I lie, then raise my bat into the air.

He flashes the cameramen two thumbs up. "Action!"

The pitcher readies himself, then underhands the ball to me. I eye the ball as it hurls toward me. Then I swing.

Crack!

My bat hits the ball just right, and the ball flies through the air until it lands on the other side of the fence. As the crowd goes wild, I go for a run around the bases. At home plate, someone dumps water over my head as my fake softball team surrounds me with cheers and slaps on the back.

The cameramen rush over to film our celebration, reminding me that I'm supposed to be smiling. *I can't look at her. I can't look at her.*

Once Mateo gets all the footage he needs, he calls out, "That's a wrap!"

Monique grabs the microphone from him. "Thank you, everyone! Extras, if you'd like a picture with the band, please line up behind this dugout."

Liz hands me a white towel as the people around me disperse. "I knew you could do it."

"I had to once I knew *she* was watching." I dry off the back of my neck, then my hair.

"She and her friend are getting into the picture line. Do you think you can handle that?"

"Probably not, but I'll do my best."

I spend the next twenty-some minutes taking pictures with fans and mentally preparing myself to see her again. What I don't mentally prepare for is not seeing her at all. When Javina appears from the other side of the dugout, she struts her way onto the field—alone.

Excited energy radiates off her as she hands her phone to Monique. We all smile for the camera, Javina says a few words of praise to my bandmates, then she leaves. The entire time, I hold my tongue back from asking her where Arella is. As the next person in line steps out, I feel Liz's eyes on me.

She mouths, "You okay?"

I only stare at her because I don't know the answer to that. Why didn't Arella come out? Where did she go? Did she not want to see me? That last thought hurts the most because I wanted to see her more than anything. Even if we didn't speak to each other, it would have made me happy just to *see* her. To get a better view of what she looks like now. To hear if she still sounds the same. Maybe I could have wrapped my arm around her shoulder for the three seconds it takes for Monique to snap a photo.

The next smiles I make feel harder to fake. Once the band is done meeting with the last person in line, I glance behind the dugout for her. She's not there. A heavy stone sinks into my stomach as I force my feet into the concession stand, where I've left all my things. The rest of the band's stuff is in here too. Otherwise, it's vacant. My bandmates are still out there, chatting with some fans who have stuck around.

I focus on sucking in deep breaths as I drag my semi-dry jersey over my head and slip into a black V-neck. Then I brace my hands against the wall and try to gather myself.

Deep breath in. Slow breath out.
Deep breath in. Slow breath out.

This deep-breathing bullshit isn't working. What else has my zerapist taught me to help control my panic attacks? I can't remember them right now. What good can those methods do me if I can't fucking remember them? Maybe I should get them tattooed onto my inner left forearm, next to the other tattoo I got recently.

Suddenly, the door pops open.

"How ya doing, T?"

I push away from the wall and plaster on a face that will make Liz think I'm not breaking down. "I'm trying not to look into it too much."

"That she didn't come to meet the band?"

"Yeah," I say somberly as my gaze dips to my feet.

"How do you feel about that?"

Devastated. Destroyed. Incinerated by a hundred fireballs. "When I look at it from her point of view, I understand. What reason does she have to see me? If I had to guess, I'm gonna say Javina dragged her here without her knowing it."

"I'm sorry, T. Do you think you can keep it together for just a little longer? There are two very eager fans standing outside, waiting for you."

"What do they want?"

"They asked if they could get a picture with just you. I told them I'd ask you first. If you don't think you can handle it, I can tell them to leave."

I draw in a long breath, then let it out. "I think I can handle that."

Liz places a gentle gloved hand over my forearm. "You are welcome to break down all you want when we get home, okay? We can order pizza and do whatever you need to feel better."

I pull her in for a firm hug. "Thanks, Liz. I love you so much."

Something I've been working on with my zerapist is getting over my fear of saying *I love you*. Through many, many,

many sessions together, my zerapist concluded that one of my biggest regrets is not telling Arella sooner that I loved her. Now I make it a point to tell Liz whenever I think of it, because someday, I may not get the chance to.

"I love you too, T-Bear." Liz stands on her toes to place a short kiss on my cheek, just as the door opens.

Kevin, our bass guitarist, freezes and stares at us, wide-eyed as the door shuts behind him. His emotions match his expression. "Uh, did I just see somethin' I shouldn't have?"

"You're good, Kev," Liz says with a nonchalant wave of her hand.

"Um, okaaay?" He looks like he's about to ask a question, then he puts his arms up in surrender. "You know what? It ain't my business."

Liz and I kiss each other in private all the time. Usually, she kisses my cheek and I kiss her hand or her forehead. It's not romantic, but if someone doesn't understand the type of relationship Liz and I have, I'm sure they think otherwise.

With all the rumors that have been spreading online about Liz and me lately, catching us in a private moment like that probably makes Kevin think those rumors are true. I don't care enough to say otherwise. I've never felt the need to explain my relationship with Liz, and I'm not about to start now.

I grab my duffel bag, then head toward the door. "I'ma go take a picture with those fans, 'kay?"

"When you're done, come back to get me," Liz says.

"Yes, Mom," I say, because she hates it when I call her that.

Liz rewards my nickname for her with an eyeroll.

As I step out of the concession stand, two women approach me with thrilled yet flustered energy.

"Trey," Pink Hair Girl says.

"Hi, ladies." I don't bother with faking a smile, because I'm gonna have to when I take the photos with them. I only have so much energy for faking it. "Liz told me you guys want a picture."

"Yes, please."

I set my bag to the side, then place an arm around Pink Hair Girl's shoulders first. Her friend snaps a photo, then they switch places and I fake smile again.

"These look great!" the brunette says as she checks the pictures.

I don't bother looking because I don't care.

"So," Pink Hair Girl says, "I told you earlier that if you hit the next ball, my friend would let you take her out on a date. You must have really wanted that date."

The brunette flashes me a hopeful smile.

I slap a hand over my chest. "Sorry, ladies. I'm seeing someone right now."

Their faces drop. "You are?"

I nod as convincingly as I can. "Yep."

"Like, is it serious?" Pink Hair Girl asks.

"Pretty serious."

"Who is it?"

"I can't say. We're, um, keeping things private."

"It's Liz, isn't it?" the brunette says. "It's gotta be Liz."

I could have guessed they'd say that. Our fans seem to think that it's impossible for two people as close as Liz and me to be single for this long and not fuck each other. To me, what's actually impossible is the idea of having meaningful intimacy with anyone but Arella. "No, it's not Liz."

"Are you sure? Because we could have sworn we just saw you two kissing when Kevin opened that door."

Of course they saw that. "Is there anything else I can do for you ladies? If not, I've gotta get going."

Disappointment slams into their guts as they shove their phones back into their pockets. "Thanks for the picture, Trey."

"You're welcome. Have a good night." I toss my duffel bag

over my shoulder, then open the concession stand door. Kevin is sitting on a chair, typing on his phone. Liz is tying up her shirt in the front.

"You ready?" I ask.

"Just a sec." Liz spends a minute switching her sneakers out for some heels, then gathers all her things into her bag. " 'Kay. Ready."

Together, we head toward the half-empty parking lot. Most of the crew is gone already. Some guys are still around, cleaning and packing up the equipment. Those two women I took pictures with are climbing into their car. I just told them that Liz and I aren't dating, yet here we are, walking to her car together, about to go home together. Sometimes, I can see why people write shit about us.

Liz and I pass a few more vehicles before we come across the trunk of one with the hood up. It's a red Toyota Corolla I've seen many times before.

"It's just a blown fuse," Javina says from behind the hood. "This happens all the time."

"All the time?" Arella says in her *are you serious?* voice.

"Once I change the fuse, this baby will be just fine again."

"Does that mean we need to go get you a new fuse?"

"Nah." Javina's footsteps round the front of her car to the passenger side. "This happens so often, I've got a stash in the glove—oh, hey, guys."

"Everything okay?" Liz asks as her heels stop clicking against the pavement.

I stop behind her with my chest pounding and my mouth dry.

"We're fine," Javina says. "My car does this thing where sometimes, this one fuse will blow and it keeps the prindle in park. Until I change the fuse, there ain't no movin' it."

Arella peeks her head out from behind the hood, and we lock eyes again. I lose my breath. She's much more beautiful in real life than she is in my hallucinations. Gone is that bright light that's always shining behind her, those stupid cockroaches, the occasional rainbow stars, and those people in suits.

Arella's long chestnut waves cascade down her ribs the way they always have. She still has those same angelical features and the same eyes that mesmerize me in every way. The only thing that's different about her is that she looks slightly older.

I resist the urge to grab her, to bring her into my chest and squeeze her and tell her that I'm still deeply in love with her and—

"Dammit!" Javina says as she finishes digging through her glove box, pulling out an empty plastic container. "I'm all out of fuses. Ari, could you call us an Uber?"

Arella snaps out of our little staring contest. "Sure. Where to?"

"Wherever the closest auto parts shop is."

Liz perks up. "I could drive you."

Javina's grin looks like the one she gave me when I treated her to a spa day years ago. "You would do that?"

"Of course. It'll be faster than waiting around for an Uber."

"That'd be great! Thank you." Javina turns to her best friend. "You wanna chill here while I go real quick?"

"Um . . ." Arella locks eyes with me again as I silently plead for her to say *yes*.

Liz butts in before Arella can come to a decision. "Trey will stay back with you and keep you company, won't you, T?"

Silently, I nod, trying not to look as eager as I feel. Then I realize it's rude to assume Arella even *wants* me to keep her company, so I clear my throat and add, "If that's what *you* want."

Arella smiles as her cheeks pinken. "Sure."

It's not an enthusiastic *yes*, but I'll take it.

19

———

ARI

I plant myself on a bench while Trey drops his duffel bag onto the ground. Then he joins me on my right, sitting as far away as possible. I'm not sure if it's because he wants to have distance between us or if he thinks it's what I want.

To say my heart is working in overdrive is to say the least. It's pounding so hard, I can practically hear it. Neither of us says anything as we stare at the parking lot, where Liz and Javina just drove out. I have so many things I want to ask him; however, I'm not sure if I *should* ask them.

Trey sucks in a deep breath through his nose, then slowly lets it out through his mouth.

Then he does it again.

And again.

I should probably say something before he passes out. "That was an impressive home run you hit."

He flashes me a warm smile that contradicts the gloom in his eyes. "Thanks."

"I didn't know you knew how to play softball."

His attention drops to his hands in his lap. "That's because you don't really know much about me at all."

He's right, and he's wrong. I know *some* things about him. Probably not as much as Alterella knows.

"I played baseball with my—" He blows out a ragged breath. "I played baseball when I was a kid. Softball is similar enough. Don't be too impressed though. That's the first time I've ever hit a ball that far. It'll probably never happen again, so I hope the camera guys got a good shot of it."

"Grant!" a man in Trey's crew calls as he heads toward a black SUV. "That was one hell of a homer!"

Trey plasters a fake smile onto his face. I know it's fake because it looks different from the genuine ones I've been seeing in my dreams. "Thanks, man."

The SUV's headlights brighten as the crew member unlocks his car, then gets in and takes off.

I run my fingers through my hair before pulling all my loose waves to one shoulder. "I'm glad I came. I had a lot of fun."

"Can I assume that Javina dragged you here without telling you why?"

"That's exactly what happened." I chuckle and flash him a small smile, hoping he'll return it.

He doesn't.

A silent moment sits between us before I ask, "When did you move back to LA?"

"I didn't. I fly in every Thursday to do band stuff and leave on Sundays."

If he has to fly, that means he's living somewhere pretty far. "Where do you live now?"

"New York City."

That's the biggest city in the states that's as far away from me as possible. Is that why he chose it? "Living in New York sounds expensive."

"It is. Especially since I live in a penthouse I never wanted."

"That sounds fancy. I bet all the dates you bring home are impressed by that."

He shrugs a shoulder as he stares at his dirty shoes. "I wouldn't know. I've never brought home a date."

"Oh. Are you one of those guys who keeps all his dates outside the home?"

"No, I'm just a guy who doesn't go on dates."

I tilt my head to the side with an *oh, come on* smile. "With a face like yours in a big city like New York, do you really expect me to believe you have a hard time finding a date?"

He shrugs one shoulder again. "I wouldn't know. I haven't tried. The only girl who's ever been inside my apartment is Liz. And the first time she ever saw it, she was *not* impressed."

"Why? Do you have a bad view?"

"The view is fine. It was the lack of any furniture whatsoever."

"Why didn't you have any furniture?"

He plays with his hands in his lap. "I had just moved in the day before—but don't tell her that. She thinks I'd already been living there for two weeks."

I'm about to ask why he would lie about something like that, but the question I actually want to ask comes out instead. "So you and Liz finally got together, huh?"

That makes him tear his eyes from his hands and look at me with furrowed brows. "What?"

"You and Liz. I'm happy for you," I say as convincingly as I can. "Friends-to-lovers is one of the best romantic relationships you can have because you guys already know each other so well."

I picture them together and try not to feel jealous. I have no reason to feel jealous, but I do.

"Wait," Trey says. "I'm confused. What makes you think I'm with Liz?"

Now it's my turn to stare at my hands. "I, um, I was waiting for Javina outside the bathrooms when I overheard you telling those two women that you're seeing someone. I heard them say they saw you and Liz kissing."

"Did you also overhear me tell 'em I'm not seeing Liz like that?"

"Yeah, but I thought you lied because you want to keep your relationship with her private."

"I lied to those girls about seeing someone because I recently figured out if I tell people I'm taken, they'll leave me alone faster than if I tell them *no*. Liz is just my best friend. Nothing more."

I side-eye him. "Best friends who kiss?"

"Not on the lips. Now *that* would be weird." He makes a genuine *ick* face that makes me *almost* believe him.

"Javina said she saw something online about how you two live together now. Is that true?"

"Kind of. I stay at Liz's place whenever I'm in LA."

If he's in LA every Thursday and doesn't leave until Sundays, that means he lives with Liz for half the week. That's living together, if you ask me. "What happened to your house?"

"I sold it to Marcus and Emmy, our drummer and pianist. They were looking for a place together, and I was looking to get rid of mine, so I sold it to them for almost nothing, furniture and everything else included. The only things I took back were my clothes and some other personal belongings, which are now in a storage tub at Liz's house."

If his house is the one I keep seeing in my dreams, then . . . "Wow. That sounds like an amazing deal."

"It was a win for both sides. They needed a house, and I couldn't step foot into mine anymore without—" His face falls as he circles his thumbs around each other. "Anyway, I was happy to give it to them straight up, but they insisted on paying *something* for it. Kevin did the same with my car. I wanted to just give it to him, but he insisted on paying *something*."

That was nice of Trey to sell his house and car to his friends for a low price. "So if you aren't seeing anyone and you're not going on any dates, then what have you been up to for the past year and a half?"

He takes a moment to think before he says, "When I first moved to New York, I spent the first six months being a bum until Liz convinced me to get my shit together. She said I needed to do three things: come back to the band, get some hobbies, and see a therapist regularly. So I guess that's what I've been doing.

"My band finished our second original album, and we just got back from tour last month. Now we're working on filming new content for our YouTube channel. At the end of July, we'll go back to playing our regular weekend shows at the Soul House."

"It sounds like you're staying busy," I say. "How do you have any time for your hobbies?"

"I have more than enough time. I go to the gym Mondays through Wednesdays. I read while I'm on the plane. When I stay over at Liz's, we watch movies. We're currently going through all the Disney canon films in order. She thought it was weird that the only Disney movie I'd ever seen was *The Lion King*. *Mulan* was last week. *Tarzan* is tonight."

"So those are the hobbies you chose? Working out, reading, and Disney movies?"

"I guess so." He kicks a small rock, and it skips across the ground. "Do you have any suggestions for something else I could be doing?"

"What are your interests?" I ask, even though I feel like that's something I should already know about him.

"Making music," he says without hesitation. "That's about it."

"What part of the music-making process do you enjoy the most?"

"Probably the writing and producing part."

"Maybe you could write and produce for other artists?"

He stares off into the distance and slowly nods. "Yeah. Maybe I could."

I pull my leg up onto the bench and turn to face him more. "Do you like it in New York?"

"It's all right."

"What made you pick New York?"

He goes quiet as he ponders that. His eyes stay glued to the ground as he says, "I'm not sure if I picked New York. I think New York picked me."

"Does that mean you've found your *place in the world*?"

He doesn't waste a second to say, "No."

"But you've been living there for over a year."

"That doesn't mean I feel like I belong there."

A group of Trey's crew members leave the softball field and wave at him as they get into their cars and leave. Now the only car left in the lot is Javina's, with the hood still up.

Trey keeps his eyes on the little rocks at his feet like they're the most mesmerizing things in sight. Why is it so hard for him to look at me while I feel like I can't take my eyes off him? I notice everything he does and doesn't do. Like the way his hands fidget like he's itching to touch me. The way he steals glances at me whenever I'm not looking directly at him. It's like he doesn't want me to see all that sadness in his eyes. I've even noticed the way he's purposely speaking softly as if he's trying not to scare me away. Little does he know, I've been anticipating the day we'd meet again. There's a question I've been dying to ask him.

"I never got your postcard." That didn't come out as a question the way I intended it to. Still, I hope this will open up the conversation about the one thing that's been running laps through my mind since he disappeared from my life.

Trey doesn't respond. Instead, his face falls. Even from the side, I don't miss the way his eyes turn more gray than blue.

"Did you forget my address?"

"No," he says somberly.

"Did you not have a stamp?"

"No."

"Could you not find any postcards?"

He still doesn't look at me. "I bought a few for you. I even wrote a message."

He actually wrote a card for me? Why didn't I receive it? I made sure to check the mail every day before Caleb could. "Maybe it got lost in the mail."

Trey bites his lip as he shakes his head. "It didn't. I—I never sent it."

"Oh." I try not to look disappointed. "Did you forget?"

"No."

"Oh." I want to ask what happened, but I don't know how to do that without suggesting I've been waiting for his postcard since the moment he left my front stoop. Every day, I checked the mail, thinking, *Today will be the day*. It never was.

Finally, he glances over at me with an ocean of anguish on his face—his gorgeous, I-want-to-touch-it-so-badly face. "I'm sorry I never sent you a postcard."

"Why didn't you?"

"I . . ." His gaze falls back to his lap, where his hands are fidgeting again. "I dunno. I just couldn't do it."

"What stopped you?"

"Anything and everything. The idea that what I wrote wasn't good enough. The idea that Caleb would see it before you and he wouldn't give it to you. The idea that even if you did get it, you'd just read it once and throw it away. Should I go on?"

It sounds like he overthought this so much to the point where it debilitated him from doing it at all.

"What did the postcard say?" I ask, trying not to sound like I'm dying to know.

"Which one? The first one or the hundredth one?"

My jaw drops. "You wrote on a hundred postcards for me?"

"It's probably closer to two hundred now."

"And you couldn't send just *one*?"

"I didn't think it mattered to you. Honestly, I'm surprised you even remember asking me for a postcard. I figured as soon as I left that day, you haven't thought of me since."

I've thought about you every day. Those words get stuck in my throat because I shouldn't be saying things like that to him. Nor should I be asking, "Do you ever think of me?"

He scoff-laughs. "Does the sun rise?"

Yes. "How often would you say you think of me?"

He gazes at me with such a deep and intense look that my lungs forget how to function. I don't tear my attention away from him as he communicates his answer to me through his unblinking eyes and silent lips.

I tell him I received his wordless answer by nodding my acceptance of it. I'd like to tell him that I probably think about him just as often, but I don't know how.

"I'll try to send you a postcard when I get back to New York," he says.

"I'd really appreciate that."

Just then, a silver Malibu pulls into the lot next to Javina's car. Liz steps out first, then Javina. They have good timing, because the tension between Trey and me was getting hard to handle.

Silently, Trey and I meet our friends at Javina's open hood.

"Did you get a new fuse?" I ask Javina, feeling Trey's stare on my back.

"Lots," Javina says. "I got a snack too. Can you hold this?" She hands me a plastic shopping bag with some chips and a root beer in it, then works to get a fuse out of its package.

With the bag in my hands, I smile at Liz. "Thanks for giving Javina a ride."

Liz offers me a warm smile back. "No problem. There's

an auto shop not too far from here, so it didn't take long. Plus, Javina bought me a snack too."

After Javina pries the old fuse out with her pliers, she sticks in a new one. Then she gets behind the wheel and starts the car.

"We're all good!" she shouts out the window. "The prindle works now." She steps out just as Trey gets her hood closed for her. "Thanks, pretty boy."

"You're welcome." He smiles, and this time, it looks genuine. It's almost like he missed hearing her call him that and it was nice to hear it again.

"Thanks, Liz," Javina says. "Next time I need an Uber, I'ma hit you up."

I hold Javina's snack bag out to her. "Here."

She tries taking it from me, but it gets snagged on my ring. I unsnag the bag's loops from the diamond as Trey sucks in a little gasp. His face falls as his eyes remained glued to my left hand.

Liz plasters a big ol' smile onto her face. "That's a pretty ring, Ari."

"Thanks." Naturally, I stick out my hand for her to see it better.

Trey's gaze follows my ring as all the color drains from his face.

"Did you pick it out?" Liz asks.

"No, Caleb did."

"When's the wedding?"

"Tomorrow." In the corner of my eye, I see Trey's shoulders slump as he sucks in a frazzled breath. His attention is still stuck on my ring.

"Congrats," Liz says. "I'll bet it's easier to find a wedding venue on a Sunday versus a Saturday."

"Oh, we didn't rent a venue. We're just having a small ceremony with close friends and family in his parents' backyard. Nothing too fancy. We picked tomorrow because it's the anniversary of the date Caleb and I met."

Liz's attention darts up to Trey, who now looks like he's going to collapse from a lack of oxygen.

"I'll be in the car," he whispers to Liz. Then he half runs, half stumbles into her passenger seat and slams the door.

"Sorry," Liz says with an apologetic smile. "He's just a little dehydrated. We've been under the hot sun all day."

We all know that's not why Trey ran away. A part of me wants to apologize to him, but for what? For getting married to Caleb? For trying to hide it from him? The entire time Trey and I sat on that bench, I kept my left hand out of his sight. I don't know why I didn't want him finding out that I'm engaged. I just didn't. Maybe it was because I wanted to avoid this awkward situation.

Javina and I say our goodbyes to Liz, then get into the Corolla. I steal a glance at Trey, who's slouched in Liz's passenger seat with his eyes closed. He's sucking in deep breaths so heavily that his chest looks pumped. I stare at him until Liz starts her car and drives away.

Javina unscrews the cap of her root beer and takes a sip. Then she places the bottle into the cup holder and opens her chips. As she crunches on one, she hands me the box of unused fuses and her pliers. "Could you put this in there for me?"

I take the stuff from her, then press the button to open her glove box and gasp. "What's all this?" At the bottom of the compartment are a bunch of fuses that look exactly like the ones in my hand.

"Oh, shit. Forgot about those."

"You had extra fuses this whole time?"

She shrugs. "Okay, sue me. I saw an opportunity, and I took it. While we were in the picture line, you said you wanted to talk to him, then you chickened out at the last second."

"Because I didn't want to talk to him in front of a bunch of people."

She flashes me a *duh* face. "Which is why I saw the opportunity and took it."

I gape at my mastermind of a friend. "Did your car even break?"

"Yes. It wasn't until they showed up and I dug through my glove compartment when the idea came to me. Without hesitation, I dumped out the fuses and presented an empty box. You can be mad at me all you want, but my plan worked. You got to talk to him without people there, didn't you?"

"Yes, but—"

"How'd it go?" She bites down on a chip.

"Fine, I suppose."

"Did you ask him why he never sent you a postcard?"

I nod as I replay Trey's long answer in my head. All his overthinking, his somber tone, that depressing darkness in his eyes.

"And?" Javina impatiently circles her wrist in the air.

"He said he never sent one because he didn't want Caleb to see it first and not give it to me." Technically, Trey said much more than that, but that's as much as I'm going to share.

Trey also said he'll send me a postcard when he gets back to New York. I plan to check my mail every day for it.

20

ARI

One year later

THE SUMMER SUN SETS BEHIND ME IN HUES OF PINK AND orange as I drive down the gravel road toward my thinking spot.

The last time I made this trip, it was because Caleb and I got into the biggest argument we've ever had. I sat under my oak tree at the top of a grassy hill until the moon came out and I felt better enough to return home.

The time before that was the month after our wedding. I had to sort through my thoughts to figure out why I couldn't stop looking for a postcard that wasn't coming and never came.

I also wanted to figure out why, as I read my vows to Caleb, I kept imagining Trey crashing our wedding. He didn't, and the wedding went as planned. Tomorrow is my and Calebs's first anniversary. Tonight, I'm heading back to my precious thinking spot because I have more thoughts I need to sift through.

When I pull my car up to the side of the road where I

usually park, there's a motorcycle already there. My heart skips a beat the way it always does whenever I see a motorcycle—especially if the person riding it is wearing a black leather jacket. It's never *him*, but my chest always thumps as if it is.

I step out of my car to examine the bike. Nothing on it screams, *I belong to Trey Grant!* but something inside me knows this is his.

More eager than I was before, I snatch my blanket from my car. Then I dash through the woods and hike up the narrow trail faster than I normally do.

When I reach the top of the hill, someone is lying under the oak tree. From the silhouette of the person, I think it's a man—a very *still* man. He's lying with his arms straight at his sides. I can't tell for sure if it's Trey, but I'm pretty certain it is. My thrashing heart says so.

As I approach him, he still doesn't move. When I get within five steps of him, I see why. He has a pair of wireless headphones in his ears. His eyes are closed, and his steady breaths tell me he's either sleeping or very relaxed.

"Trey?"

He doesn't move.

I take two steps toward him and speak louder. "Trey?"

Still no movement.

I poke his arm. "Trey?"

He jolts upright. "Ahh!"

I step back and throw my hands up in surrender. "Sorry!"

He stares up at me with his mouth agape. Then his eyebrows press together as he slowly draws out his earbuds. "Arella?"

I haven't heard someone call me that in years. The last person who did was him. "It's Ari."

He shakes his head at himself. "Right. Sorry. I didn't mean to—" He lets out a sigh. "I just—" Another sigh. "Sorry. I wasn't thinking. That just came out."

I know what he's trying to say. He only called me *Arella* out of habit. It's how he knows me, and how he thinks of me, but he can't say that because it'll make him sound crazy.

I've had over two and a half years of thinking to come to the conclusion that this man isn't crazy. If he was, he wouldn't be living in New York just to stay away from me. He respects that I don't know him, and he purposely keeps his distance. Crazy people don't do that.

"I'm sorry I scared you. I called your name, but you didn't respond."

"Sorry. I was listening to something and zoning out." He stands as he shoves his earbuds into the inner pocket of his leather jacket. "What are you doing here?"

I fidget with the blanket hanging over my arm. "What are *you* doing here?"

"I come here every Sunday."

My brows arch. "*Every* Sunday?"

"Mm-hmm."

"What for?"

He glances around at the quiet woods, then up toward the oak tree's leaves looming over us like an umbrella. "To think."

"How long have you been doing that?"

He waggles his head from side to side. "About a year."

"A whole year? How do you know about this place?"

"I . . ." His voice trails off as he gazes straight into my eyes. Then his attention travels to my neck, down my arms, past my shorts. Then he scans my legs.

What's he looking for?

His eyes meet back up with mine. "Did he hurt you?"

"Did *who* hurt me?"

"Your hus—" He clears his throat with a fist to his mouth. "Your . . . Caleb. Did Caleb hurt you?"

"No? Why would you think—" I gasp. *He knows about Nathan.* He knows my ex is the reason I found this place. He knows that sometimes after Nathan hit me, I'd drive here to get away from him. How does Trey know that? I've never told anyone about this place. Not even Caleb.

Trey grabs his backpack that was leaning against the tree trunk and swings it over his shoulder. "I'm sorry. It was wrong of me to make assumptions. I'll leave so you can have your thinking spot to yourself."

He knows I call this my thinking spot—another thing I've never said aloud to anyone. If I didn't already have enough evidence that this man came from an alternate universe, I do now. Since he knows things I've never told anyone, the only explanation is that Alterella told him before he fell down a portal and ended up here.

Now that I think about it, it makes sense that he knows about this place. I've seen us here before in my dreams. Correction: I've seen him and *Alterella* here before in my dreams.

Trey is already five steps away when I realize what's happening.

"Wait!" I run to step in front of him. "You don't have to leave. *You* were here first."

He stops and gives me a little shrug. "It's all right. I've already been here for a few hours. I'm happy to—"

"But I want you to stay."

He knits his eyebrows together. "You do?"

"Yeah. I'd appreciate your company."

"You would?"

I let out a chuckle. "Why are you acting so surprised?"

"This isn't acting. This is genuine shock. Some of the last times we saw each other consisted of a newly installed chain lock, your dude kicking me out, and your best friend meeting my band solo because you didn't want to."

I don't regret leaving the photo line that day, because what I got instead was a thousand times better. "For the record, I did want to."

"You did?"

"Yeah. I wanted to talk to you, but I chickened out at the last second."

"You *wanted* to talk to me?"

"Yeah."

He gapes at me like he can't understand that concept. "Why?"

"I wanted to ask you about the postcard. I still haven't gotten one, by the way." And I'm totally *not* bitter about it.

His eyes cast down to the grass. "I'm sorry."

"Did you forget to send it?" I ask, but I already know the answer.

"No."

"Did you overthink it again?" I flash him a teasing smile, hoping it'll help get rid of that melancholy look in his eyes.

It doesn't. "Abso-fucking-lutely."

"Did you even write me a card?"

"Yep."

I want to ask how many he wrote. Instead, I ask, "What did you write?"

"I shouldn't say."

"Why not?" I try not to sound like this is all I've been thinking about for the past year.

"Same reason I never sent it."

"Which is?"

"You're really gonna make me state the obvious?"

"It must not be that obvious if I'm oblivious to it."

"Arel—sorry." He shakes his head at himself again. "I . . . I didn't send the postcard because by the time I got back to New York, you were already married and, I dunno. It just felt weird to send a postcard with deep thoughts on it to a married woman."

"Deep thoughts?" My smile spreads from one ear to the other. "Now I *have to* know what you wrote on that postcard."

He shakes his head at me, but there's a hint of a smile on his lips—a genuine one. I want to keep seeing it. I want to spend the rest of this night making him smile until his cheeks ache.

I gesture toward the tree. "How about we sit and talk for a bit? I bet by the end of this evening, I'll get that secretive information out of you."

With a light chuckle, Trey heads back under the tree and drops his backpack at the base of it. "We'll see about that."

21

***

TREY

SHE'S A TREASURE TO LOOK AT. A GODDAMN TREAT FOR MY eyes. A sight I wasn't sure was real at first. I've visited this tree every Sunday for the last year, and not once has anyone ever come up here.

When I first saw her, I thought I was hallucinating again, even though I've been staying sober. By that, I mean everything: No drugs. No alcohol. Not even a drop. I don't trust myself. If I have even one drink, it'll easily turn into two, then ten, then I'll be too gone to make good decisions again. After that, it won't be long before I'm back to seeing bright lights and swatting away cockroaches that aren't there.

Is it miserable to live with this raw pain throbbing in my chest all the time? *Yep.*

Am I doing it anyway? *Yep.*

Am I happy about it? *Fuck no.*

Whenever I get the urge to drink myself into oblivion, I just remind myself of what Liz said: *"Is this the man she'd want you to be?"* Most days, that's enough for me. Other days, I need distractions. Having to fly to and from LA is the best at keeping my mind off self-medicating.

"You cut your hair," I say as Arella unfolds her blanket

161

and drapes it over the grass. Then she sits and gestures for me to join her. I don't hesitate to obey as a tiny-little-itty-bitty light flickers on inside my chest.

"Do you like it?" she asks.

"Yeah. Shoulder-length hair is cute on you."

"Do you like it better than my really long hair?"

"I wouldn't say I like it more or less. I'm sure you'd look cute with any hairstyle." Hell, she could be bald right now and I'd still be in love with her.

"What were you listening to before I scared you?"

"A meditation app."

"You were meditating?"

"Yeah. It's something my z—" I clear my throat to hide my almost slip of the tongue. "Around this time last year, I went into my weekly session with my therapist and asked her to teach me more methods to control my thoughts. She recommended meditating."

"I never pictured you as someone who likes to meditate."

That's because I'm not the type, but after I saw that shiny diamond ring on her finger, I was willing to try *anything* to keep myself from relapsing.

I still remember bursting into my zerapist's office that Monday afternoon. I flopped onto her couch and choked out, "She got married yesterday."

"To that Caleb fella?"

"Yep. Not only that, but they picked the date they supposedly met. The date that *I* met her."

That date is coming up again tomorrow. I bet Caleb has special plans to take her somewhere nice for their anniversary. I bet he's already picked out a thoughtful gift for her, like a new apron with her dream bakery's name on it, or maybe some custom-designed baking tools. After he gives it to her, she'll thank him by getting into the sheets. The sheets of *their* bed, inside *their* apartment, in their own little world of perfection where *he* has her and I don't.

But I have her now. She's sitting in front of me, and she's *willingly* talking to me. Not only that, but she asked me to stay. This time, it's not because she reverted back to remembering me, either. She asked me to stay as *Ari*. I don't know why. I'm not gonna question it though. I don't question miracles.

"Do you feel like meditating helps?" Arella asks. Or should I say *Ari*? I'm not sure how I should refer to this woman in my head. All I know is that I'm not calling her Ari out loud. Doing so feels like admitting she was never Arella at all.

"Meditating calms my thoughts. It's why I started coming to this tree. My therapist said I needed to find a place that was secluded to meditate at. This is the only secluded place I know of within driving distance of the two places I live."

"Are you still in New York?"

I nod.

"Do you still stay with Liz while you're in LA?"

"For now, yes, but Liz's boyfriend recently moved in. Even though they turned her office into a guest room for me, I've been looking into getting an apartment for myself."

Arella arches her brows. "Liz has a boyfriend?"

"Yep. Colton."

"Do you like him?"

"Yeah. He's a good man, and he adores Liz even more than I do."

Colton is as obsessed with Liz as I am with Arella. It's been pretty validating to know that it's normal to feel that way about your soul mate. At first, I thought that was just me. Turns out, all soul mates are like this with each other.

According to the z-net, when soul mates are separated, it's one of the worst emotional pains imaginable. Also according to the z-net, the emotional pain never goes away. When I read that, I scoffed out loud and said, "That's promising."

Liz's response was to look up at her soul mate with gratefulness that he was standing right next to her and he knew who she was. Colton gave her the same look back. I hope they never get separated, and I hope they never get their minds erased either. I don't wish this torture upon anyone, especially not Liz and Colton. They're the closest people I have to family.

Even though Arella doesn't remember who I am, I'm still grateful to be under this tree with her. I don't need her to remember me to enjoy her company or to appreciate hearing her voice.

"Have you found any potential apartments yet?" she asks.

"Some." If I really wanted my own place, I would have gotten one by now. The only reason I'm hesitating is because I don't trust myself to live alone in LA yet. Living with Liz and Colton keeps me grounded. I'll know I'm ready for my own place once I can go a day without considering drowning myself in alcohol.

"Enough about me," I say, holding back a huff. "Tell me what's been going on in your life."

She perks up with a smile that sends warmth through me. "What would you like to know?"

Everything. Where do you work now? How's your baking blog going? Do you still want to start a bakery? Are you still obsessed with bacon? Do you still always order your salads with the dressing on the side? Have you had another relapse moment of remembering me?

I don't ask any of that. I can't. What I ask instead is "What did you come here to think about?"

She gives me a narrowed stare. "I'll tell you that private information if you tell me the deep thoughts you wrote on that postcard for me."

The chuckle that leaves my mouth takes little effort to get out. "You haven't forgotten about that, huh?"

"I told you I was going to get it out of you by the end of this evening."

"You can try and beg all you want, Miss Rance, but that information is staying sealed behind these lips."

The smile on her face falls. At first, I think it's because I said something to offend her, then it hits me: Her last name probably isn't Rance anymore. The look in her eyes tells me she's thinking the same thing, but she doesn't correct me.

Like the kind person she is, she changes the subject. "If you're not going to tell me what you wrote, then at least tell me if you've been on any dates lately. The last time I saw you, you were lying to women about being unavailable so they'd stop pursuing you."

Her tactic works, because my little pang of hurt fades away. "That hasn't changed. I'm still lying to women about that. I just did it last night at my band's meet and greet, and the tipsy woman *still* wrote her number on my arm—in Sharpie. I had to scrub for almost ten minutes before it finally came off so my fake girlfriend at home wouldn't see it."

Dramatically, Arella rolls her eyes. "Wow. Must be hard to have to chase women away all the time."

I lift a finger into the air. "You know what's actually hard? Keeping up with this lie that I have a girlfriend. Last month, I did an interview for a podcast highlighting up-and-coming bands. The interviewer wanted to know more about how I met my invisible girlfriend than anything regarding my band's music."

"Naturally. That's the juicy stuff that sells."

"Yep," I say with a sigh. "Apparently, nobody wants to know about the inspiration behind our original songs or what we're releasing next. They just want to know how my girlfriend feels about my relationship with Liz and if she'll ever get over her *camera shyness*."

Arella lets out the most adorable laugh. It floods me with memories of when I used to make her laugh like that on my couch until two in the morning. "You tell people your fake girlfriend is camera shy?"

"How else am I supposed to explain our lack of pictures together?"

Arella continues laughing, and I want to keep making her do it.

"If you have enough money to buy weekly plane tickets," she says, "then you have enough to hire someone to pretend to be your girlfriend. Actually, I'm sure there's a long line of women out there who'd do it for free."

I cringe at the idea of having to talk to a real person and actually bring her places. "That sounds like more work than actually having a girlfriend. I'm not *that* committed to this lie."

"You're pretty committed to your band though. Flying back and forth every week can't be cheap."

"It's not."

"Once you get your own place in LA, do you think you'd move back here permanently?"

"No," I say without hesitation.

"Why not? What's keeping you in New York?"

It's not what's keeping me *in* New York; it's what's keeping me *out* of Los Angeles. Without me saying it, I think Arella knows that. I'm sure by now, she's guessed that the real reason I left LA wasn't to go find my place in the world. I already know where my place is; it's wherever she is. Since I can't have that, I guess I'm looking for a place where I can feel half as happy. I haven't found it yet, but I'm trying to have faith it exists.

Liz has complete faith it exists. Colton does not. Unlike Liz, Colton and I believe that trying to find a "compatible partner" after being with your soul mate is a shit idea. I'd consider finding a compatible partner if I had never found Arella at all. It's easier to settle for less when you've never had the best.

Now that I know what true happiness feels like, having anything less is like trying to use spotty dial-up that drops every two seconds after using high-speed Wi-Fi my whole life. It's just unacceptable. Can it work? Sure, but it'll take a lot of effort, waiting, and frustration to get what I want. The whole time, I'll be wishing I had high-speed Internet instead.

"Somehow," I say, "we came right back to talking about me."

"That's because you're more interesting to talk about than I am. Not everyone comes from an alternate universe."

I cock my head at her. "Huh?"

"You know, a world like this one, but not. It's Javina's explanation for how you know so much about me. At first, I thought she sounded nuts, but the idea has grown on me."

I blink at her as I attempt to grasp the concept of alternate universes. "What's Javina's explanation for how I got here?"

"You fell through a portal."

I chuckle at how nonchalantly she said that. "And what's her explanation for why there aren't two Trey Grants walking around?"

"The Trey Grant from this universe is still in prison. Basically, you just took his place."

"I see." From Arella's point of view, I guess this theory makes sense. "Do you think Javina can show me where that portal is? I'm ready to return to my own world now."

"I'm sure Alterella misses you."

"Alterella?"

She gives me a moment to put it together.

Once it clicks, I laugh. "That's clever. Who came up with that?"

"Javina, of course. I'm not that witty."

Alterella. I repeat the name in my head a few times. It rolls off the tongue nicely. "So what you're saying is that there's an alternate version of you out there somewhere?"

"Yeah, and that's the version of me who's your girlfriend. She looks, talks, and acts exactly like me, which explains why you mistook me for her. She's probably at home right now, wondering where you've been this whole time."

The idea that a version of Arella could be out there

somewhere, waiting for me, doesn't sit right. I don't like the thought of making her wonder if I'll ever come back for her or wonder if the reason why I didn't is because I stopped loving her. I couldn't stop, even if I tried.

"Well," I huff, "it's been over two and a half years. I hope she's quit waiting by now."

"Don't you *want* her to wait for you?"

"Fuck no. I want her to be happy, and waiting around for someone who's not coming is not happiness. Sounds like hell to me." *I would know. I'm doing it.*

Arella squints at me like she can't understand why I'd feel that way. "You'd rather she moved on with someone else than wait around for you?"

"If that's what makes her happy, yes."

"But what about you? What about *your* happiness?"

I shrug and pretend like the dark cavity in my chest isn't throbbing at all. "My happiness doesn't matter."

"Of course it does. Everyone deserves to be happy."

It's been so long since I've felt happy, I don't even remember what it feels like. "I'd rather she be happy than me."

"Why can't you *both* be happy?"

"Because that's not how the world works. Somebody once told me that when you love someone, you put their happiness before your own. I'm more than willing to do that for her." *For you.*

"Did you hear that line from my grammy? She says that to me all the time."

"Nah, I heard it from Alterella."

She erupts with laughter. "Oh my god. I can't believe you actually used that name."

For the next two hours, we sit on her blanket and talk while the sun sets. She makes me smile so many times, I lose count. The achy heaviness in my chest feels lighter, and I don't think about getting drunk once.

Eventually, Arella glances at the time on her phone and tells me it's time for her to go. I fake a smile to hide the way my stomach sinks and my throat goes dry.

"Could I walk you to your car?" I ask, trying not to sound as hopeful as I feel. I want as much time with her as I can get.

"Sure." If she's excited about the idea, she doesn't show it. She doesn't sound repulsed either. That's good, I guess.

I help her fold up her blanket, then together, we head through the dark woods.

When we reach her car parked behind my motorcycle, she leans her back against the driver's door and looks up at me. "You wanna know something weird I've been thinking about lately?"

I want to know everything you think about. "Sure."

"Apparently, when I bought this car, I paid for it in full—in cash."

"What's weird about that?"

"I don't remember doing that. And with my income, I could never afford a vehicle this nice, nor would I ever have enough in the bank to pay for it in full."

A lump forms in my throat because it's not like I can tell her that the car came from me. She wants to believe that I came from another universe. If that belief is what made her feel comfortable enough to stick around and have a two-and-a-half-hour conversation with me, then I'm gonna roll with it. "Maybe Caleb helped pay for your car," I say, because I'd rather give him the credit than burst this bubble of make-believe we have.

"I've asked him about it. He doesn't remember doing so, nor does he have the income to."

"Maybe your grandparents lent you some money for the car." I'm grasping at straws now.

"They can't afford anything this nice either." She looks me square in the eyes. "You know who can, though? A person who has enough money to buy things like penthouses and weekly plane rides across the country."

She gives me a moment to respond, but I don't. If I admit that I bought her this car, it'll ruin the vibe we've created. Plus, she didn't like that I bought her this car when she loved me. How will she feel about it now, when she doesn't love me at all?

"I had a great time with you," I say as an attempt to change the subject.

At first, she stares at me, probably debating whether or not to force an answer out of me. Then she relents and offers up a tender smile. "This was fun. I'm glad we ran into each other."

I take a step back toward the woods. "Drive home safe."

She unlocks her car and grips the door handle. "You too. I mean, you're flying, but you know. Just get home safe."

"Thanks." This should be when I turn and walk away, but I don't. I can't. Not while she's still here and I can still look at her.

I take another step back as she opens the door and tosses her blanket onto the passenger seat. Then she glances back up at me. "Trey?"

I lock eyes with her as my ears throw a confetti party from hearing her say my name. "Yeah?"

"Thank you for the car."

My stare tells her a silent *you're welcome*, then I take another step back and wave.

Without another word, she plops behind the wheel and starts the engine. I stare at her red taillights going down the road until she turns the corner and disappears from my sight.

Back at the tree, I flop onto the grass and gaze up at the stars. I missed my flight, but I don't care. I'm so high off joy right now, I feel like I'm floating on a cloud. Missing my flight was worth it.

22

———

ARI

"Wʜᴀᴛ ᴅᴏ ʏᴏᴜ ᴛʜɪɴᴋ I sʜᴏᴜʟᴅ ᴡᴇᴀʀ ғᴏʀ ᴅɪɴɴᴇʀ tonight?" I ask Caleb when I step out of the bedroom.

He's lying on the couch and doesn't look up at me from his phone. "Where are you and Javina going?"

"What do you mean?"

He still doesn't look at me. "How am I supposed to give you a suggestion if I don't know what type of place you guys are going to? Like, is it fancy?"

Oh. My. God. He forgot. "Caleb."

Finally, he pries his attention away from the screen. "What?"

"I'm not going out with Javina tonight. I'm going out with *you.*"

"What? But—Oh, shit!" He jerks up and swings his legs over the front of the couch. "It's our anniversary today, isn't it?"

"Yeah, and three weeks ago, you said you'd take the night off so we could go out for a nice dinner."

"Oh, muffin. I'm so sorry. I completely forgot to take it off. I have to work tonight."

I pout a little. I was looking forward to this because Caleb and I haven't had quality time together in a while. I work days at a bakery, and he works night shifts at a museum. Normally, I get off just in time to come home to make him dinner before he runs off to work. By the time he's off, I'm in the middle of my REM cycle, dreaming about a person I shouldn't be dreaming about.

Last night, my dream was the one where Javina and I were in Trey's house, chatting on his couch, when we saw him pulling into the driveway in a brand-new white crossover—the vehicle that I now own.

Javina whistled through her teeth as we stepped outside. "Damn, pretty boy. Lexus ain't doin' it for ya no more?"

Trey flaunted a megawatt smile from the driver's seat with the door open. "I'm good with my car. This one's for Arella."

I gasped. "Honey, you didn't . . ."

He beamed proudly. "I did."

"Why would you do this? After all the reasons I told you not to?"

Javina gaped at me like I was crazy. "Ari! Ungrateful much?"

Trey hopped out of the car with his arms up in surrender. "I bought the car under your name. It's all yours. Fully paid for. No strings attached."

I pretzeled my arms together. "I'm not accepting it."

"How 'bout you get in and drive it around before you make that decision?"

I was about to protest again when Javina threw her arm up. "Shotgun!"

That's the fifth time I've had that dream. The times before were the reason I thought to ask Caleb if he remembers how I paid for an expensive new car without any financing.

I mentioned it to Trey last night, and his silence confirmed he's the answer to that mystery. It's things like this that make me question my reality. Why doesn't my life add up right? And when it does, why does it always point to Trey?

"This explains why you weren't in the kitchen, making dinner." Caleb stands from the couch and shoves his phone into his back pocket. "I was beginning to wonder if you'd have food ready in time."

"I'll go see what I can whip up for you quickly."

"Don't worry 'bout it. I'll just grab something on my way to work, but that means I've gotta leave now." He leans in to peck my cheek. "I'm sorry I forgot. How about I take you out on Thursday instead? I have that night off."

"That's movie night with Javina." I think about offering to ask Javina if we can skip our movie date, but I'm not going to ditch my best friend just because my husband forgot about our first wedding anniversary. "Plus, don't you have something with Rakesh that night?"

"Oh, that's right. We're doing this tournament thing at the gym. We can win a prize if we beat the other pairs that night."

"Yeah, you told me that three weeks ago when we made these plans to go out tonight." *Which is why he was supposed to take it off.*

"I'm sorry, muffin. I'll buy you a nice gift, okay?" He kisses my cheek again, then heads into the bedroom to put on his uniform.

I'm left alone in the living room, holding back tears. *I don't want a nice gift. I want to spend time with my husband.*

LATER THAT WEEK, AS I DRIVE BACK TO MY THINKING SPOT, toxic thoughts consume my head. The one that keeps repeating is *Trey wouldn't have forgotten about our anniversary.* I scold myself for thinking that, because it's not right to compare my husband to another man. Caleb has been stressed out with work lately. I'm sure that's why he forgot.

My heart thumps wildly as I pull off the gravel road behind a motorcycle. Trey wasn't kidding when he said he comes here every Sunday.

I step out of my car with my purse in one hand and my blanket in the other. The sun is beginning to set behind the woods, looking like a Bob Ross painting. When I make it to the top of the hill, Trey is in the same position he was last time: lying on his back under the oak tree, unmoving.

"Trey?" I say as I approach him.

He doesn't respond.

"Trey?" I say louder.

He keeps his eyes closed and his earbuds in.

I don't want to scare him again, but . . .

"Ahh!" he shouts when I poke him. He jolts upright and tears the wireless devices out of his ears. When his eyes land on me, his face lights up. "You're back."

"I am." My heart flutters from how happy he looks. I didn't expect to see him smile that big.

"Did you have some more thinking to do since you didn't get to do it last time?"

"Yeah."

"Would you like me to leave?"

I unfold my blanket and lay it down. Then I gesture for him to join me. He gladly takes that as my answer.

"Were you meditating?" I ask as we settle onto the blanket together.

He crosses his legs into a pretzel. "Mm-hmm."

"Could I do it with you?"

"You want to meditate?"

"You said it helps clear your head, right? I could use some of that."

"Uh, sure." He hands me one of his earbuds, then sticks the other one back into his ear.

I put the device in but hear nothing. "How do I do it?"

"I'll choose a short guided meditation for us. Then you just listen to what the lady on the app tells you to do."

"Do I lie down first?"

"You can stay sitting or lie down. Whichever you prefer."

"It seems like you prefer to lie, so I'll try that." I settle on my back and gaze up at all the leaves and branches above me.

Trey lies next to me, making my heart beat faster. He taps on his phone a few times, then a soft melody plays into my ear. A calming female voice tells me to release every thought from my mind and focus on one body part at a time, starting with my forehead.

By the end of the ten-minute session, my entire body feels relaxed and a little tingly. We sit up and face each other.

"What do you think?" Trey asks as he returns his earbuds to their case.

I try not to admire the way the sunlight hits the curves of his cheeks just right. "That was wonderful. I feel less stressed now."

He shoves his earbuds case into the side pocket of his backpack behind him. "What are you stressing out about?"

"Same thing I came to think about last week."

"The thing you refuse to share with me?"

The person here who refuses to share things the most is him. "I made a deal with you, remember? I'll share that information if you share the deep thoughts you wrote on that postcard."

"Oh, I have a gift for you." He grabs his backpack and unzips the big pocket.

He brought the gift with him? "How did you know I was coming?" *I* didn't even know I was coming until the moment after Caleb left for work and I climbed into my car.

"I didn't," Trey says. "I just hoped."

We lock eyes as a warmth rushes down my spine. How long has he been sitting here, waiting for me to show up without knowing if I would or not?

After we break our intense stare, he pulls out a flat paper item from his backpack and offers it to me. I gasp at the colorful artwork of the New York City skyline. In the background is a silhouette of the Statue of Liberty.

"I wrote this card for you the night after my band's video shoot at the softball field."

I flip the postcard over and read it.

WHENEVER THE SUN OR MOON IS OUT.

I knit my eyebrows together. "Am I supposed to know what this means?"

"You asked me a question that day, which I never answered. This was my answer."

"What did I ask you?"

"You asked how often I think about you."

I read the postcard again.

WHENEVER THE SUN OR MOON IS OUT.

I can practically feel the nerves radiating off him as he waits for my reaction to this very sweet and personal message. I hug it to my chest. "Thank you, Trey. This means a lot to me."

The darkness in his eyes dissipates a little. "It does?"

"Yeah. It took a lot of courage for you to give me this." And now I can *finally* stop obsessively checking my mail.

"It was my therapist who convinced me to give it to you."

"You talk to her about me?"

"Technically, I talk to her about Alterella, but you come up occasionally."

Javina would love to know that Trey actually uses the name she gave my alternate-universe self. Javina doesn't know that I found Trey under my thinking tree last Sunday. Caleb doesn't know either, and I don't plan to ever tell him. This place is still my secret spot, and now Trey feels like a part of it.

"What have you told your therapist about me?"

Trey lets out a little laugh. "I can only open up so much at a time. Giving you this postcard means I've reached my limit for the week."

"Does that mean I'll have to come back next week to get you to open up again?"

He perks up. "Yes. That's exactly what it means."

"Okay, I'll put it in my calendar. Next Sunday evening is officially *hear Trey open up* time. I'll book it for seven thirty since that's the time I got here today."

That dimness in his eyes illuminates again. "Could you make it a reoccurring event?"

"Maybe," I say with a smirk. "I'll have to see if what you give me next Sunday is juicy enough to warrant a weekly visit."

"I don't open up a lot, so anything I say will be juicy."

"I'll be the judge of that."

We smile and stare at each other for a long moment before Trey forces his attention away. "So . . ." He clears his throat. "I think it's time you held up your end of the bargain and tell me what you came here two weeks in a row to think about."

Technically, I came here the first time to think. Tonight, I came to see him. "I'm not sure if you want to know. It has to do with me and Caleb."

He hides his discomfort behind another clear of his throat. "I can handle it."

"Are you sure?"

"Hey, now." He smiles playfully and narrows his eyes at me. "Are you trying to back out of our deal?"

That makes me giggle. "No, I'm just being honest with you. If you'd really like to know, I'll tell you."

"I'd really like to know."

I pause, trying to come up with a way to say it without hurting him, although it's probably going to hurt him regardless of how I put it. "Caleb and I have been trying to have a baby."

His entire face falls, and all the light that was flickering in his eyes earlier goes black. "Oh."

"We've been trying since before we got married, and still no baby. It's been frustrating and exhausting to have to track my ovulation cycle and time things right, only to get my period again two weeks later." I'm going to assume Trey knows what I mean by "time *things* right." "I've been to the doctor to get checked out for infertility, and they said nothing is wrong. As for Caleb, he refuses to get checked out."

"Why?"

"He says he knows nothing is wrong with him because we've gotten pregnant before. It was over two and a half years ago, but we lost the baby."

Something heart-wrenching breaks in Trey's eyes, then his gaze falls to the grass. "I see."

"It's been a pretty heavy and frequent topic of argument between us." That's putting it lightly. Caleb hates whenever I bring up baby stuff, so much that I've stopped mentioning it at all.

"What does he have to lose from doing a few tests?"

"That's exactly what I said. The answer is nothing. I don't know if he's scared or just being lazy."

Trey pauses to think about that. "I don't know the guy, but if I had to guess, I'd say he's scared. Maybe he doesn't wanna be told he's the problem."

"Right, but maybe if we knew what the problem was, we could move forward with a solution. My doctor has already talked to me about fertility treatments, but I don't think that's an option for us."

"Why not?"

"Because it costs thousands of dollars we don't have."

"I'll pay for it," Trey says without any hesitation.

"What?"

"I said I'll pay for it. Whatever it costs. The treatments, exam fees, medications, whatever. I'll cover the whole thing."

I gape at him. "You would do that?"

"Yep. Just tell me how much it is, and I'll send it to you."

I can't believe how easily and nonchalantly he's offering me his money. Does he not realize how much fertility treatments cost? "I didn't tell you this as an attempt to get financial help. I only told you because you wanted to know."

"And now that I know, I want to help."

"You want to help Caleb and me have a baby?"

"No," he says firmly. "I want to help *you* have a baby. Your dude just happens to be part of that picture."

"But why would *you*, of all people, want to pay for it?" I hope without me having to say it, he knows what I mean by that.

He gives me a *duh* look. "Wouldn't having a baby make you happy?"

"Of course."

"Then that's reason enough for me."

I let out a little *hmmph*. "Thank you, Trey, but I can't accept."

"Figures."

Like we did last time, we talk and laugh together while the sun goes down. Trey makes me laugh so hard, my knee's tender from how often I've slapped it.

A few stars twinkle in the black sky as Trey walks me to my car. I've got my precious postcard in my hands, and I already know where I'm going to put it: right inside that book Caleb will never open.

"Could you do something for me?" I ask.

"Anything."

My heart skips a beat from the way he says it so eagerly. "Next week, could you leave one earbud out or turn the volume of your meditation down so I don't have to scare you again?"

"Of course. I would have done that tonight, but I'd already convinced myself you weren't coming."

I stop at my car and turn to face him. "I'll be here next week. Promise."

"I'm looking forward to it."

That should be my cue to leave, but I don't. It's already past ten thirty. I stayed a little longer this time because I was making him laugh so much, I wanted to keep hearing it. Now I probably won't make it home until midnight. Then I'll have to sleep and be up by six to get ready for a day at the bakery. That's not enough sleep for me, yet here I am with a pair of feet that won't get into my car.

"What time is your flight tonight?" I ask.

"An hour ago."

"You missed your flight?"

"Yeah, but it's okay." He shoves his hands into his jean pockets. "I'll head to the airport soon and ask them to get me on the next flight. No big deal."

"I'm sorry. I should have asked when your flight was so we could get you there on time."

"It's fine, really. I'll miss a hundred flights if it means I get to see you."

The smile that curves up my lips is automatic.

23

ARI

"Hey, you." Trey smiles at me from under the oak tree. This time, he's not lying under it. He's sitting in the grass with his back leaned against the thick trunk. He had his eyes glued on me the whole time I walked over to him from the woods.

"Are you ready to open up and tell me more of your deep thoughts tonight?"

He closes the book he was reading and lets out a laugh I've been craving to hear for a week. "Is that all you came for? A glimpse into my deep thoughts?"

"Yes, and as soon as I get it, I'm leaving." I grin at him so he knows I'm joking. Then I shake out my blanket and drape it over the grass.

Trey joins me on it. "I have something for you."

"Another postcard?"

"Nope." From his backpack, he pulls out a white envelope.

I take it from him and open it, then gasp. It's a check for a hundred grand. "Nope. Nuh-uh. No way."

"Look, I already knew you were going to decline. That's why I wrote you a check. You don't have to cash it now, but I want you to have it in case the time comes and you decide you want it."

"Trey, I'll *never* want this."

"Think of it like a donation." He says that as if handing someone a check for a hundred grand is no big deal.

"I'm not a charity."

"I'm sure they have charities for infertility out there. Think of this like I'm donating to them, but this is my way of making sure all the funds go to you."

"I appreciate the thought, but no, thank you." I hold the envelope out to him.

He doesn't take it. "Could you at least keep the check in case you change your mind?"

I tear the envelope in half, then half again. "I'll never change my mind, but thank you."

Trey glares at the papers as I toss them behind me. "You've got a bad habit of doing that."

"Doing what?"

"Ripping shit in half."

"Oh, that reminds me. I have something for you too." From my purse, I slip out the taped-up photo I tore apart over two years ago. "Here."

His breathing stops as I place the photo in his palm. He stares at it with wide eyes and trembling fingers, then flips it over to read the back. As if he just remembered that he needs to breathe, he sucks in a shaky breath and lets it out. Then he flips the photo back over and stares at the front again. When he finally looks up at me, his eyes are watery.

In a soft whisper, he says, "Thank you for giving this back to me."

"You're welcome. I'm sorry for tearing it up."

"It's fixed, and I have it back now. That's all that matters." As he blinks away the water in his eyes, he pulls his wallet out of his backpack. With gentle fingers, he slides the picture into the crevices of his bifold.

Playfully, I ask, "Was this picture in your wallet when you fell through the portal? Is that why you still had it?"

"Yep," he says with a light chuckle as he returns the wallet to his backpack.

"Why did you get Alterella an angel-wings necklace?"

"Because I called her my angel." In my dreams, he mostly calls her *Arella* or *babe*. Only occasionally have I heard *angel*.

"Did you know the name Arella means *angel*?" I say, because originally, I thought that's why he bought her an angel-wings necklace.

"I didn't know that. I guess that's fitting."

"Did you know my parents named me Arella because it's a combination of their names, Aries and Bella?"

Trey stares at me, and I can practically see the gears turning in his head. Whatever thought just crossed his mind, he ignores it and says, "I've been thinking about getting my middle name changed."

"What is it now?"

"Andrew. I wanna change it to Victor—to honor my dad because he died trying to save my life."

I have so many questions about that, but I doubt he'll be open to talking about something so serious. Instead, I ask, "Is that what the letter V in your tattoo stands for?"

Trey's attention shifts to the tattoo on his left forearm. I've been stealing glances at it over the past three weeks. He doesn't have this tattoo in any of my dreams. The first time I ever saw it was when we sat on that bench outside the softball field.

His tattoo is an acoustic guitar that stretches across the entirety of his inner left forearm. The body of the guitar is shaped with a blend of fiery red flames mixed with bright blue waves of water. Going up the neck are sprigs of purple lavender that start off as guitar strings until they spread out into more lavender sprigs, surrounding the guitar's neck. At the head of the instrument is the letter V. When I first saw the V, I thought it looked like a sideways L for Liz.

Trey runs a finger up and down his tattoo. "Yeah, the V was added in honor of my dad."

"Does the rest of your tattoo have any meaning?" *More specifically, does the lavender have to do with me?* Lavender is my favorite color and scent. I use it for everything—my pillows and blankets, my shampoo, conditioner, hand soap—and it's my go-to candle scent. It's a pretty specific thing for him to have included in his tattoo.

"The guitar represents my love for music, and it was the first instrument I learned to play. The fire and water represent my friendship with Liz. She's the water; I'm the fire. She's got a matching water and fire tattoo on her forearm. Hers is just shaped into a circle instead of a guitar."

I don't miss how he avoids mentioning the lavender at all. "You guys live together, got matching tattoos, and you *still* expect your fans to think you're not dating?"

He offers me a careless shrug. "A few trolls and bad media aren't gonna stop me from doing what I wanna do. I could be dead and people would still spread rumors about Liz and I sleeping together behind Colton's back."

"Does that ever bother Colton?"

"Nah. He sees how Liz and I are in private. We're close, but even he knows the romantic feelings aren't there and never have been. He's so comfortable with it that he doesn't even care when we cuddle."

"You cuddle with Liz?"

"Sometimes. Less now that she's got Colton."

It must be nice to have such a strong platonic relationship. "Was Alterella ever bothered by your relationship with Liz?"

He pauses to think. "Eh. I wouldn't say she was bothered. When we first met, she was curious, but once she became good friends with Liz, she never questioned it."

"How close were Alterella and Liz?"

"Pretty close. They liked to talk about boy bands and

make fun of me behind my back—and sometimes to my face."

Liz seems like a really good friend and someone I'd get along with. I do love boy bands. I wonder which ones are Liz's favorites. Are they the same as mine? "In your alternate universe, did JFK get assassinated?"

Trey presses his eyebrows together. "Yeah?"

"Lincoln too?"

"Yep."

"Did your people land on the moon?"

"Yes?" He jerks his head back a little. "Why are you asking me all this?"

"I'm trying to figure out what the differences are between your world and mine."

He chuckles. "I'm amused, so please, keep going."

"Did Martin Luther King Junior say, 'I have a dream'?"

"Yep."

"Was there a Black Plague?"

"Yep."

"Did the *Titanic* sink?"

He freezes. "The Ti-what?"

"*Titanic*. You know, the ship that hit the iceberg in 1912, split in half, then went down, taking fifteen hundred people with it."

"I've never heard of such a thing."

My eyes go wide, then Trey bursts into a laugh. "I'm just fucking with you. Yes, *Titanic* sank in my universe too."

I backhand his chest. "Don't do that!"

He continues laughing as he rubs the spot I hit. I love seeing him laugh. He's doing it the same way he does in my dreams. It's light, it's beautiful, and best of all, it doesn't sound forced.

We banter for a while as the sky fades to black. Eventually, it hits me that we've been talking for so long, I forgot about getting a deep thought out of him. When I mention this out loud, he says, "All right. You can have one deep thought from me tonight. What would you like to know?"

I debate between asking him about the lavender in his tattoo and the question I asked him last week. Since I've already got a good feeling about what the lavender represents, I go with the latter. "What have you told your therapist about me?"

"Damn. I was hoping you'd forget about that."

"Not a chance."

It takes him a moment to come up with the right words. "I told her that you look like my version of Arella. She knows about what happened after I showed up at your door, thinking you were her."

I let out a *pfft*. "That's not juicy at all. I could have guessed that."

"If I give you something juicier, will you come back next week?" He gives me a hopeful stare.

I'm planning to come next week no matter what he shares with me. Still, I smirk at him. "That depends on how juicy your information is."

"Okay. Lemme think." He spends a whole minute staring at the grass in deep thought. "If I share this with you, will you promise not to judge me or get weirded out?"

I perk up. "Ooo. I like where this is going already. Yes, I promise not to judge or get weirded out."

"Okay." He sucks in a breath, then slowly blows it out. "Last week, I told my therapist that I got to see you at this tree. I told her you were planning to come back tonight and that it was the only thing getting me through the week.

"I also told her that while we were here together, I kept forgetting that the rest of the world existed. It wasn't until I walked you to your car when I finally remembered you were going home to someone else and I'd be going back to an empty apartment in New York.

"My therapist has been working with me on living in the

moment instead of dwelling on the past or dreading the future. It's been a struggle for me. All my thoughts are either about wishing I'd done things differently or how anxious I am about living the next day without . . ." He sighs as the words get caught in his throat.

"Anyway, when I'm with you, it feels easy to live in the moment and just enjoy your company. Sometimes I feel *some* anxiety because my mind drifts to when you have to leave, but when I catch myself doing that, I just do what my therapist taught me. She said to take an imaginary katana to those *out-of-the-moment* thoughts and bring myself back to living *in* the moment."

My heart leaps out of my chest over and over again. That's the most endearing thing anyone has ever said to me. I don't even remember Caleb's vows from our wedding, but I'll probably remember everything Trey just said for the rest of my life.

Without saying it, he basically just told me he wants me, and it's the most wanted I've felt in months. It doesn't feel like he wants me for anything more than my presence either. Simply being around me seems to be enough for him, which is how I feel about him too. I don't want him to give me anything, or to perform for me, or to fake a smile. I just want to sit here with him, hear his voice, see him laugh, and occasionally catch a whiff of his familiar scent.

I tuck a loose wave of hair behind my ear. "If I share something with you, will you also promise not to judge?"

"With all the shit I've done, I have no right to judge anyone, so yes. I promise."

I come out with it before I can change my mind. "I haven't had sex in three months."

"What?"

"You heard me."

He knits his eyebrows together. "But . . . I thought you're trying to have a baby."

"That doesn't mean I've had any sex."

He tilts his head to the side. "Do you not know how baby-making works?"

"Caleb and I have opposite schedules, and whenever I try, he says he's not in the mood."

"Wait, wait, wait. Are you telling me that even when you initiate it, he says *no*?"

"Basically. It's gotten to the point where I don't even try anymore because I keep getting denied."

Trey gapes at me with his mouth fully open. "Is the dude an idiot?"

I shrug with my hands out to my sides. "I think it's stress. Work has been crazy for him."

"But . . . but . . . he's got *you*." Trey doesn't expand more on that, as if saying having *me* is explanation enough.

"Maybe once work settles down, he'll get back in the mood."

Eventually, Trey forces his jaw shut and huffs out a breath. "I hate to admit this, but I've got you beat. It's been over two and a half years for me."

"What?"

"You heard me."

I don't believe him. How can a single man who looks like he belongs on a billboard advertising a diet and gym routine that actually works go that long without getting laid? I don't even think I'd believe him if he told me it's been over two and a half weeks.

"But women practically throw themselves at you."

With pursed lips, he shakes his head. "None of them are what I want."

"What are you looking for?"

"Not them." He chuckles at the way I'm still gaping at him. "I dunno why you're surprised. I've already told you I haven't been on any dates."

"You don't have to go on a date to have sex. I'm sure you've had a plethora of one-night stands."

"In the past, yes, but not anymore."

"What changed?"

He locks his eyes with mine, and it's all the answer I need: Losing Alterella changed him. Or losing *me*. I'm not sure anymore. Our worlds are blending together too much for me to keep them separated.

Trey clears his throat. "Let's just say that once you've had high-speed Wi-Fi, it's hard to go back to spotty dial-up."

That makes me laugh so much, I slap my knee. "Are you comparing women and sex to Internet speed?"

"Hell yeah. Tell me that didn't make sense though."

I laugh again. "It made a lot of sense."

"Exactly."

24

TREY

We didn't establish if she was coming back this week. As I walked her to her car last week, I thought about asking but was too afraid to. Now I'm sitting under our tree with an open book in my lap, and I haven't read a single word.

It's seven thirty-five. *She's probably not coming.*

Seven forty-five. *She's not coming.*

Seven fifty-five. *She's definitely not*—A pair of footsteps thumps against the ground in the distance. *Is it her?*

A vision of perfection appears from the woods. She's got a blanket draped over one arm and her purse in the other. All the blood rushes to my face as my lips effortlessly curve into a smile.

"Hey, you," I say when she reaches me.

"Sorry, it took me a little longer to get here. I had to stop at the store for this." She pulls out a little box from her purse. "It's called the Little Box of Questions to Ask Your Friends."

I read the colorful print on the box, and that's exactly what it says. "You consider us friends?"

She shakes out her blanket and lays it over the grass. "What else would we be?"

Good point. I guess being her friend is better than being nothing at all. I'll take it.

Once we're sitting and facing each other on her blanket, she unwraps the box of question cards from the plastic. The way the light from the setting sun hits her face makes her look like she's a hallucination. Sometimes, I'm *still* not sure if she's real. It's only once she speaks that I'm positive I'm not hallucinating. It's just hard for me to believe that she's actually here in front of me and that she has come four weeks in a row. *What did I finally do right?*

"Is this a game?" I ask.

"Yeah, but better, because it's the type of game where we both win. All we do is take turns pulling a card from the box, then we both answer the question. Would you like to go first?"

"Sure." I slip a card out from the middle of the box and read it. "What is one of your biggest regrets?" I think about my answer, then I playfully glare at her. "Is this another one of your sneaky ways to get me to open up?"

Her mouth spreads into a guilty grin. "You caught me."

"Is that really why you bought this question-box thing?"

"Let's just say that one deep thought a week is not enough for me. I want more, and I figured this was a subtle not-so-subtle way of asking for it without actually asking for it."

If she wants more, I can give her more. Hell, I'll give her all of me if that's what she wants. I just expect the same back. "You answer this question first."

"Okay. One of my biggest regrets is staying with my ex for as long as I did. I should have left as soon as I saw the red flags. Instead, I made excuses for him over and over, until I was trapped."

I could have guessed she'd say that. We've had multiple conversations about Nathan before, and they all ended with the same conclusion: No matter what, she's never going to stay in a relationship where she's abused or feels unwanted ever again. She vowed to herself that as soon as she saw the signs, she'd get out, even if it means starting over. I'm proud of her for that.

"Your turn," she says, leaning in to me with an eager look.

"Okay. One of my biggest regrets is waiting too long to tell someone I love them." I keep it vague on purpose and hope she won't ask me to elaborate. If she does, I won't. This is already too much opening up for me, and we're only one question in.

She must read my mind, because her face tells me she wants to ask a follow-up question, but her hand pulls a card from the box instead. "What is the first thing you noticed about me? This time, you have to answer first."

I make a stank face. "I dunno if I like this question. Your answer will have a completely different vibe from mine."

"How so?"

"Because when you met me, I was a stranger at your door, saying things you thought were insane."

"But that's not the first thing I noticed about you."

Suddenly, I'm a fan of this question. "Then what was?"

"Nuh-uh. You have to answer first."

"All right, fine. The first thing I noticed about you was your captivating eyes. Sometimes they tell me things your mouth doesn't."

"Your eyes do the same."

So I've been told.

Arella shyly tucks some hair behind her ear. "The first thing I noticed about you is how protectively you wrapped your arms around me. It felt desperate and possessive."

Because it was. For as possessive as I am with her, I give myself an A-fucking-plus for staying away from her for as long as I have. This shit isn't easy.

"Are you that way with Liz too?"

I waggle my head from side to side. "Protective? Yes. Possessive? No." I pull another card from the box, ready to stop talking about the moment I heard her say *"Who are you?"*

Those three words echo in my head constantly, eating me alive from the inside out. I hold the card up and read it. "If you had the option to live forever, would you?"

"I wouldn't," Arella says without putting any thought into it. "I'd hate to watch all the people I love die and to have to go on without them."

"Yep, that would be hard." It's basically what I've been doing with her. She's not exactly dead, but the part of her that remembers me is.

"What's your answer?" she asks.

I let out a scoff as I fling the card next to the box. "My answer is fuck no. I hate my life. Why the hell would I *choose* to do this shit forever?"

"You hate your life?"

The fact that she's surprised by that means she doesn't know anything about my past. "I haven't really been dealt a good hand of cards to play with in this game of survival."

"But you seem to have enough money to buy or experience whatever you want."

"Money isn't worth anything when you've got no one to share it with."

She creases her face together and slumps her shoulders. "Oh, Trey . . ."

"Please don't look at me like that. I don't want pity." *Nor do I deserve it.* I pick up the little game box and scowl at it. "Are there any questions in this damn thing that will solicit a positive answer? I'm done with this depressing shit."

"Let's see if I can find one." She pulls out a card and reads it to herself. Then she shoves it back in. "Nope." She slides out another card. "Definitely not." She pulls out a third card. "Um, maybe. Tell me if this is okay. The question is, Who has had the most positive influence on your life?"

"That's easy. My answer is Liz."

Arella adds the card to our pile of used ones. "Tell me more."

"Liz taught me that when life gets shitty, you can still make something of it. When we first met, I was a drug addict. She helped me clean up. Then two years ago, when I fell back into drugs, she helped me get sober again."

"You were an addict?" Arella says, her jaw dropped.

"Are you really that surprised?"

"Like, how bad?"

I don't want to go into deep details about this with her, so I say, "Pretty bad."

"Do you still struggle with it?"

"Sometimes." *All the time.* It's been easier to overcome my urges lately—for the last four weeks, to be exact. Whenever I feel the urge to silence my chaotic mind with a substance, I just imagine seeing her at this tree on Sunday evening, and the urge fades away.

"What did Liz do to help you sober up?"

"It's not what she *did*. It's what she *said*."

"Which is?"

I eye her playfully. "That's enough opening up for one night."

"What? You're gonna leave me hanging?"

"That question was supposed to elicit a positive answer. Talking about my past is not positive. Why don't you tell me who's had a good influence on your life? Maybe that'll lift the mood."

"Sure. Growing up, my answer would have been my grandparents. They love me more than I've ever seen two people love someone. As an adult, my answer is Javina. She's been there for me from the moment we met, and she's part of the reason why I'm stronger now. Plus, if it wasn't for her, we wouldn't have had that conversation on that bench. Did you know Javina had extra fuses the whole time?"

My face contorts. "What?"

"Yeah, she dumped out her box of fuses and pretended to

need more because she wanted me to be able to talk to you without an audience."

I swear, Javina is one of my favorite people in the world, and she doesn't even know it. "Was her car even broken?"

"Yes. That, she didn't fake."

I let out a soft *hmm*. "Remind me to treat that woman to a spa day sometime."

"She'd like that. Did you know whenever we talk about you, she always refers to you as *pretty boy*?"

A wide smile spreads across my lips. "You guys talk about me?"

Arella glances away as her hair falls to cover her blushing cheeks. "Sometimes."

"What do you guys say?"

She laughs and shakes her head. "I'm not telling."

"What? I just confessed to you that I had a bad drug addiction. It's only fair that you confess something too."

"Okay, fine. Most of the time, we just talk about you coming from an alternate universe."

"Does she know about *this*?"

Arella doesn't need me to specify what *this* is to know what I'm referring to. "I haven't told her, and I don't plan to."

"Does your dude know?"

"No, and I think it's funny that you call him my *dude*."

Because it stings to have to call him her hus—Yeah, I can't even do it in my head. "Liz doesn't know about *this,* either."

"Why haven't you told her?"

Because I already know what Liz will say. She'll tell me this is a bad idea. She'll tell me that when this ends, because it eventually will, I'll be left with a larger gaping hole than before. I already know that, yet here I am, plunging headfirst. Whatever the consequences are, I'll deal with them later. Right now, I'm too happy to care.

25

TREY

"Hey, you."

It's exactly seven thirty. She didn't make me wait for her this time. I wasn't even sure if she was coming tonight. When I walked her to her car last week, I weaseled out of asking her because I'd rather live on the hope that she *might* be coming than go through a whole week knowing she won't.

"Do you greet me like that because you're trying to avoid calling me Ari but you can't call me Arella either?" My perceptive woman lays her blanket over the grass, then sits on it.

"How would you like me to greet you?"

"You could try saying, 'Hey, Ari,' or 'How's it going, Ari?' "

My face remains impassive as I plant myself next to her. "I think I prefer *Hey, you.*"

"Try calling me Ari, just once."

Fuck no. "Why?"

"Because I want to prove to you that it won't kill you."

Maybe not physically . . .

"Just say something simple like 'Hey, Ari. How's your day?' "

To appease her, I force it out. "Hey, *Ari*. How's your day?" That name sounds foreign coming from my lips. The only times I ever called her Ari was when I was introducing her to someone new. Even when I talked about her to my bandmates, I usually referred to her as *my girl*.

"You know what? That sounded awkward. You should just call me Arella."

"But you always correct me." *And it hurts like hell every time.*

"I won't correct you anymore. From now on, you have my full permission to call me Arella."

I lock eyes with her to check if she's serious. Her sweet smile doesn't falter, making my insides throw some balloons in the air. If she's going to allow me to call her Arella, that means she's letting her walls down around me. Is it because I've been letting mine down around her?

Last week, I was the most open with her since her memories were scrubbed. I told her about my biggest regret and my addictions. In turn, I got to hear that the first time she remembers meeting me, she could feel how protective I was of her. *I still am, baby.*

I also found out that no one knows she comes here to see me. I don't know why that makes me feel so good—it just does. It's almost like this place is something only she and I share and, without saying it out loud, we've agreed to keep it a secret.

That means she puts a lot of trust in me. If she thought I had intentions to hurt her, she wouldn't come here, and she especially wouldn't do it without telling *someone* where she is and who she's with. I plan to do everything in my power to keep her trust.

"Do you think you're up for some more questions today?" Arella pulls the box of deep-thought-revealing cards from her purse.

I sit up straighter. "Sure."

"Ooh. Is that enthusiasm I hear? I would have thought you'd dread this game because it makes you open up."

"It makes you open up too, so I'm okay with it. I don't think you would have told me about the way I made you feel when you first met me otherwise."

She purses her lips together and thinks. "Yeah, probably not."

"So the real question is, Do you think *you're* up for some more questions today?"

With a grin, she plucks a card from the box and reads it. "What's the hardest thing you've ever had to do?"

"Whoa!" I dramatically jerk my head back. "*This* is how we're gonna start tonight off?"

"I can pick a lighter question, and we can come back to this one?"

"Yeah, let's do that. I'm not ready to dive into something that heavy yet."

She sets the card aside and plucks out another one. "What do you think is your best quality?"

"Easy. I have none. Next question."

"What? You have lots of great qualities."

I scoff. "Name one."

"You can play lots of instruments."

"Those are skills, not qualities."

"Learning an instrument, especially as many as you have at the level you can play them, means you have patience, determination, and a good work ethic."

"Or it means I grew up without any friends, so I had nothing else better to do with my time."

She rolls her eyes at me. It's something I've missed in our time apart. "Fine. Here's another one: You're generous with your money."

"That's because I don't think I deserve it, so I'd rather give it away than spend it on myself."

"You're protective of Liz, which means you're caring."

"I'm protective of Liz because she's all I have. If anything happens to her, I'll have no one. My protection is selfish."

She rolls her eyes again. "The next time you see your therapist, you should ask her to psychoanalyze why you feel the need to downplay all your good qualities."

"Eh, anything good about me is because I'm self-preserving or it was forced upon me due to situations out of my control."

"Don't you think you have *some* good qualities if someone as amazing as Liz chooses to be best friends with you?"

"Nah. Liz is the type of person who thinks she can fix people. I'm an ongoing project for her."

The first and only time I ever said that to Liz, she got really offended. She claims we became best friends because we bonded over shared trauma. That may have been the surface reason, but deep down, there's a part of her who befriended me because she saw a broken man who needed fixing. I bet she didn't realize how much fixing I'd need.

"Why don't we list off your good qualities instead?" I say, desperate to talk about anything except me. "For example, you're strong, and kind, and you're really good at baking."

Arella slides the box of questions toward me. "According to you, being good at doing something is a *skill*, not a quality."

I pick up the box. "In that case, being good at baking means you're creative, and you're really good with your hands." If she was the Arella who remembers me, I'd make a dirty joke right now.

"Did you know I'm starting my own bakery soon?"

"Really?" Owning a bakery is one of the first things Arella told me she wanted in life. She used to talk my ear off about what colors she wanted the walls to be and what she was going to name it.

"I've already written out my business plan, and I hired a woman to help me create a logo and marketing plan. My next step is getting a loan for a location. I've got two places in mind. The first one is in a great area, but the space is smaller than I want and needs remodeling. The second spot is a little bigger. It only needs some minor cosmetic fixes, but the location is terrible."

"Why don't you find a place that's the size you want in a location you want that only needs the right paint color?"

"Because I've already been to six different banks and I don't qualify for enough financing to—"

"I'll pay for it." I already know she's gonna turn me down.

"No, and don't you dare show up next week with a check, either. This bakery is important to me. I want to do this on my own."

Of course she does. Arella used to tell me that Nathan only bought her things to be able to hold them against her later. I'd never do that to her, but because of him, she feels the need to make purchases without anyone's help. I respect that she sticks to that, even though it's frustrating for me.

"If you ever change your mind, my offer never expires." I slide my finger over the top of the cards and select one from the middle of the box. "What is one of your happiest memories?"

Arella tilts her head back as she thinks. "My happiest memory . . ."

I prepare to fake a smile in case her dude gets mentioned. She doesn't mention him often, or at all, really. I'm not sure if that's because she's not thinking of him while she's here or if it's for my benefit. Either way, I'm not complaining.

"My happiest memory is probably when I first moved to LA," she says. "My grandparents are super protective of me, so I had never been that far from them before. Moving was scary, but it also felt freeing. What about you?"

Almost all of my happiest memories were made with her. How do I pick just one? "Could I share two memories with you?"

Arella perks up like I'm giving her a gift wrapped in sparkly paper and fancy ribbons. "Please."

"It was hard for me to feel happy again after my parents died, but the first time I felt true joy after their death was the first time I performed for a crowd with my band. We were so new that we weren't even Flames in the Night yet. We just called ourselves the Five. We performed at a bar to people who weren't even listening to us, but I didn't care. It was the way we all worked together so seamlessly, and our harmonies just felt right. My second happiest memory was my first kiss with my first love."

Arella waits a second before she circles a hand in the air. "You're not going to give me details about that second one?"

"What details do you want?"

"Whatever you're willing to share. I just feel like I got a whole backstory with the first one and nothing with the second."

"There's not much to share. We were in my kitchen, and she was teaching me how to bake cookies. After we got them into the oven, we playfully threw flour at each other. It got so heated that we ended up kissing for the first time. That's it."

That's not it.

I could tell her so much more, but it feels weird to talk to her about *our* first kiss.

Arella's eyes go wide as her mouth opens slightly. A thought has crossed her mind, but I can't tell what. Even if I was a Mind Reader, I still wouldn't know.

"How many times have you been in love?" she asks before I can ask her what she's thinking.

"Just once."

"But you said *first* love. I assume that means there's a second."

"Nope. It's just been the one." I don't think I'll ever fall in love again, nor do I want to. According to the z-net, it's possible to fall in love with people who aren't your soul mate.

It doesn't make the love any less real; it just means you're in love with someone who isn't a perfect match. I don't want that.

"I've been in love twice," she says.

Technically, she's been in love three times, but to her, I don't count. Is her love with Caleb even real if it's something a Scrubber forced into their minds? It must be real if they're still together.

For the rest of the evening, Arella and I take turns pulling out more cards and talking until the sun is gone and it's time for her to go.

Like I did the previous four weeks, I ask if I can walk her to her car. Like usual, she says yes.

Side by side, we head away from our tree, still talking, still laughing, and still enjoying each other's company. I think about asking her if she's planning to come back next week, but don't. I won't be able to handle it if she says *no*.

When we reach her car, I try not to let the sinking feeling in my stomach get to me. I feel this way whenever it's time to watch her leave. As an attempt to prolong the high, I always head back to our tree and replay every moment from that night in my mind before I leave for the airport. I plan to do that again tonight.

Arella stops at her car and turns to face me. "You know what I just realized? We never went back to that first card I pulled out."

I was hoping she'd forget about that. "What was the question again?"

"What's the hardest thing you've ever had to do?"

"Oh. Why don't you go first?"

"The hardest thing I've ever had to do was go through a three-year-long abusive relationship and have to find myself again and relearn that I'm strong."

"You've done it. You are strong." *One of the two strongest people I know.*

"Thank you. That means a lot. Now you answer."

"The hardest thing I've ever had to do is . . ." *let you go.* I've been keeping my answers to these cards pretty vague. Either that or I tell her a version of the truth and hope she doesn't ask for more. I'm not sure how to spin this one to avoid saying too much.

Arella stares up at me, patiently waiting for me to finish what I started.

It takes me another moment. "Um, the hardest thing I've ever had to do is what I'm doing now."

"Which is?"

I knew she wasn't gonna accept that answer. "Which is . . . ya know, living. Moving on. Letting go of the past and stepping into the future. Sometimes I feel like I gave up, but Liz tells me I did the right thing."

Arella cocks her head at me, trying to read between the lines and figure out the deeper meaning behind my words. "Liz seems to know what she's talking about, so I trust that she's right."

"Yeah, but," I say, staring at the gravel I'm standing on, "that doesn't make it any less hard."

She slides a tender hand up my chest and stops over my pec. "You're so strong, Trey. And I see your strength growing with each smile you make. Just keep going."

Every nerve in my body sparks to life. My skin tingles from where she trailed her hand up, and it's on fire where she's keeping her hand now.

I don't move. I *can't* move. I'm too afraid it'll make her pull away. I want her to keep her hand on me for the rest of my life. If she does, I'll die a happy man.

26

TREY

"Arella." It feels good to be able to say her name to her. She smiles when I do.

"Trey." It feels even better to hear her say my name, especially because she's not saying it like she's wondering who I am. She's saying it like she knows me and is happy to see me.

This is the sixth week in a row she's come to our tree. It's been a whole month and a half of breathing easier and feeling the weight on my shoulders slowly chip off. I try not to think about how much it's going to destroy me if I lose her again—*when* I lose her again.

I'm not trying to fool myself. I know this won't last forever. That's why I'm imprinting everything she says and does into my mind so I can replay it over and over when I inevitably return to hell.

"Were you meditating?" she asks as I put my earbuds back into their case.

"Yep. I had the volume on low so I could hear you coming."

"I could tell. I didn't have to scare you this time." She shakes out her blanket and lays it down for us. "Did you finish your session?"

"No, but I can finish it later."

"Let's do it together."

I'm about to return my earbuds to my backpack when I stop. "Really?"

"Yeah. I've got some thoughts that need calming."

I hand her one of my earbuds, then we lie on her blanket next to each other and I hand her my phone. "Pick out a session for us."

She scrolls through the app, then chooses a guided meditation that's ten minutes long. As the soft music plays into my ear, I close my eyes and steady my breaths.

The point of meditating is to release all the thoughts clouding my head. With Arella next to me, it's near impossible. All I can think about is how close our hands are and how easy it would be to grab hers and hold it. I resist the urge to open my eyes and stare at her.

Halfway through the meditation, I lose the fight. As the lady in my ear tells me to focus on breathing deeply, I steal a peek at Arella through half-closed eyelids. She still has her eyes shut as she draws in a deep breath and slowly lets it out as instructed. I wonder what thoughts are storming through her head that need calming. *Do any of them have to do with me?*

At the end of the meditation, I close my eyes and slowly flutter them open as if they hadn't already been open for the last five minutes.

"Thanks, Trey," she says as she offers the earbud back to me.

"Did that help calm your thoughts?"

"It did."

"Do you want to talk about them?" *Please say yes. Please say yes.*

"If you want me to open up, you'll have to open up about something too."

Am I willing to do that? "How deep do I have to go?"

"I'll give you the freedom to decide that."

"All right. Deal. You share first."

She takes some time to think, then says, "I think my husband has turned into my roommate."

Hearing her call someone else her husband feels like accidentally touching a hot pan. The burn won't kill me, but the sting will linger for days.

She continues, "Lately, I feel like we're two people who just happen to live in the same apartment. I only ever see him during dinner, and most of the time, he's just scrolling through his phone. Whenever we happen to have the same day off, he's usually got plans at the gym with Rakesh."

Her dude hasn't made love to her in *months*, and when they're together, he's not even *looking* at her? What the fuck is wrong with him? "Who's Rakesh?"

"Caleb's best friend. They work out together almost every day."

"So he makes time for his friend, but not you?"

"I don't mind that they go to the gym together. I'm at work whenever they do, anyway. However, it does bother me that he makes plans with Rakesh, even when he knows I've got the day off."

It's official: The dude is an idiot. He has everything I want, and he's not even appreciating it. "Have you tried talking to him about this?"

"A few times, but it hasn't changed anything."

"Maybe you could suggest a system. Like whenever you both get your work schedules, you can sit down together and block out time to spend with only each other. Then talk to him about staying off his phone."

"A system . . ." Her voice trails off as she thinks about that. "That's really good advice. Thank you. Have you ever thought about being a relationship counselor?"

I burst into a loud laugh because that's the funniest shit I've ever heard. "Me? A relationship counselor? I haven't been able to keep a girl around for more than three months. No one would hire me with that track record."

"I would, judging from that one piece of advice. It means a lot coming from you."

What she's saying is that it means a lot coming from someone who would love to take Caleb's place. Technically, he took *my* place. I'd just be taking it back.

I might've given her different advice if I was certain we could have a future together. With her memories gone, that diamond ring sparkling on her finger, and no solid plan of how I could keep an intimate relationship with an Ordinary off the zovernment's radar, a future together is not a possibility. That doesn't stop me from yearning for it though.

"It's your turn to share something deep," she says.

"What would you like to know?"

"There's a question you refused to answer before that's been on my mind." She pauses, silently asking me for permission to continue.

With that curious glint in her eyes and the way her entire body is turned toward me so attentively, I eagerly grant her the permission. "Let's hear it."

"You said that Liz said something that helped you get sober a second time. I'm curious what she said."

I suck in a deep breath then slowly let it out. "Liz said a lot of things, but the winning line was, Is this the man she'd want you to be?" I don't need to specify who *she* is for Arella to know.

"And that's it? You went sober, just like that?"

"Basically." I say that like it's been easy for me, when in reality, it's a battle I'm fighting every day that sometimes feels like accepting an L wouldn't be the worst thing.

"If Alterella thinks similar to the way I do, then Liz is right. That isn't the man she'd want you to be."

That dark place in my chest floods with light. Suddenly, all those lonely sober nights of miserably living through my zero sense of purpose feels worth it. Just being here with her is worth it.

Arella tilts her head to the side, then softens her tone. "What's something you would say to her if you could?"

There is so much I would say. Most of them are things I write on postcards that never get stamped. I guess if I had to summarize all those handwritten notes, there would be one central message.

My words come out barely above a whisper. "I'd tell her that I miss her."

"What do you miss about her?"

"Everything."

"Could you be more specific?"

A shorter list would be what I don't miss. "You already got one deep thought from me tonight. Are you saying you wanna trade one more?"

With a smirk, she digs through her purse and pulls out our little box of questions. She slides the lid off, then plucks out a card from the middle and reads it. "What is something you'd say to anyone in any universe if you could? And be specific."

I burst into a laugh. "That's not what that card says."

"That's *exactly* what this card says. Word for word."

I hold my palm out. "Lemme see it then."

She hugs the card to her chest. "Nuh-uh. You have to answer it first."

"Lemme see the card first."

"Nope." She shoves the card down her shirt as if that's a deterrent. If she was mine, I'd have my hand down there already.

I drop my outstretched hand. "Fine. My answer is that I miss this. I miss being with her. I miss her playfulness. I miss how we used to cuddle in bed and talk for hours. I even miss arguing with her over stupid things, like which way to correctly hang toilet paper and whether putting icing on a muffin makes it a cupcake."

"First off, putting icing on a muffin does *not* make it a cupcake. They're completely different recipes. And second, the correct way to hang toilet paper is going over, never under."

I can't hold back the smile that spreads across my face. "Alterella had the same strong opinions."

"What's your opinion?"

"That I don't care if you call it a muffin or a cupcake as long as I get to eat it. I also don't care which way the toilet paper gets hung as long as I get to use it." Because I know it'll get a reaction from her, I add, "I tend to just put the TP on the holder whichever way it happens to be facing."

She leans back with a gasp. "That's even worse than going under. It's never consistent."

I chuckle lightly. "I don't give a fuck which way it's facing. At the end of the day, it's just toilet paper."

She narrows her eyes at me. "Are you one of those people who thinks pineapple belongs on pizza?"

"I don't mind pineapple on my pizza, but I wouldn't go out of my way for it."

"Ew!" She makes an *ick* face. "That's gross."

"Hey. At least I'm not a weirdo who pours their milk in before the cereal."

She slaps an offended hand over her heart. "Excuse me. I don't like soggy cereal. If I pour the milk in first, I can add a little bit of cereal at a time, then eat it while it's still crunchy before pouring in more. That's smart, if you ask me."

I don't think I've ever been more in love with this woman. The level of happiness and comfort I feel right now is beyond measure. I just wish I could get rid of the feeling that this happiness is coming to an end soon.

27

ARELLA

"Caleb . . ."

"What?" He glances up at me from across our little kitchen table. He's got his phone in one hand and a fork in the other.

"Remember what we talked about on Monday?"

He thinks, then sets his phone down. "Right. Sorry."

I took Trey's advice and talked to Caleb about being more intentional about spending time together and staying off his phone. Caleb agreed, and tonight, we're having a date night. Unfortunately, it's a Sunday, but this was the only night Caleb could take off work.

Around this time, I'm usually on my way to see Trey. I hope he's not sitting under our tree right now, waiting for me. I wish I had a way of telling him that I'm not coming. I don't have his phone number or email, and neither of us use social media.

With my fork, I push some of the rice around on my plate. I need to get Trey out of my head so I can think of something to talk about with Caleb. "How was your workout today?"

"Fine." He takes a bite of his rice and beans, barely even looking at me.

"What do you want to do for date night?"

"Whatever you want."

I thought I asked *him* to plan something for us, but I suppose I can do it at the last minute. "Would you rather stay in or go out?"

"Either." He stares blankly at his water glass as he takes another bite of his dinner.

I set my fork onto my plate. "Caleb?"

"What?"

"Is everything okay?"

"Yeah, why?"

That's a lie. He's more distant tonight than most nights. "You're barely even looking at me."

"I'm just stressed about work. That's all." He says it so nonchalantly, I almost believe him. Even if his stress was only about work, it still doesn't make it okay that he's letting it affect our relationship.

We haven't been actively trying to have a baby for four months. Correction: *He* hasn't been actively trying. I've been actively getting rejected. It takes two for this baby thing to happen.

"I'm ovulating?" I meant for that to sound sexy, but it comes out more like a question.

"Sorry, muffin. I'm not feeling it tonight."

"You haven't felt it for four months."

"It's hard to feel it when I'm stressed out."

I'm beginning to think this stress thing is just an excuse. I get stressed out at work too, but I don't allow it to affect my sex drive. All he has to do is walk laps around a closed museum at night. What's so stressful about that?

Maybe he doesn't find me attractive anymore. I've gained a few pounds since we met. I wouldn't say I'm big, but I've definitely filled out. *Is that it?*

"Do you want to talk about what's going on at work?" I ask.

He finishes eating the last bite of his dinner. "Not really. I don't want to put that burden on you."

But you are—indirectly. "Do you want to cancel date night?"

"We haven't had one for a while, so we should have it."

We *should* have it. He sees this as something we *should* do, not something he *wants* to do. I'm beginning to question if this date-night thing is something *I* want anymore.

Caleb stands and brings his dirty plate to the sink. I push my half-eaten food away because suddenly, I'm not hungry anymore.

After the kitchen is cleaned up, Caleb and I sit on the couch to pick out a movie together. By that, I mean it's him scrolling through movie options in four different streaming services before finally deciding on something.

We are three streaming services in when Caleb's phone vibrates on the coffee table. I don't have to look to know it's Rakesh calling.

Caleb doesn't hesitate to pick up his phone. "Hey."

The phone is loud enough that everything Rakesh says goes straight into my ears. "It finally happened, man."

"What?" Caleb tosses the TV remote onto the coffee table. "Just now?"

"Yeah. I just got off the phone with my brother. He was with her when it happened."

"Oh, I'm sorry."

"It's okay," Rakesh says through a sniffle. "She's not in pain anymore, I guess."

"Do you need anything?"

"Could you come over? I'd really like some support right now."

"I'll be right over." Caleb ends the call, then turns to me. "Rakesh's grandma just died."

I've never met Rakesh's grandma, so I pretend to sound like I care. "What happened?"

"She's been in hospice for the past few weeks."

News to me.

"Her colon cancer got really bad."

I didn't even know she had cancer. Honestly, I didn't even know Rakesh had a grandma.

"Are you cool with me going over to see him?"

"Of course." It's not like I can say no. He already told Rakesh he was coming.

Within seconds, Caleb has his shoes on. As he grabs his keys, he says, "Don't wait up for me." Then he's gone.

As his car engine rumbles to life, my heart sinks. He didn't even say bye or give me a kiss before he left. Just "don't wait up" as if he plans to be out all night. *Does he?*

I suppose it wouldn't be out of the norm. Lately, Caleb has been having game nights with Rakesh and a few other friends. On those evenings, he usually doesn't return home until almost two in the morning.

I press a button on the remote, and the TV goes black. Then I'm left alone in a dark living room, questioning all my life decisions. Being alone was not part of my plan tonight. I pictured this evening filled with fun and laughter. I even hoped for some baby making.

Now I'm not even sure if I want a child with Caleb anymore. If this is how he's going to act when we don't have kids, how is he going to act when we do have them? Will he be an absent father? Will he leave me to take care of them every night while he goes out with his friends? Will he even look at our children when they talk to him, or will he just scroll through his phone?

Caleb hasn't been physically present in our relationship for four months. Now that I think about it, he hasn't been mentally present for even longer. Is this how it's going to be for the rest of our lives? I can't live like this.

Within seconds, I've got my shoes on and I'm out the door.

28

ARELLA

The stars are shining by the time I park my car behind Trey's motorcycle. The entire drive here, I was worried he had left already. I'm thrilled to know he hasn't.

When I get up to the tree—*our* tree—he's not there. His backpack is though. *Where did he go?*

I lay out our blanket, then set my purse down.

"Trey?" I call, because maybe he's nearby.

The crickets are the only things that answer me.

I glance around the oak tree toward the woods that always stretch behind us, but there's no movement.

Since his backpack is here, he's gotta come back for it, right? With a sigh, I sit on the blanket and wait.

Thankfully, I don't have to wait long. Barely five minutes later, the sound of footsteps comes from behind the tree.

When Trey rounds the trunk, he stops and jumps back with a hand to his chest. "Fuck. You scared me."

"Sorry," I say through a giggle.

"How long have you been here?"

"Only a few minutes." I pat my blanket and gesture for him to sit. "Where did you go?"

He drops down next to me and crosses his legs together.

"My therapist suggested that I go for walks whenever the meditations don't work. So that's what I did."

"How often do you go for walks?"

"I used to almost every day. Sometimes twice a day. I haven't been on a walk in . . . seven weeks."

It takes me a second to understand the significance of seven weeks. Then that same warmth I've been feeling lately around Trey eases through me, filling my stomach with little flutters. "Why did you walk tonight?"

He blinks at me, and his eyes tell me his answer: He went for a walk because he thought I wasn't coming. He waited for me and overthought it so much that even the meditations didn't calm his mind.

"Did the walk help?"

"Not really, but I'm good now." He offers me a tender smile that says, *I'm good now that you're here.*

"I'm sorry. I didn't know how to contact you to let you know I wasn't going to be here. Maybe we should exchange numbers."

He twirls his thumbs around each other. "I've thought about that, and I don't think it's a good idea."

I try not to look disappointed. "Why's that?"

"Do you want to guess, or do you want me to just say it?"

"Um, is it because you don't think you should have a married woman's number?"

"No. It's because I don't think I can handle it. If I have the ability to text you, I won't be able to do anything else. I'll just stare at my phone all day, waiting for you to text me back. If you don't right away, I'll obsess over it, and I don't think that's healthy for me."

I can see where he's coming from. If I had his number, I'd probably spend all day texting him too. We never seem to run out of things to talk about. I wouldn't be able to get anything else done.

"So," he says, "you weren't planning to be here tonight?"

"Not originally."

"What changed your mind?"

Nothing really *changed* my mind. I've wanted to be here all week. Even when Caleb told me he took tonight off, I asked him if there was any other night he could take off instead. "I took your advice from last week. I talked to Caleb about spending more time together and staying off his phone. Tonight was supposed to be date night. Then Rakesh called. His grandma died, so Caleb ditched me to go be with him."

"I see." Trey's eyes cast down with a somber look.

I hate seeing him like that. "Why do you look so sad?"

He blinks like he's trying to arrange the right words in his head, then he bails. "It's nothing."

"It's *not* nothing. It's probably deep if you're not openly sharing it with me."

"It is deep, but it's also an inappropriate thing to say to you, so I should just keep quiet."

Now I *have* to know. I dig my hand into my purse and pull out our questions box. Then I take the lid off and pull out a card. I barely even look at it as I say, "What deep thought crossed your mind just now?"

Trey shakes his head at me, chuckling. "This tactic again, huh?"

I smirk a little. "It worked last time."

"If I share this deep thought with you, you're gonna have to fork one out too."

"Deal. Now spill."

He focuses on his hands in his lap for a while before finally saying, "The thought that crossed my mind was that the only reason you came here tonight was because your other plan fell through. To you, I'm just a backup plan. But to me, you're . . . well, you're not a backup plan. That's for damn sure. I shouldn't take it too hard though. I'd rather be your backup plan than no plan at all. I should just take what I can get."

Each of his words is laced with a brokenness I can feel in

the depths of my heart. I'm sure his thoughts run deeper than what he was willing to share. I'm grateful that he shared *something*, though, because I need to correct him.

I place a tender hand over his knee so he can *feel* how much I mean my next words. "Trey, you are *not* a backup plan. I wanted to be here tonight, but this was the only night Caleb could get off. The entire time I had dinner with him, I was thinking of you."

"You were?"

"Yeah. I didn't like the idea of you sitting here, waiting for me. That's why the second he left, I came straight here."

Trey places his hand over mine on his knee. His warmth sends a tingle up my arm. "I would wait forever for you, even when I don't know if you're coming. The possibility that you *might* is enough for me."

My heart melts into a little puddle. That's the most endearing thing anyone has ever said to me.

My eyes lock with his. I recognize that intense look between all the chaos and misery in his blue-grays. It's the way he looks at me in my dreams—right before he kisses me. My breath hitches at the idea. His gaze drops to my eager lips and lingers there. I can practically see all the wild thoughts racing through his head as he battles with himself. Eventually, he leans back, clears his throat, and takes his hand off mine.

My skin feels cold where his hand used to be. I retract my palm from his knee as my throat goes dry. *Maybe it's for the best.*

To lighten things up, I say, "Does confessing that I was thinking of you during dinner count as forking out a deep thought?"

"Hell no. I'm gonna need something more than that."

"What would you like to know?"

He takes a moment to think. "Tell me a secret of yours. Something no one else knows."

I try to think of something I haven't told anyone else, not even Javina. She knows almost everything about me. The only thing she doesn't know is anything that's happened here with Trey. Lately, it's been getting harder to keep this from her. "A secret just came to mind, but it's not really a secret. It's just something I'd like to clear up with you."

"I'm listening."

"I don't have any food allergies. Nor do I have a birthmark. I've never had a dog either."

"But . . . you . . . when I came to your apartment—"

I offer him an apologetic shrug. "They were trick questions."

"I feel bamboozled."

I giggle at his funny word choice. "I'm sorry. At least you know now."

"You know, I drove myself insane trying to remember if you had ever mentioned having a dog."

He didn't say if *Alterella* had ever mentioned having a dog. He's talking about *me*. Usually, when he brings up the past, he's pretty good about keeping Alterella and me separated. I do the same. That way, we can continue living in our own little world where alternate universes explain why I don't remember him. A world where we don't have to talk about this unexplainable and unbreakable connection we have.

It's easier that way. I like being able to pretend like he's just an old friend I'm reconnecting with—a friend who appears in my dreams all the time. Because of those dreams, I feel like I know him. I don't know many facts about him, but I know his mannerisms, his tells, and the many thoughts he doesn't say aloud—things that people only know about each other after spending enough time together. Technically, I haven't spent that much time with Trey, but I have in my mind.

Despite that we've barely touched each other, I know his body too. I know what it feels like to have his muscular arms wrapped around me after a hot make-out session that leaves us panting. I know what it feels like to run my fingertips up and down the ridges of his abs. I even know what it feels like to wrap my palms around his thick shaft. These aren't things I remember doing in real life. They're things I've done only in my dreams, which I suppose could have been real life. I'm not sure anymore.

Trey said he can't tell me how I lost my memories because the government would throw him back in prison. If I guess it right, would he tell me? I have theories. Some are plausible; others are downright insane.

My craziest theory is that Trey is from the future—a future where they visit the past like it's a fun recreational activity, as if it's the same as taking a little vacation or going on a road trip—and on one of Trey's visits to the past, we met and fell madly in love. Since people from the future are forbidden from getting personally involved with people from the past, the future government wiped my memories using a memory-zapping device like the one from *Men in Black*. Then the future government banished Trey from returning to the future and said if he ever told me what happened, they'd imprison him.

Their memory zapper must not be that powerful if my memories have been returning in my dreams. Trey must know it's possible to beat it, because he once said, "Whatever they did to you, you can fight it. Look into my eyes. Try to remember me."

I wish I could fully remember him. My dreams only give me a tiny snapshot of the full picture. Sometimes my dreams are clear. Other times, they're blurry, like I'm watching things happen through a dirty lens. Occasionally, I have dreams where everything sounds muffled like everyone is speaking into a voice distorter.

My worst dreams are the ones where I can hear everything clearly but all I can see is black. Those are typically my dreams where Trey is screaming like he's being attacked by vicious animals. I can't see that it's him, but I know in my heart that it is, from how much it kills me to hear him in pain like that. If my other dreams of us actually happened, does that mean my dreams of him screaming happened too? If so, why was he screaming?

"You okay?" Trey asks.

"Yeah. I'm just a little cold." It's the middle of July in California. My shivers have *nothing* to do with being cold. I just get chills whenever I think about my dreams of what I'm assuming is Trey getting tortured. Who or what was hurting him? And why do I get the feeling that they were torturing him because of me?

He takes off his leather jacket and drapes it over my shoulders. His manly scent surrounds me like a warm blanket of comfort and ease. "Better?"

"Kind of." I'm not sure if *better* is the right word. His jacket over me is only jumbling my thoughts more. Why is his scent so familiar to me? And why does it spark up a desire between my legs?

"I don't mind sitting in the grass. Why don't we wrap this blanket around you too?"

A thought pops into my head, and I say it before I can think about the consequences. "Actually, could you just hold me?"

He freezes and stares at me like he's trying to figure out if he heard me right. "Hold you?"

"Yeah. Penguins keep warm by cuddling. They live in snow, so it must work, right?"

"Right . . ." Slowly, as if not to scare me, he lies down and pats his chest. "Come here."

I don't hesitate. Keeping his jacket around my shoulders, I scoot toward him, then lay my head over his chest. His tattooed arm circles my back and rests over my hip.

I nuzzle my face into his shirt, taking in more of his sweet scent. This is the first time he's ever cuddled me—that I can remember—yet it feels so familiar.

At first, Trey just lies there with his body stiff. It's like he's afraid if he moves too much, I'll disappear. As an attempt to make him feel more comfortable, I rest my hand over his abs the way I always do in my dreams.

"Arella?" He says my name all breathily.

"Yeah?"

"Is it okay if I put both my arms around you?"

"Mm-hmm."

Without wasting another second, he wraps his firm arms around my back and crushes me against his chest. He does it so tight, the air leaves my lungs. This feels like it did the first time: desperate, possessive, protective.

I give him a moment, but when he doesn't release me right away, I let out a stifled, "Trey, you're suffocating me."

He relaxes his boa-constrictor arms a little. "Better?"

"Yeah."

His chest rises with a deep breath. When he exhales, it sounds ragged. He breathes in again, and on the exhale, his breath comes out shaky, like he's trying not to cry.

"Are you okay?" I ask into his chest.

"Mm-hmm." He sounds choked up. "I'm just—um, overwhelmed."

"By what?"

"Happiness. It's been so long since I've held you, I forgot what it felt like."

I've never felt so comfortable in someone's arms like this. I've never felt so safe and protected either. "When was the last time you held me?"

"That day you looked at me with recognition and said my name like you knew me. Then you asked if I could stay and hold you until you woke up."

"I don't remember that, but I know it happened." *Only because Caleb said so.*

"I know, and that's okay."

"Is it though?" I tilt my head back to look at him.

His eyes are glistening with surface tears. He blinks them

away, then clears his throat. "There's nothing I can do to change the situation, so I *have to* be okay with it. Besides, it doesn't matter how I feel, as long as you're happy."

It bugs me that he doesn't see his happiness as something important. He matters just as much as anyone else. "How would you know if I'm happy or not?"

"You have to be. Otherwise, going through hell wasn't worth it."

Going through hell. Is he referring to when he was being tortured? Or maybe when people were attacking me? A few times, I've had dreams of people throwing flaming objects at my face or a knife at my arm. I've done a thorough check of my arms and haven't found any evidence of a knife wound. Then again, Caleb said I remembered Trey getting stabbed, and there's no evidence of that either. Did whatever healed him heal me too?

"Did you leave LA because of me?" That question has been burning on my mind for years. I already know the answer; I just want to hear it from him.

"I left LA so you could be happy."

For the most part, I am happy. I have amazing friends, I love my job, and I'm planning to open my dream bakery soon. The only thing is that when I'm with Trey, I feel like my life is complete. I don't feel that way with Caleb, and now that I think about it, I never have. Minus the past few months, Caleb makes me happy. However, there's a difference between feeling happy and feeling complete.

"I think you should move back to LA."

Trey pulls me in closer and breathes into my hair. "Why?"

"Because I don't like the idea of you living in New York just to stay away from me. You don't have to do that anymore. We're friends now." The word *friends* sounds wrong to describe this relationship I have with Trey—a relationship that exists only on Sunday evenings under this tree, where it feels right to be held by him.

"Thanks, Arella. I appreciate your friendship, but I think I've gotta stay in New York."

What he means is that being friends with me isn't enough of a reason to move back. He wants more. *Do I?* "Is New York where you see yourself in five years?"

"Probably not."

"Where do you see yourself then? Or maybe a better question is, What would you like to see?"

"Like, in terms of life?"

"Yeah. For example, in five years, I see myself as an established bakery owner. Maybe I'll have a second location. I see lots of fun employees who enjoy coming to work every day the way I do at the bakery I currently work at." I also see myself as a mother, but at the rate I'm going with the man I'm with, that'll never happen.

"Do you want my realistic or unrealistic answer?"

"Both."

"Realistically, I see myself still making music, whether that's with my band or not. I've been thinking about what you said last year—about writing and producing for other artists. I've been playing around with the idea of starting my own production company."

I lean back with a wide grin. "That's a wonderful idea! Now, what's your unrealistic answer?"

"To have a family."

That's what I want too. "Why is that unrealistic?"

"Because to have a wife and kids, I'd need to have a girlfriend first."

I make a *pfft* sound. "Have you looked into the mirror lately? Finding a girlfriend can't be hard for you."

"Finding the *right* girl is. I don't want to have a family with just anyone. What I want is to have a family with *the* one, but . . ." He lets out a deep sigh. "Anyway, it's just not in the cards for me."

But what? But she's already with a man who spends more

time with his best friend than his wife? A man who barely looks at her while he eats the dinner she makes for him every night? A man who doesn't even know his wife's been hanging out with another man every Sunday for the past seven weeks?

Even if I told Caleb about Trey, he wouldn't care. He'd probably just go back to scrolling on his phone. What does it mean for my marriage if my husband doesn't care what I do or who I'm with?

29

ARELLA

By the time I get home from my thinking spot, it's well past two in the morning, and Caleb is still gone. I call him, but he doesn't pick up, so I fall asleep without him.

When I wake up around nine, I'm *still* without him. *Did he stay the night at Rakesh's?*

After I brush my teeth, I call him, but he doesn't answer.

Twenty minutes later, I ring him again. Same thing.

Due to being out late, I called in sick to work, so I'm home when Caleb finally returns around noon.

"Is everything okay?" I ask when he strolls through the door.

"Yeah," he says as he kicks off his shoes. "Why are you home? I thought you had work today."

"I got the day off."

"Oh." He barely looks at me as he rushes into our bedroom.

I follow him. "How's Rakesh doing?"

"He's all right." After unbuttoning the top three buttons of his pastel shirt, Caleb drags it over his head and tosses it into the hamper. "We took a trip up to Bakersfield to visit his family last night. He felt better after that."

I climb onto our bed and sit with my legs to the side. "Is that why you were out all night?"

"Yeah. We stayed at his mom's place."

It would have been nice if Caleb had told me that. I suppose it's not like I was up all night worrying about where he was though. "I called you a few times."

"I saw. Sorry I didn't pick up. I fell asleep in the car on the way back."

But you didn't pick up last night either. "Do you think we could look at our schedules today to see when we can reschedule our date night?"

"Uh, sure." His tone comes out somewhere between hesitant and forced. "Let me take a quick shower first. I feel gross right now."

I'm on the couch when Caleb comes out of the bathroom from his longer-than-usual shower. He doesn't look at me as he heads straight past me and into the kitchen.

He opens the fridge. "I'm going to head to the gym, then Rakesh wants me to come over after that. I'll probably get dinner with him before I head to work tonight, so don't worry about me for food, okay?"

He already spends more time with Rakesh than he does with me. Now he's getting dinner with Rakesh too? During the only time I ever get to see him? Seriously? Do I even know this man anymore? I wouldn't even consider us roommates at this point. He's like a stranger to me. More of a stranger to me than Trey the first time I saw him standing on my doorstep. There's always been a part of me that's felt connected to Trey. I thought I felt like that with Caleb, but now I don't feel connected to him at all.

I step into the kitchen to find the stranger I happen to live with munching on a granola bar. "Can you pull up your work schedule?"

"What for?" he asks through a mouthful.

"So we can compare schedules and plan our next date night?" *What we said we were going to do before you showered.*

"Oh, that's right. Could we do it later? I'm supposed to meet Rakesh at the gym soon."

I suck in a deep breath, resisting the urge to roll my eyes. "Fine. Whatever."

Turning on my heel, I storm away. I expect him to stop me or ask what's wrong, but he doesn't. This is what I mean when I say he doesn't care. He hasn't cared for a while, so I don't know why I keep trying.

After Caleb leaves, I try not to cry as I write down a list of the things I want to hash out with him. I vowed to myself after Nathan that I would not stay in a relationship where I felt abused or unwanted ever again. Caleb doesn't abuse me, but he doesn't want me either. And if he does, he's got a crappy way of showing it. I'll tell him he's got one month to make things better between us or I'm out.

The next day, I bring out my list during dinner and hand it to Caleb.

"What's this?" he asks with his fork halfway to his lips.

I play with the mashed potatoes on my plate. "It's a list of all the things I think we should work on as a couple."

He stares at the piece of paper in his hand. "Make spending quality time together a priority. Actually look at each other when we're having a conversation. Have more conversations. Have monthly date nights. Be intimate again." He sets the paper down, then goes straight back to eating his steak.

I wait a moment before asking, "Sooo . . . ? What do you think?"

"I don't know."

"What do you mean, you don't know?"

"As in, I don't know," he says, clipped. "You keep saying you want to spend more time together, but it's hard to do that when you work days and I work nights."

"That's why I suggested that we make it a priority. Like yesterday, I had the day off, but you went to the gym with Rakesh."

"I always go to the gym with him on Mondays. It's our leg day."

"Yeah, but you had dinner with him too, which is supposed to be our time together."

"Because I was going to his place after the gym, and then I had to work after that. It just made more sense to get dinner with him so I wouldn't have to drive back and forth."

"You didn't have to go to his place after the gym. You could have come home if you wanted to." And that's the problem. He didn't want to.

"Rakesh wanted me to come over because he wanted to talk to me about going to the funeral with him this weekend."

"Are you?"

"Yeah. The wake is on Sunday, and the funeral is on Monday. We're going to leave Saturday morning and stay at his mom's place. I should be back Tuesday afternoon."

That seems like a long time to be gone for one funeral. "Are you going to be able to get the days off for that?"

"I already did. I asked my boss last night."

How was it that easy for him to get three nights off in a row at the last minute? Whenever I ask if he can take one night off for me, he always makes it seem like it's a hassle to even ask. "What about all the other stuff on my list?"

He cuts into his steak with a knife. "What about them?"

"Do you think we could try to work on them together?"

"How do you want to do that?"

"Well, I was thinking for the intimacy one, we could start with cuddling more." *Or at all would be nice.*

"Sure," he says halfheartedly.

I pretend like he said it with enthusiasm. "Do you want to cuddle after dinner?"

"Not for long. I've gotta go to work soon."

I suppose that's better than *no*.

After I get the kitchen cleaned up, I sit on the couch and wait for Caleb. He comes out of the bedroom in his security guard uniform and plops onto the cushion next to me. When he puts his arm around me, it feels forced, not eager. When I lay my head against his stiff chest, it feels awkward, not comforting.

We get about two silent minutes in before Caleb says, "I've gotta go before I'm late."

I push myself off him and try not to frown. "Okay. Have a good night at work."

He gets his shoes on and rushes out the door like he couldn't get away from me fast enough. For being held by a security guard, I didn't feel safe or protected once.

30

ARELLA

Since Caleb is out of town, I don't have to wait until after he's fed and off to work to head to my thinking spot. I don't know what time Trey usually gets there, but he's always already there when I arrive around seven thirty. Tonight, I want to spend as much time with him as possible, so I leave my apartment early with hopes that he'll already be there.

And he is.

When I emerge from the woods at the top of the hill, Trey's gaze flicks from the book in his lap up to me, then his expression brightens.

"Hi." I'm breathless from the way he's staring at me so intently.

"Arella." I'll never get sick of hearing him say my full name. He peels his eyes off me to glance at his phone. "You're two hours earlier than usual."

"Are you complaining?"

"Fuck no. I'm ecstatic." It's good to know that *someone* feels that way about seeing me.

I lay out our blanket as Trey shoves his book into his backpack. "How far did you get in your reading?"

"About halfway." He sits across from me on our blanket

with his legs crossed. "I'll probably finish it on my flight home tonight."

"What time is your flight?" I hope it's not early, because I plan to stay here for as long as he stays.

"Whenever I get to the airport and purchase one."

"You don't have a flight booked yet?"

"Nah. They've got flights leaving LA to New York every few hours. I'm willing to pay whatever, and I don't care if I have to wait, so lately, I've been getting on whatever is available."

I'm flattered that he makes so many accommodations just to be with me. "Do you ever have to wait long for a flight?"

"Sometimes, but I don't mind. I'm never in a rush to get back to New York. The only thing I've got going on there are my Monday afternoons with my therapist. The rest of the days, I'm basically just killing time until I fly back to LA."

I imagine him in his big fancy penthouse all alone. The scene depresses me, so I imagine myself there with him. *That's better.*

"Do you still talk to your therapist about me?"

"Occasionally." In Trey speak, that means *all the time.*

"What's the last thing you told her about me?"

"That you let me hold you, and that it wasn't because you suddenly remembered me."

"Do you have any idea how that might have happened?" *Because I'd like to make it happen again.*

"Not a goddamn clue." The pang of sadness that crosses his eyes tells me he's speaking the truth. It also tells me he wishes he knew just as much as I do.

My guess is that seeing that spider triggered my traumatic memory of being attacked by spiders, which must have triggered my mind into remembering him. I've seen more spiders since then, but my mind has stayed the same.

Suddenly, Trey perks up with a smile. "Can I show you something?"

I return his smile and eagerness. "Sure."

He stands, then offers me his hand. I don't hesitate to take it. "Do you know how to climb a tree?"

"Not really."

He gestures toward the lowest branch of the oak tree. If I stick my arm up, I could touch it without having to step onto my tiptoes. "I'll give you a boost, okay?" he says.

"Why are we climbing this tree?"

"Because I wanna show you somethin'."

"And we have to climb a tree to see it?"

His smile drops as he gives me a *come on* look. "Put a little faith in me, will ya? You're gonna like it. I promise."

With his help, I hoist myself onto the lowest branch, then climb onto the next one.

"Don't go any farther. Wait for me." Trey makes climbing the tree look easy. With one swift motion, he's already up and next to me. His warm hand presses against the small of my back to steady me, but I don't need the support. I'm clinging onto this tree so tightly, a hit from Thor's hammer couldn't make me fall. "You good?"

I nod.

"Cool. Now climb up three more branches."

My eyes go wide. "Three? That's pretty high, Trey. If I fall, I'll break something."

He lets out a little scoff. "Do you really think *I* would let you fall?"

Good point. I reach for the next branch and climb up. Three branches later, I've got leaves in my face.

Trey climbs up next to me with a huge grin. I don't know why he's grinning like that. This branch we're standing on could break any second. I'm surprised it hasn't already.

I cling onto the branch next to me. "All right, mister. What's so cool that we had to climb a tree to see it?"

"Shh." He places a finger against his lips. Then he whispers, "Turn around."

I match his hushed tone, even though I don't know why he's whispering. "Um, I'm not sure if moving on this branch is a good idea."

He places a hand over my waist. "I won't let you fall, baby. Promise."

He just called me *baby*. And it felt so normal.

With his confidence in the sturdiness of this branch, I slowly turn around, then gasp. A plump bird is curled up in her little nest, sleeping.

"Oh my god," I whisper. "She's beautiful."

Trey keeps his voice low too. "She's got eggs beneath her. I saw 'em earlier."

"How did you know she was up here?"

"I noticed her flying in and out while I was reading, so I climbed up to check it out."

I resist the urge to pet the bird. "Aw. I can't wait to see when her little babies hatch."

"See? I told ya you'd like this."

"How did you know I would?"

"You find joy in the little things in life, and this is one of them."

We stay in the tree, watching the mama bird sleep for another minute before Trey helps me climb down.

Once my feet have returned to the ground where they belong, we sit on top of our blanket and talk as the sun sets. It's not until after the stars are twinkling that I realize I haven't needed to take out our questions box yet. There hasn't been a single lull in our conversation.

We've talked about nothing yet everything at the same time. Trey told me the story of how he met Liz. He shared stories about some funny things that happened while he was on tour with his band. I cried from laughing so hard. He even willingly told me about seeing his parents' death, which was a huge step for him.

Now he's telling me about the time he woke up in a hotel

room with a naked bartender in his bed. "I left that hotel with my head spinning, feeling pretty disappointed in myself."

I gaze at him, admiring his perfectly trimmed stubble and the way he's so comfortably sharing things with me. "Why were you disappointed?"

"Because it shouldn't have happened, and I told her so. She assumed I was married."

"Why?"

"Probably because I didn't fuck her that night and was sober enough to ask her to leave the next morning."

I'm not complaining, but . . . "Why didn't you have sex with her?"

"According to her, I couldn't get it up."

My jaw drops with a laugh. "What?"

"I was so wasted, I don't even remember it. How do you expect me to perform under those circumstances? She said I was a good kisser though."

If he kisses anything like the way he does in my dreams, that woman is right. "Was she good?"

"Hell if I know."

For my benefit, I'm going to tell myself she was terrible. She probably used too much tongue and was sloppy about it.

My stomach rumbles so loudly, it makes Trey chuckle.

"You hungry?" he asks.

"A little." I tuck some hair behind my ear.

"Maybe you should go home and make something to eat." He pulls his phone out from his backpack to check the time. I don't miss how he hasn't taken out his device once since I arrived. "Shit. It's almost midnight. Shouldn't you be gone by now?"

Usually, I'm *looong* gone by now, but tonight is special. "I can stay as late as I want. I have tomorrow off." *Because I took it off with the intention of staying out late.*

"When does Caleb usually get home from work?"

"Around four in the morning."

"Shouldn't you be home before he gets there?" It's endearing that Trey cares enough about me to even *think* about making sure I'm home before Caleb is. I'm sure if it was up to Trey, he'd keep me here forever.

"You don't have to worry about Caleb. He's out of town."

"What for?'

"Rakesh's grandma's funeral." I found out yesterday that Caleb never even met Rakesh's grandma, so I don't understand why he felt the need to go to her funeral. Even if it was just to be supportive for Rakesh, taking three days off work to be at the funeral of someone he never met seems excessive.

Trey's eyes light up. "So what you're saying is that you're free to get some late-night pancakes with me?"

I nod eagerly. "That's exactly what I'm saying."

31

TREY

I can't believe my luck right now. First, she arrives two hours early. Then, she stays two hours later than usual. Now we're going to get pancakes together? Seriously? Is this real life, or have the last eight weeks just been a long hallucination?

When we step out of the woods and onto the gravel road, Arella unlocks her car and tosses her blanket onto the backseat.

"Do you want to drive separately?" I ask, because maybe she'll want to head home after we eat.

"Actually," she says, "could we take your bike?"

I can't hide my shock. "Really?"

"Yeah. I've never ridden on a motorcycle before. It looks fun."

I swallow because it's moments like this that remind me she doesn't remember me. Sometimes when we're together, I forget about what's happened to her memories, because things feel like we've picked up right where we left off. "I've only got one helmet, but there's a diner not too far from here. Are you cool with me riding without a helmet?"

"If you're okay with it, then I am."

After we stash my backpack in her car and stick her purse

and my wallet under my bike seat, I help her get my helmet on. It's a little big on her, but it'll keep her alive if we crash, which I don't intend to. As extra protection, I take my leather jacket off and hold it out to her. "Put this on."

She doesn't ask why. She simply takes my jacket and slips into it like she's been wanting to all night.

I mount my bike and pat the empty spot behind me. She throws her leg over the seat and wraps her arms around my torso the way she has before. A rush of warmth and tingles races down my legs and lingers there.

"Ready?" I ask. I almost call her *babe* but stop myself. I slipped up earlier, and even though her eyes lit up, I don't want to overdo it.

"Ready."

I start the engine, then we're off.

Riding my motorcycle with Arella takes me back to the good ol' days, when we used to do this all the time. Arella rode with me to work plenty of times. We'd take my bike to get dinner, or I'd take her back to her apartment on it. I even bought her a helmet, which later became one of the many things that disappeared from my home after the Keepers scrubbed her.

A cute twenty-four-hour diner sits on a quiet main street in the town next to where our tree stands. I pull into a front parking spot and kill my engine. Then I wait for Arella to hop off before I do.

She yanks my helmet off and hands it to me with a grin. "That was so fun."

I'm glad she enjoyed that. Probably not as much as I did though. She didn't trace her fingertips in figure eights over my abs the way she used to, but that's okay. I can't expect her to do *everything* the same as before.

Inside the cozy diner, some '70s music plays over the speakers in the ceiling. Two of the tables are occupied. One has a couple sitting on the same side of the booth, speaking in low voices to each other while they eat their waffles. The other table has a gray-haired man downing a burger.

Arella and I get seated in a corner booth.

"I'll be back with some water," our waitress says as she hands us our menus.

Once she's gone, I glance at the menu, see something I want, then set it back down. Why look at a sticky laminated piece of paper when I can stare at the delicious snack sitting across from me?

It only takes another minute for Arella to set her menu down, which means I got a full minute of uninterrupted time to admire her.

Our waitress returns with two glasses of water. "Y'all ready?"

I order my pancakes with extra whipped cream, some sausages, and eggs over easy. Arella asks for pancakes with a side of bacon. *Shit.* I should have ordered bacon too, in case she wants mine, like she has in the past. I think about changing my order, but the waitress is already gone.

Arella takes a sip of her water with a far-off look in her eyes. She's thinking about something heavy, and I wish I knew what.

I'm too curious not to ask. "What are you thinking about?"

She stares out the window at my bike. "I've been on a motorcycle with you before, haven't I?"

"What?" I say, not because I didn't hear her, but because I can't believe she just said that. Our unspoken rule is that we pretend we don't have a history and that she and Alterella are two separate people.

"Earlier, when I said I've never ridden on a motorcycle before, you got this look in your eyes."

Damn my eyeballs for always giving me away. "What look?"

"The look you always get when I say something that contradicts what you know. You got that same look when I told you I've been in love twice and again when I mentioned my pregnancy loss." She stares at me to gauge my reaction.

I keep my face impassive as I play with my hands in my lap. "I dunno what you want me to say."

"Can you tell me if I've ever been on a motorcycle with you?"

A knot tightens in my chest. If we drive down this road, I have a bad feeling we'll crash and it'll break this magic between us. Pretending that I came from an alternate universe is what's keeping our weekly slivers of heaven from feeling tense and awkward. Is she going to keep coming if things get complicated? If I start confusing her with stories of the past? Or mentioning things I know about her she doesn't recall ever telling me?

"You know what?" she says. "I don't need to hear you say it for me to know the answer. The second I sat on your bike and put my arms around you, I knew it wasn't my first time. It felt too familiar."

We never should have left the solace of our secret tree. The second we did, it changed things. She and I exist in peace there. It's a place no one else knows about, where we can be together without acknowledging the rest of the world. How am I supposed to find peace with her out here when there are thousands of things threatening to tear us apart?

"Can you at least tell me why you got that look when I told you about my miscarriage? What do you know that I don't?"

That knot in my chest pulls tighter, threatening to suffocate me from the inside out. "I, um, I don't think we should talk about this."

"Like right now in this diner or at all?"

"At all."

"Don't you think I should know?"

Yes, she *deserves* to know. *Should she know?* is a different question. This knowledge won't change anything. She'll still be married to someone else, and I'll still be forbidden from being with her. It's better if she lives in ignorance. That way, she won't have to carry all the pain and burden that comes with knowing the truth. One person doing it is enough.

"Arella, I think we should keep pretending like—"

"It was *our* baby, wasn't it?"

My bubble of bliss cracks straight down the middle. I'm about to lose my perfect little world of paradise that exists on Sunday evenings with sunsets under a tree. I can't allow this to happen. I won't.

"Arella, I—"

She slides out of her booth, climbs into mine, then throws herself into my chest. I hold her close as she quietly cries into my shirt. Her shoulders shudder, and I tear up as I let out a deep breath into the top of her hair. I can't break down right now. If I do, I might not be able to crawl out of that hole for a while.

"I'm so sorry," she whispers into my pec.

I caress little circles into her back. "You have nothing to apologize for."

"Yes, I do. I left you to grieve the loss of our baby all on your own. That must have been so hard."

It was. I lost my baby, my dad, and then Arella, all in a matter of days. But none of that was her fault. The entire situation was something neither of us had control over.

Arella wipes her wet cheeks off with the bottom of her shirt, then tilts her head back to look up at me. "Did you want to have a baby?"

"With you, yes."

"Was it something we tried for?"

"It was an accident." An accident I wish I would have known the truth about sooner. If the zovernment didn't lie to the Zordi world, saying it's impossible for us to reproduce with Ordinaries when we actually can, I never would have questioned Arella's faithfulness.

"Did you know it was a girl?"

My body goes rigid. "What?"

"After my surgery, the doctors sent the embryo to pathology. When the test results came back, it included a note that stated the embryo had **XX** chromosomes. That means it was a girl."

An invisible hand grips my lungs and squeezes all the air from them. I chomp down on my bottom lip as a debilitating wave of agony takes over my body.

I could have had a baby girl. She would have been two by now. I could have known what it's like to hold my own child in my lap and kiss her forehead. I could have known what it's like to hear a little girl call me her daddy. I could have had a family.

Hearing that our baby was a girl makes the loss more real. It makes the pain more real too. I was so close to being a father, and then it was torn away from me in the worst way possible. This miscarriage didn't happen naturally like Mia Wang said probably would have happened. Someone drugged and dropped lightning balls onto Arella until our unborn baby couldn't take it anymore.

I will never forgive Jodi for that or anything else she took away from me in her diabolical scheme to get revenge on my dad for having an affair. My mom and dad were soul mates. I used to think the soul-mate thing was just a ploy to justify adultery, but now I think it's valid. My mom and dad were meant to be together. Why get in the way of that? Why take it out on their son? Jodi could have gone off to find her own soul mate. Instead, she swapped minds with my dad and locked him up with intentions to torture him. Then she pretended to be him for over twenty years. That decision destroyed many lives and ended countless others.

The waitress returns to our table to find Arella sniffling into my shirt. She flashes me an understanding look, then without a word, she places our plates onto the table and leaves.

It takes Arella a few minutes to gather herself. Once she does, she sits up but doesn't leave my side, giving me a tender smile. "I'm ready to go back to pretending now, if that's what you want."

I return her smile. "Yes, please."

32

TREY

"I CAN'T BELIEVE THEY HATCHED ALREADY," ARELLA SAYS, smiling at the baby birds sleeping in their nest.

"The incubation period for small birds is only ten to fourteen days."

"You seem to know a lot about everything. How are you so smart?"

"Google," I say simply, and it makes her laugh.

We stand in the tree, watching the beauty of Mother Nature do its thing for a while. Eventually, the mama bird returns and sits on her babies to keep them warm, and Arella and I take that as our cue to leave them alone.

When our feet return to the ground, we immediately go back to the position we were in before I suggested seeing the nest. I lie first, then Arella nuzzles into my side with her head in the crook of my shoulder and her hand over my stomach.

We started off week nine like this. Within a minute of her coming out of the woods, she had her blanket over the grass and asked if we could cuddle. I didn't hesitate to pat my shoulder and gesture for her to come to me.

I put my arm that's not wrapped around her back behind my head like a pillow. Then I close my eyes and bask in the euphoria that comes from feeling her body against mine. It's a high that no amount of drugs has ever given me. This high also lasts longer than jaderro. After my Sunday nights with Arella, I've found myself feeling light and full for at least three days. By the fourth day, I'm still in a good mood but I'm definitely ready for my next dose of Arella.

"Trey?"

"Hmm?"

She traces a figure eight over my abs, and I couldn't be more thrilled about it. "Do you think we're soul mates?"

I know we are. "Why do you ask?"

"Because I've been doing some research on it. Did you know that soul mates can feel a connection to each other that's stronger than any other force in the world?"

"Yep."

"Did you know that my body felt it when you got into that motorcycle accident?"

"Yeah, I know." When I decided to live in New York, there was a part of me that didn't want to, in case I ever felt the glimmer again. How was I supposed to protect her from all the way across the country?

"I also read online that if soul mates are torn apart, it feels like losing a part of yourself. Do you think that's true?"

"Yes." *That's how I feel whenever I'm apart from you.*

"Did you know that just because you're soul mates, it doesn't mean you end up together?"

"Yep." My dad spent more years trapped in darkness than he spent freely in the light with my mother.

"Did you know that whenever your soul mate misses you, they appear in your dreams?"

"That, I didn't know."

"Well, it's on the Internet, so it must be true."

That gets a chuckle out of me. "If that's true, then you must dream about me a lot."

"I do."

"You do?"

"Yeah." She tilts her head back to meet my eyes. "Multiple times a week."

"For real?"

"Yeah. For the past two and a half years."

My body freezes as I gape down at her. How can she say that so nonchalantly? "Wait. Wh—what do you dream about?"

"Sometimes we're just doing mundane things like cuddling in bed or driving in a car. Other times, I've dreamt of us hanging out with your band or hanging out here at this tree."

"What was the last dream you had of me?"

"I dreamt that you beat up Nathan so badly, he left my apartment with a bloody nose and a limp."

My eyes go wide. Did it happen the same way in her dream as it did in real life? "What else have you dreamt about?"

"A few days ago, I dreamt that we were in a dark basement with an older Chinese couple, looking through a photo album."

My breath gets caught in my throat as I try to understand what the hell is going on. Are her memories returning to her in her dreams?

Arella continues, "Sometimes, I see the same dream over and over. One that has recurred a few times is the one where I'm in a kitchen with you, baking cookies, when all of a sudden, we're throwing flour at each other."

"What kind of cookies were they?"

"Snickerdoodles."

I let out a sharp gasp. Has she dreamt about everything that's happened between us? If she has, what does that mean for us? If she *hasn't*, what does that mean for us?

She keeps her eyes trained on me. "They aren't just dreams, are they?"

I clear my throat as I try to pull myself together. "If you have to ask, then you already know the answer."

"I think I've known for a while."

I put my hand over hers on my stomach as I let this sink in. "Why didn't you tell me about your dreams sooner?"

"I was afraid it would ruin what we have."

I totally understand. That's the same reason why I don't say half the shit I want to say to her either. "Why are you telling me now?"

"Because you actually talked to me about losing our baby instead of keeping up this charade that we don't have a past together. I understand why, because I do it too, but I felt like you should know about my dreams."

"I'm glad you told me." *Even though I have no idea what to do with this information.* At the end of the day, this changes nothing.

She pushes herself up and sits with her legs to the side. "Can you tell me what happened to my memories?"

I sit up too, then cross my legs. "I can't."

"Because you'll be taken to prison by the government from the future?"

I let out a laugh. "You think I'm from the future?"

"It's a possibility."

This reminds me of the time she asked if I was a superhero or an alien. Is that moment something she's dreamt about too?

"You've been watching all the Disney canon movies with Liz, right?" she asks me.

"We finished that already." Like six months ago.

"You saw *Snow White and the Seven Dwarves*, then?"

"It wasn't a favorite, but yes."

"Do you remember how Prince Charming broke the spell that was cast on Snow White?"

Where is she going with this? "Yep. True love's kiss."

"What if that's what can bring back all my memories?"

I sigh a little. "It won't."

"How do you know?"

"Because you're not under a magic spell. Plus, that would be too easy, and I've had twenty-nine years to learn that nothing in my life ever comes easy."

She rubs the ends of her hair between her fingers. "Don't you think we should at least try?"

Try what? To break a magic spell she's not under? One that doesn't even exi— *Wait* . . . "Are you saying you want me to kiss you?"

She nods and whispers, "Desperately."

That's all the permission I need. I seize her face and crash my lips against hers. She clutches my shirt and pulls me into her as our lips dance with each other like they've been waiting to for their entire existence.

I claw at her to come closer, and she does. She climbs into my lap, straddling me as she plunges her tongue into my mouth. My need for her has never been so strong.

My hand slides up her back, then I yank her closer to me, desperate to feel her breasts against my chest. Her fingernails scratch up the back of my head, then she pulls my hair at the top.

I groan as my cock hardens in my jeans. "Arella . . ."

"The spell isn't broken yet," she says breathlessly against my mouth. "Let's keep trying."

I don't need to be asked twice.

With my lips attacking hers, I gently lower her back to the ground until I'm on top of her. Then I straddle her and kiss her like a starving beast as she moans beneath me.

My lips travel down her neck, and she arches her head back to give me more access. I nip and suck on her skin as she lets out breathy groans and claws at my back. I want to feel her skin against mine, and I hate that all this fabric is in the way.

As if reading my mind, she reaches under my shirt and

slides her palms up my bare chest. That does it for me. I do a push-up over her, then hold myself up with one arm as I tear my shirt over my head. It goes flying somewhere behind me.

I'm about to go back to kissing her neck when she drags her shirt over her head too. Then she throws it in the general direction I threw mine. Two perfectly plump breasts peek out at me from behind a purple lace bra. My hands itch to grab her tits, but I don't. What if that's too far for her?

She must see my hesitation, because she makes the decision for me. Within seconds, she unhooks her bra and flings it to the side. "It's not like you've never seen them before."

She's right. It's not like I've never sucked on them before either. She lets out a gasp as I drop my mouth over her nipple and suck it in. My other hand cups her other breast, then I roll her nipple between my fingers.

If someone would have told the man I was two and a half years ago that this is what I'd be doing right now, it might have been easier for me to get sober. This moment is worth all the agony I felt as I forced myself to stay away from her. I never thought she'd ever be so willing to let me touch her like this again.

"Is the spell broken yet?" I ask as I switch to tasting her other nipple.

She clutches the back of my head and presses me to her chest harder. "No. Just keep going."

I can't disobey her, so I suck her nipple into my mouth even harder. She tastes as good as I remember—maybe even sweeter because I waited so long for this.

My hips grind against her body before I even realize they're doing it. As I go back to kissing her lips, she fights with the button of my jeans, wins, then yanks my zipper down. After I kick my shoes off, she shoves the denim down my legs. Then I yank my socks off and climb back on top of her in only my boxers.

I return to nipping at her neck as she slips out of her shorts. They thump onto the ground behind her head. I pepper kisses down her chest and stomach, then gasp. I didn't realize she took her panties off too. I didn't even get to see what color they are.

I'm about to ask for permission to lick her when she grips the back of my head and slams my face into her clit. *So. Fucking. Hot.* I suck her clit into my mouth as she moans my name.

"Trey. Oh, god. That feels so good."

I stick two fingers into her only to find she's already wet. *God, this woman. She's going to be the end of me.* I pound my fingers into her, making her writhe beneath me.

"Yes," she says all breathily. "Don't stop."

"I won't, baby. Not unless you beg me to."

I stare at her with utter admiration as my fingers slam in and out of her. She keeps her eyes closed and her head back as she accepts all the pleasure I'm giving her. I want to keep giving it to her. I want to see her satisfied and hear her scream my name.

"You like that, baby?"

She nods and slides her thumbs between the elastic of my boxers. I stop fingering her so she can wrench my boxers off. My thick cock bounces up, the tip already wet. She's about to grab it when I seize her wrist and slam it above her head.

My voice comes out husky. "If you touch me, I'm——"

"Own me, Trey."

Those are the same words she said to me the first time we ever made love to each other. "Are you sure?"

"Yes." A flame of desire spreads within her eyes. "I want you, Trey. I've wanted you for a long time."

"I've wanted you for even longer." I pull her legs up and place my tip at her damp opening, sliding it up and down. "Once we do this, there's no going back."

"I know."

I don't think she knows what I mean. If we do this, there won't be any more Sunday evenings here where I talk to her and only *pretend* she's mine. Once we do this, I'm going to *make* her mine. "Are you sure this is what you want?"

"Yes, Trey. I'm sure."

I lean down to kiss her lips until it turns into a frenzied act of desperate need again. I want this woman with every fiber of my being, and I'll never feel complete until I have her back. I need her to be a part of me, not apart from me. I need her to be my rock, my savior, my sun to shine bright on all my darkest days. In return, I'll be hers, and I'll never falter from the duties that come with that. Never.

She pulls away from my lips and pants. "Trey?"

"Yeah, baby?"

"Don't be gentle with me."

That's all I need to hear to stop hesitating. I plunge my cock into her, making her scream out. She wraps around me, all tight and wet. I gasp as the pleasure ripples through me, and my climax threatens to explode out of me.

"Oh, fuck. You feel amazing."

Her fingernails dig into my back as I pull back and thrust into her again. I take deep breaths to hold back my release. I can't come this soon. I've barely had her.

She moans my name, and it brings me to the brink.

Fuuuck. "I don't think I can last long, babe. It's been so long for me."

"That's okay. We'll just have to do it again."

"You're going to let me have you twice?" I can't believe my ears.

"Yes, Trey. I want you twice."

I'm gonna need to find out what I did to deserve this, because whatever it is, I need to keep doing it. I take her waist into my hands and hold her still, then I pound into her over and over. She screams as her body takes every inch of me slamming into her.

The orgasm builds inside me, and I try to hold it back, but I can't anymore. I need to get one out. After that, I'll be able to focus on her pleasure instead of mine.

I'm almost there. "Babe, where do you want me to come?"

"Inside me."

"But what if—"

"Trey, just come inside. Please."

Hearing her beg is what does it for me. I continue thrusting until the pleasure becomes too much and I groan as my orgasm consumes me. I know she can feel me pulsing, because she moans and clutches my arms the way she used to. I pour every drop of my load into her, then I collapse on top of her.

Our heavy breaths sync together as I spiral down from my orgasm. She holds my head against her chest as if she's not ready for me to go anywhere yet. I wouldn't, even if I could. I can barely feel my arms right now. I'm too high from being inside her to feel anything except her beating heart against the side of my face.

Once we catch our breaths, she asks, "Were you going to say, 'What if you get pregnant?' "

"Yeah." *Word for word.*

"You don't have to worry about that. I'm not ovulating."

I'm not worried about getting her pregnant. I'm more worried that I *won't* be able to again. Either way, that's not something I want to think about right now. I kiss her, then grin. "Does that mean I can come inside you again?"

Her face lights up with an eager smile. "Yes, please."

33

ARELLA

"Oh, Trey," I say through a moan.

His face is buried between my legs while his fingers work their magic inside me. The way he licks me with the perfect amount of pressure is sending me to the edge. It's only been a few minutes, and I'm already about to burst.

My hands clench the back of his hair as I arch my head back against the blanket and let out a guttural moan. This is exactly how he pleasures me in my dreams, and I wouldn't have it any other way.

"I'm going to come," I pant toward the branches above us.

Trey peeks his head up as his fingers keep moving inside me. "Not yet, baby."

"What?" I open my eyes, just to gape at him. "Why?"

"Because I haven't gotten my fill of you yet."

"But I'm so close."

"Not yet, babe. Hold it back." His mouth dips to suck my clit again, and I writhe beneath him. The more the pleasure builds up inside me, the more I dig my fingernails into his shoulders.

I've imagined him doing this to me for weeks, and my imagination is *nothing* compared to the real thing. This man knows exactly how to touch me. He knows exactly where to put his fingers and exactly how hard to press. How many times have we done this for him to learn all that?

With his fingers still inside me, he pops up to take my nipple into his mouth. I shout his name toward the stars. My body tingles from head to toe, and I'm dripping wet. I feel it running down my butt cheeks.

I need to release. "Can I come now?"

"Not yet," he says, then reburies his face between my thighs.

I clench my hands in the blanket. "But I want to come so bad."

"Almost, baby. Just let me enjoy this a little longer."

"Oh, god. I can't hold it back any longer."

His fingers rub little circles over my clit in a steady rhythm. "Keep holding it, babe."

"Trey, please! I'm . . . Oh, god. I'm . . ."

"Okay, baby. Come for me." He rubs me a little faster, using the same pressure.

I moan his name and feel the pleasure rising inside me until I finally jump over the edge. I scream out as ripples of bliss take me over. My legs shake. My hands tug at the blanket. I'm panting like my lungs are fighting for their next breath.

When I open my eyes, I'm disoriented. I can't remember the last time I had such a powerful orgasm.

Trey stares at me with a look of satisfaction. Then he grips his hard cock and gives it a few strokes. "You ready for me again?"

Breathlessly, I nod.

Without another word, he pulls my legs over his shoulders, then plunges his cock back inside me. I let out a deep moan and arch my head back as he thrusts his thick erection in and out of me, over and over.

I'm still sensitive from my orgasm, so he feels even better this time. Our chests slide against each other as he grunts out his pleasure. I love being able to hear him like this. So raw and unfiltered.

"You feel amazing, baby," he pants into my neck.

I'm veering off the blanket and into the grass, but I don't care. I just don't want him to stop.

Trey kisses the soft spot behind my ear, then peppers his lips down to my collarbone. His breath sends tingles down my spine as he keeps a steady rhythm thrusting into me.

He's about to lean back when I seize the back of his hair and force him back down to me. He doesn't need me to ask before he returns his lips to my neck. I arch my head the other way to give him more skin to play with, and he takes it as permission to suck a little harder. I whimper from the pain that quickly turns into pleasure.

"Are you ready for more?" he asks into my collarbone.

"Mm-hmm."

He pushes himself up, then grabs my hips to keep me securely against him. Then he relentlessly slams his dick into me.

In, out, in, out.

Harder, faster, harder, faster.

I scream out his name over and over as he arches his head back, taking all the pleasure he can get from me.

"Fuck, baby," he growls. " You make me wanna come so bad."

"Come inside me, Trey. I want to feel you."

"Can you take me harder?"

"Yes."

With that, he positions my legs over his shoulders again and props himself up on his hands. Then he pulls his hips back and drives himself into me as hard as he can. His cock hits my back wall over and over until he groans to the stars and I feel him pulsate inside me again.

He cries out as he hammers every last drop of his orgasm

into me. I wrap my legs around his back, making sure I get all of it.

Only once his cock stops throbbing does he slide out of me, then he falls onto his side, panting. I'm left in that dazed state again, feeling a large empty hole where his thick cock used to be.

He grabs me by the shoulders, wrenches me against his body, and breathes into my hair. I melt into his chest, feeling more protected by him than I would if I was surrounded by an army. With Trey, I feel peace. With Trey, I feel like I can be anything I want to be. Like I can accomplish anything. Like I can—

"Arella." With a finger, he tilts my chin up until our eyes connect. "Will you come home with me?"

My body stiffens. "What?"

"Come home with me, baby. Be mine again."

Something in my chest locks up, and suddenly, I can't breathe. His words sound like a question and a request all in one. Go home with him? Like, forever? "I . . . I can't."

"I promise I'll love you and take good care of you. I'll make sure that you're happy. I'll help you reach all your dreams and goals, and I'll encourage you whenever you're down. You'll never have to doubt my love for you because I'll show it to you every minute of the day."

That all sounds wonderful. Any other woman would love to hear those words come out of a man's mouth. But me, I want to hear them from my husband's mouth. *Don't I?*

Oh, god. My husband. Caleb. I forgot that he existed. It's easy to do that whenever I'm with Trey. Under this tree, I forget about the rest of the world and all my troubles that come with it. Here, I'm safe and I feel wanted. Out there, I feel like something's missing and—

"We could have a family." Trey clutches my face and plants his forehead against mine. "I want that more than anything, and I know you want it too. I'll work hard to be a good father. I'll take parenting classes and read lots of books. I'll protect you and our babies like—"

"Trey, stop." *Please.*

"Arella, we belong together."

"But . . ." The words get lost on their way out. I clear my throat and try again. "But I'm married."

"Leave him," he says like he's been wanting to for weeks.

I sit up, feeling more naked than ever. "I . . . I can't just leave him."

"Why not? He doesn't even appreciate you."

Trey's not wrong, but that doesn't mean I should give up on Caleb. "What am I supposed to tell him?" Or Javina? Or my grandparents? My friends from work? They all love Caleb. *I* love Caleb . . . *don't I?*

"Tell him you've found someone who wants to love you right. The way you deserve to be loved."

"I can't do that. It'll hurt him." I stand to search the grass for my clothes. I find my panties first and put them on, ignoring how damp my inner thighs are. Then I pick up my bra and hook it on.

Trey slips into his boxers with a hard look on his face. "You weren't ever supposed to marry him anyway. What happened to your memories only made you *think* you were in love with Caleb."

Again, he's not wrong, but that doesn't mean Caleb and I haven't built a life together. We love each other now, and we're partners. I know it hasn't looked that way recently, but it's just a phase we're working through. *Isn't it?* "That doesn't change that I still married him."

"Only because you don't remember being with me."

"For reasons you refuse to tell me," I snap and instantly regret it. I'm not angry at him. I'm angry at myself. At all these answers I don't have.

Trey hands me my shirt, and I slip into it. Somehow, he's able to keep his chill. In a gentle tone, he says, "I refuse to tell you because I can't. But you remember me in your dreams. Maybe that means you can try to remember what happened to your memories."

"Don't you think that if I could remember, I would have by now?"

The air goes silent as we finish getting dressed. I'm about to pick up my blanket when Trey takes my hands into his. "Maybe being together will help trigger more memories for you. And even if it doesn't, I don't care. I want to be with you whether you remember being with me or not. We can leave the past in the past and start from here."

"But what about Caleb?" More guilt eats at me with each second I spend here, talking about my husband with the man who isn't. "I can't just leave him, Trey."

He drops my hands and takes a step back, putting a whole arm's length of distance between us. "Then why did you seduce me?"

"I . . ." That's a good question. *What was I thinking?*

"If you didn't want to be with me, then why did you allow me to make love to you?"

"I'm sorry. I got caught up in the moment, but now that my head is clear, I'm realizing I shouldn't have done that."

This isn't like me. I'm not the type of person who does these types of things. Why did I tonight? Am I just frustrated about my relationship with Caleb feeling like a train wreck? Am I allowing his recent distance to dictate my actions?

Trey drags a palm through his hair, unintentionally showing me his veiny arm muscles. Those muscles were wrapped around me barely a minute ago as I moaned his name to the starry sky. How did I do all that and not once think about Caleb?

"I don't understand," Trey says with a huff. "If you don't want to be with me, then why did you—was that a test? Did you just want to see if I'd do it?"

"Of course not." *I think.* I'd like to say I'm a faithful

woman, but if I can't say that anymore, then am I the type to play mind games too?

"Is it because you haven't had sex in a while and I was an easy target?"

"No." *I think.* I'm not sure anymore.

"I don't want to be used, Arella. I allowed someone to use me before, and I told myself I'd never allow that again."

"I wasn't trying to use you, Trey. I don't know why I did that or what I wanted from it. I just—it felt right in the moment."

"And now it doesn't?"

My eyes fall to the grass. "I . . . I don't know."

Trey takes my hands again and gives them a comforting squeeze. "Look, baby, I know you're confused, and that's okay. You've got two conflicting parts inside you: the part that thinks you're in love with Caleb, and the part that's actually in love with me. I understand that, and I've been patient about it. Hell, I let you go for almost three years without knowing if you'd ever come back to me. But you did, and I don't want to ever let you go again. You belong with me, Arella. I know you know that. You've said it yourself. We're soul mates."

I choke up because there's so much truth in those words. However, the other truth is that I've already made a commitment to someone else. Caleb's recent emotional absence and lack of physical attention don't mean I shouldn't honor the vows we made to each other. *Right?*

Or is that just my past self talking? Am I doing that thing again where I make up excuses to stay with a man who doesn't treat me the way I want to be treated? Am I doing that thing again where I convince myself to stay in a relationship because it's easier than getting out? Or because I have hopes that he will change?

Maybe it's *me* who needs to change. Maybe I should be a better wife to Caleb. I have been pretty naggy lately. I suppose

I could lay off bringing up all the things that bother me about him.

Maybe he needs more space. I suppose I could spend more time alone or with my friends. I need to work on getting a loan for my bakery anyway. I could put more time into that.

I could stop asking him for intimacy too. It's not like I *need* to have sex with him to know he loves me. He still tells me enough. I don't remember the last time he did, but it's within the last week for sure.

The bottom line is that Caleb loves me, and I think I should give him more time to . . . well, I don't know. Figure out how to work through his stress without letting it affect our marriage?

Whatever it is, I don't want to hurt him. Unfortunately, someone in this situation is going to get hurt, and if it's not Caleb, that means it has to be Trey.

"Not all soul mates end up together," I say with a lump in my throat.

Trey's shoulders slump as he drops my hands. "That's the excuse you want to stand on?"

"It's not an excuse. It's true."

"But you're with someone who doesn't truly love you. He only *thinks* he loves you because he had his memories altered that way. But *me*, Arella, *I* love you. Deeply. I feel it every moment of the day. Please, baby. Come home with me. I know there are logistics we'll have to figure out, but I'm confident that as long as we're together, we can make it."

For a split second, I consider it. I picture myself running home, packing up what I own, and running off with Trey. Then I picture the conversation I'd have to have with Caleb. I imagine telling him that we need to get a divorce. That everything we have together no longer matters. I picture my sweet husband sobbing from the heartbreak, and it kills me. I can't do that to him.

I look into Trey's eyes and hope he can see how much it kills me to do this too. "I'm sorry, Trey. I just can't."

"So that's it then?" He throws his arms out, letting them drop back to his sides. "You're just gonna go home and pretend like *we* never happened?"

"I have to."

"But do you *want* to?"

Not really. "I don't have a choice. I made a vow to be with Caleb."

Trey scoffs like that's the most ridiculous thing he's ever heard. "Vows can be broken. Half the married people in this fucking country do it."

"That doesn't mean I want to be one of them."

He huffs and shakes his head. "So let me get this straight: When you asked me to kiss you, you did it knowing you wouldn't leave him for me, and not once did you stop to think about how that would affect me?"

I didn't, and now that he puts it that way, I feel even worse. This whole time, I've been so focused on feeling guilty about betraying Caleb, I didn't think about how I was betraying Trey too.

He continues, "You know how I feel about you. It's not a fucking secret. Didn't you think it was wrong to play with my heart like this?"

"I'm sorry, Trey. I made a mistake." The second that comes out of my mouth, I know it's a lie. Everything I just did with Trey didn't *feel* like a mistake. It felt right. This is the first moment it has ever felt wrong—and only because society would say so. Inside, I'm not entirely convinced. Being with Trey has always felt right. Letting him touch me feels right. Even picturing a life with him feels right. So why can't I bring myself to do it?

"You just slept with me *twice*, Arella. That's not a mistake. That's a choice."

"I won't let it happen again," I lie, because if he kissed me right now, I wouldn't stop him.

He takes a step back as if he needs more distance from me. "So that's all I am to you? A mistake?"

"No. That's not what I meant."

"Then what did you mean?"

"Just that I shouldn't have let things get that far."

"But you did." He gapes at me like he can't believe what's happening.

I'm with him on that because I can't believe what's happening either. What have I done? And why do I feel so conflicted? My head is telling me I should leave while my heart is begging me to stay.

Trey swallows hard, his breaths going ragged. "You wanna know something I've learned in my fucked-up life? It's that when other people make *mistakes*, somehow I'm always the one who ends up paying for them." In one swift motion, he scoops up his backpack and tosses a strap over his shoulder. Without another look at me, he marches away.

I run after him and stop in front of him with my hands up to his chest. "Where are you going?"

"The airport." He doesn't stop. He only swerves past me.

I stay where I am. "You can't just leave like this."

He twists around with his arms out to his sides. "How do you want me to leave? Do you want me to tell you that my heart's not broken? Do you want us to go back to the way things were when we were living in our own little world of make-believe? Do you want me to walk you to your car and die inside as I watch you drive back home to *him*? I can't do that, Arella. I told you once we went that far, there was no going back. So—this is me—not going back." He hurries toward the woods again.

I catch up to him and stop him with a hand to his chest. He feels hard under my palm. "I don't like ending things like this."

"How do you want to end things, then?"

I lower my hand because I don't like feeling how tense he is. "On a good note."

"There is no good note. At least not for me. You know what's stupid is that I've always known this was going to end badly. Right from the start, I knew that eventually, you would leave and I'd be left with nothing.

"Yet every single week, I showed up here, willing you to come out of those trees. You know why? Because I'm so fucking in love with you that even knowing I would get hurt in the end couldn't stop me from yearning to see you.

"The stupidest part is that even if someone had told me at the beginning that this is a thousand percent how it would end, I would have come here to see you anyway. Because these last nine weeks with you are worth all the pain I'll have to endure trying to let you go again."

For a second time, I consider taking the other path—the one where I choose Trey. I can vividly see us in my new bakery together. I can picture myself getting to know his friends and supporting him in his musical career. I can picture us growing old together. In a perfect world, that's how it'd be.

But we don't live in a perfect world, and things happen. What if it doesn't work out between us? What if our relationship turns toxic? What if he ends up changing his mind? What if he gets too busy for me, and we drift apart the way Caleb and I have? I would have left my marriage for nothing, and I'd be right back where I am now.

"Why don't we try to come up with a solution that will make us both happy?" I say.

"The only thing that's going to make me happy is you saying you'll be with me. So I'm going to ask you one last time, Arella. And if you say anything other than *yes*, I'm heading straight to the airport, and I'm not looking back." He sucks in a deep breath, then blows it out. "Will you, please, leave him for me?"

I can't believe he's trying to force me into a big decision like this on the spot. Even if I knew that everything would work out for us, that doesn't mean I can just drop my husband without even talking to him first. "I'm sorry, Trey. I just can't."

The light that's been shining in his eyes for the last nine weeks suddenly goes dark. He takes one long look at me as if he thinks it's the last time he'll ever be able to. Then, without a single word, he turns and disappears into the trees.

I'm left stunned and speechless.

By the time I've gathered myself enough to realize I should chase after him, it's too late. When I run out to the gravel road, his bike is gone.

34

TREY

She's not coming. I mean, why would she? She has no reason to. The way we left things last week didn't exactly cultivate the most welcoming environment to elicit her return.

I shouldn't have said some of the things I said. I shouldn't have walked away like that either. What I should have done is given her more time to think about it. After a whole week of brooding over this, I realized that I pushed her too far, too fast. I got too caught up in the moment and all the feels of having her back that I didn't stop to think about how I was making her feel by asking her to drop her husband for me. Just because I'd be willing to drop everything for her doesn't mean I should expect the same.

I confided in Liz about the whole situation. At first, she was ticked that I never told her about my Sundays with Arella. Then she told me I was an idiot for thinking Arella would up and leave her marriage in a snap. At the end of the conversation, Liz encouraged me to write a letter with all the things I'd like to say to Arella the next time I see her—*if* I ever get to see her.

Slumped against our oak tree, I take my earbuds out of my backpack and shove them into my ears. I need to calm my mind because it's eight thirty. If she was coming, she'd be here by now.

The sun has almost set for the evening. If she's not here by midnight, I'll head to the airport and accept that I'll never see her again. And if this meditation doesn't work, I'll go for a short walk through the woods. Short because I don't want to miss it if she does show up.

I find a meditation that's an hour long because that's how much time I'm gonna need to calm my mind.

"Focus on your breaths," the lady on the app says as I lie back on the grass and shut my eyes. "Breathe in deep. Breathe out slowly."

I do what she says as relaxing music plays in my ears. I've got the volume all the way up because I need it loud enough to block out the screams in my head telling me I'm not good enough. Maybe if I was, she'd be here.

I haven't gone a single second without thinking of her or regretting the way I stormed off. I was just hurt, and I didn't know what else to do. Staying there with her when I knew she wasn't leaving with me felt like torture. Even so, the second I mounted my bike and rode off, I wanted to go straight back.

But there was nothing to go back to. She told me I was a mistake. I stood there offering her my whole heart and soul, and she didn't want it. I still don't know what she wanted from me or why she would let me make love to her without any intention of staying with me. Maybe she just wanted to feel loved because she's not getting it at home. Maybe she wanted to see how easy it'd be to seduce me.

Turns out, I'm easy. All she had to do was ask, and I was all over her. She should have known that I'm a weak man—especially when it comes to her. She could ask me to do anything, and I'd—

"Ah!" I scream when something pokes my arm. I jolt upright and yank my earbuds out. What's left of my shattered heart thumps wildly in my chest. "Arella."

She offers me a tender smile. "Sorry."

I stand and stash my earbuds in my jeans pocket. "You came back."

"Yeah. I didn't want to leave things the way we did."

"I didn't either. That's why I wrote down a whole list of apologies and other things I want to say to you." From the inner pocket of my leather jacket, I pull out a folded sheet of paper and hold it up.

Arella smiles warmly as she slips a piece of paper out of her back shorts pocket. "I wrote down some things I want to say to you too."

I hope that's a good sign. I mentally prepare to hear what she has to say. "Would you like to go first?"

"No, you go first."

"Sure. Would you like to sit?"

She hesitates, making my eyes drift to her empty arms. *Where's her blanket?* Its absence makes all my hopes deflate. Before I can think about it too hard, she plops onto the grass, and I join her.

With shaky hands, I unfold my letter and read it aloud. "Arella, I'm sorry for what happened. I didn't mean to make you feel uncomfortable or push you to do something you didn't want to do. I'll never make you feel that way again, because I don't ever want to make you feel like you *have* to be with me. What I want is for you to *want* to be with me.

"That's why I'm going to give you time. It was wrong of me to try to force you into making a big decision that night. I should have simply told you how I felt about you, then let you make that decision yourself. So please, take as much time as you need. In the end, if you choose me, I promise I'll love you until my last breath. I promise I'll—"

I stop reading because Arella's face drops. That's not the reaction I was hoping for. I'm not even halfway through my letter yet, and I don't think I should continue. The rest of it includes all the reasons why she should choose me, but maybe it's too much to ask her to love me back this soon. I've been in love with her for years, but she's only gotten to know me within the last nine weeks. This might be moving too fast for her. I guess I don't *need* her to love me back right now. *I could settle for less . . .*

With a long sigh, I crumple up my letter and shove it back into my inner jacket pocket. "You know what? I just realized that I don't need much from you to be happy. I don't need you to choose me, if that's not what you want. Seeing you once a week is enough for me. Actually, even if you only come once a month or once a year, I'll be fine with that. Honestly, I'll take whatever you're willing to give me."

I pause for a moment to see if she'll say something. She doesn't, so I continue speaking from the heart. "Arella, you've made me feel so alive lately, because without you, I always feel like I'm missing something. I think you kept coming here because you felt like you were missing something too, and whatever that was, you were getting it from me.

"So tell me what you want from me, and I'll give it to you. If you want me to pretend like last week never happened, I can do that. If you want to go back to being friends and live in our little bubble where we just talk and answer question cards, I'll make it happen.

"Hell, I'll even let you use me, if that's what you want. Just tell me what you need me to be for you. Whether that's a big part of your life or a small one, I'll learn to accept it. I'll learn to be happy with it. Because the bottom line is, I just want *you*. However I can get that, I'll settle for it."

"Oh, Trey . . ." She rubs her hair between her fingers, barely looking at me. "Maybe I should have gone first."

That doesn't sound good.

She unfolds her paper and is about to read it when I push it into her lap.

I hold back the tears threatening to fall as I choke out, "I've got a feeling that your letter is your way of letting me down softly." I give her a moment to deny that. When she doesn't, the shattered pieces of my heart break more. "This gaping hole in my chest can only take so much, okay? Can you just skip the fluff and give it to me straight? Did you come here tonight to say goodbye to me?"

The way she creases her eyebrows together with sorrow is all the answer I need, but she verbalizes it to me anyway. "I came to give you a proper goodbye because I didn't want to leave things the way we did last week."

The world stops turning and fades to gray as Arella continues talking. She goes on for a while, but I don't catch it all. What I hear are snippets of her explanation as to why she can't see me anymore.

"I owe it to Caleb and our marriage to try to make things work." She says some other bullshit about how she spoke to him last week, and how they've agreed to work harder on their relationship. She even gives me some examples, like how they're going to have more date nights and make an effort to actually converse with each other. The more she talks, the more I spiral into a deep hole I'm not sure I'll ever be able to crawl out of.

Since this is the last time I'm ever going to see her, I stare at her face as she continues explaining shit to me. I memorize the curve of her cheeks and the shape of her nose. I reminisce on how it felt to finally kiss her plump lips again. I try to ingrain every little detail of her into my head so that whenever I need it, I'll be able to conjure up an image of her at will within seconds.

During our years apart, I started to forget what she looked like because I never got the chance to memorize her face. Maybe doing so now will help me remember her ten, twenty, or even fifty years from now. *Fuck. Fifty years without her?* That sounds like hell. Can I make it that long? Probably not. At least, not without some self-medi—

She pats my forearm. "Trey?"

"Hmm?"

"Did you hear me?"

I nod slightly as an invisible snake slithers around my lungs, strangling me from the inside out.

"What did I just say?"

"You said that you're . . ." The words get caught in my dry throat. "That you're never coming back."

"Did you hear anything I said after that?"

Mostly, sorta, not really. "Yeah, I heard you."

"What did I say?"

I swallow thickly, then bite the inside of my mouth. *You said that you love Caleb and that . . .* My tone comes out broken. "Please don't make me repeat it out loud." I can't even do it in my head.

"Did you hear my question?"

I suck in a ragged breath. "What was your question again?"

"I asked if you understand why I made my decision this way."

I definitely was not listening when she asked that, nor do I understand. "Yeah, I understand."

"I'm really sorry."

My breathing turns shallow, and my head feels like gravity is pulling me toward the center of the earth. There, I'll get swallowed whole and die an agonizing death. That'd be better than staying up here, forced to live out the rest of my life in my own personal hell.

My hand trembles against my thigh, and it takes me a few seconds to realize what's happening. I can't allow this panic attack to take control of me right now. Not while she's still here.

If it's bad enough, like to the point where I feel like I'm having a heart attack, my powers will go wack. If Arella sees a tree catching fire out of nowhere and the zovernment finds out about it, she's going to get scrubbed again. I can't let that happen. We've made some great memories here together, and I want her to remember them.

I close my eyes and take in three long, deep breaths.

In . . . out . . .

In . . . out . . .

In . . . out . . .

Once my breathing is under control and my hands are less shaky, I ask, "Will you go on a walk with me?"

"I'd love to."

I stand and think about offering her my hand, but I don't. I won't be able to handle feeling her skin like that. Not even if it's for a second.

Arella stands on her own and offers me a sweet smile.

I don't return it. It's taking everything in me to keep from falling over right now. I don't have the capacity to steady my breaths and fake a smile at the same time.

I head toward the dark woods behind our tree with Arella at my side. The black sky hangs above us with a dirty yellow moon and no stars.

My throat feels muggy as I work on sucking in more air. I don't think my body is getting enough oxygen, because I'm feeling a little light-headed. Or maybe that's the panic attack? Who knows?

The trail going through the forest is just wide enough for Arella and me to hike side by side. I shove my hands into my jeans pockets in an attempt to keep them from accidentally touching her. Then I concentrate on my feet the way my zerapist told me to: *"Just focus on putting one foot in front of the other. And if it helps, you can count your steps."*

So I do. *One . . . two . . . three . . .*

Twenty-one . . . twenty-two . . . twenty-three . . .

Arella taps my arm. "Trey?"

I force my head up. "Hmm?"

"Did you hear me?"

"Sorry. What did you say?"

"I asked if there's anything you'd like to talk about."

I shake my head. "Is there anything you'd like to talk about?"

"I think I said everything I wanted to earlier."

"Okay." The air goes quiet as I start my unhelpful step-counting activity from the top. *One . . . two . . . three . . .*

"If there's nothing you want to talk about, then why'd you ask me to go on a walk with you?"

I think about coming up with a filtered answer, but that would require more effort than I have to give right now. My words come out slow and somber like I've just woken up from a deep sleep. "I just needed to walk because I felt a panic attack coming. I also wasn't ready for you to leave yet, and it felt like you were about to." *This was my way of getting you to stay longer.*

"You get panic attacks?"

"Occasionally." *All the time.* "Let's not talk about it though. The point of walking is to help me forget about it."

"Right." She ducks under a branch, then says, "Why don't we talk about what you're working on with your band?"

I appreciate her attempt at trying to lighten the mood, but . . . "I'm not really in a good mind-set to talk right now, but if you want to talk, I'm happy to listen."

"I was talking earlier, but it didn't seem like you were listening."

"Sorry." I swallow some pain, then let out an unsteady breath. "It's just a little hard for me to concentrate right now."

She stops in the middle of the trail, making me stop too. "Trey, you're scaring me."

"How so?"

"For starters, you're quiet, and that's not like you. The Trey I know is always keeping up a conversation with me."

That version of Trey is the alive one—the one who was living under a false pretense that he could handle the consequences of losing the love of his life again. When I told myself I could handle it, it was because at the time, I was too high off the joy to care.

Turns out, I was wrong. I can't handle this. I feel like I've got a searing-hot knife sticking out of my chest and the weight of the world on my shoulders.

She continues, "When you answer my questions, you say the bare minimum, and you're doing that thing again where you answer my questions with a version of the truth instead of the full truth."

I let out a huff as I toss my arms into the air. "What would you rather I do?"

"Be open with me."

"I've been open with you! Look what that got me. I've got a one-way ticket back to nothing." I don't mean to raise my voice at her, but, goddamn, is it hard not to. "I don't think you understand that before you came back, I was drowning. Sometimes, if I was lucky and if I swam hard enough, I was able to come up for a single breath of air—only to get pulled right back down. I was constantly fighting to live and to feel any sense of belonging or purpose.

"Then one night, you came out of those fucking trees like a goddamn lifesaver. I didn't have to fight for my next breath anymore. I was exactly where I needed to be, doing exactly what I needed to be doing.

"For a whole week after that, I felt like I was standing in the shallow end. I was able to breathe without fighting for air, but still headed toward the depths. Then you showed up a second time and—" I snap my fingers. "Just like that, I'm saved again."

I shove my hands through my messy hair, shaking my head at myself. "I'm quiet because I'm scared, okay? I'm scared of what it's gonna be like to fall back into the deep end. This time, it'll be like my feet are tied to bricks. I'm afraid of returning to the bad habits I've worked so hard to fight off. I'm afraid of the person I'll become when I finally lose that battle. But mostly, I'm fucking terrified of not submitting to the numbing remedies because it means suffering through the raw misery of every day I have to live without you."

Tears glisten in her eyes. "Oh, Trey . . ."

"No." I turn my head away and aim my gaze at a tree. "Don't look at me like that. I don't want pity."

"I never meant to hurt you."

"I know." I soften my stance, then sigh and lower my voice. "I'm sorry for raising my voice at you. I'm not mad at you; I'm mad at myself. Deep down, I always knew you'd leave and that once you did, it would destroy me. I made the choice to continue seeing you anyway, and that choice came with consequences I'm gonna have to live with."

My breathing sounds like I'm suffocating. The anxiety is consuming me again. I need it to stop, so I don't think about it as I seize Arella's hand and cup it against my cheek. She allows me to hold it there while I close my eyes and work on some deep breaths.

It takes me a minute to steady my heart rate and reopen my eyes. A pair of beautiful brown ones stare back at me.

"Did that help?" she asks.

"It always does."

For a moment, I imagine throwing her over my shoulder and taking her home with me. I'll convince her that she belongs with me, and after a while, she'll believe it. She'll fall madly in love with me like I am with her. She'll want to have my kids, we'll support each other in our careers, and then we'll live happily ever after.

I let out a long sigh as I mourn the loss of the life I want so badly. Maybe in an alternate universe somewhere, another version of me has all that. Sadly, I'm stuck here, where Arella can't be mine and I can't do anything about it.

I gesture toward the trail we're stopped on. "Let's keep walking."

For a while, we trudge through the woods with only the sounds of our breaths and the crickets wailing in the tall grass.

I stare at my feet and count my steps again because it gives my mind something to focus on other than the idea of masking this ache with the first illegal substance I can get my hands on.

One . . . two . . . three . . .

Arella keeps a steady pace next to me. "Do you regret it?"

"Regret what?"

"Any of it. Our time together."

"No," I say without missing a beat. "If given the choice, I'd do it all over again, even knowing what I know now."

"Why?"

"Because I didn't deserve a single moment of it, but you still gave me nine weeks of pure joy, which is better than none at all. I'm grateful for what I got." *Even if it means falling into a hole that's darker than before.* At least I got to experience what it's like to live in the light with her again.

How long is it going to take for me to get over this woman? Is it even possible to get over losing a soul mate—again? Honestly, this whole soul-mate thing is bullshit. Why tie two people together and not allow them to be together? What's the fucking point?

"Do you regret it?" I ask.

She doesn't hesitate. "No. I feel guilty sometimes, but it's not enough guilt to wish we never happened. The only reason I came here in the first place was because I wanted to sort through my thoughts about how Caleb was refusing to be intimate with me. If he actually paid attention to me, I don't think you and I would have gotten that close. We probably wouldn't have had this time together at all."

"Did you tell him about us?"

"No."

"Do you plan to?"

"No. What happened at our tree stays at our tree."

I didn't know she thinks of it as *our* tree. The idea makes me want to smile and sob at the same time. "I'm glad you didn't tell him. You don't need to give him a reason to not want you. He seems to have enough reasons already, and he doesn't need another. Whatever it is that fell apart between you two, I hope you two can fix it and move on to be happy together."

"What about you? Where are you going to find your happiness?"

I keep putting one foot in front of the other as I think about my answer. "I already have. I've got nine weeks of it to replay in my head whenever I feel down. Every Sunday, when I'm back at our tree, I'll just imagine that you're there with your little questions box. I'll answer the cards and imagine that I made you laugh so much that you slap your knee like you sometimes do. It'll be great."

She shakes her head, giving me a sorrowful look. "That doesn't sound great to me."

That's because it's not ideal, and it actually fucking sucks. "Well, that's all I've got, so . . ."

"You'll find someone someday."

"I don't want anyone else."

"What if there's someone out there who could make you as happy as I do? What if you're missing out on her because you're refusing to let anyone else in?"

I let out a scoff. "I'm done letting people in, but I appreciate that you care enough to—I dunno. Whatever it is you're trying to do."

"I'm trying to encourage you to move forward."

"I will." *Begrudgingly, but I will.* "It just won't include some random chick who won't make me feel even half as whole as you do. Besides, I'm fine with being alone. I've done it my whole life, so don't worry about me. I'm more concerned about your happiness than mine anyway."

"Why?"

Because you're the one who's running back to a man who doesn't love you. I don't say that. The last thing I want is to start a conversation about how I'm right for her and he isn't. It'll make things tense between us again, and I'd rather end this evening on a good note. "Let's just say that if you ever find yourself in a place where you feel like something's missing again, you know where to find me on Sunday nights."

She's quiet after that. I hope it's because I made her think about the possibility that she's making a mistake. Maybe the more she thinks about it, the more she'll convince herself to leave him. *A man can hope.*

When we return to our tree, Arella picks up her purse and slides it over her shoulder. Then she locks her eyes with mine in an unspoken request. I know what she wants from me, because I want it too.

"Can I walk you to your car?"

She perks up with a relieved smile. "Yes, please."

We get there together in silence. Normally, silence irks me; it reminds me that I'm lonely, and it encourages all the raging thoughts of my worthlessness to beat me up inside. But when I'm with Arella, the silence doesn't bother me. Even now, as I walk her to her car where she'll end up driving away from me forever, this silence with her still comes with a teeny-tiny sense of peace.

After she sets her purse in her car, she shuts the door and turns to me. "Do you want a goodbye hug?"

Do I want one? *Fuck yeah.*

Can I handle holding her knowing I'll have to let her go? *Absolutely not.*

"I'm not sure if that's a good idea."

"Right. I understand." Her face falls more than I expected it to. I thought she asked if I wanted a hug for my benefit. Now I think she might have asked for hers. "Take care of yourself, okay?" she says.

I won't. "You too."

"And stay sober."

"Sure." *No promises.*

"And stay out of prison."

That one gets a chuckle out of me. It's small, but it's something. "I'll try."

She smiles at me like she's grateful to hear my laugh one last time. I'd like to hear hers too.

The idea comes to me easily. "You know what else I'll do?"

"What?"

"I'll start putting the toilet paper on the correct way."

She rewards my quick thinking with a giggle. "Of all the things I just mentioned, that one is the most important."

I take a step backward, keeping my eyes trained on her. I want to look at her for as long as possible. She grabs the door handle and pulls the door open. I brand the shape of her body into my mind. The length of her hair. The curves of her waist. The way her legs look in those shorts. When I'm old and gray, I want to remember all these little details about her. When I'm on my deathbed, I want the last thing I picture to be her.

She's about to step into her car when I can't hold back anymore.

"Arella?" My voice comes out like shattered glass.

She freezes and looks up at me with wide and eager eyes. My feet make their way to her before I can stop them. They pause once I'm in front of her again. I clear my dry-as-fuck throat. This is a bad idea, but I'm gonna do it anyway.

"I, uh, changed my mind. I think I'd like a goodbye hug. You know, if you're still offering."

With glistening eyes, she nods. I don't need more permission than that. I yank her toward me so hard, she collides with my chest with a thump. Our arms clutch each other like we're a couple in the 1940s and I'm about to go off to war.

I want to ask her why she's doing this. Why she's torturing

us both. Why she feels like she owes anything to a man who didn't fall in love with her of his own free will.

But I don't.

I can't.

She's made her decision.

Maybe this is for the best. I'd probably only have her for a few short months before the zovernment takes her away, anyway. Unfortunately, this is our fate. Two souls meant for each other but fated to be apart.

I fist her hair and squeeze her against me so tight, a strangled breath leaves her mouth. I don't care. I keep crushing her anyway. Apparently, she doesn't care either, because even though I'm probably suffocating her, she doesn't pull away.

I breathe in her sweet scent one last time, then my words come out through held-back tears. "Count down from three, and I'll let you go. Slowly, please."

She nods against my pec. "Three."

Fuck, why is she counting so fast? I wasn't ready for her to start yet.

She waits a few seconds before saying, "Two."

I hug her tighter. Since I can't say it out loud, I hope she can feel how much I love her through my body.

"One."

I release her and march toward the woods so she can't see the tears dripping from my eyes. I feel her gaze on my back as I order myself not to look at her. If I do, I might drop to my knees and beg her to stay.

35

TREY

I KICK A ROCK ON THE GROUND. IT TUMBLES ACROSS THE TOP of the cliff and over it. Then it's gone forever.

The sky draped over the forest is a swirly mix of pinks and purples intertwining with the dusty blue behind the trees. The October sun is about to set for the evening. Tomorrow, it'll return to shine on another day of me just trying to make it through.

My zerapist says I need to focus more on living in the moment. Whenever I dwell on the maybe-I-should-haves and what-if-I-hads of the past, I get depressed. Whenever I think about having to do this bullshit for another day, week, or year, I get anxious.

I've spent every Sunday over the last two months at our tree, waiting for her to appear out of the woods.

She never does.

Tonight is the first night I've told myself I'd stop looking. That's why I went for a walk. I needed to stop staring at those damn trees like they hold the answer to all my troubles. What I really need is to stop living my life as if she'll come back into it. She's not, and it'll do me some good to accept that and move on.

On the outside, I've been trying to move on. I've been working on my new career goals. I've also been looking into getting more involved with my foundation for kids with deceased parents.

On the inside, though, I'm still with her. It's like I'm stuck in the mud there, and no tow truck on Earth is strong enough to drag me out. A part of me doesn't even want to get out, but I have to. It's not healthy for me to keep hoping for a life I'll never have.

Liz keeps telling me that time will heal and eventually, things will get easier. Time hasn't done anything except make me realize that even when I offered everything I had to the only person I can see a future with, she only saw me as a part of her past.

The only thing that's gotten easier is my ability to hide the pain. I came up with some systems because I got sick of people asking me if I'm okay.

Whenever a bandmate catches me staring off into space, instead of apologizing for it, I tell them I was thinking up lyrics for a new song. It's been working to get them to leave me alone because I'm "in the zone."

Whenever a crew member asks me how my week has been, instead of saying *fine* like I have been, I tell them it was fantastic. I even add a whole bunch of enthusiasm into it, then ask them a question to take the attention off me.

I've gotten better at faking smiles too. I learned that if I do it while squinting my eyes, it's more believable. Many nights of practicing in the mirror helped me figure that out.

My hope is that the more I can make people believe I'm okay, the more I'll be okay. I lied when I told Arella that my unrealistic want in five years is a wife and kids. Sure, having a family would be great, but what I truly want is inner peace.

I just want to be able to wake up without feeling this constant weight on my chest. I want to be able to brush my teeth and take a shower without it feeling like a chore. I want to be able to perform in front of a crowd without feeling like I don't deserve to.

I envy the people who can get through their day without second-guessing everything they do or what they have, or wonder why they're even here. I'm jealous of the people who can wake up every morning with genuine vigor to live. And the people who never question their worth. And the people who've got all their shit together. How can I be like them? What's their secret?

When I said all that to Liz, she told me that part of their secret is that they didn't witness their parents' murder in a mushroom of fire when they were seven. And they didn't grow up with their abusive uncle who was really their spiteful aunt. And they didn't lose the love of their life to memory scrubbing.

"Everyone has shit they've been through," Liz said. "You've got a little more shit than most, but that doesn't mean some inner peace isn't achievable."

So that's what I'm working toward: *some* inner peace, because *some* is better than none. However I can achieve that —without getting high—I'm willing to try it. I even went on a date last week. I'm pretty fucking proud of myself for it too.

It was with the thirty-two-year-old Zordi woman who owns the sandwich shop near my penthouse. I go there almost every day while I'm in New York. Usually, she makes conversation with me about food or Disney movies while she puts my sandwich together. Last week, she asked if I'd like to get dinner with her sometime.

I was about to politely decline when I stopped myself and said, "Why not?" Later that night, I took her to a nice Mediterranean place.

We had a fine conversation over chicken pitas and hummus. She told me the entire story of how she started her sandwich shop, and I told her about how I started my band. She laughed at my lame jokes, and I pretended to be interested in her cat. Overall, I'd say the date served the purpose I was going for: to do more in New York than sit around my apartment, waiting for my next flight back to LA.

I didn't feel that spark with her that I do with Arella, but I didn't expect to. Part of the reason why I haven't wanted to date other women is because I keep looking for my next Arella. Since there is no such thing, I'm setting my expectations lower, like someone I can hold a conversation with. Sandwich shop lady met that expectation.

We didn't make plans for another date, mostly because I told her I'm moving back to LA full-time. Once that's done, I plan to focus on my new career goals, and then maybe I'll work up to going out with another woman I can hold a conversation with. Who knows? Maybe one day, I'll even get to the point of being able to kiss someone—soberly.

No, I don't have plans to find my "compatible partner," but I might be able to handle a casual, friends-with-benefits, no-strings-attached type thing. There's gotta be *someone* out there who's looking for that too. And if not, that's okay. Being alone is my destiny, and I've accepted that.

The sun is gone, and a few dim stars are trying to peek out from the depths of the black sky. I think I've stood on this cliff, staring aimlessly at the trees below, for long enough. It's time to head to the airport.

With my hands in my jeans pockets, I turn toward the trail, then jump back and gasp.

"Sorry!" A woman of angelic beauty throws her hands up in surrender as she stumbles out of the tree line. "I didn't know if it was you. It looked like you from behind, but I didn't want to say something in case it wasn't you."

I probably wouldn't be this jumpy if I could sense her emotions. I always know when someone is near—unless that someone is her.

"What are you doing here?" I ask. Not that I'm unhappy to see her. My chest is thumpy all of a sudden.

"I sat under our tree for a really *looong* time, and when you didn't show, I thought I'd look for you."

The one fucking time I go for a longer walk . . . "I hope I didn't make you wait too long."

"That's okay. I made you wait two months, so we're even."

I close the distance between us to get a better look at her. Her wavy hair looks more wavy than usual, like she spent extra time curling it. She's wearing more makeup than she normally does too. Not that I mind. I'll take her any way I can have her.

"I was just about to head back to our tree," I say, specifically using the word *our*. "You wanna head back with me?"

"Of course."

We get about ten steps through the woods before she asks, "How have you been?"

"Fantastic," I say, coupled with enthusiasm and one of my smiles with the squinty eyes.

Her shoulders perk up. "That's great to hear."

All that practice in the mirror is paying off. "How have *you* been?"

"Good. I finally got a loan for my bakery, and I found a location that's a good size in a decent location."

"Congrats. What's the next step?"

She keeps a steady pace beside me. "I'm meeting with the landlord tomorrow to sign the lease."

"Wow. I'm excited for you."

"Me too. This is something I've wanted for a long time."

That peace I always feel when I'm with her eases into me like sweet honey. I wish I could capture this feeling and turn it on whenever I need it. "Can I tell you somethin' cool?"

"Of course."

"I bought a studio."

"What?" She stops in the middle of the trail. "Seriously?"

I stop too. "Yeah. I just signed for it on Thursday. My

band is outgrowing the backstage area of the Soul House anyway, so it'll be a good space for us to write and record our third original album. It's also where I'll start my new production company."

"That's wonderful! Where is it?"

We continue down the trail as I say, "Pasadena. Pretty close to where Liz lives."

"So what you're saying is that you've been keeping busy?"

"Trying." I think about mentioning the first date I had in almost three years, but I don't want Arella to think I'm unavailable. To her, I'm as available as available can be. "How about you? Have you been keeping busy?"

"I have. Lots of life changes, but they're all good."

I'm about to ask her if things are better at home with Caleb, then I stop. I don't want to know. Most of me hopes everything is good because I want her to be happy, but I'd be lying if I said there isn't a part of me that wishes things aren't good so she'll come back to me. It's better to wonder than to know.

When we make it to our tree, her blanket is already draped underneath it, next to my backpack. Her purse is also here, next to our little box of questions.

"You came prepared." I take a seat on top of her blanket because fuck the consequences. She's here, and I'm ecstatic about it. I don't give two shits that it's going to rip me apart when she leaves tonight. I don't even care that I might have to start the healing process all over again. I just want to enjoy her company while I've got it.

She pretzels her legs together, then hands me the box. "Would you like to go first?"

"Sure." I pluck out a card and read it. "If you could go back in time and change one thing, what would it be?"

Arella does that cute thing where she squints at the sky as if the stars will give her the answer she's looking for. "I think I'd stop all those people from getting onto the *Titanic*."

"The Ti-what?"

She lets out a little *ha!* "Very funny, mister. I know you know what that is."

"Nope. In my universe, no one has heard of the *Titanic*."

"Ha. Ha. Ha," she says with a sarcastic tone. "What's your answer?"

"My answer is more selfish than yours."

"That's okay. No one said you couldn't use your one imaginary trip back in time on yourself."

"There are a lot of things I'd wanna change, but the biggest one is that I'd get my mom to marry my real dad."

She cocks her head to the side. "What?"

"Long story short, I found out that the man I thought was my dad wasn't actually my dad. My mother had an affair with my dad's older brother, who's actually my dad. So if I could, I'd go back to make sure they got married instead." Then again, changing that could mean I wouldn't have met Arella. I wouldn't trade never knowing her for a better childhood.

"Wait . . . your mom had an affair with your uncle?"

"Yep."

Her eyes go wide. "And she got pregnant with you?"

"Yep."

"But they told everyone that your father was—"

"Yep.

Her mouth falls open and she goes silent. It takes her a moment to gather herself. "How did you take that crazy news?"

"At the time, my life was too chaotic to think about it. I've had more time to reflect on it since, and I'd like to think I'm taking it well." Finding out that Victor is my dad wasn't the hard pill to swallow. Finding out that my aunt swapped minds with him for twenty years was.

"There's something I've been meaning to ask you, but I haven't because I figured if you wanted to talk about it, you would."

"Go ahead and ask," I tell her. "If I don't wanna talk about it, I'll just say so."

She straightens up. "Okay. When we had that conversation about your tattoo, you said that the V is in honor of your dad because he died saving your life. What's the story behind that?"

"My dad saw me getting attacked by my aunt. He saved me but died in the process." I left out every important detail, but that's as much as she should know.

"Interesting."

I want to ask what she means by that, but if we keep talking about this topic, we'll get into illegal territory, so I push the questions box toward her. "Your turn."

She pulls out a card. "If you could have any superpower, what would it be?"

"Easy. I'd like to be able to teleport wherever I want, whenever I want. I'd save so much money on plane tickets." If I actually had that power, I'd also need a lot of self-control to make sure I wouldn't keep appearing outside Arella's apartment every day.

"I'd like to have telekinesis."

Ironic. "That could be handy."

"I'd also want the ability to make fire come out of my hands."

My eyes flick up to meet hers. Does she know? Is she trying to tell me that she knows?

What's next? Is she gonna tell me she wants to be able to sense people's emotions too? I can't tell what she's thinking from the impassive look on her face.

She hands me the box. "Your turn."

I clear my throat as I pluck out a card. "What are your relationship deal-breakers?"

"Abuse. Gaslighting. Manipulation."

"Damn," I say with a chuckle. "Take a moment to think about it, will ya?"

"I've had a lot of years of thinking to know what I never want again."

"I'm proud of you for that. As for me, I only have one deal-breaker."

She gives me a second to expand on that. When I don't, she says, "Are you going to leave me hanging, or . . . ?"

"I think you could guess it."

"You've mentioned that one of your exes is a lying bitch. Is that it?"

I chuckle because she used the word *bitch*. "Nope."

"You don't want someone who's after your money?"

"No." *I don't want someone who's not you.* "Let's talk about something else."

"Fine. How about we talk about the fact that you have yet to ask me why I came here tonight."

"I don't question miracles."

She giggles as her face lights up. "That's what you think this is? A miracle?"

"Why else would you be here? Honestly, a part of me is questioning if you're even real."

"I'm not. This is actually a simulation."

I let out a real laugh for the first time in two months. "If this isn't real, does that mean anything goes?"

"What would you do if you could?"

Take you home with me. Kiss you until you're breathless. Make you mine again. "Things I shouldn't."

"Aren't you even the least bit curious why I'm here?"

"Yes, but at the same time, I don't care *why* you're here. I'm just glad you are."

I'd like to think she came here tonight because she missed me. I'd also like to think she's going to keep coming on Sundays again, but that's probably wishful thinking. If she does, I'll do better about mentally preparing myself for the impending end. Maybe this time, it won't hurt as much.

"Whose turn is it?" she asks.

"Yours."

She lifts the box, picks out a card, and reads it. "Will you take me home with you?"

My body tenses. *Did I hear her right?* I'm not sure, so I say the most intelligent thing I can. "Huh?"

"I said, will you take me home with you?"

There is no way she just said what I think she said. "That's the question on the card?"

She slams the card against her chest with a grin. "Word for word."

"Lemme see."

With a laugh, she sticks the card down her shirt. "Answer the question first."

"I . . . I don't understand the question."

She pulls the card back out of her shirt and stares at it. "The card says, 'Will you, Trey Grant, take me, Arella Rance, home with you?' "

I blink at her as all the blood rushes from my head. "What?" I snatch the card from her and read it. What the card actually says is, What are your biggest strengths?

I'm about to ask her what's going on when something hits me. She just called herself Arella *Rance*. Isn't her last name . . . ? My attention flicks to her left hand.

No ring.

My breath gets lost on its way out as my eyes lock with hers. Where's her ring? What does this mean? Did she leave him? *When? Why? How?*

She answers all my silent questions with "Our divorce was finalized on Wednesday. I'm officially—"

I launch myself at her, toss the card in my hand somewhere behind me, then pin her back to the blanket. She laughs beneath me as I straddle her.

"Are you coming back to me?" I can barely get the words out through my shaky breaths.

"If you'll have me."

I'm getting light-headed. "Are you planning to stay with me forever?"

"Forever," she says with so much conviction, it doesn't feel real. She wasn't lying earlier; this really is a simulation, and I don't give a fuck. I'd rather live in whatever this fake world is than the real one.

"Yes, baby, I'll have you." I lean down and plant a hard kiss over her lips. She kisses me back with a breathless sigh as she claws at my shirt to pull me closer. I snake my arm around her back and hold her tight against my chest.

I must be hallucinating, or I'm dead and somehow made it to heaven. She's kissing me. She's letting me touch her. She said she's going to stay with me forever. I don't deserve this. I don't deserve her, but I'm taking her anyway.

It takes me a minute to gather enough willpower to pull away. "Tell me you're mine."

"I'm yours," she says with dazed eyes.

"Tell me you're going home with me."

She doesn't hesitate. "I'm going home with you."

"Tell me you're never leaving me again."

"I'm never leaving you again."

An overwhelming wave of tears takes over my body. I lean back down to kiss her as they drip from my eyes.

"I love you so much, Arella." I trail kisses down her throat.

She arches her head back. "I love you too, Trey."

I suck on her neck, pulling moans from her that make my dick ache. I'm throbbing to be inside her, but I won't make that mistake again. There's no way I'm going to make love to her until she's got all her shit in my house and is lying in a bed that's *ours*. I need some sort of guarantee that *this* is it.

Panting, I flop onto my side and tug her against me. "How did this happen?"

36

———

ARELLA

IT'S BEEN A MONTH SINCE CALEB AGREED TO MAKE SPENDING time together a priority. This is our second date night since, which is more than what we've had in the past six months.

Tonight's date night feels as bland as the last one. During dinner, neither of us could stay focused on the conversation. The silences between us felt awkward, and the way he kept staring off into the distance bothered me.

I wasn't much better. My mind kept wandering toward a man with dark hair and a sadness in his eyes that's been haunting me since the moment he stormed off and left for the airport.

I thought that after four weeks, I'd be able to forget about the way I saw his soul die when I said I wasn't coming back. I haven't forgotten. I also haven't forgotten about how for the rest of that evening, Trey got lost in his own thoughts and barely heard anything I said. I wanted to take it all back and ask him to whisk me away with him as if Caleb had never existed.

But Caleb does exist, and now we're on our couch, watching a movie.

Correction: Caleb is snoozing like he has been for the last

twenty minutes. I'm staring blankly at the movie we were *supposed* to watch together, wondering what the heck I'm doing.

Why am I forcing my husband to spend time with me when he clearly doesn't want to? Why am I putting so much effort into fixing something I'm not even sure can be fixed? I have no idea why we fell apart or why he's been so distant, but I can't live like this anymore.

I told myself after leaving Nathan that I'd never subject myself to another relationship where I was abused or felt unwanted. Caleb wouldn't lay a finger on me that way, but I don't feel wanted by him either. Lately, I've also been questioning what I want.

I spend more time thinking about Trey than I do thinking about Caleb. I spend more time wishing Caleb was Trey than I do wishing this marriage will work. Caleb and I still have yet to have sex again, and even if we did, I'd probably imagine he's Trey the whole time.

What am I doing? This marriage is over, and now that I think about it, it's been over for a while—long before I even saw Trey at our tree.

Before I can talk myself out of it, I shake Caleb's arm.

He startles awake and upright. "Sorry. I didn't mean to fall asleep."

My heart thrashes in my chest—in a good way. "I need to talk to you about something."

He rubs his eyes, then straightens his back. "Okay?"

I try not to think about how this is going to hurt him. If I think about it too much, I'll chicken out. Yes, this is going to burn, but it's for the best. Our relationship isn't healthy anymore. I don't think Caleb has the courage to leave me, which means I have to be the one to leave him.

I suck in a deep breath, then let the words out. "I'm in love with someone else."

Caleb's body freezes. "What?"

"I said, I'm in love with someone else."

I expect him to freak out and ask me who. Instead, he says, "Me too."

"What?"

"I said, me too." From the way his face remains impassive, I don't question the validity of those two little words.

"Who are you in love with?"

"Rakesh." He stares at me for my reaction.

"But he's—oh . . ." It all clicks together: Caleb's late nights out with Rakesh. His lack of physical intimacy with me. His eagerness to drop me to be with Rakesh. It all makes sense now. "Is Rakesh gay too?"

"Yes."

"Does he also have feelings for you?"

"Yes."

"Have you guys . . . um, done stuff?"

Caleb sighs and picks up the TV remote, then turns the movie off. The room goes silent as he stands to flip the light on. When he returns to the couch, he folds his hands together in his lap. "How much do you want to know?"

"Everything."

"Are you sure? I don't want to hurt you." This is why I don't think he'd have the courage to leave me. He's too nonconfrontational for that.

I give him a firm nod. "I'm sure, Caleb. Just tell me everything."

He stares at his hands, trying to figure out how to start. "Um, it wasn't until after our wedding when I began developing feelings for him. I always chalked it up to how close of friends we are. Eventually, I couldn't ignore the feelings anymore. The more time I spent with him, the more I didn't want to leave him. The more I saw him shirtless at the gym, the more I wanted to touch him.

"It scared me at first because I've never looked at a man like that before. I also didn't know he was gay, so I suppressed my urges. I told myself I was just being ridiculous. I mean, I was already married to a woman, and he was my best friend, who I assumed was straight.

"As time went on, it got harder to suppress my urges. It also got harder for me to be with you because the idea of touching a woman just didn't appeal to me anymore. That's why I pulled away, and I'm sorry for that. You've been trying so hard to make this work, and I've been an asshole."

I lean in to him and lower my voice. "Caleb, you could have told me. You know how I feel about stuff like this."

"I was scared though. When I finally admitted to myself that I'm gay, I spent months keeping it to myself."

"When did you finally tell Rakesh?"

"When his grandma died. You remember how I went over to his apartment that night? I found him crying, so I gave him a hug that was meant to be consoling, but once our bodies connected like that, it was like something sparked between us. The next thing I know, we're making out in his kitchen."

In any other situation, I might feel betrayed to find out that my husband kissed someone else, but all I feel is happiness for Caleb. That kiss was a long time coming for him and Rakesh. It must have been a huge relief.

"Rakesh has known he's gay since middle school, but he never explored it because his very traditional Indian family won't accept it. He never came out to his friends either, because with his siblings at the same school, he didn't want it to get back to his parents. As for me, he's the only person I've told. And now you."

I place a gentle hand over his forearm. "I'm really glad you told me. That was really brave of you."

"Brave? No, Ari. I've been a coward. You're an amazing wife to me. You're everything a man wishes for in a woman. You're caring, loving, attentive, and you're an amazing cook. You deserve better than this. I should have told you much sooner, but I was too afraid of hurting you."

Obviously, I wasn't *that* attentive, because I missed seeing that my husband is gay. "Hurting me is better than killing yourself on the inside for being untrue to who you are."

He lets out a breath as he rubs his sweaty palms off on his pants. "Jeez, you're taking this way better than I thought you would. I suppose whoever you're in love with has something to do with that."

"A little."

"Can I guess who it is?"

Caleb is never going to get it right, so I say, "Sure."

"It's that Trey guy, isn't it?"

"What? How did you know?"

"You didn't see the way he looked at you, Ari. I mean, maybe you did, but you don't remember it. That man looked at you like you were his entire reason for existing."

I wish I could see the way Trey looks at me from the outside. If it's anything like the way Gramps looks at Grammy, then I'm making the right decision.

Caleb continues, "I still don't know what happened that day you acted like you knew him and tried to kick me out of our apartment. What I do know is that you looked at him like you loved him. At the time, I was freaked out by it, but I also loved you so much that I just wanted to forget it ever happened."

"I think I'm supposed to be with him."

"I think you are too, and despite how weird this may sound, I think you were with him before." Caleb stands and waves for me to join him. "Come on. I need to give you something."

I follow him into the bedroom, where he stops at his nightstand. He pulls out the second drawer, then grabs a little black box that used to hold a watch. He flips open the lid, then pulls out a shiny diamond necklace with gold angel wings.

He drops it into my open palm. "Read the back."

I gasp as I stare at the engraving. *Paris? T.G.* "Where did you get this?"

Caleb snaps the old watch box shut, then tosses it back into his drawer. "Do you remember the day of your surgery, when the nurses in the pre-op room asked you to change into a hospital gown?"

"Yeah?"

"After you changed, the nurses handed me a bag with all your clothes and personal belongings to hang on to. When you got out of surgery, I pulled your clothes out for you and found this necklace. I meant to give it to one of the nurses, thinking they must have accidentally put someone else's jewelry into your bag, but I forgot to.

"Later, we got home and were eating burgers when Trey showed up. The second he said his name, I thought about the initials on the back of this necklace and found it strange that some guy appeared at our door with the same initials as what's engraved onto a necklace that appeared in your personal-belongings bag from the hospital."

I run my thumb over the diamond. This is the same necklace I wore in that picture I gave back to Trey. It's also the same necklace I keep seeing in my dreams. How did this end up in my bag from the hospital?

"Why didn't you give this to me a long time ago?" I ask.

"Because I was weirded out by it. I mean, seriously, Ari? The whole situation is a little freaky, don't you think?"

It felt freakier to me three years ago. Thanks to my dreams, now I have a better grasp on the full picture. While it's still a little weird, I've accepted it.

"What do we do now?" Caleb asks.

"Now," I say, "we move forward."

Trey's been listening to me tell my story without a single interruption.

"After I told him that I'm supposed to be with you, he agreed, then said he needed to give me something. From his drawer, he pulled out this." I drag the necklace out of my pocket.

The loudest gasp I've ever heard comes out of Trey's mouth. "He had it this whole time?"

"Yeah."

Trey gapes at me with his mouth fully open. "And he's gay?"

"Yeah, and Rakesh is moving into our apartment next week. That means I've got a week to pack up and move out."

"Give me one day, baby. That's all I need. I'll call the movers first thing in the morning."

"Most of my stuff is packed already. I started getting my things into boxes while Caleb and I worked out our divorce. It'll be expensive to get all my stuff shipped to New York."

Trey's face crinkles into hard lines. "New York? No way. You don't belong in New York. You belong here."

"But isn't that where you live?"

"Yes, but I've also got a house in Pasadena."

What? "When did you get a house in Pasadena?"

"Two days ago. With starting a new production company here, I figured I was ready to be back in California full-time. I was planning to go back to New York tonight to pack up."

"Is there room for me at your house in Pasadena?"

"Hell yeah. And if you need more space, I'll buy us a new house. Whatever you want, wherever you want."

I had already mentally prepared myself to move to New York with him during the week and work on getting my new bakery going over the weekends. Living in Pasadena sounds way better. "I'm sure the house you bought will be just fine."

"It's only got two bedrooms. I wasn't expecting to need more. We can use one as ours and share the other one as our office. You can have a desk where you do all your bakery business stuff. I can have my guitars on the other side."

"That sounds perfect."

He takes my hands into his, giving me a short kiss on the knuckles. "I can't believe this is happening."

"I can. I've been waiting for this moment for four weeks."

He shoots me a hard scowl. "Why did you wait so long?"

"I wanted to start our lives together without taking a single thing from the past with me. That included my marriage. Plus, I needed time to sort things out. This is a big transition for me. I had to tell people that Caleb and I were getting divorced, which was really scary."

"How did everybody take the news?"

"My friends at work were shocked. Javina wasn't surprised at all. I've been keeping her in the loop about Caleb, so she saw this coming. What she didn't see was that he's gay and that I'd been seeing you on Sundays. When I told her my plan to come straight here after the divorce was finalized, she was thrilled. Her first question was, Do you think he'll give me free tickets to see his band's shows?"

Trey throws his head back with a laugh. "Tell Javina that pretty boy is happy to give her free tickets for life—with spa days included."

"She'll love that."

"How did your grandparents take the news?"

I let out a long sigh as I recall the rough conversation I had with my grandparents. Rough is putting it lightly. They went on and on about how Caleb and I needed to try harder to make the marriage work, even though I explained multiple times that Caleb isn't interested in women anymore. "They didn't know that Caleb and I were having problems, so this came as a shock to them."

"Can I assume they don't know about me either?"

"Nope. My plan is that in a few months, I'll introduce you to them as if we just met."

Trey nods his approval. "That sounds like a good plan."

"Wonderful. Now before we get too ahead of ourselves, I need to ask you an important question."

"Before you do that, can I, please, put that necklace around you?"

I perk up and hold out the diamond. He takes it from me, then I gather all my hair to one side. Our eyes lock as he hooks the jewelry around my neck. Once it drapes down from my collarbones, he plants a tender kiss against my forehead, then my lips, then my nose.

I giggle as he continues pecking me all over my face. I don't stop him.

"Okay, I've had my fill for now." He straightens his back as if he's ready for anything I'm about to say. "You may ask your important question now."

I come straight out with it. "How are we going to keep the zovernment from finding out about us?"

As expected, his eyes go wide. "H—how do you . . . What?"

"For the past two months, I've been having dreams of us flying on a floating tire. On it, you tell me things that don't make sense but make everything else make sense. I've had that dream three times now. The last two times, I woke up and wrote as much of it down in my dream journal as possible."

"You have a dream journal?"

I adjust to sit with my legs to the side. "Yeah, to record all the dreams I have about you. I feel like my dreams are pieces of a puzzle, and I've been trying to put it together without most of the middle and only half the edges. Once I had this dream of us on a flying tire, everything finally came together. I'm still missing a lot of puzzle pieces, but I think I can see the main picture."

"Which is?"

"That we live in a world with two kinds of people: ones with powers and ones without. That you're one of the people who has powers and I'm not, and for some reason, I'm immune to everyone's powers. I know that you can create fireballs with your hands and move things without touching them. I know I was kidnapped and that you saved me. I even know that after the Enforcers captured us, I was interrogated for three days about everything I know about your world."

With every piece of information I say out loud, Trey seems to lose more air in his lungs. "Holy shit."

I place a gentle hand over his forearm. "Trey, if all my dreams over the past three years are things that actually happened, then I want you to know that I fought them when they tried to scrub me. I begged them to give me an exception. I even punched someone in the nose and made them bleed as they dragged me to the procedure room. I'm going to assume that's how I woke up in the hospital and that's the first time Caleb and I ever saw each other.

"I think I'm going to continue seeing the past in my sleep and eventually, I'll remember everything. Every few months, I see something new instead of a repeat, and it gives me more pieces of the puzzle." I hope that, through being with Trey, I'll be able to learn everything I used to know, and then some.

Trey lets out a long breath, taking this all in. "So what do we do now?"

"Now," I say with a grin, "we move forward."

"But what about staying off the zovernment's radar?"

"We'll figure that out along the way."

37

———

TREY

"Please behave," Arella says as I pull her car into the driveway of a corner house—one that looks *waaay* too nice for a former mechanic and a stay-at-home grandma.

The large property is surrounded by blooming flower gardens and lawn gnomes. Thank fuck they're the cute cartoony gnomes and not the creepy grinning ones that look like they come alive at night. Some of the gnomes are even wearing Santa hats.

Christmas lights hang from the edges of the roof. A decorated tree with an angel on top sits just inside the living room window. I admire the cozy family-friendly vibes this house is giving. I could see myself raising kids with Arella in a house like this. Our current house is too small for that.

I turn the car off, unbuckle my seatbelt, then turn to face my girl for the last twelve weeks. "You don't trust me to charm your grandparents into liking me?"

"Honey, you're not about to meet Javina for the first time. My grandparents will need a little more convincing than some free spa days. They figured it out that I left Caleb for you, and when they asked me about it, I didn't want to lie. To them, you're what ruined my marriage."

300

I scoff. "Did you tell them that I moved across the country for three years just so I wouldn't ruin what you had with Caleb?"

"No. They think we met recently, remember?"

"Shit. You're gonna have to help me keep our story straight."

"Just go in with the knowledge that they think Caleb and I could have made things work but I gave up on him because I met you."

"Didn't you tell them Caleb's gay? Unless you're going to magically grow a beard and a penis, that man is not interested in you anymore."

The last I heard, Caleb and Rakesh told their families about each other. Unfortunately, neither family took the news well. Caleb's parents even called Arella, asking her to take him back.

I overheard the conversation and felt so proud of my girl for kindly explaining to Caleb's parents how they could be more supportive of their son instead of attacking him for something he can't control. Love is love, no matter the gender or lack of powers. Maybe if Caleb's parents can see it that way, the zovernment can too. More wishful thinking, I know.

Arella and Caleb have been keeping in touch, which I don't mind. Not just because I'm confident that he won't ever try to steal her back, but because they really do care about each other, and not because their minds were altered to care.

"My grandparents don't think Caleb is actually gay," Arella says. "They think it's 'just a phase,' which really rubs me the wrong way. But I'll work on getting them to understand that another time. For now, let's just focus on having a good Christmas dinner and getting them to like you."

I slash a nonchalant hand through the air. "Don't worry, babe. They'll like me."

"Okay. Remember that Grandma Roxy likes it when

people compliment her garden and Grandpa Phil likes to talk about baseball."

"Garden. Baseball. Got it." I flash her a thumbs-up.

"And above all else, do *not* swear."

"Damn, babe. You didn't tell me your grandparents are prudes."

She slumps her shoulders and scolds me. "Trey, please. Just behave, okay?"

I throw my hands up in surrender. "All right. Don't say *fuck*. Got it."

Together, we exit her car. I don't need my powers to know my girl is nervous. She's rubbing the ends of her hair between her fingers and biting her lip. She's got nothing to worry about though. From what she told me, it seems like her grandparents are mostly concerned that what we have is a fling. They're concerned about whether Arella is going to be loved and treated right. I have every intention of loving and treating this woman right, so getting her grandparents to like me is gonna be a piece of cake.

Arella is about to knock on the front door when it opens. Her grandma is on the other side, wearing a huge smile on her face.

"Ari, dear! I'm so happy to see you."

Arella gives her grandma a tight bear hug. "Merry Christmas, Grammy."

The seventy-something-year-old woman drops her smile when her eyes land on me. I drop my friendly smile too, because all of a sudden, the zense in my chest is tingling.

38

———

TREY

"Is this your new boyfriend?" Roxy eyes me up and down. Her panic spreads through my body like wildfire.

If Arella notices Roxy's clenched jaw, she probably thinks it's just because her grandma is tense over the Caleb situation. I know better; that prickling in her chest is freaking her out. It's freaking me out too. The last thing I expected to find on the other side of this door was a Zordinary.

"How about I introduce Trey inside?" Arella says. "With Gramps."

"Um, sure . . ." Roxy hesitantly steps aside to allow us in. "Grandpa is in the living room."

As I step into the large entryway, I offer up one of my many charming smiles. Roxy's expression remains stony. She slams the door shut, then races down the wide hallway ahead of Arella and me.

"Phil! Ari's here."

A deep voice replies from the next room. "Wonderful. Let's meet the bastard who convinced our grandbaby to leave a perfectly good marriage."

Damn. He sounds like a fucking delight.

Arella gives my hand a reassuring squeeze as we enter the

living room. The Christmas tree by the window is slightly smaller than the one Arella and I picked out for our place. Red stockings hang over the mantel, where a gaslit fire sits. Christmas-themed blankets are neatly folded and draped over the back of the couch and chairs. Every surface is covered in picture frames.

In a recliner sits an old man, who sets his book down on a side table and stands. He plasters a fake smile over his lips as if he didn't just say a rude comment he very much wanted me to hear.

His fake smile remains on his lips until the second I get within two steps of him. As the zense activates in my chest, his face falls, his back straightens, and his shoulders square. A rush of horror radiates off him. Just like me, he also expected to meet an Ordinary today.

As an attempt to ease the tension, Arella fakes a smile of her own. "Grammy, Gramps, this is the *amazing* guy I've been telling you about."

I play along, sticking my hand out to the gray-haired man. "Nice to meet you. I'm Trey."

The man takes my hand, shaking it like he's trying to squeeze my hand to death. Next, I offer my hand to Roxy. She shakes my hand a little gentler, yet still stony-faced.

Arella doesn't acknowledge their rough demeanors. "Trey, these are my grandparents, Phil and Roxy."

I almost scoff out loud. *Her grandparents?* What a joke. I've got half a mind to hoist Arella over my shoulder and run her out the front door. Save her first, ask questions later.

I don't do that because, based on the many loving photos surrounding me, this couple hasn't done any harm to my girl. From the many stories Arella has told me about them, they took good care of her after her parents died. I'm not leaving here until I find out why two Zordis would bring an Ordinary girl into their lives like that.

A long silence fills the room as Phil and Roxy's frenzied

energy swirls around me. I'm waiting for one of them to say something. Neither does. They just keep staring at me as if waiting for me to make the first move. What move? I'm not sure, but they look ready to hoist Arella over their shoulders too.

Arella is the first to break the silence. "Why don't we all sit down and get to know each other?"

In silence, Arella and I claim the love seat behind us. I feel the need to grab her hand and hold it in my lap, so I do. I don't miss the way Phil scowls at our conjoined hands as he stiffly returns his ass to his recliner. Roxy eyes her husband as she settles on the couch across from us. It's as if she has a feeling Phil is going to attack me and she needs to stop him before he does.

"Tell us how you two met," Roxy says with a forced friendly tone.

I'm not gonna win any points by telling them that Arella and I originally met on the side of a highway while I was working a top secret **ZIRDA** mission to find out what makes her immune to Zordi powers, so I keep quiet.

Thankfully, Arella has all the right words. "We met at the Soul House, a music bar in downtown LA. Trey's a musician, and his band plays there on the weekends."

Phil's hard glare flicks from Arella to me. His tone comes out displeased. "You're in a band?"

"Yes, sir." Calling the man *sir* doesn't seem to win me any points either.

He scowls at me so hard, his entire forehead creases into thick folds. "Do you happen to have a *real* job on top of that?"

"Grandpa," Arella scolds. "Trey's band does really well online. They've also released two original albums, and all their shows always sell out. Just because it's not a regular nine-to-five doesn't mean it's not a *real* job."

I don't care what this wrinkly fart thinks of my career

choice. I have well beyond the means I need to take care of the woman beside me.

Phil narrows his gaze on Arella. "You left a hardworking cop for a man who sings songs on the Internet for money?"

Simply stated, that does make me sound bad.

"Grandpa," Arella scolds again. "First of all, Caleb isn't a cop. He's a security guard at a museum. Second, Trey doesn't sing songs on the Internet for money. Being in a band is like running a business. What he sells just happens to be the music he writes. And third, you promised you'd behave today."

It's good to know I wasn't the only one who received a behavior lecture before this meeting that's going *sooo fucking well*.

Arella continues, "How about you give Trey a chance?"

Phil sighs and rubs the back of his neck. "All right, boy. Tell us. When you met Ari and she told you she was married, why did you still pursue her?"

"Phil . . ." Roxy says at the same time Arella drops her jaw.

"Grandpa!"

I really wish she'd stop calling him that. Everyone here knows this man isn't really her grandpa—except her.

Phil doesn't quit. "What kind of man steals a woman away from her husband?"

"Grandpa, stop."

"Not a real man, that's for sure. What made you think you had any right to dig yourself into a perfectly good marriage and—"

"Grandpa!" This time, Arella yells, and it shuts him up. "Stop saying my relationship with Caleb was *perfectly good*. It wasn't."

"He put a roof over your head, didn't he? He loved you, cooked for you, and made you happy. What about that wasn't good?"

"First of all, I had my apartment way before I even met

Caleb. He's the one who moved in with me. Second, I did *all* the cooking. He's terrible at it. And third, I've explained it to you already: Caleb and I weren't good for a while. A woman needs more than just a roof and food."

Phil lets out a condescending *pfft*. "What else is there?"

Arella loses it. "Affection! Passion! Complete and utter devotion! Caleb stopped giving me any of that months before Trey and I started anything. There was absolutely no passion in our marriage, and neither of us were devoted to the other.

"For god's sake, Grandpa, the man is gay! And he's already dating his friend Rakesh. Now stop talking about Caleb. I came here today so you could meet Trey, the man who's sitting right here. The man who I'm passionate about. Who's devoted to me and has promised to take care of me better than anyone can."

Phil rolls his eyes. Now I know where Arella gets it from. He shoots me a skeptical glare. "If this band thing doesn't work out, how are you planning to take care of my granddaughter?"

I'm so fucking close to aiming a fireball at him and accusing him of kidnapping an innocent three-year-old Ordinary girl. I almost do, until Roxy slaps her thighs.

"How's about we all take a break, huh?" Roxy grimaces at her husband. "Phil, how's about you and I meet in the kitchen?"

Phil stays where he is. "And leave her alone with *him*? Are you crazy?"

What the fuck? Does he think I'm gonna hurt Arella? Or is he more afraid I'll spill their secret? *It's definitely the latter.*

Roxy grits her teeth together. "If he wanted to hurt her, he would have already. Now come."

Okay? Maybe he *is* worried that I'll hurt her. If that's the case, this grumpy asshole knows nothing about me.

Roxy's words give me a little confidence that, on some level, we all want the same thing. These people don't want anything to happen to Arella any more than I do. Having *one* thing in common is good, I guess. Well, technically, we have two things in common, if I count having powers.

The second her "grandparents" stomp down the hall and disappear into another room, Arella turns to me. "Oh my god, Trey. I'm so sorry. I don't know what's gotten into Gramps. He's not usually this mouthy. He promised me he'd try to like you."

Her "grandparents" liking me is no longer what I'm concerned about. "Um, babe, do you remember when your grandparents took you in, or is that just what they told you happened?"

"I was three. I don't remember anything that happened at that age."

My eyes scan the room, looking at every picture frame in sight. I don't see what I'm looking for. "Are there any pictures of your grandparents with you as a baby? Like from before your parents died?"

"Um, I dunno. Why does that matter right now?"

"Are there any pictures of your grandparents with your parents?"

"What does that have to do with anything?"

I stroke my stubbly chin as the gears turn in my head. "I dunno. Maybe nothing. Maybe everything."

I haven't told Arella what I know about her parents yet. Mostly because whenever I bring them up, it doesn't seem like she remembers our conversation about how her name was Hannah Calder at one point. I've been waiting for either her to dream about it or a good time to tell her. We've been too busy being happily in love for me to want to drop a bomb that big on her.

Arella throws her head into her hands and groans. "This is a disaster."

I'm still trying to piece things together as I drape an arm around her back. "Everything will be okay, babe."

"Nope. Gramps is still stuck on the fact that I left Caleb to be with you."

Actually, I think he's now stuck on the fact that she's with a Zordi, but I'm not gonna tell her that. Not yet. First, I need to figure out why and how two Zordis got their hands on an Ordinary girl and have pretended to be her grandparents for the past twenty-some years.

A pair of light feet shuffles down the hall until Roxy reappears in the living room. She locks her eyes on me. "Phil would like to speak to you in the kitchen, please. Just you."

"No!" Arella shouts. "I'm not going to allow Grandpa to keep talking to my boyfriend like that."

I love the sound of that. *My boyfriend.* I'd like the sound of *my fiancé* better, but boyfriend is acceptable for now.

Arella and I have been careful about only showing affection to each other in private. My band doesn't know about her yet, but Liz and Colton do. Basically, we're trying to keep the number of people who know about our relationship as low as possible. Hopefully, that will help keep us off the zovernment's radar. Introducing me to Arella's grandparents was something we debated for weeks.

When I get to my feet, Arella does too. "I'm coming with you," she says.

"No, Ari. Grandpa wants—" Roxy starts.

"Relax, babe." I place a gentle hand over her shoulder. "I can handle him. Just let us talk, man to man." *Zordi to Zordi.*

She stares at me for a long heartbeat before finally relenting. "The second he gives you *any* flak, you come straight back here, and we're leaving, okay? I don't care that it's Christmas. The way Grandpa's acting is unacceptable."

I plant a tender kiss against her forehead, and just because Roxy's watching, I make sure it's extra-long. When I finally draw back, I cup my girl's cheek. "I'll be fine, babe. Did you forget my childhood? Nothing he can say will break through my thick skin."

Roxy steps aside as I pass her to find the kitchen.

At the square table, Phil is seated in one of the four chairs. He points to the chair across from him, and I take it. For a few breaths, he doesn't say anything. His eyes never leave me either.

It's times like these when I wish I could read minds, not emotions. I want to know what he's thinking, not what he's feeling. I don't need my powers to know he's furious. The death glare he's shooting my way is evident enough.

"How much?" he asks.

I wait for him to finish, because is it just me, or is "how much" not a complete question? "How much what?"

From his lap, he lifts a checkbook and a pen. "How much will it take for you to walk away?"

Is he serious? The idea that anyone thinks it's possible to pay me to leave Arella is so ridiculous, I laugh.

"You think this is funny? I'm not joking, boy. Now tell me, how much? Name your price. I'll write you a check. You walk out this door"—he hooks a thumb toward the exit behind him—"and you never see or speak to my granddaughter ever again."

My granddaughter. Such audacious words.

I lean toward him over the table as my laughter dies. In a low tone, I say, "There's not enough money in this world to get me to walk away from her."

Phil doesn't hear a single word from my mouth. "How's ten thousand?"

I shake my head.

"Twenty?"

"No."

"A hundred?"

"Nope."

"Come on, boy. You're a good-for-nothin' musician. Imagine what a hundred grand could do for you."

I laugh deep in my chest. When I'm almost done laughing,

I laugh some more, just to drill in my point of how fucking stupid this is. "Your money isn't worth anything to me. I make more than a hundred grand a month."

"Yeah, right!" Phil half sneers, half scoffs. "How the hell do you make that kind of living?"

"Royalties."

"From what? You're not the guy who invented the Internet."

"Nope. Better. My parents invented healing products."

Phil's entire face falls as his eyes turn to slits. "What did you say your last name was?"

I never said my last name earlier, but if he knows Zordi history, he should already know my last name. "It's Grant. Trey Grant. My parents are—"

Phil's chair tumbles behind him with a loud *crash!* He seizes me by my neck and pins me against the wall before I can take another breath. I gasp for air as he tightens his vise grip around my throat.

"How did you find her?" he growls into my face for only me to hear.

This man is lucky that Arella thinks he's her grandpa. Resisting the urge to punch the gray-haired motherfucker in the face, I claw at his fingers clenched around my neck.

"How did you find her?" he repeats louder.

"What . . . are . . . you . . . talking about?" I say through the little breathing space I have.

Arella bursts into the kitchen, screaming as she grabs Phil's arm. "Stop! Stop!"

Phil barely moves. He's strong for a guy in his late seventies.

"Grandpa, stop!" Arella punches at his arms, but it does nothing.

"Phil!" Roxy shouts. "Let the boy go!"

My relentless attacker finally releases me. I brace myself

against the table, coughing as my lungs take in the precious air they were deprived of.

"What is wrong with you?" Arella scolds the man she thinks she's related to. She puts a hand over my shoulder. "Are you okay, honey?"

Nope. I'm still gasping for air as I force a nod. "I'm okay."

"Get away from him!" Phil grabs Arella by the arm and yanks her toward him. At least, he tries to.

She jerks her arm back and locks it and her other arm around my bicep. "What are you doing?"

"Protecting you! This man is dangerous!" Phil tries to grab her again, but she refuses to allow it.

I'm not dangerous—not to Arella—but I'm about to be pretty fucking dangerous to him if he keeps trying to touch her like that.

Arella stomps her foot. "Will you stop and tell me what's going on? Why are you acting like this?"

Phil turns to his wife. "Go make the call. We need to end this now."

"End what?" Arella shrieks so loudly, it hurts my ears.

Roxy doesn't move.

"Rox!" Phil's face is turning red. "I said, go make the call!"

Roxy looks at Phil, then at Arella, then at me, then back at Phil. I wish I knew what she was thinking, because it's definitely not about making a phone call. Who the hell does Phil want her to call, anyway? It's not the zovernment, because then, they'd be in just as much trouble as I'd be.

"Will someone tell me what the fuck is going on?" Arella screams to the ceiling.

Hold on. Did she just say *fuck*? After she warned *me* not to swear?

"I'll tell you what's going on," Phil says. "This man is not who you think he is. You need to get as far away from him as possible. He's using you."

"No, he's not!" Arella shouts with so much conviction, I

don't feel the need to defend myself. "Trey loves me, and I love him."

"It's true," I add, intertwining my fingers with hers. "I love Arella—with all my heart."

The room goes silent as Phil and Roxy digest that. They gape at me with their mouths wide open. I think I've put them in shock.

Phil keeps his glare on me as if the second he looks away, I'll turn into a monster and eat Arella alive in front of him. "Rox?"

The old woman shakes her head. "I—I can't tell."

"What do you mean, you can't tell? Obviously, the boy is lying! I was only asking you for confirmation of what we already know."

"Well, my alarm didn't go off."

"What the hell are you talking about? Of course it did! You just missed it!"

A slow smile spreads across my cheeks as the realization dawns on me. Suddenly, a plan begins forming in my head.

Phil shoots a killer look my way. "Wipe that stupid grin off your face and get the hell out of my house."

Arella tugs on my arm. "Let's go, Trey."

"No!" Phil points a stern finger at her. "Not you."

"Seriously, Grandpa? Trey has done nothing wrong, and you're treating him like he's a rabies-infected wild animal."

"Wild animals are more humane than the Grant family."

Roxy gasps. "The Grant family?"

"Yes, Rox. They've finally found her. This boy is related to the Grants."

Roxy slaps a hand over her chest. "Oh no! Ari, please listen to your grandpa. Get away from that man."

"What?" Arella's face falls. "Just now, in the living room, you said you would give him a chance."

"That was before I knew who he was," Roxy says.

"He's manipulating you!" Phil yells. "That's what he does. That's what the entire Grant family does."

"Everybody shut up!" My yell silences them all. "I think I know how to clear this up. Well, some of it." I try to free my arm from Arella's grip, but she only hangs on tighter. "It's okay, babe. You can let me go."

"No."

"Trust me. It's okay."

Slowly, she releases me, and I take a step to the side to make sure our skin isn't touching and, more importantly, that her immunity isn't projecting onto me. Then I clear my throat, square my shoulders, and look straight into Roxy's eyes.

"I am *not* in love with Arella." I give Roxy a moment to process that before I continue. "I do *not* currently have a diamond ring in my pocket—one that I haven't been carrying around for the last two weeks."

"Honey, what are you doing?" Arella asks me.

I put my hand out to Arella, palm forward. "Just trust me." I lock my attention back onto Roxy. "Every day for the last two weeks, I have *not* been asking Arella to marry me because I do *not* have plans to spend the rest of my life with her."

"Trey," Arella says.

"Hold on. I've got one more. Arella is *not* currently pregnant with my baby, and I'm *not* thrilled out of my mind about starting a family with her."

Arella backhands my chest. "Trey!"

Last night, Arella and I agreed that we wouldn't mention the baby to her grandparents, but since we're letting everything air out, I made the split-second executive decision to air that one out too.

A huge grin spreads across my face. "Tell us, Grandma Roxy, how many of those were lies?"

Her eyes are watery. "All of them. Every single one."

"What?" Phil wheezes. "How is that possible?"

Keeping my grin wide, I close the gap between Arella and me, then I circle an arm around her waist. "Great! Now that that's settled, if you still wanna kick me out, I'll happily leave now. But I'm taking my girl with me, and if either of you try to stop me"—I drop my voice into a low growl—"I'll blast you with a fireball."

Arella's jaw drops. "Trey!"

"Oh, shit! I forgot one." I let go of Arella's hand and step away again. Looking back into Roxy's eyes, I say, "Arella does *not* already know about our kind."

Roxy gasps, slapping both hands against her chest. "Lie."

39

—————

ARELLA

MINUTES AGO, MY GRANDPA WAS CHOKING MY BOYFRIEND against the wall. Now Trey is making a ton of backward statements, told my family I'm pregnant, and just threatened to blast them with a fireball. What is going on, and how did my life unravel so quickly?

The kitchen is silent. Gramps looks like he's about to strangle Trey again, and my man has a smug grin on his face like he's challenging Gramps to do it. I'm too confused to move.

Like usual, Grammy's the only one with her head on straight. She gestures toward the table before the men— excuse me, *boys*—can start fighting again. "Why don't we all sit down?"

Trey doesn't miss a beat. He twists on his heel to pull out a chair for me. I sit, then he pulls out another chair, moves it next to mine, and plants himself on it. He even makes a show of putting his arm around the back of my chair and resting his hand over my shoulder. Still smiling, he locks his gaze onto Gramps as if daring him to say something about it.

My grandparents take the seats across from us. Both of

their expressions are like they've seen a baby get thrown off a skyscraper.

"I just made a bunch of confessions," Trey says, "all of which Roxy has confirmed are lies. I think it's time you two made some confessions of your own."

Gramps and Grammy swivel their heads to each other. They seem to say something with their eyes. What I gather from it is that neither of them know what to say and they're hoping the other will take the lead.

"No confessions?" Trey asks.

The room stays hushed.

"Not a single one?" He waits another moment. "All right. If you want, I could say my theories, but I think Arella would rather hear it from you."

Hear what? What am I missing?

Trey continues, "Let's see. I don't know the whole story, so I'll just have to fill in the blanks myself. What I don't know is how the fuck you came into her life and why. And what reason you two possibly have to think I'm dangerous to her."

Like a reflex, my arm flies to backhand him in the chest. "Trey!"

"Ow!" He rubs the spot I hit. "What?"

"No swearing, remember?"

His head jerks back. "Oh, *now* that rule is in effect? What about earlier when you swore?"

"Things were heated," I say defensively, straightening up. "It was necessary."

"What do you think, Phil?" Grammy asks in a soft tone, biting her lip.

"I think this boy is a good liar and has fooled you. I think I'm two seconds away from killing him. And while I'm dragging his body into a ditch, I think you should go make the call."

What call? And excuse me? Drag Trey's body into a ditch? I'd like to think Gramps is joking, but the daggers in his eyes tell me otherwise. "Grandpa! This is the father of my unborn child you're talking about murdering."

Gramps doesn't take his attention off Trey. "Ari, you are not pregnant with this man. It's impossible."

"What makes you think—" I gasp. He knows about Zordinaries. He thinks it's impossible for me to carry a Zordi child. But how does he know that?

"Phil," Grammy says calmly, "I think we've gotta tell her."

"We will do no such thing! We swore from day one that we would protect her. We won't stop just because some deceiving asshole has crashed into the picture. Now go make the call. They'll help us take care of this."

"But Phil . . . He loves her."

Bang! Gramps slams a fist against the table. "He's lying!"

"He's not," Grammy says with calm conviction.

"Seriously, Rox? He's already manipulated her. Now you're gonna let him manipulate you too?"

I've gotta hand it to Grammy, she doesn't allow Gramps's fury to affect her. Her voice stays even as she says, "My internal alarm went off as the boy made all those backward statements. You can't fool my gift."

Finally, it hits me. "Oh! You're a Detector."

Grammy nods. "Yes, dear. I am."

"But that means . . ."

"Yes, dear. We are."

My grandparents are . . . Zordis? How? Does that mean I am too? I don't have any powers though. Plus, my body functions like an Ordinary's body. Then that means . . . "You're not my grandparents."

Grammy's gaze falls to her lap. "No, dear. We aren't."

"Roxy!" Phil shouts, slamming both fists against the table. "What the hell are you doing? I did not agree to this."

Grammy isn't having it anymore. "Phillip, you need to exit the kitchen, and you are not to return until you have a handle on yourself. You're embarrassing me in front of Ari and her boyfriend."

Trey lifts a finger. "Actually, I'm not just her boyfriend. We're soul mates. Confirmed by the glimmer on multiple occasions."

Gramps grits his teeth together as he turns to Grammy. "Rox?"

"Truth," Grammy says.

"Jesus fucking Christ!" Gramps's chair squeals as he shoves himself away from the table. "I'm going for a walk."

"Good," Grammy says. "And don't come back until you've cooled down."

Gramps makes a grunt as he slips into a pair of shoes near the back door. He continues muttering swearwords to himself as he slams the door shut and stomps across the yard.

"I apologize for his rudeness," Grammy says. "I'll have a strict talking to him later tonight. Now, Ari, I owe you an explanation, and I'm happy to tell you everything, but first, I just realized I've been a bad host. Would either of you like something to drink? Or a snack? I've got Christmas cookies and milk."

"Milk and cookies would be great," Trey says with a sweet smile.

I only nod because I can't get any words out. My grandparents aren't really my grandparents? *What?*

Behind me, Grammy rummages around the kitchen. A moment later, three glasses of milk appear on the table. Trey grabs one of them. After he takes a long drink, Grammy tops off his glass, then returns to the table with a large Tupperware of home-baked cookies.

Trey grabs one from the box and pops the entire thing into his mouth. "Delicious."

"Thank you," Grammy says as she settles back into her chair. "I feel like there's so much to say. I don't know where to start."

My mouth is dry as I say, "I know where. Why don't you start with the part where you and Gramps aren't actually my grandparents?"

Trey places his hand over my thigh, offering me a small slice of comfort.

"Ari," Grammy says with a soft pouty look on her face. "I hope you can understand that while we aren't biologically your grandparents, it doesn't change that in every other way, we are. From the moment you were placed into our care, we vowed that we'd protect you with our lives and love you as if you were our own. If anything, you're more like a daughter to me. When you came to us, Grandpa and I were already in our fifties, so we had to claim to be your grandparents."

"Why did you have to claim to be my family at all? What happened to my real family?"

Grammy tears up a little, making me feel bad for what I said. She places a hand over her heart. "We *are* your real family, dear. Maybe not biologically, but Grandpa and I are the ones who raised you and made all the sacrifices we needed to for your safety."

"Safety from what?"

"Not what, dear. *Who.* And that who is the Grant family."

Trey's body stiffens. I put my palm over the top of his hand on my thigh, offering him my comfort in return. He doesn't ease into me the way he usually does, so I give his hand a little squeeze and shoot a scowl at my . . . well, the person I *thought* was my grandma.

"Don't lump Trey in with the rest of the Grants," I say. "Whatever happened back then, he had nothing to do with it."

"I suppose you're right." Grandma turns to Trey. "How old would you have been back then?"

"Seven," he says. "I was seven when my parents were killed. On the same day Arella's parents died."

Wait. What? It was on the same day?

Grammy furrows her brow as she thinks. "Ah, yes. It was the same night, wasn't it?"

Trey's body goes rigid. "Can you tell us what you know?"

"Are you sure you're ready for this, honey?" I ask, because this poor man has spent most of his life wondering what happened the night his parents were killed. I never thought it'd be my grandparents who might have the answers.

Trey closes his eyes, sucks in a deep breath, then slowly releases it. When he reopens his eyes, he nods with vigor. "I'm more than ready."

Grammy takes a drink of her milk, then begins. "Phil and I were living in San Diego. He was an Enforcer. I also worked for the zovernment, but in foreign affairs. We had been married for quite some time and had no children. We'd had a child at one point—a daughter. She died when she was fifteen from a severe case of zmonia. It's like the Ordinary pneumonia, but for Zordis, and worse. The mortality rate is about forty percent, and our little Cassie didn't make it."

Grammy locks her watery eyes on me. There's nothing but pain on her face. "Your grandpa and I were devastated. We only had one child, so when we lost Cassie, it felt like we'd lost our entire world. That's why when our longtime friend Rita came to us with a child who had just lost her parents and needed protection, we didn't hesitate to say yes.

"Rita had told us she was a graphic designer until she showed up that night on our doorstep with you in hand. She explained that she was really a ZIRDA agent and that she was working on this mission to discover what made some rare Ordinaries immune to Zordi powers.

"You were the youngest of the Ordinaries they were studying. Your parents were told that you were part of a top secret medical study led by the government. Your parents were assured that the research would cause you no harm. As you can guess, they were lied to. The tests were not safe whatsoever. ZIRDA was doing everything from cutting the

Immunes open to pumping them with drugs and raping them."

I gasp with a hand covering my mouth. "No."

"Yes, dear. I would never make up something that vile. ZIRDA thought that if an Immune could block Zordi powers, then maybe they could also block our inability to mate. If it was possible to mate with an Immune, they figured they could create some of the most powerful Zordis on the planet. Could you imagine a Zordi immune to other Zordis' powers? That person would be unstoppable.

"Naturally, once the Immunes realized that the tests were unsafe, they tried to back out—your parents included. However, ZIRDA wasn't about to let the youngest Immune in their research pool go that easily. They offered your parents millions of dollars to give you up.

"When your parents still refused, like any good parent would, ZIRDA killed them. More specifically, Victor Grant killed them. He also killed another little Ordinary girl who looked just like you. Then his agents strapped all three of them into a car and rolled it off a cliff. The police were none the wiser. They ruled it as an accident and quickly moved on to their next case like it was nothing."

I glance at my man, who seems to be processing this information the same way I am: in shock.

Grammy continues, "When the other ZIRDA agents found out what Victor had done, the organization split into two groups. One half agreed with Victor that the Immunes project needed to continue as it was, involuntary surgeries, nonconsensual drug tests, rapes, and all. The other half believed that the project needed to end. Rita—and Suzie and Andy Grant—led that second group. On the same evening your parents' bodies were shoved off that cliff, Rita, Suzie, and Andy, with a number of other agents, made plans to save you.

"While some of the agents distracted Victor and his

group, the others snuck you away. What Rita didn't know was that Suzie and Andy weren't actually on her side. Secretly, they wanted the Immunes project to continue, just in a more humane fashion. So they double-crossed her."

"No!" Trey shouts so loudly, his voice booms against the kitchen walls. "They wouldn't have done that."

"Oh, I can assure you," Grammy says, "they did. The original plan was that Rita would sneak Ari away to a location only Rita knew of. The less everyone else knew, the better. That place was with your grandpa and me," Grammy says, looking back at me.

"We didn't even know she had plans to bring you here until she showed up. At the time, we hadn't seen her in almost a year. We were friends, but we weren't *that* close. However, she knew us well enough to know that if she showed up with a precious little girl in need of care, we wouldn't say no. And she was right. Once she finished telling us everything that happened, we didn't hesitate to make you some food and a place to sleep."

"Can you tell us more about the part where my parents apparently double-crossed Rita?" Trey asks. "How did that all go down?"

"After Victor killed Ari's parents," Grammy says, "he locked her up in his ZIRDA hideout. While Rita and her team worked to sneak Ari out of there, that's when your parents tried to take her for themselves. I don't know everything that happened, but according to Rita, it sounded like a bloodbath. Some lives were lost."

Grammy locks her gaze on me. "In the end, Rita was able to get you out and away from the Grants, unharmed. While she made her way to us, Victor's team assumed it was Suzie and Andy who took you, so he ordered his people to the Grants' home, which was what allowed Rita to disappear without anyone stopping her."

Trey's hand trembles against my thigh. "That's why those

men came crashing into my house that night. They were looking for Arella. When my parents realized that, they probably rushed home to save me and ended up getting killed instead."

Tears roll from my eyes. "Oh god, Trey. I'm so sorry."

"Rita told me about the explosion," Grammy says. "I have to admit, at the time, I was pretty dang happy about it. With Suzie and Andy gone, there were two fewer people in this world who wanted to hurt the innocent little girl who had just been dropped into our laps. The only people left that we needed to keep her away from were Victor and the people on his side."

"How did you do it for so long?" I ask.

"Well, within a week of having you, Grandpa and I quit our jobs and got new identities. We gave you one too. Your birth name was Hannah Calder. Your parents were Stanley and Robyn Calder, two very brave and loving people. Of course, I never met them, but I can only assume that of them for refusing to give you up for any amount of money.

"We named you Arella because Arella means *angel*. To us, you were our little angel. Our second chance at having a daughter or, since we were already in our fifties, a granddaughter. We gave up so much to keep you safe, dear: our careers, our names, our friends, and any connections we had to the Zordi world. We did everything and anything necessary to protect you. No expense was too big."

Trey raises his hand like we're in a school. "I have a question."

"Hopefully," Grammy says, offering him a sweet smile, "I have an answer."

"If you were trying to keep Arella safe from Victor, why would you stay in California? Why not move to the other side of the country or a different continent?"

"Good question. It's one that Phil and I have debated a lot over the years. We've lost countless nights of sleep over the many reasons why we had to get Ari away from California, but the answer was simple: Uprooting seventeen people's lives and tearing them away from their families was where we drew the line.

"Unless we were going to raise this little girl out in the middle of nowhere, there was always a chance that Victor or *someone* would come around knocking. We considered the isolation method, but that's not the life we wanted for you. Therefore, Rita and the other sixteen people on her team vowed to protect you for the rest of your life. Together, we agreed to remain in California so everyone could stay with their families. Then, if the day ever came, they'd only be one phone call away."

Things are starting to come together now. "That's the call Gramps kept asking you to make."

"Sure is. There are only twelve of them left. Some have passed. Some ended up moving away. The people who remain have named themselves Ari's Guardians. We moved around the state every year to be closer to each one, because every year, they rotated being your main guardian—from a distance, of course. We've been careful to ensure that if Victor's people ever tracked them down, they'd have no relationship with us to track back to you. Moving around the state also helped make you harder to find."

"Somebody somewhere was slacking," Trey says with a scoff, "because somehow, Victor found her, and that's how I came into her life."

That's not the way I would have said that, but okay . . .

"It sounds like you two have a story to tell as well. Maybe you can explain how this"—Grammy wiggles a finger between Trey and me—"happened."

"Yes," I say, "but I want Gramps to hear it too. Maybe once he does, he'll be more willing to accept Trey."

"You still want his acceptance? Even after finding out he's not really your grandpa?"

I nod firmly. "Of course, Grammy. Like you said, biological or not, you are still my grandparents. I still love you as much as I did before. Actually, I think I love you more now, knowing you took in a little girl you'd never met and sacrificed so much to give her a good life."

That does it for Grammy. She loses it, bursting into tears. I slide off my chair to wrap my arms around her. She stands to meet me, and we embrace in a long, tearful hug. After we step back, I wipe the salty water from my eyes.

We chat about lighter things as we wait for Gramps to return. Trey enjoys more of Grammy's cookies while she tells us some funny stories of the things I did growing up.

Eventually, Gramps steps back into the house and kicks off his shoes. He doesn't look like he's fuming anymore, but his expression is still hard.

"I told them the truth," Grammy says gently. "The kids have a story to tell us too. Are you ready to hear it?"

Gramps responds by sitting in his chair and giving Trey and me a nod.

Together, we tell my grandparents everything.

Trey starts by telling them that he was a **ZIRDA** agent. Big mistake. The way Gramps's face turns to stone makes me think he's going to start a war, but he keeps his cool and doesn't say a word. He relaxes once Trey gets to the part where he felt the glimmer and realized he was in love with me.

By the time I talk about how I was kidnapped by Victor's people, Gramps is back to fuming. He doesn't shout, but his hands turn to fists over the table. Those hands slowly unclench as Trey tells the details of how he rescued me.

When we get to the part where we were running to Las Vegas to hide from the Royals, Grammy's on the edge of her seat.

"You *know* we made it out okay," I say, trying to ease her. "I'm sitting right in front of you."

"That doesn't change that the Royals were right above

your heads while you were crouched in an underground crawl space in a ginseng store. What happened after that?"

"Actually," Trey says, "I think we should go back a little. We skipped the part where I find out that Victor's not my uncle and is actually my dad."

Trey tells a shortened version of that part, and then we get to the part where we found out that his aunt Jodi had swapped minds with Victor for twenty years.

"You've got to be kidding me," Gramps says. "All those things Victor did to those Immunes . . . it was Jodi the whole time?"

Trey nods. "Yep. Everything from the brutality of the Immunes project, to killing Arella's parents and mine, to abusing me as a child, to running ZIRDA as a Royals camp, to kidnapping Arella, and everything else in between. It was all Jodi."

We give my grandparents a moment to digest that before I tell them about the zovernment erasing my memory and planting Caleb into my life.

"How is that possible when you're immune?" Grammy asks.

"According to the Executive Keeper I spoke to," Trey says, "they have a way of turning off her immunity by pumping her with a bunch of drugs and hormones to shut down her fear."

Thankfully, Trey doesn't mention how my immunity walls come down whenever he makes me orgasm. I don't need my grandparents knowing that.

"I swear," Gramps says, "the zovernment is full of corrupt bastards. They keep so much information hidden from the general public, and they—"

Ding-dong!

All four of us straighten up like rods as we glance at one another.

"Are you expecting anyone?" I ask.

Grammy shakes her head. "Nope."

Gramps is the first to rise from his chair. "Stay here. I'll go see who it is."

"I'll come with," Trey says, squaring his shoulders like he's ready for battle.

Gramps doesn't protest as the two of them disappear down the hall.

"It's probably just a package," Grammy says, rubbing the back of her neck. Judging by the way we all snapped into alert mode, I don't think it's just a package.

We listen intently as the door opens and Gramps says, "Can I help you?"

"Hello," a sweet voice says. "My name is Mia Wang. I'm a Keeper here to speak with Mr. Ward, Mrs. Ward, Miss Rance, and Mr. Grant. May I come in?"

40

TREY

THIS DAY CANNOT GET ANY MORE INSANE.

At the sight of Mia Wang, I almost bolt back into the kitchen to rush Arella out of here. I don't, only because if a Keeper is here, that means the zovernment already knows about Arella and me. Now I've got the feeling they've known for a while.

Phil's back stiffens as he narrows his gaze on the woman on his doorstep. "Can I see your badge?"

I'm surprised he can think clearly enough to ask for credentials. Phil has been on information overload since the moment I started my and Arella's story with *So, I used to be a ZIRDA agent.*

Mia unbuttons the top button of her silky blouse, then drags the fabric to the side.

"Oh, you're not just *any* Keeper," Phil says as he glances at the branded crest over her heart. "You're one of the top dogs."

"Yes, Mr. Ward, I am. And no, I'm not here to take her away, nor am I here to arrest you. I'm just here to talk."

Phil goes silent as he thinks. He must come to the

conclusion that he has no choice, because with a sigh, he steps aside and waves for the Keeper to enter.

"She claims she's not here to take away our little girl," Phil says as we return to the kitchen.

"I heard that claim," Roxy says, standing in front of Arella like she's guarding precious artwork. "I don't believe it."

"You can relax, Mrs. Ward. I promise you, if we wanted to take Miss Rance away from you, we would have three years ago when we found out you had kept an Ordinary hidden in your home for most of her life." Mia turns to me. "You can relax too, Mr. Grant. If we wanted to take her away from you, we would have the first night you two met at your oak tree."

My eyes have never been wider. How much does the zovernment know? Right now, it seems like they know everything.

Mia smiles warmly. "It's nice to officially meet you all, and you again, Mr. Grant."

I keep my expression tight. "Don't know if I can say the same. Not until I know why you're here."

"May I sit?" Mia asks, pointing to one of the kitchen chairs. She doesn't wait for permission before taking a seat and glancing around the room. "Your home is lovely. I've been admiring the gardens outside."

Dammit. I haven't had a chance to compliment Roxy's gardens yet. Every moment in this house has been wild. I'll be sure to mention her flowers before we leave—assuming I *can* leave, because I'm not stepping a foot outside this house without my girl.

Like Roxy, I don't trust that Mia is simply here to *talk.* I think that's just a ploy to get our guard down. When Mia gets the chance, she's going to snatch Arella away from us and scrub our minds before we can stop them. I won't go down without a fight, and I've got a feeling Arella's grandparents won't either.

As impatient as ever, Phil grumbles, "How's about we cut

the small talk and get straight to the point? Tell us why there's an Executive Keeper in my kitchen."

"I advise you to keep your emotions in check, Mr. Ward." Mia's tone is tender yet firm. "I have no problem leaving without explaining anything. To be frank, fifty of the Keepers voted to leave this situation be and to not intervene this early. The other fifty-one believed it would be in everyone's best interest, especially Miss Rance's, that we stepped in. You're currently looking at the person who made that swing vote. So why don't you all sit down so we can have a nice chat?"

Arella is the first to move. She's either brave as fuck or just doesn't realize that having a Keeper here isn't good. She takes the chair straight across from Mia. I sit down too, only because I need to be as close to my girl as possible. If anyone tries to take her, I'll be right there with a fireball.

Roxy takes a moment to weigh her options before finally settling onto the last open chair. With a huff, Phil leaves the room. He comes back seconds later with a clanky folding chair and sticks it at the end of the table, next to his wife. Then he plops into the chair with another huff as if he needs to make it clear that he hates all of this.

"Do you need to take another walk, Phillip?" Roxy asks.

"No," he grumbles. "I'll keep it together."

The tension shooting at me from Arella's grandparents makes me a tiny bit more confident that they'll fight alongside me if this Keeper tries anything. When I first got here, I felt like it was me against them. Now it's us against this Keeper—except I highly doubt Mia came here alone. I'll bet there are other Keepers and Enforcers stationed outside this house right now, waiting for us to make a move. I expand my empathy power to check. Everything seems normal. Does that mean Mia is actually here to talk?

Mia flashes us an overly sugary smile. It makes me trust her even less. "Where should I start? I'm thinking this situation calls for a little Zordi history lesson. How does that sound?"

We all look at each other, then back at the Keeper and nod.

"Miss Rance, my understanding is that you can recall bits and pieces of the things that happened before you were scrubbed, is that right?"

Arella flicks her eyes to me with a look: *Do I lie?*

I give her a look back that says I have no idea.

Arella is smarter than I am, so I trust whatever decision she wants to make. She turns back to Mia. "Yes, that's right."

"Do you remember if Mr. Grant ever explained what caused the Grand Separation in 1326?"

"Not really."

"Great. Let's start there. The Grand Separation is what divided our kind from Ordinaries. What Zordi schools teach their students is that the separation was started by Ordinaries poisoning our alcohol, causing two million people to die within a year. Zordi schools also teach that we cannot reproduce with Ordinaries. While there are truths to both statements, neither is completely true. Yes, Ordinaries tried to eradicate us, but for a valid reason: We were killing their women." Mia stops there, letting us process that last statement.

"You're lying," Phil says, breaking the silence. "Our kind would never do that."

Mia flashes a smile toward Roxy. "Have I lied, Mrs. Ward?"

Roxy lets out a little sigh. "No. Not once."

Since Roxy has no reason to lie about this, I believe her.

"I should add that the killings were unintentional," Mia says.

"What does that mean?" I ask. "How did our kind *unintentionally* kill Ordinary women?"

"I'm so glad you asked." Mia straightens her back. "Let

me explain. You've been taught that Zordi sperm does not recognize an Ordinary egg as a suitable host for reproduction. In addition, you're taught that Ordinary sperm is not strong enough to penetrate a Zordi's egg to conceive. While that is mostly true, it doesn't mean it's impossible. Occasionally, there are Zordi sperm that are less picky. There are also some Ordinary sperm strong enough to fertilize the Zordi egg.

"Back before the Grand Separation, the chances of conception were much higher than they are now. About one in every ten pregnancies between our kinds successfully produced a healthy child. Due to our separation over the centuries, the gap between our biological makeups has grown even farther apart, making one in every hundred pregnancies between our kinds viable. Again, difficult, but not impossible."

Roxy's jaw falls. "Are you saying there are people out there who are half and half?"

"No," Mia says. "The children are always born as one or the other—Zordinary or Ordinary—never both. As soon as the embryo is implanted, it has already determined for itself whether it's going to be a Zordi or an Ordi."

"Can we get to the part where you explain how our kind was unintentionally killing Ordinary women?" Phil asks.

"Yes. When a Zordi female becomes pregnant with an Ordinary male, there are usually no complications. The Zordi body can handle growing either type of fetus. The problems only arise when it's an Ordinary who becomes pregnant with a Zordi fetus. It's too hard on the Ordinary mother's body. If the mother doesn't die during the pregnancy, she usually doesn't make it very long after the birth. The chances of survival are about fifty percent."

Everyone at the table snaps their gaze to Arella, who has suddenly gone pale. I take her hand into mine, but it does nothing to ease the panic in her eyes. I don't blame her. Inside, I'm panicking too.

We've been trying to get pregnant since we got back

together. Both of us are more than eager to start a family. Because it didn't happen right away like the first time, I was beginning to think it wasn't going to happen at all.

Yesterday morning, Arella's test came back positive, which I remember from prior experience means she's *positively pregnant*, not positively *not* pregnant. We've barely had time to celebrate it, and now I'm being told this could kill her? Having a baby is not worth losing her again.

Mia continues as if the rest of the table isn't losing their goddamn minds. "Before the Grand Separation, there were already plenty of Ordinaries who believed that Zordis didn't have a place in this world. Can you imagine how much deeper that belief became whenever an Ordinary woman died from giving birth to more of our kind? The worst of them was Sir William Knight. Do you remember learning about him in your Zordi history classes?"

"Yes," I say. "He was an Ordinary supremacist who believed all people with powers must be eradicated at all costs."

"Correct," Mia says, "and anyone who agreed with his beliefs joined his anti-Zordi cult. Unfortunately, when enough racist people unite, cloaking their bigoted message behind Christianity, they gain enough followers to become a problem.

"Their crusade began with refusing to give Zordis access to basic needs until they eventually graduated to murdering innocent Zordis, starting with the children. The young ones were easy targets, and they believed if they eliminated the kids first, then there would be fewer Zordis in the future to create more of our kind. It goes without saying that the Zordi community was not fond of Sir William Knight or his people.

"Now the person you aren't taught about in Zordi history class is Richard Taylor. He was the Zordi who raped William's wife, his two sisters, and his mother. Some say Richard did it as revenge for all the dead children. Others say he was hoping for one of the women to fall pregnant with hopes that if William had a Zordi in his family, he'd stop the killings.

"If that was Richard's intent, it failed, because he only made things worse. One of the four women did fall pregnant and carried the baby to term. That woman was William's oldest daughter, and she did not survive the birth. This was the event that caused William and his followers to produce the poison that triggered the Grand Separation."

No wonder I never learned about Richard Taylor in my Zordi history classes. His actions were no better than what the Ordinaries did to us. But come on. Murdering innocent, defenseless children? Really?

Mia continues, "When the zovernment made the decision to hide our world and scrub all the Ordinaries, they also altered all Zordi minds to believe that procreation between our kinds is impossible. We were also taught to start calling the regular people Ordinaries. Before then, everyone was considered to be either a human or a gifted human. The people who hated us called us *freaks*. The zovernment hoped that the new language would foster natural distance, while at the same time, not separate our worlds too much that a future reintegration would be impossible."

I shoot Mia a dirty look. "That's some bullshit. The zovernment is keeping people away from their potential soul mates."

My glare does nothing to faze Mia. "While there is some truth to your statement, Mr. Grant, it's not completely true. With our kinds being separated for so long, we've naturally found soul mates in our own kind more often than outside of it."

"So why are you here?" Phil asks. "I've got a feeling you have more of an agenda than to give us all a history lesson."

"Correct, Mr. Ward. I'm here because Miss Rance is pregnant." Mia flashes Arella a soft smile. "Despite how hard the zovernment works to keep our world hidden, our goal is to eventually bring our worlds back together. That's why when these pregnancies happen, we fully support them. The more Zordis there are in the world, the better. Our belief is that if we can get the Zordi population equal to the Ordinary population, then Ordinaries will be more likely to accept us again. We're currently nowhere near that, but it's a work in progress.

"Typically, we Keepers wait until the second trimester before we offer support, guidance, and medications to ensure the health and growth of your child to term. Because you're a rare Immune, it's our priority to do everything we can to increase your chances of survival."

I don't like the word *survival*. Arella shouldn't have to fight to *survive* the birth of our child. Especially not if the chances are fifty percent. With the way my life has gone, I can almost guarantee she won't make it. *Am I cursed?* Is it my fate to see everyone I love die?

"What about Trey and me?" Arella asks. "I'm not going to have this baby if the zovernment separates us again."

"Ah, right. Maybe I should have addressed that first. Have you heard of Augustine Island?"

"Yes," I say. "It's a hidden island where the entire population is Zordis."

"Correct. That island is common knowledge for our people. The hidden island that isn't common knowledge is the one called Jetty Island. It's where all the crossbreeding couples go to live with their children. Many generations of crossbred people live there now. It's a pretty nice place, in my opinion. There, our kind is free to be with whoever they want. Zordis can freely use their powers too. It runs like its own little country."

Arella tilts her head to the side. "Are you saying that if Trey and I want to be together, we have to move to this island?"

"Yes. In addition, the choice is permanent and there is no

contact with the outside world. This is how we're able to keep this place hidden. Your current friends and family will have their minds altered to believe you're dead. If you don't choose this, your other option is to terminate your pregnancy, and we'll have to scrub you again."

"No!" Arella and I shout at the same time.

"I predicted you'd say that," Mia says with a chuckle, even though there's nothing to be chuckling about. "That's why I've come with a secret third option. With Miss Rance being immune, you have the ability to fool the Zordi world by claiming you're one of us. You can say your mind power is the ability to block powers and the zense. If you choose this option, my team can begin the process of getting Miss Rance added to our Zordi systems as one of us."

"What are the downsides to that?" I ask, because this sounds way too good to be true. There's gotta be a catch.

"The downside is that if this secret third option becomes a problem for the Keepers, we will force option two onto you without discussion. You'll both forget that any of this ever happened. As for any children you might have, they will also be scrubbed and placed into someone else's care."

Arella and I glance at each other. It only takes us a second for us to silently agree on which option we want.

Mia nods her approval as if she heard the conversation we just had with our eyes. "That's wonderful. As soon as I leave, I'll have my team begin the paperwork."

"Wait," I say. "Does this mean Arella and I have full permission to be together now?"

"There are certain rules you'll have to follow. For example, with Miss Rance pretending to be a Zordi, all Zordi laws will apply to her. Otherwise, yes, you are free to be together."

"Does that mean I can legally marry her too?"

"On paper, Miss Rance will appear as a Zordi, so, yes, you may legally marry each other."

I jump out of my chair with both arms in the air. "Fuck

yeah!" I seize Arella's face and plant a long, hard kiss against her lips. I don't even care that everyone's watching. Neither does she, because she kisses me back just as hard.

Every day for the last two weeks, I've asked Arella to marry me. She's been rejecting me because we wouldn't be able to have a "real wedding" or be "legally married." I didn't care. I just wanted to see a ring on her finger. I wanted us to at least *pretend* to be engaged.

Now she has zero excuses to deny my proposals. I'm going to make the next one so special, she'll want nothing more than to say yes.

Arella has a giant smile on her face as I sit back down and take her hand into my lap. I can't stop smiling either. I never thought I'd see the day when a zovernment official told me I have permission to be with an Ordinary. I want to take Arella home and make love to her right now. After that, I want to show her off to my bandmates, then the rest of the world.

"Do the Keepers know what makes Ari immune?" Phil asks.

"It's as much of a mystery to the Keepers as it is to you," Mia says. "I can share our theories with you; however, nothing has been scientifically confirmed."

"Please share," Roxy says eagerly.

"Sure. Theory one is that while Ordinaries were developing the poison to kill us, they were also developing a drug that could make them immune to Zordi powers. It's possible that they succeeded and the drug altered the DNA of those people before the worldwide scrub. Now that gene has been passed down this far to Miss Rance. We don't have confirmation of this theory because we have yet to create an immunity drug ourselves, so we're unsure how a bunch of Ordinaries could have done it back in the 1300s.

"Our second theory is that Miss Rance and the other Immunes are merely an anomaly. There's no pattern to it, and it happens so rarely that we haven't been able to gather enough data about Immunes to make any firm conclusions."

"What data do you have?" I ask.

"We know about as much as you know," Mia says, and I don't believe her one bit. "The only thing I know more than you is the data involving Immunes and soul mates.

"Within the system of Keepers, my official title is Soul Mate Specialist. I lead a team of other Keepers who research and study how the soul mate connection is built, how it affects people, and how the glimmer works, especially when it's between a Zordi and an Ordinary.

"As you can imagine, with Zordis believing that our kind should stick to our own kind, that type of connection is pretty rare. Being immune is even rarer, which means being an Immune who has built a soul mate connection to a Zordi is the most rare. To this day, you are the third couple in history who fits that criteria, and the first to happen in my lifetime. That's why I, along with our Immunes specialist, have been keeping a special eye on you two over the past three years.

"When you were arrested by the Enforcers outside Shadow Ridge, word spread that they had found an Ordinary woman who seemed to be immune to Zordi powers. Once that word spread up to the Keepers, Grace, our Immunes specialist, went to check it out. You both might remember her. She has blonde hair with a strip of purple going down the front."

At first, I shake my head, and then it hits me: That's the woman I hallucinated the last time I got high. Was that woman actually real? Was the man with the goatee real too?

As if she can hear my thoughts, Mia says, "Yes, Mr. Grant, they were real."

"I saw that woman in my dreams once," Arella says. "All I remember is that she kept asking me a bunch of questions."

"Yes," Mia says. "You were in the middle of being interrogated by an Enforcer when Grace figured out through your informative answers that you and Mr. Grant were soul mates. And that's when I got called.

"Ordinaries who get scrubbed are never able to regain their memories. Immunes who get scrubbed are the same. However, when an Immune with a soul mate connection to a Zordi gets scrubbed, their memories return in their dreams. At least, that's what I gathered from the data from the two previous couples like you. Since this hasn't happened for over two hundred years, Grace and I weren't sure how accurate that data was.

"That's why we allowed you to keep your memories, Mr. Grant. That's why I allowed you to keep your photo with Miss Rance's writing on the back. That's also why I slipped that angel-wings necklace into her hospital bag. I hoped that leaving you two with those items would help keep your connection alive so we could see if Miss Rance would regain her memories or not."

I shoot Mia a nasty look. "So this whole time, we've just been a part of your little experiment?"

"I can understand why that might make you angry," Mia says calmly. "However, I have good news for you. Three Immunes with a soul mate connection to a Zordi is a small sample size, but it's a big enough pattern for me to conclude that permanently scrubbing an Immune who has made a soul-mate connection with a Zordi is impossible. That means the next time this happens, the zovernment will proceed differently. I suspect that Miss Rance will regain all of her memories over time and it'll be like she was never scrubbed at all. At least, that's how it was for the other two like her."

"But she *was* scrubbed," I say. "I went through three years of hell without her."

Mia doesn't look like she cares. "At the end of the day, Miss Rance was still an Ordinary who found out about the Zordi world. She would have been scrubbed regardless. Grace and I simply kept an eye on you two afterward."

"But you let it go on for three years. Why not just tell us your plan? Then Arella and I could have worked on getting her to remember me faster."

"That's not the way Keepers work. We intervene as little as possible. Also, we wanted to see how long it would take for Miss Rance's memories to return and at what capacity. We also wanted to discover what factors might play into her memories returning. That's all valuable data we wouldn't have been able to collect if we intervened. Letting you keep that photo and the necklace was already intervening too much. Saving your life after you tried to kill yourself was pushing it too."

"What?" Arella gapes at me. "You . . . what?"

I never told Arella that I used to purposely overdose. I also never told her about the many times I contemplated jumping out the window of my penthouse or the times I thought about tying bricks to my ankles and *accidentally* falling into the Hudson River. I've kept that information from her because I don't need to share the darkest parts of my past with the lightest parts of my future.

"Mixing alcohol with jaderro is a deadly recreational activity," Mia says. "Not only did you do that multiple times a week, but it went on for months. We tried diluting your supply a few times, but it only made you take larger quantities."

That explains why I kept having to up my dosage.

Phil's tone turns to ice as he glares at Arella. "You're dating a drunk musician with a jaderro addiction?"

I'm about to open my mouth to defend myself, but Arella beats me to it. "Trey has been sober for a long time now."

"I can confirm that," Mia says. "And please apologize to Liz for me. A Scrubber altered her memories to make her think she flew to New York and found you in a bad state on the floor of your apartment. In reality, we had already brought you to the hospital and pumped the drugs out of your system. Then we knocked her out and flew her there ourselves. We needed her to talk you out of doing it again. I'm pretty impressed by you, Mr. Grant. You quit cold turkey, and you haven't relapsed once."

"It's really fucking creepy that you know that," I say.

"I wish we knew more. Even with the information we have now, it's still unclear how Miss Rance is able to reverse the scrubbing." Mia smiles at Arella. "We can only assume it has to do with whatever makes you immune and the unique way our bodies function after building a soul-mate connection."

"How did you gather your information?" I ask. "How can the Keepers watch us without me knowing it? My empathy power would have been able to detect whenever someone was nearby."

"Your empathy power can't sense Astral Projectors."

Arella glances around the room, then at the ceiling. "Is there someone watching us now?"

"Yes," Mia says. "It's a normal practice. How else do you think the zovernment knows anything?"

Roxy gives Mia a motherly shake of her head. "Just because it's normal doesn't make it right."

I couldn't agree more.

"It's done with the intent of our kind's protection, Mrs. Ward. And obviously, things do slip through the cracks. For example, it's hard for us to keep up with all Royal crimes when there are more of them than there are of us. I mean, you raised an Ordinary child in your home without us knowing it. Our limited number of Astral Projectors can only see so much."

Mia glances at her watch. "I need to wrap this up, so I'll end with this: Over the centuries, we've learned that it's easier for our kinds to produce a healthy child together if the couple are soul mates. Since you've already gotten pregnant once before and that fetus was using her mind power in the womb, I've got a good feeling your current pregnancy will grow to term. Most pregnancies between our kinds don't even get that far. That's why it's crucial that we stepped in early. With our zoctors handling your prenatal care, we expect your survival rate to rise to almost seventy-five percent."

Almost? "That's it?"

"Seventy-five is much better than fifty, don't you think, Mr. Grant?"

I scoff. "But that means Arella still has a twenty-five percent chance of dying in the next nine months."

Mia ignores me and turns to Arella. "Why don't we start your prenatal visits as soon as the holiday is over? I'll have our medical team get in contact with you. If it gives you any hope, your chances of surviving this pregnancy and the birth are much higher if your child is an Ordinary. Around week ten, we will do a genetic test. If those test results come back with an elemental chromosome, that'll mean your baby is a Zordi."

Arella lets out a long breath. "I guess we'll find out in six weeks."

41

TREY

Arella's groans of pain echo against the walls of our kitchen. Last month, we turned this room into a birthing station in anticipation of our Ordinary child coming into the world. We don't know what gender we're having yet. Arella wanted it to be a surprise. I don't care what gender our baby is. I'm just excited to become a dad.

My girl has been in labor for almost fifteen hours. Four highly trained medical zoctors have been coming in and out of our house all day, doing everything they can to help ease Arella's pain. They're now surrounding her feet, ready to catch our baby when he or she pops out. Arella's midwife and two nurses are also at her side, coaching her through what looks and sounds like a goddamn horror movie.

I'm near Arella's head. She's crushing my hand in hers as I try to stay strong for her. I hate seeing her in misery, especially knowing there's nothing I can do to stop it.

"You're doing great!" the main zoctor says. "Your baby is almost here. Can you give me another hard push?"

Arella sucks in a deep breath, then pushes again. She squeezes my hand so hard, I internally yelp. The zoctors at her feet smile as an infant's cries fill the room.

My heart swells as my eyes fill with happy tears. That's my baby crying. *My* baby. *My* little boy or girl. I lean down to give Arella a kiss on her forehead. "You did it, babe! I'm so proud of—"

She lets go of my hand as her head drops against the bed. The machine she's hooked up to goes off with a loud siren.

"She's passed out!" a nurse shouts. "She's not breathing either."

"She's losing a lot of blood!" says a zoctor.

A nurse pushes me out of her way, and I stumble backward into the wall. *Passed out? Not breathing? Losing a lot of blood?*

We've had multiple conversations about this being a possibility. When Arella and I debated whether or not to continue her pregnancy, we decided to put trust in the zovernment to keep her and our baby safe and healthy. Now I'm thinking we might have made the wrong decision.

My vision blurs as muffled shouting and an infant's cries consume me. All the people in my kitchen yell things at each other I can't make out. They surround Arella with machines and cords I have no idea what to do with.

The head zoctor hooks an oxygen mask over Arella's face. At least, I *think* it's an oxygen mask. If it's not, what is it for?

If Arella doesn't make it through this, what does that mean for me? For our baby? I haven't thought much about that because I haven't wanted to consider it as an option. I've been living off the hope that seventy-five percent is enough.

Someone shakes my arm. "Mr. Grant?"

I glance up at the nurse from the kitchen counter I'm bracing myself over. "Huh?"

"Did you hear me?"

"I'm sorry." My voice comes out as shaky as my hands. "What did you say?"

"I asked if you could do skin-to-skin with your daughter?

It's important that the baby gets it immediately. We typically do that with the mother, but . . ."

My daughter?

The nurse holds up a tiny human who's crying at the top of her lungs. She's so loud, I can barely hear the nurse ask me to take my shirt off.

Get yourself together, Grant. Your baby needs you. After sucking in a deep breath, I tear my shirt over my head, then the nurse hands me my daughter. I erupt into tears as I hold her against my chest and feel her skin against mine.

I'm a dad now. I'm a fucking dad.

I bounce my baby girl in my arms as the nurse rushes back to Arella's bedside. My hands tremble against my daughter's back while I wait for someone to tell me whether my wife is okay or not.

I stare at the canvas print of Arella and me hanging on the wall near the fridge, hoping it'll give me some peace. Arella looks like an angel in her long lacy white dress. At the time, she wasn't showing yet, which was why we had our wedding barely a month after Christmas. In the photo, I'm dipping her back, making her laugh so hard, she squints her eyes and drops the bouquet of flowers in her hand.

That was one of my favorite moments from our wedding because it was right after I was told I could kiss my bride. We had a small wedding at our oak tree at sunset with our closest friends, Arella's grandparents, my bandmates, and Li and Tao. Javina's maid-of-honor speech made people laugh so hard, they cried. Liz's best-woman speech was so heartfelt, I cried.

Now Arella and I have our wedding photos plastered all over our house—the house we moved into two months ago. It's much bigger than the previous one, and we chose it because the second we stepped into it, Arella said she could see us raising our kids here.

I can't live here without her. Correction: I can't live without her. We've had the most amazing eleven months together. I can't lose her. Especially not today. It's September fifth, the anniversary of my parents' death, which is now also the birthdate of my first child. It's crazy how the world works this way. Is the world crazy and cruel enough to give me my daughter and take away my wife on the same day it took away my parents?

My baby's cries mellow out the longer I rock her against my chest. "You're okay, baby girl. Daddy's got you."

Holding her is calming me just as much as it's calming her. I wish I could tell her that her mother is gonna be okay. I don't want my baby to grow up without—

Wait a second . . . I'm at least five steps away from all the other people in this kitchen. Why am I feeling the zense?

I glance down at my baby. It's her. The zense is coming from *her*. But how? Throughout Arella's pregnancy, she never felt the baby use any mind powers. Also, the genetic test came back confirming that our baby was an Ordinary. The test looked for the chromosome that determines what elemental power the baby will develop by the age of one. Our baby didn't have that chromosome at all. How am I feeling the zense from her?

"Mr. Grant?" the main zoctor says.

I turn to find her with bloody gloves and a pale expression. *That can't be good.*

"She's stable."

"What does that mean?"

"It means we've sedated her." The zoctor puts her bloody hands up in surrender. "It's okay. It's just to help with pain relief. Her body went into shock after the birth and she had a postpartum hemorrhage, but she's going to be okay."

A postpartum what? I don't recall hearing that term during any of our prenatal visits.

The zoctor must see the confusion on my face, because she says, "It just means she had heavy bleeding after birth. Remember, we planned for anything to happen. Therefore, we already had the right things in place to give her a blood transfusion if we needed to. The other zoctors are working on that now. She'll be fine."

I let out a long breath as I force myself to nod. If the head zoctor is saying Arella's going to be fine, I'm going to believe her. That's all I can do right now.

"May we take your daughter to get her cleaned up?"

Silently, I hand my baby off. The second I let her go, her cries fill the kitchen again.

I keep an eye on my baby as I make my way back to Arella's side and take her hand. As if she can hear me, I speak softly into her ear. "She's beautiful, Arella. I can't wait for you to meet her."

TREY

"Liz?" I say when she answers my call. I'm lying on the couch with my baby sleeping on my chest. I hope she won't wake up again.

"Hey, T-Bear."

"Can you come over?" I ask softly.

"Um, sure. Is everything—Oh my god. Is Ari in labor?"

"No."

"Damn. I thought for sure that's why you called. She's like, what, three days overdue?"

"Liz, she's not in labor because . . . well, she's done."

"What?" Liz shrieks so loudly, I have to pull the phone away from my ear. "Since when?"

"About two hours ago."

"Oh my god!" She switches to shouting. "Colton! I'm going to Trey's! Be back later!"

In the background, Colton shouts back, "Cool. Send me pics!"

A door slams shut, then Liz says, "Okay, T. I'm getting in my car now."

"Good," I say, "because I really need you."

"What for?"

I stare at my daughter, who looks just like her mother. "You know how to change a diaper, right?"

"Yeah, but don't you?"

"Arella and I took some parenting classes together. I practiced once on one of those fake dolls, but I can't really remember it right now. I don't wanna fuck it up. I'd ask one of the nurses here, but I'm too embarrassed to admit I don't know how to change my own baby's diaper. It's not urgent because the diaper's not full yet. Honestly, I just really need you here. Arella is . . ." I hear Liz's car engine start up in the background as I work up the courage to tell her what happened.

"Just take a deep breath."

I do, then let it out. "Arella is currently sedated."

"What?"

As Liz makes her way here, I tell her everything that happened, from the start of Arella's contractions to all the chaos during and after the birth.

"They said she's gonna be okay, so I'm trying my damnedest to believe them."

"Just hang in there, T. I'll be there soon."

When Liz arrives, she uses her key to get in so I don't have to move.

"In here," I say from the living room. My voice startles my baby so much, she wakes up with a wail. *Fuck.*

Liz drops her purse onto the floor as she enters the living room.

"Please help me," I beg as I sit up, holding my crying baby against my chest. "Tell me you know how to do baby shit."

"Oh, T. I'm sure you're doing just fine."

"I'm not. She keeps waking up and crying every ten minutes. Earlier, when I tried to feed her, one of the nurses had to step in because I couldn't get her to latch on to the bottle."

"That's pretty normal."

I hold my daughter out. "Just take her, and tell me what I'm doing wrong."

"Um . . ." Liz lets out a chuckle. "First off, that's not how you hold an infant."

"What? The nurse said I need to keep her neck supported. That's what I'm doing."

Liz offers me a gentle smile. "Here. Lemme help."

Five minutes later, Liz is on the couch with my baby calmly drinking from a bottle.

"I swear, you're a baby whisperer."

Liz giggles, never taking her eyes off my daughter. I don't blame her. It's been hard for me to look anywhere else too. "Becoming a parent isn't easy, T. Just be patient with yourself. It's a big learning curve."

"I don't think you realize how big my curve is. Until that nurse handed me my daughter, I'd never even held a baby."

"Seriously?" She gapes up at me from the couch. "Actually, now that I think about it, that checks out."

With the lightest plop I can manage, I settle onto the couch too. For a while, neither of us says anything. We just admire my daughter with light smiles on our faces.

Eventually, Liz breaks the silence. "What's her name?"

"I don't know. Since Arella did all the work to grow our baby, I wanted her to come up with a name. She told me she had some in mind but wanted to surprise me. The nurses and I have just been calling her *baby girl*."

"That's cute."

I bite my lip before asking, "Liz, do you notice anything strange about her?"

"Strange? Like what?"

"Like this." I head across the room, standing well over an arm's length away.

At first, Liz crumples her eyebrows together with a *what the hell are you doing?* face. Then she gasps and stares down at my baby. "Oh my god. She's one of us!"

"Yep." I return to the couch.

"But—"

"I know."

Liz pauses to think, then says, "Do you think the genetic test came back wrong?"

"I dunno, but—"

Ding-dong!

"Who the hell is here?" I pop up to answer the door.

On my front stoop is Mia Wang wearing another silky blouse tucked into her black skirt. "The test was not wrong, Mr. Grant."

"Jeez. Remind me to never talk shit about the zovernment. Not even under my breath."

"We've heard it all. Trust me." She lets out a light chuckle. "May I come in?"

Back in the living room, I offer Mia the recliner. She accepts it with a smile toward Liz. "It's nice to officially meet you, Miss Hart."

I've told Liz all about how the zovernment watches us through Astral Projectors.

While the smile Liz flashes toward Mia is friendly, it's not her friendliest. "I'm guessing you're Mia Wang?"

"Correct."

"Are you here to tell me that my child is Dormant?" I settle back down next to Liz, who's still feeding my daughter like a pro. The milk in the bottle is almost gone, and my baby hasn't gotten fussy once. Seriously, what was I doing wrong earlier?

"Even Dormant Zordis have an elemental chromosome," Mia says. "They have the genetics to produce mind and body powers as well. They just have a condition that prevents them from doing so. Most Dormant children will develop their powers later in life. Unfortunately, being Dormant is not the case with your daughter."

"How long have you known that my daughter is a Zordi?"

I ask, because even though the zovernment has been taking amazing care of my wife throughout her pregnancy, I still don't fully trust them.

"I got a message from your main zoctor about thirty minutes ago."

From what I can tell, Mia's speaking the truth. It's good to know this wasn't something the zovernment knew about and chose to keep from us. "So if my daughter isn't Dormant, what is she?"

"Since we've only had thirty minutes to theorize, we aren't a hundred percent sure, but we suspect your daughter might be the Helio."

"The what?"

"The Helio. It's a rare Zordi who does not have a mind, body, or elemental power. Instead, they *are* a power."

Liz perks up. "Oh! I read about this in Zordi school when we were learning about Zordinary myths and legends. Isn't the Helio like the sun or something?"

"Correct, Miss Hart. And just like the sun, there is only one. Think of the Helio as the sun in human form with the power to give energy to others. The Helio was once a living, breathing Zordi, just like us. When they died, they turned into an invisible wisp with its own thoughts and feelings. Because it takes its energy from the sun, it never fully dies. It just floats around the world until it finds its next suitable human host to latch onto. Once it does, it gives that host all of its powers, turning that host into the Helio. Once that host dies, the wisp moves on to find their next host."

I take a moment to process that. "So, um, you're saying there's a wispy thing inside my daughter?"

"If our theory is correct, then yes."

"How can we know for sure?"

"Like our limited knowledge about Immunes, we don't have much knowledge about this either. The legend says that because the Helio draws its powers directly from the sun, the host's skin will glow slightly when under sunlight."

I glance at Liz, then at the bit of sunshine coming through the living room window between the curtains. As if reading my mind, Liz stands and strides across the living room. I wave a hand at the curtains, and they slide apart all the way.

As soon as the sunlight hits my daughter's face, I gasp. Her skin instantly brightens and gives off a subtle glow.

"That's enough proof for me," Liz says.

"During the quick five-minute briefing session I got about the Helio before arriving here," Mia says, "I was told that the Helio used to be the most powerful Zordi to ever live. They had the power to do things like control the weather and bring people back to life."

I imagine my daughter growing up, running around gravesites, raising zombies out of the dirt. The scene doesn't sit right with me.

Mia continues, "However, there haven't been signs that the Helio has been active for centuries, so it's most likely that your daughter may never develop any Helio powers at all."

"Is there a way to get this wispy thing out of my baby?" I ask.

"Not that we know of."

"What does this mean for her then?"

"That depends entirely on if she develops any Helio powers or not. If she does, we'll have to make sure she's safe and under control. If she doesn't, she'll simply live out her life as if she's Dormant. Over time, her skin brightening under the sun should lessen, but it won't ever fully disappear. It shouldn't be noticeable unless someone's really looking for it."

None of that sounds ideal. I was thrilled about having an Ordinary child. This Helio thing sounds like a whole lot of chaos I wasn't prepared for. Not only do I have to learn how to be a father who can correctly hold an infant, but now I have to learn how to handle having the one and only sun wisp inside my daughter?

I really need my wife right now. She'd know what to do.

A NURSE KNOCKS ON THE DOORFRAME OF MY BEDROOM. "MR. Grant?"

I finish swaddling my baby girl, then pick her up and support her against my chest. "Yes?"

"Your wife is awake and asking for you."

Thank fuck! I've been sitting at Arella's bedside for hours upon hours, waiting for her to wake up. Of course it's when I'm upstairs, changing our baby's clothes, that she rises.

I race down the steps and into the kitchen to find my wife sitting up in her medical bed. The nurses and our midwife are gone, but they haven't gone far. Their low murmurs of conversation and light emotions are floating into me from the living room.

When Arella sees me, her face lights up. "Is that our baby?"

"No, ours is upstairs. This one is a simulation."

She bursts into a laugh that instantly lifts my mood. "I'm glad you still have a sense of humor. The nurses just told me I've been out for a while."

"Yeah, and I've needed my sense of humor to be able to get through it." I choke up a little, grateful that she's okay. "Would you like to hold our daughter?"

"Daughter?" Arella takes our baby from me, cradles her, then tears up. "She's beautiful."

Seeing the person I love the most in the world hold a child we created together—there aren't enough words in the dictionary to describe all the joy rushing through me.

"Liz said she looks just like you," I say as I gently tuck some of Arella's hair behind her ear.

"Is Liz here? Tell her to come in."

"No, she left a while ago. Earlier, she taught me how to properly strap on a diaper."

"Did she teach you how to properly hold a baby too?"

I let out a laugh. "Yes, she did."

"Thank god. I saw the way you were doing it in our parenting class with a fake baby. The whole time, I told myself you'd come into it naturally with a real one."

"I got some good tips from Professor Google too. I'm like a pro now."

Arella cups the side of my face, and I lean into her palm. Her touch erases all my anxiety. "I'm so proud of you, honey. Thank you for taking care of our baby while I couldn't."

"Don't give me all the credit. Without Google, Liz, and all these trained women around, I might have poked at you until you woke up to help me."

She gives me a knowing smile. "Did you think you were going to lose me?"

"Yep."

"Did you think you were cursed for almost losing your wife on the same day you lost your parents?"

"Abso-fucking-lutely."

She chuckles and rolls her eyes. "Come here, honey."

I lean over our baby to give Arella a kiss. The second our mouths collide, every swarm of nerve-wracking thoughts from the past gut-wrenching day disappears. *My wife is alive, she's awake, and she's going to be okay.*

I only stop kissing her once our daughter gets a little fussy. I call our midwife back in to help Arella breastfeed for the first time—another sight I never imagined could give me so much fulfillment.

The entire time she feeds, I stand back in awe of everything my woman is. I hope that every morning she woke up nauseous, the constant lower back pain, and those fifteen hours of labor she went through are worth it for her. Everything I had to go through to get here is already worth it, just to see my wife looking at our daughter like she's the most precious thing in the world.

Once our baby falls asleep in Arella's arms, the midwife returns to the living room. I take the time to fill Arella in on finding out that our daughter is a Zordi, and not just any Zordi, but possibly the most powerful Zordi on the planet.

When I get to the part where our daughter could have the power to bring people back to life, Arella makes the same *ick* face I did.

"Are you saying our daughter can make zombies?"

It's nice to know her mind went there too. "Mia said the Helio hasn't shown signs of being active for centuries. She said our daughter is merely a host for it to exist."

"Aren't you a lucky man? You've got two of the rarest humans in the world under one roof."

I'm not sure if *lucky* is the right word, because I don't *feel* lucky. Mostly, I just feel the need to enclose my wife and daughter inside an impenetrable dome. Since they are so rare, they must be protected.

That's when it hits me: I know what my purpose is now. This is why I survived the explosion that killed my parents. This is also why I survived all the other shit I went through, especially those three years I spent without Arella. The world kept me around to protect my wife and our little girl.

I take a moment to let that realization sink in. My eyes close, and I bask in the rush of warmth that spreads through me. I imagine the rest of my life with my little family and silently vow that I will do everything in my power to give them the best and protect them at all costs. It feels good to know I was meant for something all along.

"Would you like to know our baby's name?" Arella asks.

I open my eyes, blinking away the happy tears. "You have a name picked out already?"

"Yeah. I had a name picked out for both genders. If our baby was a boy, I was going to name him Victor."

My heart swells up as I think about the loving man who deserved so much better than what he got. "That would have been a great way to honor my dad with more than just a letter in my tattoo."

"Yeah, but since she's a girl, her name is Katie." Arella has been seeing a lot of Katie in her dreams lately. Like many of her dreams, they don't give her the full picture, so I've been filling in the blanks as much as possible. Together, we have cried and mourned over the loss of the brave young woman who's a huge reason why we are here today.

"Do you like the name?" Arella asks.

I place a tender kiss against her forehead. "Yes, baby. Katie is perfect."

ACKNOWLEDGMENTS

To my **husband, Joe***:*
The way Trey will always choose Arella is how you are with
me. The way Arella feels completely safe and loved with Trey
is how I feel with you. Thank you for giving me the time and
encouragement I need to write my books and for all the good
dicking in between.

To my team of **beta readers** *who stuck with me to the end:*
Thank you for being the firsts to feel each break of Trey's
heart with me. I loved all your reactions and funny comments
throughout this trilogy. Kaycee Racer, Priscillah Bancy, Kelsey
Davis, Whitney Tanner, Mads Arlow, and Annie.

To my **readers***:*
Trey and Arella's journey to a happily ever after lived in my
heart for over ten years, and I'm thrilled to finally share it with
you. The fun's not over yet though. Trey appears as a side
character in book four of the Zordi world. Can you guess
whose story it is?

To **Enchanted Ink Publishing***:*
Natalia, for turning my crappy blurbs into something that
actually sounds good. Stephanie, for your amazing attention
to detail. Christian, for taking my vague request of "green oak
tree" and nailing it on the first try! Lisa, for being the final
pair of eyes every author needs. Greg, for dealing with me. ;)

To my **Secret Keepers**:
You make my author life so much more exciting! If I had to describe my street team in two ways, it would be: hilariously supportive and a little unhinged.

To my **ARC team**:
You chaotic bunch of thirsty book lovers. I've never had so much fun seeing people finish my books in real time. The way you all rushed to our Instagram group chat to rant about the cliff-hangers and beg for the next books will live in my head rent-free. Sorry not sorry to those who cracked their screens after throwing their devices at the wall.

To **Sara Bendickson**:
Thanks for being my supportive bestie in all endeavors, my vacation buddy, my *let's do nothing together* partner, my person to laugh at everything with, and my baby's pillows.

To **anyone who wants to write a book**:
Just do it and see where it takes you. :)

ABOUT THE AUTHOR

Melissa Lam loves reading and writing romance books that take the reader on an emotional roller coaster full of mystery, suspense, and heartache.

As an extroverted introvert who doesn't like to leave the house (because it requires wearing pants), Melissa enjoys playing strategic board games and taking long showers. When she does find the will to put pants on, she can be found traveling, enjoying bubble tea, or experiencing the world through food.

TL;DR I like to eat and write about heartbreaking shit.

Website: authormelissalam.com
Instagram: instagram.com/authormelissalam
Facebook: facebook.com/authormelissalam
Newsletter: authormelissalam.com/newsletter

SUPPORT INDIE AUTHORS

The best way to support indie authors is to leave reviews, because it helps other readers discover us! If you enjoyed this book, please consider leaving your feedback on Amazon, Goodreads, and anywhere else readers hang out.

Grab the next book in this series at
www.authormelissalam.com